AERYN E. CHRISTIE
SHADECURSED
THE BESTIARY BOOK ONE

Shadecursed

The Bestiary :: Book One

Aeryn Christie

NO PART of this book has been produced using generative technology.

Aeryn Christie/KirinZoo Publishing
www.shadecursed.com

Publisher's Note: This is a work of fiction. Names, characters, places, and incidents are a product of the author's imagination. Any resemblance to actual people, living or dead, or to businesses, companies, events, institutions, or locales is completely coincidental.

Hardcover Book Jacket prepared by R.A. Meenan

Shadecursed / Aeryn Christie -- 1st ed.
ISBN: 979-8-9894226-2-3 (Hardcover Edition)

Dedicated to R. A. Meenan
Whose honest critique made this book
The best it can possibly be.

Thank you also to the many people who believed
In this story and in me: To my friends and family
And to my Kickstarter backers who funded the publication.

Special thanks to **Elizabeth Jarvis**, whose generous Kickstarter
pledge funded almost half of my production.

THE FOLLOWING PAGE contains
CONTENT WARNINGS

These warnings contain
SPOILERS.

You may skip them if you do not need them.

CONTENT WARNINGS by CHAPTER

(Contains spoilers!)

CHAPTER TWO + CHAPTER THREE: Violent attack meant to harm.
CHAPTER THREE: Body horror (Transformation).
CHAPTER FOUR: Self-defense with attempt to harm. Blood.
CHAPTER SIX: Minor character death (peaceful).
CHAPTER TEN: Suicidal ideation and attempted suicide due to accidental envenomation. Blood.
CHAPTER TWELVE: Threat of drowning.
CHAPTER TWENTY-ONE: Blood/Accidental injury.
CHAPTER TWENTY-EIGHT: Thoughts of murder.
CHAPTER TWENTY-NINE: Injury/blood.
CHAPTER THIRTY-TWO: Minor injury.
CHAPTER THIRTY-THREE: Existential terror.
CHAPTER THIRTY-FOUR: Deep wound.
CHAPTER THIRTY-SEVEN: Main character experiencing memory of abuse as a child. Severe injury/blood.
CHAPTER FORTY: Blood/injury/burning/broken bones/dislocation/Body horror/dismemberment/Traumatic character death.
CHAPTER FORTY-ONE: Healing of severe injuries, including burns.
CHAPTER FORTY-THREE: Body horror.

The Continent of
KYRNIS
Veil
Wheriae's Break
Fayre Ocean
Lunarilis
Ge'Elo Cliffs
Valor Run
Hya Resort
Kipanic Sea
Greysky
Old Lunarilis/ The Meerit Den
Unseelie Fae Court
Gulf of Anroot
Split
Alysdrecca Fae Court
Seelie Fae Court
Shadow
Ghaspir
Straight of Faerlost
Dead Forest
Alamont Valley
Alysdrecca Bay
Ziro's Spine
D'Rana
Border
Gwulo
Faded Dunes
Skymesa
Summerfeld
Syren Oasis
Fade Desert
Fearless River Gorge
Marshe
H'grit Den
Oeliran
Edge
Opkin
Fearless
Grai
G'z'e'n
Rona Sea
Faun-faun
Rivermeet
Prairieville
Grai Power Relay Plain
Falcon Bluff
Tyl
Harrier Point
Falcon Point
Faun-ir Forest
The Betweenroads
Faun-tala
Reinoaken
Phoenix Estuary
Great Faun Lake
Faun-anin
Faun-ir
Forvanis Watch
Xaytoll Falls
Razorclaw Den
Faun-eila
Sunset
Emerald Bay
Solani
Ocean Den
Rune
Moorlunae Fae Court
Vanndos
Archipelago
Mount Godforge
Zedric
Kaliten Mountains
Ghoust Sea
Kaliten Foothills
Ghoust
Kobla Penninsula
Antirrhopus
Ravenfrost Sea
Approx. 1000k
Kobla's Talons
Only the largest cities and settlements are noted.
All distances are approximate.
Continent of Rhogot

Contents

PROLOGUE

A Letter to the Emperor

Dear Emperor Gwilym,

I hope this letter finds you and the empress well. May your reign be long and peaceful.

Now that the formalities are out of the way, I must apologize! I'm sorry I haven't written in the past couple spans. I've been busy translating that text I spoke about in my last letter. It turns out it wasn't Duarrow or Orcish—it was written by gnolls!

They have *three* languages: A complex language which indicates emotion and ideas, a simple language historically only used in conversation with other species, and a language specifically used for naming themselves. And gnolls learn all three of these languages from birth.

Luckily, this book was written in the simple language, or it would have taken me a whole aur to translate. I've submitted the translation and a copy of the text to the history museum here in Faun-ir, and I've returned the original back to Ghaspir for repatriation. The postmaster told me that it would likely be returned to me, though, as the gnolls tend not to accept parcels from other nations. Apparently, the book was quite a find since the study of gnolls is sort of the "in" thing at the moment.

Last time we spoke in person, you indicated some curiosity about The Defeated, which the gnolls call the Old Gods. The book contained a poem I thought you'd find interesting, which I've translated for you below. Some words (like certain names), I was unable to translate, but I hope you still enjoy reading it.

Plea to Our Gods for Reprieve

Oh, faithless, look what you've done! If not for you, we could still bask in the glow of our creators, those who built us from the clay of the earth and breathed into us their own breath.

My sisters, I beg! Please keep vigil. Remember the old ways, that upon the return of the gods, you shall be rewarded for your faith. Rejoice that their sights fell upon you and created you in their very image.

Oh, Kt'arr'ghar, keeper of the winds and rain, of the sun and shadow, how we miss the kiss of your lips upon our brow.

Oh, H'nrreegh, guardian of life and death, keeper of health and disease, we mourn the loss of your spirit to the aether.

Oh, Lr'engh'ereh, patron of the animals and plants, of the very earth upon which we stand, we fall down before the lack of your guidance.

Oh, Rr'roorit'hroggj'r'oritih, authority of law and of the chaos inherent to the universe, how can we survive without your strong hand?

Faithful sisters, shun the magics of the Thieves. Depart from your treaties and dishonor your debts as they have dishonored us. Those who murder the creators have no place at our table.

Faithful brothers, bow down and acknowledge your sorrow. Keep the flame of your ire fresh for the prosperous time to come. Do not let the endless days discourage you, as we will feel the touch of the gods again.

Remember the codir of the gods. Remember their gaze. Remember their will. Break free of the chains that pull you from their grace, and you will be lifted up upon their return.

Faithful sisters, faithful brothers, do not succumb to your misery, but let it feed you. Your time shall come.

The author isn't listed, sadly.

From what I can tell, this poem has been passed down orally from generation to generation and was an important part in the formation of their oracle clades. I don't know more than that, though, and the book is pretty tight-lipped when it comes to their society.

I almost feel sorry for them. Isn't the skull of one of the gods on display in Herractir? Even the most skilled mages of Faoliia can't bring someone back to life, and having your skull out for the whole world to see is pretty indicative that you're really, really dead. Can you imagine holding onto such anger for thousands of aurs? Wow.

Anyway, I hope to see you soon. I promise I'll write quicker next time!

With respectful affection,
Benji Wild
First Sacrifant Son of Imperial Lunarilis

Take That Leap

A SONG WRITTEN BY BENJI WILD

I had my chance, and I wasted it.
There was no warning or siren;
Just a calm flow from one minute to the next.
Then it was gone.

And they stutter when they find that moment
But I say "go for it"
Because you never know when the minute will pass
And your moment will fade.

Relative to nothing and no one,
Relevant to nowhere at no time,
The ocean of "What ifs" and "Might-have-beens"
is swept away by the tide.

And the clear sand beach
Paints a picture of opportunity,
But you know more than most
That the canvas lies.

CHAPTER ONE

The Shadow in the Garden

Meadow Halfhorn experienced a weird *twinge* in his brain just after breakfast. It was the type of twinge that demanded immediate attention, but much like the check-drive light in his car, he chose to ignore it.

Never mind that his car shortly thereafter became an *ex*-car. He had things to do and no time to worry about twinges.

He scribbled a note for Luka and Ptery, who would arrive while he was out. After sticking it to the fridge where one of them would hopefully see it, he hurried out the front door of his treehouse. As usual, he was running late.

By choice, he'd insist to anyone who asked. After all, who in their right mind would arrive early for *anything?*

Pure coincidence led him through his garden instead of down the path. Meadow reasoned that by cutting through the overgrown and disorganized chaos, he could save a few seconds—at most—and reach the Festival Plaza in reasonable time.

His hooves sank into the dirt while burrs caught in his tail. As he whirled around to give a clinging vine a hearty piece of his mind, he noticed something peculiar.

Well, more peculiar than usual. Meadow's garden was chock full of all sorts of weird and wonderful disasters, all home-grown with his special brand of flora magic. In fact, Meadow grew the very tree in which he lived, as well as many of the other Halcyon Oak apartments in the forest. Yes, he was a faun of many talents, and all his plants thrived under his care.

So he found it particularly odd that something on his property had *died*.

Moreover, a few sparks leapt around the plant like it was frog-catnip.

Sparks were the heralds of the water god, Wheriae, and no one wanted them around. They were noisy, obscenely bright yellow, left slime *everywhere*, and made general pests of themselves without even trying. Most logical beings considered them a nuisance, but they were the water god's chosen creatures, which meant, in some regard, they were sacred.

That didn't stop people from punting them, though, especially when they set up camp around your home. Or, gods forbid, *inside* your home.

"Shoo!" Meadow ordered, waving a hand at them. "Or I'll get the spray. Then you'll be sorry."

They scattered, leaping out of his garden. Their webbed feet smack-pattered against the forcefield-shielded dirt road, then they disappeared into the forest's dense underbrush on the other side.

"That's better," he muttered, shaking his tail free from the burrs. Crouching down next to the dead weed, he narrowed his eyes. The leaves were black and strangely matte, as if they consumed all light and reflected none of it.

Through his connection to the goddess Petalvine, Meadow sensed that the leaves weren't dead, but altered. Caught within another plane of life. Horrifying. Far be it from him to describe something with excessive hyperbole—although he described things with excessive hyperbole *excessively* and *often*—but all he sensed from the diseased foliage was darkness.

Cliche, but apt.

He tilted his head and scratched at the base of one of his horns as he pondered, then he did what any self-respecting faun would do: he reached out and poked the thing.

It wobbled as a normal leaf should. Unlike a normal leaf, however, it made Meadow want to tear off all his skin and roll in the dirt to escape its sheer *wrongness*. Just in case he'd somehow misinterpreted the first poke, he did it again. This time, he was overtaken with the desire to ask a dracotherex to chew his hands off.

This was the opposite of a plant. No, not an animal, or dirt, or anything else with a viable definition. This was a *not-plant*.

"Weird," he understated, trying to banish the shiver worming its way up his spine. He didn't remember growing *that.*

True, occasionally his experiments would breed and produce something even more horrendous than before, but such were the hazards of flora magic. At least none of his plants had ever eaten anyone. Yet.

In any case, he could un-magic the thing when he got home.

As Meadow rose, a car glided around the corner onto his street, and the glow from its Ghiscaer Drive briefly sparkled off something metal half-buried in the ground.

Interesting.

He could have ignored it, but what sort of faun would he be if he did? Then someone else would find it, and he wouldn't have the satisfaction of a mystery well-solved. That wouldn't do.

"All sorts of surprises today," he muttered, kicking at the dirt hiding the shiny thing. Crouching again, careful to avoid touching the not-plant, he brushed the soil away until he unearthed a copper-chain pouch. It was the kind sometimes carried by acolytes of the goddess Ziro and roughly the size of an apple.

Hoping to find an apple inside, Meadow untied the cord and peered within, only to find a handful of stones instead. Inedible. Drat. Still, his curiosity got the best of him, and he upended the copper bag onto his palm.

A trio of stones rolled from it. Pretty but unremarkable, they were rough and uncut and certainly not the type Ziro's followers usually used as leystones. In fact, they were so fresh from the mine that dried mud still dappled their surfaces, so much so that Meadow could barely see the colors of them. Scratching the mud away, he uncovered an emerald, a deep red garnet, and a lump of onyx.

For most fauns, finding such a treasure would mean *finders-keepers,* and given Meadow's natural affinity to onyx—he wore quite a bit of onyx jewelry—he was tempted to keep it. But the stones seemed valuable, and he did have an inkling of a conscience, so he checked the bag for evidence of an owner. After all, he liked the followers of the earth goddess. They were kind, pleasant to talk to, and their godmark made them smell like the forest after a refreshing rain. He'd never steal from them.

After tilting the bag toward the light, he found a scrap of parchment stuck within the links of the copper chain. Fishing it out with his hoof-horn nails, he unfolded it, the scent of rain still fresh upon it. It was recently written.

"Meadow," he read aloud, "take these with you."

Well, then! He wasn't about to refuse free rocks. Satisfied with his find, he rolled the stones back into the bag.

That's when he noticed the dirt shifting beneath him.

Alas, he'd stood in one spot for so long that tiny pink flowers now bloomed from the ground surrounding his hooves. His own godmark was much flashier than the godmark of Ziro's chosen, and its appearance meant he'd wasted too much time studying the strange offerings in his garden.

Now he was running *even later.*

Stowing the copper bag in one of his pouches, he hopped over the garden's short retaining wall and set off at a decent clip toward the Festival Plaza. Benji would, of course, excuse his tardiness because Benji was the most laid-back person Meadow had ever met. Even so, there were limits to his rudeness, and he refused to cross that self-imposed line.

Out of breath and sweating, he slid through the plaza gates and wound his way through the crowd to the competition grounds. With any luck, he'd make it in time for his friend's victory. With even greater luck, he would have missed all the boring stuff that came *before* the victory, like the posturing, the deafening silences, and the gods-forsaken *thinking*.

CHAPTER TWO

Champion

Whether by luck or through the cultivation of a lifetime spent learning, Benji was about to achieve the nigh-impossible feat of besting a sphinx at a puzzle-solving competition.

He'd tried for aurs to beat her, becoming an expert at all kinds of puzzles and trivia. Anything he could study, he'd studied. Any workshops he could attend, he'd attended. Even so, each competition threw different challenges at him, and no one could ever anticipate the form a competitive puzzle would take.

Today it was a game played on a holographic map.

The sphinx lounged across the table with the confident poise of a champion. With thirteen victories in this competition alone, she had little to worry about from the upstart elf who sought to claim today's trophy. As she tapped her claws on the gameboard, her golden eyes flashed upward to stare at him.

"You could yield, Aeora," Benji croaked, with all the confidence of a lost tadpole baking in the sun.

She smiled at him and arched her eyebrows.

He tried to ignore the intimidating set of her feathered wings. Those sharp teeth. The incessant hammering of his own heart, which filled his ears and drowned out all the peaceful ambience of the forest. After all, he had reason for his confidence, having decimated every bracket of the competition thus far. She had no right to doubt him.

He needed a quick break. He'd fail if he didn't take a tick or two to breathe.

Rubbing his temples, he gazed out into the Faun-ir Forest, admiring the immense trees and the multitude of apartments grown directly into the trunks and branches. Each tree connected to its neighbor with sturdy rope bridges, shaded by the cool leaves of the generous canopy far above. Usually, the bridges were peaceful and empty; today, they dipped under the weight of dozens of spectators, who gazed down from their perfect vantage points to gawk at the competition.

Their chattering droned in Benji's ears.

At least the people in the nearby bleachers stayed quiet, respecting the stress-inducing urgency of the competition. Most of them waved Aeora's red and yellow standard, which was disheartening, although a few held pennants of Benji's purple and gold. It made him smile.

He almost worried that he didn't see Meadow until his friend barged through the gathering of onlookers and clambered up onto the bleachers. His hooves made a terrible clattering as he went.

Once settled, Meadow grabbed another fan's pennant and waved it around, a huge grin plastered on his face. How typical. Yet his presence put Benji's mind more at ease.

The late afternoon sun streamed through the canopy, casting dappled light across the plaza's shielded, packed-earth floor. Gauging the time by the pattern of lengthening shadows, Benji turned back to the table, his respite spent.

You can do this, he thought. *You can do this. Make your dads proud.*

Gods, why hadn't he invited his parents? Surely their presence would have helped his nerves. But what if he took silver *again?* They always had such eager—albeit *embarrassing*—praise for him when he took second place, but they never understood his hunger for a victory against Aeora. Against her, second place only signified a loss. He couldn't bear it if they saw him lose again.

You can do this. Without them here. It's better this way.

Better that he won first, and then he could celebrate by telling them all about his victory.

But first, he had to win.

He forced himself to concentrate on the non-sensical clues, drawing his high-strung mind back into the game.

Aeora smiled, her heavily lidded eyes taunting him. Did she already have the answer? No. She would have already called the arbiter if that were the case. But perhaps she was close.

Which meant at *best,* Benji had a half hour. At worst, she'd call the game in a few short ticks, and he'd be taking home yet another silver trophy.

Not this aur. Not again.

With new determination, Benji shuffled through his notes. Of all the types of puzzles, the ones based on stories were his favorite. His specialty. If he made sense of the last few clues, he could move his paladin to the finish line on the board and claim victory. Of course, he had to locate the finish line first.

He stared at the holographic map in the middle of the table, reaching into it to poke his avatar, setting it to spin. Both he and Aeora sat within the game board's dilapidated steel factory, where they'd each found a small com-pad containing either a hint for the conclusive answer... or a red herring.

Benji wondered if he'd missed something along the way. After a quick once-over of the map, though, he concluded that the com-pad held the information he needed, as frustratingly lackluster as it was. He tapped its smooth, black surface and reconstituted its projection.

The sphinx kept checking hers as well, as she sorted through a thick stack of papers with claws that were ill-fitted for the work required.

Benji twirled his pencil around his fingers, glad for his hands. Finding a blank sheet of paper, he wrote the clue from the last round.

Four letters. I-E-R-P.

He supposed the letters sorted out to *PIER*. The problem was, the imaginary puzzle-city was landlocked, without any rivers or lakes where a dock could serve as a small wharf.

Originally, he thought the letters spelled *RIPE*, but when he used one of his questions to ask about the presence of a grove or other source of fruit, the arbiter told him there wasn't one.

He also had a piece of amber, won by defeating his opponent two rounds prior. As he rubbed his thumb across it, he stared at the com-pad's holo-image again.

It was a short brick and mortar pillar with a glimmering lantern atop it. He couldn't manipulate the image—no zooming or enhancing—which meant the building behind the pillar remained out of focus no matter what Benji did.

He tried to set the amber on the com-pad's plate, but that only scattered the projection into water-like droplets for a few ticks before it re-coagulated into the same useless brick pillar.

Maybe the pillar wasn't the clue. Benji narrowed his eyes and turned the com-pad, studying the garden underneath the pillar, which was unkempt and empty.

Except for an empty crystal stein lying on its side. Hm.

He stood up, stretching as far as possible over the map. Despite the lack of detail in the three-dimensional image, each of the signs had pictures on them, representing the purpose of the building behind them. One of them had a stein on it.

The clues resolved in his mind. Benji took a deep breath and typed his last question into his special contest terminal. If the answer to the question ended up being another negative, there was no way he could win.

His heart leapt when the answer came back to him a few seconds later.

With the other clues, including a sheet of impossible fractions which now made perfect sense, Benji solved the whole thing. Without wasting a single tick, he scribbled the answer down, leapt up onto his bench, and waved the answer for the arbiter.

He couldn't resist a smug smile when the sphinx glared at him.

His smugness faded—and Aeora's grin reappeared—when no one came to collect the answer. Benji scowled at the snoozing arbiter as a few chuckles from the crowd reached his ears. Ears which were surely turning a deep, embarrassed black by now. Wonderful.

"*Meadow!*" Benji hissed as he stomped one insistent foot against the bench. The faun stopped waving the stolen pennant and blinked in confusion until he realized Benji's plight, then he stretched out a hoof and nudged the arbiter with gentle insistence. Once. Twice.

When politeness failed, he aimed a rough kick, and the arbiter jerked forward, his forehead colliding with the table.

The chuckles became a chorus of laughter. Meadow puffed up with pride; Benji rolled his eyes.

Aeora remained frozen, her paws overlaid on the table, her ears folded back against her head. Benji ignored the prickling discomfort that crept up the back of his neck. "Please don't—don't look like that..." he said as the aged arbiter pushed himself from his bench and toddled over. When Aeora didn't budge, Benji muttered an apology under his breath.

The sphinx narrowed her eyes, gaze flicking past Benji toward the arbiter, who cleared his throat. The old faun smiled, eyebrows arched as he held out his hand for the answer.

"Right," Benji said, hopping down from the bench. He couldn't allow himself to be intimidated by his rival, not this close to victory. Turning his back to the sphinx, he pressed his answer into the arbiter's hand.

A hush fell over the crowd as the arbiter adjusted his glasses, ample brows descending so low on his forehead that they almost obscured his eyes. A hundred hours passed as Benji waited for the verdict.

The arbiter nodded, his thoughtful expression relaxing into a smile.

Benji allowed the elation to overtake him, forgetting the stress that led him to the finals, forgetting all his doubts, even forgetting Aeora. He fought back a squeal of victory as a sudden vertigo nearly knocked him over. He'd done it!

The arbiter tucked Benji's answer into his pocket and announced, "Our young challenger moves his paladin to a distillery called 'The Pier.' He intercepts the smuggler and prevents the—"

Aeora's snarl of rage sent a shiver up Benji's spine. He turned in time to watch her leap onto the table, paws the size of his own head scattering the game pieces in all directions. Papers flew into the wind as various knick-knacks clattered to the shielded earth.

Terror seized him as her eyes bore into his. He was about to die.

CHAPTER THREE

The Dreadful Manticore

Aeora crashed into Benji, her weight throwing them both to the ground.

Let it be quick, he prayed, hoping Aurapax or Drowlian might grant him just one little favor. If he'd offended the sphinx, he'd accept his fate, but he didn't want to suffer. *No pain. Please, no pain. I don't want it to hurt. Please...*

Time ground to an unsettling halt as Aeora breathed against his neck, her claws piercing flesh. His breath hitched in his throat as she snarled.

A weak "Help!" squeaked out from between his teeth.

Her feathered wings unfurled like a shadowy cape, smashing into the two associate judges who rushed to Benji's aid. As they toppled into the trees, Benji rasped, "You can win! You can have it!"

She pressed against his chest. His ribs cracked, robbing him of breath as his lungs collapsed, burning for air. He gasped. Nothing. He tried again. Nothing. The agony darkened the edges of his vision and caused the panicked cries of the crowd to fade away.

Someone called his name. Benji barely heard it through the ringing in his ears but instinctively turned toward it. It was Meadow, his fingers laced through the shield and into the dirt, working to draw life up from the packed earth.

Please, Benji thought.

But the sphinx's wing lashed out again, and Meadow went flying.

Aeora leaned down and whispered the first words Benji ever heard her speak, her voice strained: "This must happen."

Then she crushed his heart with her full weight.

His consciousness teetered, pain ebbing away as death tried to claim him. For a tick or two, Benji felt almost peaceful as he accepted his fate. He even thought about what he'd write later—about how strange it felt to die and how he really wished he hadn't.

A dense static embalmed his veins, the numbness turning to discomfort, then annoyance, then a rather unusual ache. Magic coursed through him, piercing his heart and causing it to stutter and skip as if it meant to explode. *No*, he thought as the pain returned. *Let me go. It was so peaceful...*

Bright flashes assaulted his vision, bringing the world back into focus. Adrenaline flooded his senses, ensuring he was wide awake as the ache became a dizzying anguish impossible to ignore. A scream bubbled up from his throat; he lacked the fortitude to prevent it from bursting past his lips in an agonized wail.

Aeora's weight lifted as she slunk alongside him instead. Her voice whispered a hair's breadth from his ear, "It'll be over soon."

"Now," Benji demanded. "Now."

"No. Soon."

Every centikip of his body burned as needles skewered his veins. Ancient magic welled within him, lashing out against his very bones and twisting his organs. His back spasmed and distorted, the sensation as confusing as it was painful, while his limbs cracked and elongated to impossible proportions.

Just as Benji thought the magic would rip him to shreds, something pushed against his back—or rather, his back bucked against the ground—flipping him over onto his stomach. His body stretched as his ribs tried to burst through his chest.

Some dull, pain-drunk part of his brain understood.

No. Please, he begged. *Not this.*

Benji's clothes tore at the seams, falling off him in strips. He tried to free himself from his precious gold-inlaid vest before it, too, fell to tatters, but it was too late. He couldn't shrug it from his ever-expanding shoulders before it pulled apart into mere threads and flitted to the surrounding ground.

He tried to scream, but the chain around his neck choked his words away. Even in the throes of torture, he somehow worked a single digit under the noose and snapped it; liquid-platinum beads spilled to the ground like raindrops.

The misery abated for a moment, long enough for him to feel himself—to realize that his thick, curly hair now enveloped his neck and chest, much like a mane.

"What—wha—" he managed before pain exploded from his shoulders. His vision flared white, and he saw stars. Strangely, someone saw fit to throw a blanket over him, but as he tried to shrug it off, he realized the blanket was attached. His eyes focused on the shimmering, scaly membranes of his own wings.

Wings.

He felt the muscles building around them, lifting them from the ground.

"Please be over," he said. His fingers—now barely recognizable anymore—curled against the shield, sending up snaps and sparks as he dug furrows into the ground below.

As one last insult, the magic stretched his spine, muscles seizing as a tail curved up and over his back.

Finally, blessedly, the pain relented. Its echoes persisted, though, smoldering in all his limbs, making him loathe to move. He saw Meadow's hooves in front of his face but lacked even the minuscule effort of strength it would have taken to meet his friend's eye.

Instead, he stared at those hooves, finding each scratch, each bump, each irregularity standing out in stunning, impossible detail like he was looking at them through a microscope.

And the whispers of the crowd... He could pick out actual conversation, even in the tumultuous din.

How could she?

What about their code?

Are we next?

He moaned, trying to shut out the noise as the sphinx paced in front of him. She said, "You are quite handsome, you know. I expected something more gangly."

As Benji tried to look up at her, he accidentally locked eyes with the arbiter, who peeked out from behind the tree where he'd been hiding. As if spurred into action by that glance, the arbiter leapt forward on tottering legs, gesticulating wildly at Aeora. "You!" he cried. "You're disqualified!"

"I think I'll live. Or not. It isn't up to you to decide."

The red uniforms of the Enforcers were so bright, Benji had to close his eyes as they surrounded the clearing. They'd never glowed so much before.

"She's broken a law," Meadow said. Though he whispered, his voice thundered in Benji's ears.

"R-remind me not to—" Benji couldn't form the rest of his sentence. Meadow hushed him, but that was okay. He couldn't remember what he wanted to be reminded of, anyway.

When Meadow swore and scrambled away, Benji forced his eyes open only to find Aeora's face a couple centikips from his. She no longer wore a smile, but a rather serious scowl. Although *she* should have been the one apologizing, Benji found himself eking out a rather strained, "I'm sorry."

She gave no indication that she even heard him, save for the flick of an ear. Without another word, she launched herself upward, into the trees. Leaves and branches rained down on him, so he instinctively raised his hand to cover his face.

There was a paw at the end of his arm. Not his, surely. Elves did not have paws. Did they? His head hurt so terribly that his memory failed him. All he could think about was... Something about a sphinx...

The sphinx is getting away!

Her powerful wings slashed through the vinegrowth as she fled to the sky.

"No—wait! Come back!" Benji pleaded, using his inexplicable paws to scramble to his feet. Naturally, he rose up onto two legs like a proper person, only to find his center of balance... *missing*. After staggering for a couple ticks, he crashed back to the ground, crushing his wings against the dirt.

He rolled over, gritting his teeth. If he had to, he'd climb a tree and chase her down! About to do just that—once he figured out how to properly stand—he felt a gentle hand on his shoulder.

"Hang on, Ben," Meadow said.

"I don't want to 'hang on.'" Benji stared petulantly at the ground. Little yellow flowers sprung up around Meadow's hooves, their petals exhibiting such stunning detail that Benji couldn't help but stare. Strange. Alluring. He reached out for them and caught sight of his hand again, which was, indeed, a lion's paw.

Apparently, elves *did* have paws.

"Uh..." he started.

"Just... don't freak out, okay?" Meadow said. "Don't move for a tick. Get your bearings."

"What?" Benji asked. "What'd she—I mean, how... Am I...?"

"You're a liori."

Oh. That made perfect sense, and none at all.

Despite Meadow's instructions to stay put, he tried to get up again, as if he could run away from this nightmare. And, even understanding that he'd be stuck on all fours for the foreseeable future, his body wanted to walk upright. The dissonance made him sick, and he gagged. Thankfully, his stomach was empty.

"Shh." Meadow crouched next to him again, running his fingers through his hair. Through his *mane*. Gods, he had a mane! And broad shoulders, and wings! And—

All around him lay the remains of his clothing, which resembled a smattering of scraps from the floor of a tailor's shop.

He was naked!

His face and the tips of his ears burned, although if he was a liori—and he had no reason to believe he wasn't—he'd be covered in fur. He glanced back to check out his rather luxurious grey pelt.

Still naked, although not quite as embarrassing.

He didn't know how to solve this problem. Although "solve" seemed like an odd word, it was the first one that materialized in Benji's exhausted thoughts. It was, after all, a puzzle of sorts. And part of the solution lay in the pile of clothing scraps, which he dug through with desperation.

"Ben," Meadow said.

"I need it. I need the—"

"Benji!" Meadow snapped. "What are you doing? There's nothing left!"

"The crest. I need to find the royal crest." His claws snagged in the torn fabric. When he shook his arm to rid himself of the cloth scrap, he glimpsed pale pink pawpads where his fingers should have been. He couldn't tear his eyes away. "Are these my hands?" he asked, unable to keep the wonder out of his voice.

Meadow sorted through the scraps and picked the moon-shaped pendant out of the dirt, along with Benji's wallet and terminal. The latter two items he placed in a pouch, then he held up the silvery pendant. "It's here, see? I got it." A few more of the pearl-like, platinum beads fell from the chain before he doubled it up, tied it, and draped it over his shorter, broken horn. "I'll hold on to it for you until later."

Benji wiggled his fingers, sick and curious at the same time. "Look at my hands. Look at my *feet*."

When he held up a leg, he unbalanced himself and fell over onto his side. He caught sight of his wing, which ever-so-slowly draped down across his face.

"C'mon, Benji." Meadow's hooves shuffled across the ground, kicking sparks up from the shield and crushing the pretty yellow flowers. "C'mon. We gotta get you... somewhere. To my place. We can hide you there 'til you've rested a little."

Benji stood up, but despite his four-legged stature, he still met Meadow's eyes.

No, he couldn't think about that. If he let himself experience what he'd become, it'd make it too real. He ignored his own thoughts and peered past Meadow, toward the other fauns leaping through the trees. Some of them wore the red of Enforcement. They were looking for the sphinx, and when they caught her, they'd bring her back, and...

"Benji, look at me," Meadow said. He took handfuls of Benji's mane in his hands and stared at him with mismatched eyes. One green, one blue. A mishap in his youth. A magical anomaly. A—

Meadow gave his hair a sharp tug.

As his mind escaped him, floating somewhere in the ether above his body, Benji recognized the fascinating symptoms of shock. Incredible! Although—how could he hope to take notes with paws for hands? Perhaps he could dictate to Meadow, and Meadow could...

He shook his head and brought himself back into his body. "I don't know what to do."

"We need to get you out of here." Meadow nodded toward the cavalcade of frightened, albeit curious, onlookers.

Benji's face heated up again. "I'm... There's not—I'm—no clothes."

"I'll find you some pants at home." Meadow gave him an insistent shove.

Unbidden to his will, one of Benji's wings lashed out and struck Meadow's shoulder, sending him sprawling. Again.

"What'd you do that for?" Meadow demanded.

"I didn't mean to! They're—they don't..." Benji tried to tuck his wings in where they would be less likely to do damage, but his muscles didn't seem to understand what he wanted. He accidentally smacked himself across the nose with one of the massive membranes. "I was just trying to—"

If he could complete a sentence today, Benji would consider that a gods-blessed miracle.

Numbness set in as Meadow guided the outer edge of each wing toward Benji's body. He had wings. Wings. *Wings*.

"Is that better?" Meadow asked.

"Huh?"

"Can you follow me?"

It took Benji a tick to remember what they were supposed to be doing. "To your house."

"Right. Can you do that?"

He could, he thought, if he let his mind wander into calm nothingness and concentrated on trailing after Meadow. He took a step with one front paw, then the other, then a back paw, then the other, until he found himself walking. Not as he'd prefer to go, sure, but at least he was moving forward.

Most disturbing was how his mind sort of floated along after him, like a balloon on a string. In that moment, he felt nothing.

"I'm not a sphinx," he said.

"Male liori are manticores," Meadow said. "You know that."

"Right. Right. I can't think..."

"I don't expect you to right now. It's all right. We'll get you settled, then you can think."

They were so close to making their escape into the trees when the voice of the arbiter stung Benji's ears. "Wait!" he called, leaving two Enforcement agents at the edge of the clearing. The old faun huffed and puffed on his hooves until he reached them. "Don't you want your prize? You've won!"

Benji couldn't imagine anything he wanted less than a fake gold trophy and a certificate of victory, even if he spent the last few aurs training for this prestigious honor. Compared to what just happened, it was painfully insignificant, and a reminder of his curse.

"No," he said.

Stunned, the arbiter stood out of his way to let him pass.

CHAPTER FOUR

Banshee

Meadow had a problem.

In actuality, Meadow had *several* problems, which he allowed to stack up unto infinity until he couldn't avoid the solving of one or another. In this case, though, Benji feared he couldn't fit through Meadow's front door. This was a problem that required immediate attention.

"Well, that's dumb," Meadow scoffed reassuringly. "You can fit. You just have to squeeze your wings in."

Benji's eyes—once a deep, midnight purple and now a glowing, incandescent amber—stared plaintively. His long ears folded back, disappearing into his curly, charcoal-grey mane, and he stuttered a few incomprehensible syllables before finding his voice. "I can't get them to do what I want them to do. How'm I going to get them to squeeze?"

Meadow scratched his chin. "You're gonna have to watch the tail, too."

Benji sat, craning his neck to look up at the telson, which was mostly grey, although splotched with a bright, warning cerulean. Quills the length of Meadow's forearm swept from the underside, surrounding a blade-like stinger on the end. "Elves," Benji said, "don't have tails."

"You're a manticore at the moment."

"Oh." Benji narrowed his eyes, contemplating. "Yeah—yeah, I remember."

The poor guy was in shock, and Meadow had no idea how to snap him out of it, nor did he know if snapping him out of it was even possible. So he tried placations like, "Don't worry, we'll figure out how to change you back," even though he'd never heard of such a thing happening. He also tried, "Once you're inside, we'll get you something to eat, and you'll feel better," which he knew to be true. Food always helped in any situation.

Unfortunately, Meadow had one more problem. One more dire than the one he was currently trying to solve. And even *more* unfortunately, he'd forgotten about it until it was too late because the space in his brain could only accommodate so many active problems at once.

As he stood to one side, debating whether or not to use magic to widen the entrance to his house, the door flew open to reveal Ptery standing in the frame.

Right. Ptery and Luka were supposed to meet them at home after the competition. He should have realized they were here since Luka's sleek green car now floated idly a couple centikips above the driveway.

The previously-forgotten-about problem was that Ptery did not like manticores.

Meadow knew this, but he didn't expect the depth to which this hatred ran. The expression on the banshee's face turned from pleased to surprised in an instant. The burnished bronze feathers on the crest of Ptery's single wing fluffed in consternation, and a look of terrible rage crossed their face. Meadow only had a fraction of a tick to cover his ears before the scream split the air.

Entire flocks of birds took flight as the aftershock echoed from the trees; several deer bounded from the forest in a panic, only to disappear into the copse across the path. It was quite the force of sound and an entity in its own right, causing Meadow's knees to buckle with its sheer power.

Benji's ponderous body absorbed most of it, and he fell like a whole sack of stunned galluds. His chin smashed against the walkway, causing the transparent shield to ripple while his eyes rolled back in his skull. As he fell over onto his side, the giant, segmented scorpion tail slammed against the ground, leaving quills embedded in the grass.

Though Meadow's ears still rang from the assault, he held out one hand to Ptery, urging them to stop. And although Ptery's lip curled, their rust-red eyes wide with terror and anger, they didn't scream again. "What is this *thing* doing here?" they demanded. "And what are you doing here *with it?*"

Too concerned to answer, Meadow crawled around the prone manticore on shaky limbs. Blood leaked from Benji's nose and ears, which spread in a crimson stain across the path. Meadow, sure his friend was dead, forwent gentleness and dug through Benji's mane until he found the warm throat, and there, he also found a pulse. "Oh, thank the gods." His heart unfroze as he took a deep breath. "He's alive."

"Pity," Ptery said. "If this beast thinks to take my other wing, it's got another thing coming. I'll bludgeon it if I have to. Believe me, I will!"

"I can't believe..." Now assured his friend was okay, Meadow rubbed at an ear, then checked his hand for blood. Nothing. "You could have hurt *so many people*."

"Nonsense!" Ptery crossed their arms. "I have *expert* line control. No *person* was ever in danger—"

They stumbled forward, shoved from behind, as Luka stepped out onto the porch. "I heard that from *upstairs*. 'No one was in danger' my *ass!* What in the Darkrealm are you..."

She trailed off, studying the manticore with intent curiosity. Meadow, unable to find the words to ask for help, pleaded with his eyes. It only took her a moment to understand, and she swore. "There's people staring," she said.

Meadow nodded. "Help me get him inside."

"You can't possibly be serious!" Ptery snapped, talons curling. Their claws dug into the tree's living wood, drawing lines of sap from within. Meadow, his head pounding and, frankly, tired of the bullshit, smacked Ptery upside the head with his tail. Ptery staggered away, rubbing their cheek. "What in Faoliia's name was *that* for?"

"If you're not going to help, go get Efrit," Meadow said, gesturing in the general direction of the old healer's house.

Benji groaned, and Meadow turned his attention back to him. "C'mon, buddy. We gotta get you inside. Help me here."

"*Buddy.*" Ptery spit the word like it was poison. They leapt up onto the banister and crouched, neither helping nor running to get the healer, as Meadow suggested. "And who is this *buddy* I've never heard about?"

Luka pressed on Benji's backside, and ever-so-slowly, he staggered to his feet. As she mopped her forehead, pushing red hair out of her eyes, she glared at Ptery. "Do you ever *look* before you act? Or are you just naturally careless?"

Here, Ptery took a moment to study the manticore's features, during which Benji mumbled, "remind me never to piss 'em off."

It was the last clue Ptery needed. Their feathers puffed up again, and their talons curled straight into the banister, splintering it. "Of all the—*fuck!* Fuck you, Meadow! And you, Benji! I'll get myself home!"

They leapt off the banister and stomped down the path, each footstep sending up sparks from the shield with an electrical *skrak!* as their talons dug into it. Meadow sighed and met Luka's eyes. She said, "Go. I'll get Ben inside. Stop 'em before they do something stupider."

Meadow nodded and pursued, each footfall sending a stab of pain all the way up his spine to his head. Gawkers shuffled out of his way as he rushed past, until he closed the distance enough to reach out and grab Ptery's sleeve.

They whirled around, lip curled into a sneer. "Don't. Don't touch me, don't *talk to me*. You know how I feel about liori. Vicious, horrid, violent creatures. You've all agreed with me before. Ugly souls. I can feel the evil radiating from him. I can feel it, Meadow!"

"Would you listen for a second?" Meadow pleaded, But Ptery was already lost in another tirade.

"And he's been what, training with them under my nose? Is that it? Learning to be one of those things? I thought it was a competition you were going to. One of those puzzle-things. But you went to the liori, didn't you?" They pouted, anger burning away into confusion. "Surely I would have noticed. I *should* have noticed. You can smell when someone's been around those beasts. And that hideous... *ritual.* I thought we were friends!"

"You *are* still friends! If you'd just listen to me for a tick—" Meadow tried to grab Ptery's shoulder, but they shook themself loose and stomped away.

"They're all—"

"It was an *accident,* you idiot pigeon," Meadow snapped, his temper spent.

Ptery blinked, affronted, but they were stunned silent long enough so that Meadow could take their shoulders and explain. "He wasn't training. He wasn't doing anything under your nose, *I promise*. He doesn't want this either. Have you ever seen any indication that he was talking to the liori?"

Ptery calmed, the feathers on their wing lying flat again. A few coverts molted away and drifted to the ground. "Well, just because I haven't seen anything doesn't mean he wasn't... Cavorting with some sphinx."

"He wasn't. You think Benji would do that? That he could keep that secret?"

"No."

"Good." Meadow held up a finger in Ptery's face. "Now. I need you to go get Efrit."

"*I'm* a healer," Ptery argued.

"You're a baby healer. Benji's bleeding from his ears. I need someone who knows what they're doing. Go get Efrit. Please."

Ptery scowled. "I wouldn't have—If I'd known it was Benji..." Still, they turned, heading down the path. With a look over their shoulder, they said, "Tell him, won't you?" then disappeared around a stand of shrubs and undergrowth.

CHAPTER FIVE

Listen to the Band

Since Meadow grew his own Halcyon Oak, he was allowed to do whatever he wanted with it. That included, among many other quirks, adding as many rooms to it as he pleased. Bedrooms, bathrooms, bedrooms that were also bathrooms, rooms full of shelves and storage space, a Serkitball court, a *second* Serkitball court in case of company, rooms where he'd grown furniture onto the ceiling for a laugh...

Sure, he knew he had the whole tree to himself *mostly* because no other rational, intelligent being would risk living with him, but the tree's spirit loved his originality. And really, what else mattered?

In any case, right now Benji needed a perfectly empty room, of which there were many.

Getting to one was an issue, though, as Meadow had a lot of stuff, and Benji's wings would not obey him. The moment Meadow let go of one wing, it sprang out, shattering a lamp and sending the pieces flying.

"Sorry!" Benji said. He spun toward the broken lamp, whereupon his tail slammed into the back of a leather chair, cutting a hole right through it.

"It's okay! It's fine! It's just *things,"* Meadow said, gathering Benji's wing up again. Several quills stuck out of the chair's plush backing, each of them oozing a deathly black ichor, which dribbled onto the floor. Meadow winced.

Luka held the other wing tight to Benji's side. "Just think of your wings as two more arms," she said. "Feel them in your mind. They're yours. You control them."

"Easy for you to say." He sneezed, a red mist spraying from his nose. As he wobbled, Meadow lost hold of the wing again, and it flopped to the floor. Benji groaned. "I think I'm gonna pass out."

"Stay with us, buddy," Meadow said. "We're almost there."

It took longer than anticipated because Benji was heavy and sometimes leaned on them with most of his weight. Still, they finally guided him into one of the empty rooms, and Meadow got a blanket for him to collapse onto, which he did with grateful exhaustion.

With Benji asleep, the tail and wings lay placidly on the floor.

"We've gotta do something about those quills," Luka said. "Pretty sure they're venomous."

"They got something in 'em," Meadow agreed, sliding against the wall to the floor. "Do you... know anything about liori? About manticores?"

"Not a lot," Luka admitted. "Enough, though. How'd this happen?"

He would have told her, but one of his ears picked up the opening of his front door, even through the ringing. "In a minute. They're—"

"Hello!"

Had Meadow *not* been expecting Efrit's arrival, he might have jumped through the ceiling. As it was, he leapt back to his feet, dancing around and brandishing his fists at the ancient faun in the doorway. He never understood how she could sneak up on someone so silently on those old hooves.

"They're back," he concluded, breathless. Luka rolled her eyes.

Efrit tottered amicably into Benji's room with little regard for the gigantic manticore splayed across the floor. Even though her face was weathered, her horns knobby and cracked, and her posture stooped, her eyes were still blood red and alert, as intelligent as they'd ever been. If she had any caution for liori, she showed none of it as she crouched down in front of Benji, gently rubbing his ears. "Young Pterylae said you had quite the conundrum, though I don't suppose I'll have to look too far to find it!"

She chuckled at her own wit as Ptery followed behind her, pausing in the doorway.

Meadow couldn't help a small bow of respect for the accomplished healer. "Ah, Luka... You remember Efrit. She's..."

How did one show respect to an idol when they were standing in your presence? "She's quite... ah..."

"Old?" Efrit guessed. She smiled a toothless grin.

Meadow smiled, embarrassed. "No, elder. No, I meant that you're just... You're quite a respected healer..."

"Then that's what you say, boy." She lifted her walking stick—which, rumors said, was made from the horn of one of her long-dead mates—and gently cuffed Meadow atop the head with it.

"I'll remember, Efrit."

She knelt with some difficulty, setting her walking stick on the floor and slinging the bag from her shoulder. As she dug through it, she glanced at Ptery. "Aren't you training in the healing arts?"

Caught off guard, Ptery blinked. "Er, yes, ma'am. How did you—"

"Why aren't you healing?"

"We didn't trust them with this one," Luka answered. Ptery's face fell, although they said nothing in response.

"Ah, trust will be important in the coming days," Efrit said. "There is a bright part of yourselves, sometimes buried deep, that must find and cling onto that trust. Do that, and you can never be led astray. Now..." She cupped Benji's chin in her hands, raising it from his paws. "Come then, sweet child," she said, her voice like the comforting folds of a blanket. "I need you to wake up for me."

Benji stirred, his eyes squeezing shut in discomfort, then opening. Despite their black depths, one yellow iris was bloodshot. "Please let me sleep," he mumbled.

"Not now. Soon. What's your name?" Efrit asked.

"Benji. Wild."

"Yes, yes, I know. I just wanted to see if *you* remembered after such an accident. You've changed. Taller, perhaps."

He smiled a bit.

Efrit drew a thin vial from her bag. It was filled with a thick, red elixir, which might have been blood if not for the soft, red glow it emitted. "This will help. Come, now, handsome boy. You've got to take it."

Reluctantly, and quite possibly because the potion looked very much like the blood he'd just let out, he raised a paw to the vial, taking it as carefully as possible with his thick fingers.

"All of it," Efrit said.

Benji downed it, made a face, and dropped the vial. It clattered to the floor as he gagged.

Meadow couldn't help asking, "How was it?"

"Like eating old socks," Benji said, coughing.

"There, now you can sleep, and I can tend to your ears." Efrit gave him a gentle pat, then looked at the others. "This will be very boring, and I can already feel young Ivrian's temper about to boil over. Go bicker elsewhere."

Luka blinked.

Meadow motioned them out, then down the ramp to the living room, where most of his furniture still stood. He righted a table and kicked aside a few stray quills before stretching out on the couch with a relieved sigh. "Old Efrit'll take care of 'im," he said. "He'll be good as new."

Luka sat in the chair that had been run through by Benji's tail. The front of it maintained its purpose well enough. "She knew my last name?"

"Oh, Efrit knows everything," Meadow said. "I wouldn't be surprised if she knew your great grandma's maiden name, too."

"Yeah, that's just unsettling," she said.

Ptery selected a chair as far away from the quills as they could find. "You're going to tell us what happened now, aren't you?" they asked. "How this was all some *accident?*"

They said "accident" as if they still couldn't believe it. Luka scowled, sitting forward on her chair, her fair cheeks red from restrained anger.

Despite being human, and thus unequipped with the slashing claws or sturdy hooves of other species, Luka never shied away from a fight. Sometimes even a fight against her own friends, if she thought they needed sense knocked into them.

"It *was,*" Meadow interrupted before she could start throwing punches. "Benji won the contest."

"Well, of course he did," Ptery said. "He's a genius."

"He was up against a sphinx named Aeora. When he won, she got mad and turned him."

The irritation drained from Ptery's face as they uttered a soft syllable of disbelief. Their head twitched to one side in a negative, after which they glanced at Luka to gauge her reaction.

Her fingers dug into the leather of the chair. She gritted her teeth, her eyes narrowed like she was trying to hold herself together.

"It's impossible," Ptery said. "Liori only change people of their own free will. It's the one thing that makes them civilized—and I use the term loosely, of course. It's the only law they have!"

"I bet it's on the news." Meadow fished into one of his pouches, finding his terminal. Opening his WorldVS module, he searched for the competition. Aeora's attack on Benji was the number one result. "Here."

Ptery took the terminal, tapping play. Although Luka refused to leave her seat, she heard Benji's screaming and the panicked cries of the crowd, and she shivered, lip curling in disgust.

Meadow took his terminal back.

"This doesn't happen," Ptery said, although the doubt had left their voice. The sharp claws on their fingers mussed into their black-purple hair, sending the barbs on their feathery crest askew. As acceptance crept into their demeanor, their wing puffed out again in anger, the blue pinions shimmering in the light. "We'll... we'll have to find her! Bring her to justice! Make her change him back!"

Meadow looked at Luka. She looked back at him and said, "You know that's not possible. I mean, that's the one thing everyone knows."

"You don't mean to suggest we stand here and do *nothing!?*" Ptery snapped. "After she made him into an animal against his will!"

"He *was* the same guy you've always known 'til you popped his eardrums out!" Meadow argued. "And what do you mean, *animal?* He was walkin' and talkin' before you showed up!"

"You can't trust manticores. Something changes in them when they choose that life." Distressed, Ptery crossed their arms over their head, sliding off their chair and crouching close to the floor. "It's a barely held... *civility* that they use to pass in proper society. It's just how their minds work. Even if it's Benji. And even if he didn't... Even if he—"

Ptery's voice lowered until they were unintelligible.

Meadow sympathized, considering everything Ptery went through. And to be fair, liori were all capable of extreme violence if they so wished. With their size and strength, they could do some serious damage. But not Benji, who fit the cliche of the gentle giant better than anyone, especially now.

"He's not a fucking animal," Luka all but hissed, once again sitting forward on her chair.

"And!" Ptery said, ignoring her. "And how's he going to play bass anymore with... with..." Reaching out with both hands, they wiggled their fingers.

"Please. Petals, Ptery. For the love of gods, don't bring that up right now," Meadow pleaded. "He's been through enough. You're his friend. Act like it."

"But we have to..." Ptery trailed off, their attention on Luka, who stared daggers at them, her luminous eyes wide with anger. Cowed, Ptery sat back on their chair, rubbing the back of their neck. "It'll come up at some point."

"Not. Now," Luka said.

Ptery said nothing, which Meadow took for agreement.

"It's not as if everything hasn't been turned upside-down anyway," Luka said. "You think any of us are going to be able to rehearse now? It's not just Benji. The *last* thing I want to do is band stuff."

Ptery spat, "Fine."

They sat in silence until Efrit appeared from Benji's room. Toddling down the ramp and using her walking stick to aid her, she said, "He's sleeping soundly and well on his way to healing. Make sure he gets water, and that he eats. He's quite disoriented."

"He'll be okay?" Meadow asked.

"Liori are possessed of a great many instincts, but some must be taught. Here. On your travels..." She pulled a sealed, crimson-red envelope from the folds of her sleeve and tucked it into a natural alcove formed by the tree's walls. "This is the address of a rather wise old manticore who lives in the Betweenroads. Make sure Benji speaks with him as soon as possible. I'd call it *necessary*, even."

Meanwhile, Luka narrowed her eyes and mouthed, *"Travels?"*

Meadow shrugged.

Efrit re-situated her bag on her shoulder, then reached down and curled her fingers around the back of Ptery's tunic, lifting them to their feet with surprising strength. "You're coming with me. For a while, perhaps. Maybe for longer. Come."

Thusly plucked from their seat, Ptery looked to Meadow for help, but Meadow could only shake his head.

CHAPTER SIX

In the Lap of the Gods

Ptery regretted following the old faun almost immediately.

They thought she'd lead them to a little treehouse like Meadow's, but as they entered a village cluster, she veered off through the scrub brush and thorns, into the forest.

Sure, the scales on Ptery's legs protected them from cuts and scratches and poison ivy and the like, but it was the principle of it. They were getting plant matter crammed into their claw beds, and it *rankled*.

"Oh," Efrit said ahead of them. She moved surprisingly fast for such an old bat with a cane. "Such a beautiful day. Keep up, dear! Come on now!"

Ptery's wing threw off their balance; as they tried to regain equilibrium, they tripped over a rotted root and fell, one arm landing right in a cluster of stinging nettles. One toe, still stuck on the root, twisted enough to send a stab of pain all the way up their leg.

"That's it. I'm going back," they growled. Though Ptery had little patience left, it certainly took all they had to painstakingly separate their arm from the nettles and untangle their foot from the root. Stupid forest. Stupid leaves. Stupid *everything*. Plus! They were still worried about Benji, although they ought not to concern themself with such a perilous predator.

Finally standing, Ptery wheeled around to escape the green pit of pain, during which a thick, clinging vine grabbed onto their wing.

"Oh, that's. Just. Wonderful. Let *go*, you green son-of-a-Darkspawn. Let *go!*"

The bristly branches were tearing the fine barbs apart, turning the pristine plumage into a matted mess. And by this time, their arm was blistering, each pin-prick sting emitting an irritating pinch of pain.

"Don't fight the forest, child," Efrit said, making her way back. She chuckled, using the twisted old walking stick to pull the vines apart. "You'll never win. It's much older than you or I and so very, very wise."

Ptery didn't have the energy or the audacity to argue. Grumbling a declaration of disgust, they tried their best to smooth down the feathers that were sticking up. They'd have to preen! For hours! Granted, they often spent hours preening anyway. One wanted to look their best when leaving the house.

Irrelevant.

They stalked away, but Efrit followed. "We're not going that way, Pterylae," she said. "Besides, if you're trying to return to the village, you're going the wrong way."

"Nonsense," Ptery replied, but they had to admit, all these trees looked troublingly similar, and their sense of direction had abandoned them. "Eventually, I'll run into someone who can take me back."

"Come now." The old faun gently took their hand. "You must attend."

"Attend what?" Ptery asked, but Efrit only chuckled.

"You'll have to forgive me for being so very excited," she said. "It's not every day... Well, you understand. Of course you do... A smart young thing like you."

Ptery didn't, but they said, "Yes. Definitely."

"Good! We won't have to make introductions then!"

What in the Darkrealm did this old goat mean?

Before Ptery could inquire, she was off again, trailblazing a path through the vines and brush and fallen foliage on her way deeper into the darkness. The sun didn't quite reach the ground here. When Ptery looked up, they could see its bright brilliance through the leaves, but the canopy was so thick that the light stopped before it could reach the forest floor. Ptery could barely see their feet, let alone the old faun in front of them. They followed the sound she made, though, as she pushed the overgrowth aside.

Sometimes she'd pause to tut-tut at a blackened stalk or vine or sapling. Ptery knew little of the forest, it was true, but they still sensed something wrong with the aggrieved greenery. It was gnarled and twisted. Brittle and bizarre. In the low light, Ptery couldn't be entirely sure what they were seeing, and Efrit always hurried on before they could ask.

Soon, she stepped out onto a path and stopped. Ptery nearly ran into her.

The brush here had been cut or cropped short between multiple radiating paths, which zig-zagged up a hill toward a single standing stone at its peak. Somehow, the canopy parted far above, casting a golden glow upon the stone and a spiral of scarlet flowers which surrounded it. Ruby-winged butterflies flitted from one flower to the next and then vanished into the shadowy realm beyond the hill.

If nothing else, Ptery could recognize the significance of a stone like that. It wasn't the same one they'd found with Meadow back when they were tiny, but it had the same shape. Square-ish. Old. Covered in moss and vines.

"You know what this is?" Efrit asked.

The dirt paths were not well-traveled. The pebbles on the surface skittered down the rise as Ptery climbed toward the stone, and they were struck with a sense of awe and deference they only reserved for matters of magic. "I'm sorry," Ptery said. "I know it's one of the stones of the gods, but I don't know..."

"Surely you can guess."

And they knew. The overabundance of red provided them with the answer. "Faoliia," they said.

"Indeed," Efrit replied. "She's kept me alive for this moment, I wager. After all this time, I finally have my answer."

She passed them, her hooves barely disturbing the pebbles at all, as if she'd made the ascent many times before. When she reached the stone, she set her walking stick against it and knelt in the flowers, sighing contentedly, looking up into the ray of light from above. "Come, Pterylae." she patted the flowers. "I have something for you."

Her red eyes seemed to glow.

Ptery continued up the hill, kneeling next to her. They brushed their fingers through the flowers; despite practicing healing for many aurs, they hadn't seen any blossoms quite like these. Perhaps they were unique to this small area around Faoliia's stone, which made them rare indeed. And particularly beautiful.

"You'll take one with you when you go," Efrit said. "It will remain alive as long as you need it to. And when the moment comes, you'll know how to use it."

Ptery felt like the two of them shouldn't be kneeling in the flowers and crushing them if they held so much power. Still, Efrit remained, tracing her fingers along the long-eroded inscription upon the stone. No one seemed to have any particular dedication to the stones; they'd been abandoned in the forest to deteriorate for hundreds of aurs. Perhaps thousands. Yet the faun revered them as they revered their pristine temples. "Did you want to clean it?" Ptery suggested, with some disappointment. "Is that why you've brought me here?"

Efrit only chuckled and reached into her robe.

She withdrew a wrapped package, the white weavings yellowed with age. Setting it in the flowers, she untied the twine holding it all together. Inside was a dagger. Its pommel wasn't particularly ornate, though it had an inscription carved into the leather in runes Ptery couldn't read. A round stone was affixed to the end of the handle, which Efrit had used as a mortar at some point, judging by the stains on its surface.

Efrit reverently removed the blade from its nondescript leather sheath. Ptery gasped.

There were only a handful of daggers like this on the entire planet. Many had tried to forge them, but Ptery's eye knew the genuine article when they saw it. The ruby surface was as smooth as ice, though the *inside* of the blade appeared to be faceted—cracks and imperfections ran through the entire thing, causing it to refract the sun in a stunning spectrum of reds, oranges, and yellows. Many said that each of the gods in Faoliia's circle contributed to the creation of this dagger, and that the earth god himself had crafted the impossible blade.

"It must never harm, only heal," Efrit said.

"You can't mean to give this to me," Ptery said matter-of-factly. "This blade is as archaic as the gods themselves."

Efrit gave Ptery a pointed look and continued, "This is not a weapon. You must understand. It is a tool blessed by Faoliia herself and carries her power within it."

Ptery still felt uncomfortable with such a burden, and their bravado fled them. "I have a dagger. A good one. It's... Well, I've been told it's blessed."

The old faun smiled gently. "Ah, most of them are. Most of them have been consecrated by her disciples, but this one... This one is special. Made by her own hands. And she sees what is to come. What's already in motion." Efrit drew the edge across her palm. A thin scratch appeared; she clenched her hand into a fist and allowed the droplets of red to fall into the flowers. "She knows that my time on Erit is finished and that it is time to bestow the dagger onto another. One who is driven. One who has reason to fill themself with her magic beyond the prestige and gain it could bring."

Ptery couldn't help a glance over their shoulder, where their missing wing should have been.

"You are not as selfish as you project," Efrit said with a smile. "Faoliia knows."

"I can't heal it," Ptery said. They felt so vulnerable before this old goat, while all their deepest regrets poured from them unbidden. "I can't. The time has passed."

"Perhaps. For you, and for many others, but that isn't why you took up her mantle, is it?" Efrit passed the dagger to Ptery, who took it with a shaking hand. "Tell her the dagger is yours now."

Ptery had often fantasized about receiving such a beautiful dagger. They would have even taken an imitation just to have the gorgeous blade displayed in their home—in a place of prominence, of course, where everyone could see it. But if they were being honest, they never expected to hold the real thing. "I can't," they said.

"You must. It is her will."

They still hesitated, staring at the blade that sparkled in front of their eyes as if it had a life of its own. *Her will.* As if Faoliia had chosen them personally. It made Ptery feel a little important, but also terribly uneasy. Why would a god have shown interest in them, out of all the people in the world? Out of all the caregivers on the planet? Out of every healer who had ever existed?

After calming their trembling, Ptery drew the blade across their palm.

It cut deeper than they expected, given how thin the edge must have been. They didn't even have to squeeze their hand for the blood to drip into the flowers as Efrit's had. Surprisingly, it barely hurt, though with each passing moment, the sting made itself more and more apparent.

The flowers glowed as brightly as Efrit's eyes, their blossoms reaching up toward the sun.

Ptery felt the weight of the gift. The responsibility. The fact that no one else would be able to use this dagger as they could, because it was linked to the goddess, and the goddess chose Ptery on which to place her favor.

"This one has belonged to the faun since the birth of the New Gods," Efrit said. "I do not know why she chose you, but she always has her reasons."

Within seconds, the bloody gash on Ptery's palm slowed to a trickle, then sealed entirely, scarring over as if it was an old wound. Soon, even the scar would vanish, Ptery knew. Those who followed the healing goddess weren't expected to carry the scars of their craft forever. Only a reminder here and there.

"She will guide you back," Efrit said. "The path will be open to you now. You will see every step you must take."

Ptery laughed, placing the blade back in its sheath. As they wrapped it back up, they said, "To be safe, I think I'll follow you."

Efrit picked a flower and placed it within the package as Ptery folded the last yellowed flap over the dagger. "I'm sorry, child. I won't be going with you."

"Well, then I'll stay until you're ready," Ptery said. "I can't navigate this place by myself."

She smiled and took their hands. "I have lived almost four hundred aurs, Pterylae. Long past the point I should have died. All for this moment. All for you. And now Faoliia is calling me to my final rest, and I must heed. Just as you have accepted her call, just as your acolyte will accept her call one day. Just as we all have, and will, for the rest of time."

Her eyes closed, and she leaned forward. Ptery caught her, only because of the way she fell.

Fear filled them, and along with it came the intense terror born from loss. They didn't know what to do or where to turn and certainly hadn't asked for *any* of this. "Please," Ptery said to Efrit. Without anyone here to see them, they allowed themself to break, shaking the old faun without gentleness. "Wake up. Please!"

But her dead weight pressed on them.

"Help!" Ptery called. Someone must be here. Someone must tend to the stone.

"Help! Someone?" They gave Efrit another shake, but they already knew she was gone. Ptery could feel the panic rising in their chest. *"Help!"*

The sunlight flashed across the scarlet flowers.

Faoliia made her presence known only for a moment, but Ptery felt her cool, guiding hand against their back and experienced peace beyond what they could even comprehend.

Then they knew what they had to do. Reciting old harpy words of blessing, Ptery lowered the faun's body into the flowers, where Faoliia herself would tend to it and give Efrit her final rites.

It was all meant to happen this way. Even through the peace, however, Ptery could feel the stirrings of something greater, and couldn't shake their terror.

CHAPTER SEVEN

Heart

Benji woke to his mouth being wrenched open. Blinking, he focused on Meadow, who was doing the wrenching. Like all fauns, Meadow possessed a very lax understanding of personal space, especially when interest carried him away.

"Hrroo-oong?" Benji asked.

"Counting," Meadow said, turning his friend's head from side to side.

Benji blinked. "Wrry?"

"Luka told me that manticores have a lot of teeth, and I wanted to see for myself."

"I told him not to," Luka said. She sat cross-legged nearby, with one strap of her overalls flopped down around her upper arm. Benji could see all the detail within it. Each individual thread. Every minute tear where age had snapped the fibers. And, he could smell Luka's worry like a stinging thistle jammed into his nose.

At that point, he remembered the events which led to him lying on the floor of Meadow's house, and he sighed.

"There's two rows!" Meadow exclaimed. "No, wait. Maybe three. The third row is just bumps, but they look rough. Wow. Look at this."

Despite herself, Luka leaned over to look. Benji helped by trying to open his mouth a little wider. He growled a note of protest, though, as Meadow turned his head sideways and resumed his counting.

The growl surprised him. It sounded so much like that of an animal that he actually felt his heart skip a beat. Had he made that noise? *How?*

"All right, Meadow." Luka pushed him back. "Enough. He's probably still sore."

As Meadow let go, Benji stretched his jaw from side to side, rubbing the joint with a paw to work out the discomfort. Although grateful for Luka's interference, he had to ask, "How many?"

"That's the spirit." Meadow clapped him on the shoulder. "Honestly, all I can say is 'probably less than a hundred.'"

"Wonderful," Benji said. He grunted, brain still muddled from sleep and shock. Closing his eyes, he tried to picture himself without a beast's body and lacking a beast's terrifying growl.

This failed, as it must. After all, he was now *greater* than he'd been, with the sum of his limbs totaling a number almost double what they were before. Even lying perfectly still, he could sense the tent-like wings and the serpentine tail.

So, he thought, he must think of it as a puzzle. If he reasoned it out as a game, perhaps he could remain calm, even in the face of impossible odds. In fact, he could see the pieces fitting together in his mind because all puzzles carried a solution hidden deep within their myriad clues. If he figured out the logistics of this, the *greatest* of his challenges, he could perform the implausible and return to his own body.

The moment he stopped thinking of it as a problem to be solved, he'd cry. He had to maintain his hope, or he'd—

"Ben?" Luka said.

"I'm just thinking," Benji replied. He glanced toward the crystal window closest to the ceiling, which let in the dappled light of morning. It had enough of a reflective surface, though, that he'd be able to see himself in it.

He hoped. He wasn't sure he had enough control over his limbs yet to reach a bathroom mirror.

His joints protested as he rose and turned. Paying special attention to his wings and tail, he kept them as close to his body as possible, although Luka and Meadow shuffled out of the way. As he rose up onto his hind paws, one wing shot out to help him maintain his balance, skimming the top of Luka's head.

He muttered an apology as the tips of his ears brushed the ceiling. Then, he turned to face his reflection and bared his teeth, studying the two tiny tusks that stuck up from his bottom lip. "I think..." he said after some studying, "it'd be easier for me if I had a lion face, too. I wouldn't look so much like two completely random things just stuck together."

Neither Meadow nor Luka replied.

"And I've got spots on my face," he went on. Even though he tried to keep himself from crying, he couldn't hold back a single tear, which trailed down the dark smudge that ran from the inner corner of his eye down to his chin.

"And on your butt," Meadow said helpfully.

Benji turned and, in the same motion, rubbed his face against one fluffy shoulder to hide the tear. Then he stared at his back half, where a whorl of tiny, leopard-like spots decorated his flanks. "Oh," he said. "Look at that."

"Are you okay?" Luka asked as if she already knew the answer.

He slid down from the window, paws reaching for and fluffing the blanket before he lay down on it. He felt his wings, albeit distantly and as if they weren't quite part of him yet, and pulled them into his sides. He also curled his tail around itself and out of the way. "I feel like I'm puppeting someone else," he said. Turning a paw over, he stared at the pink pads underneath and wiggled his stumpy fingers. They weren't useless, but they also lacked much in the way of dexterity. He'd need practice if he wished to use them.

Related to nothing, and with a voice flat as glass, he said, "I can hear your hearts beating."

"Creepy," Meadow said. "But that's cool. You know, you're holding yourself together awful well. Don't you want to scream or something? Uh, bite someone? Not me. I can get Ptery for you if you want."

Benji shook his head. He wasn't okay, but how could he tell anyone? He didn't want to sound helpless. "Ptery's still here?"

"They were out late, but they slept over," Luka said. "We're not eating Ptery today, though. No matter how much they deserve it."

"I wouldn't—" Benji started.

"I know," Luka said. "Meadow's just an idiot. Meadow, could you leave us alone for a bit?"

"Sure. I'll be outside. I got somethin' to look at in my garden, anyway." He snapped off a salute and wandered from the room, his hooves clattering down the ramp outside it.

Benji worked his wings into a more comfortable position, even though the muscles still confused him. He supposed they couldn't be part of him if he couldn't control them, though, a point for which he was thankful. Once he sorted himself, Luka leaned against his side, and for a while, they enjoyed a companionable silence.

"Remember when you accidentally called me your soulmate?" Luka asked.

Benji felt the tips of his ears warm. "Er. There's no good translation from elvish to faunii," he said. "It's not—"

"I think you were right," Luka interrupted. "When I saw what happened to you... When I realized it was *you*... I was scared. More scared than I'd ever been. It was like I felt your fear."

He turned to look at her, arching his eyebrows in curiosity. Then he truly studied her, seeing her as never before. The minute scrapes on her hands from her aurs of work on machines stood out in stark white from her already pale skin. Her green eyes shined more brilliantly, and the pale streak behind one ear stood out even brighter against her auburn hair.

He could smell her, too.

Earthy. Fearful. Cautious. He could put an emotion to those scents now. Beyond that, he could smell his own blood, which really should have been inside of him rather than staining the floor.

Then his eyes were drawn once again to the crystal window set inside the growth of the tree; he marveled at how each facet sparkled with incredible, unreal beauty. How had he never experienced life in this way before? He reveled in it and feared it at the same time.

Would he miss these senses when they were gone? No, he'd be glad to be rid of them, of course.

"You think we're soulmates?" he finally asked.

"Yeah," she said, wrapping her arms around his neck. They barely reached the full circumference, and she had to squeeze to make her fingers touch. "I think we might be."

He smiled. It helped to hear such an admission, especially considering what happened with Ptery. Although he really never feared Luka would react in a similar fashion, it put his mind at ease to hear her say something so comforting.

"I know this might sound, uh. Hollow, after what happened," Luka went on, "but congrats on your win. I know you've been trying for a few aurs."

While it did seem like an empty victory, considering everything he lost, Benji's heart leapt with pride. Despite his situation, he'd bested a *sphinx*—one of the greatest puzzle solvers on the planet! And Aeora was known for her fierce competitiveness. "Yeah," he said, then stopped short of wishing Luka could have been there to see it. He slumped.

"I don't see your trophy," she said.

"I left it behind."

"We can go get it later."

"I don't want it."

She shuffled on her knees until she was sitting in front of him and took his front paws in her hands. "None of what happened changes who you are, okay? Sometimes shit happens, just like this. And you have to realize that the world keeps spinning, even if you want it to stop so you can get off."

Of course she was right and wiser than anyone her age should have been. But how could she understand? How could *anyone* understand? "I... I have to—I have to feel sorry for myself right now," he said. "Just for a little while. Then I can figure out what to do. Maybe how to fix it. I can't—Right now I can't deal with any of it."

She nodded, smiling. "I guess that's fair. But we're gonna get your trophy. You earned it."

Today, facing the scope of his assault was akin to an ant staring up the side of a mountain. Insurmountable. But with some proper rest and a bit of thinking, perhaps the climb wouldn't be so daunting.

"Tomorrow. Maybe," he added, pulling the blanket up over his face.

That was as good an answer as she was going to get.

CHAPTER EIGHT

Garden Variety

Meadow crouched next to the black-leafed plant in his garden. His hooves dug into the dirt, making a crackling sound that reminded him of Benji's ribs breaking. He shook his head to clear it, but the horrifying noise continued to rattle around in his brain as he pictured the terror in his best friend's eyes.

One particular guilty thread wove through the memory: Meadow was glad it wasn't him. He was okay. He was spared. It was someone else's problem.

Benji's problem.

Meadow lifted Benji's pendant over his broken horn and brushed his hand across the cool, moon-shaped crystal face. Within it, a golden dragon crest floated on a field of color, which constantly shifted from ocean blue to sea green to midnight violet.

The royal crest. A gift from Benji's birth parents and one of his most treasured possessions.

Like all good jewelry of elven make, each individual platinum bead was separated from those next to it by tiny interstitial knots, which themselves shimmered like silver. Replacing it with a duplicate would be too expensive and much too delicate for a manticore. Plus, even if it hadn't broken, the chain was much too short now.

Meadow tucked the crest into his pocket. He'd have it restrung with a heavy cord so Benji could wear it again. That would alleviate his guilt!

It wouldn't.

When he shifted his feet to take a step, something snagged his fur, causing him to stumble.

Grumbling, Meadow reached down to free himself, only to find razor-thin tendrils curled into his fetlocks. They continued to spring up around his hooves, each one blooming with dozens of miniature black flowers.

Usually, his god-mark produced pink or yellow blossoms. Sometimes blue or white, but *never* black. And these were such a deep, shadowy black that they might have been tiny little voids strung along a vine.

Also, his god-mark usually didn't *grab his legs*.

He didn't believe in ill omens like the elders did, but he felt a flutter of trouble in both his stomachs. It was a sort of flip-floppy portent he didn't appreciate, kind of like that time he ate a whole ham just to see if he could.

Fauns were not meant to eat hams.

"Well," he said to the dark little blooms. "If you're not going to give me any answers, you can just go away."

He waited for their wisdom. They neither divulged it, nor did they leave.

Because they were Darkrealm-damned plants.

"Well, fine!" he went on, ripping his fingers through the vines. "You know, I'm pretty shaken, too! It's not just Benji. A sphinx almost ate me. And, you know—" He paused, weighing whether or not sharing a heart-to-heart with his god-mark was crazy. Probably. "Sometimes I think Ptery's right. I mean, they're an ass about it, but liori are pretty dangerous with the... Claws and such."

He let his legs slip out from under him, wincing as his backside collided with the ground. The vines slithered further up his legs, demanding and unrelenting.

How could Meadow have let the sphinx maul his best friend? How could he have been so paralyzed with fear that he'd been unable to act? Meadow usually wielded magic like a kid wielded a paper sword—quick and reckless. Hindering Aeora should have been as easy as spitting on the temple steps. Which he did often.

Is that why the flowers were black? Because he failed?

You tried, he reminded himself. *She was stronger.*

Resting one arm over his knee, he swept his fingers over the encroaching vines and coaxed them together, their tendrils glowing and twisting into each other until they became one single sprout. With less thought than it took to remember his own name, he nurtured his creation as it unfurled shimmering golden leaves and finally blossomed into a thousand-petaled turquoise chrysanthemum.

With a mere whim, he split the blossom into a dozen writhing, thorny vines, which curled and twisted in on themselves like wriggling snakes. He could have used that little trick to capture Aeora.

But he hadn't.

He had the ability.

One hand danced an elaborate air-ballet over the vine, directing the thorns to bloom into flowers of all types and colors, each set between a rainbow of waxy leaves.

The elders never thought he'd achieve *eminent creation* in addition to every other clade of flora magic, so they left him to learn on his own. Maybe he'd learned better without them.

Or maybe, with their tutelage, he wouldn't have balked when he needed his magic the most.

"What if he blames me?"

Unlike Meadow, who would come to terms with the whole thing in a day or two, Benji loved dwelling in the past. And not just dwelling but sleeping, eating, and *drowning in it*, too. But Benji didn't begrudge anyone, so even if Meadow deserved the grudgiest grudge in the whole world, Benji wouldn't be the one to hold it.

No, Benji would blame himself, and that was even worse.

Damn.

To distract himself, Meadow turned his attention back to the black-leafed plant. Once again feeling its strange malevolence, he directed his magic around it and down into its roots, trying to shift it into something more benign. To heal it.

Nothing happened.

Out of the corner of his eye, he saw a number of sparks lurking at the edge of his garden around more of the strange plants. One, the vine he clearly remembered yelling at yesterday, was no longer green and healthy, but black and rotten.

"What in the Darkrealm...?" he muttered. Getting to his feet, he approached it and brushed the sparks away. They chirped and croaked with excitement, hopping back onto the affected vine and up his legs.

Bracing himself, Meadow grabbed hold of the vine and pulled.

It snapped in half, both ends leaking a black, shimmering sap. It ran down Meadow's arm, dragging with it a feeling of cold death that made his tail thrash involuntarily. He flung it off. The goo spattered on other plants in his garden, and they, too, began to wither.

Meadow swore, but the sparks' chirping intensified. One of them hopped onto the torn end of the vine and croaked as loudly as something so tiny could possibly croak, pulling Meadow's attention toward it.

The void within the vine contained oily darkness rather than the fibers one might expect to see within such a stalk. It also bled an endless stream of viscous, black fluid, unlike any matrix he'd ever seen in the history of all flora.

He held his hand under the sap again. The droplets danced with frictionless zeal atop his skin, neither soaking in nor leaving any part of themselves behind. When they contacted each other, they coalesced. When he let the droplets fall into the dirt, they evaporated into silvery smoke.

Okay. That was weird.

Meadow gave the sparks a scathing glare. He didn't want to be wrapped up in any business of Wheriae's, even if Petalvine was also somehow involved. But their bulbous, rainbow-colored eyes begged him. Pleaded with him.

And he did have a soft spot for animals, even animals as annoying as the sparks.

Fine.

The plants weren't killing him. They just made him *wish* he was dead. Sure, they might cause him to break out in a rash later or sprout a second head, but that was a problem for Future Meadow to worry about. He could deal with them now.

Standing, he plucked several of the afflicted plants from the ground, each one making him want to throw his hands into the sun to be rid of the chill. As their sap coursed down his arms, he whined like a child just out of the creche.

Meanwhile, the sparks chirped and chittered, anxious.

"All right," he said to the annoying little heralds. "You win. I'll take these to the temple. Go on. *Git.*"

Satisfied, the sparks vanished into the scrub, leaving no sign that they'd been there at all. Not even a farewell or a *thank-you-for-endangering-yourself* croak. Ungrateful little bastards.

Well. It was time to take a beautiful, disturbing bouquet to the elders.

CHAPTER NINE

Temple of Petalvine

The flora temple, nestled within a grove of mighty oaks, was draped top to bottom with fluffy moss and lichens. Combined with overgrown ivy and climbing roses, the diversity of plant life hid the entire structure from anyone who didn't know what they were looking for.

Glittering jade and emeralds, set into the stone at various intervals, revealed the temple to its faithful. Visitors could also look up to find a more obvious guidepost; the elders' homes were embedded within the high oak boughs around the temple itself. Their little lights twinkled in the canopy as the families of the priests went about their lives.

Meadow took the steps three at a time. Unlike the temple walls, the stairs were worn clean from constant foot traffic, with not a bit of Petalvine's characteristic moss carpeting them. Divots and grooves peppered the surface in places that endured higher use, which was logical for a structure that was several centuries old. The imperfections worked with the temple's natural charm.

Meadow and religion didn't mix. Given the circumstances of his magic and the tug-of-war over his soul, he had a rather unique and unfavorable perspective of the gods, which made him irreverent at best.

Even on the steps of Petalvine's temple.

"You disrespectful *toad*," came a voice from just inside the open wooden door. A thin, ram-horned faun slunk outside, shoulders hunched in a laughably threatening posture. Far-Leap. He barred Meadow's way inside, glaring down his ample nose at the withered bouquet in Meadow's hand. "This isn't fit for an altar! This is a joke!"

Far-Leap was a joke, but Meadow didn't say that. "It's not for an *altar*. It's for..." Damn. Which elder would take him seriously? Or, at the very least, not scoff at his findings? "Stonebuck! Elder Stonebuck!"

"That's even worse," the acolyte said.

"No, I mean... Look. Just..." He held out the bouquet. "Touch it."

"I'm not touching your slimy tribute."

"It's not a *tribute!* Petals, Far-Leap. You don't even have to touch it; just look at it a bit."

Meadow set it down on the temple steps, glad to be rid of the thing. Intense relief followed—the kind he didn't even realize he'd missed since the rotted flowers twisted their darkness so deep into him, he could barely remember existence without it. Shaking his arms to free himself of the last vestiges of their rot, Meadow backed away and sighed with unrestrained contentment.

With a shuffling of skeptical hooves, Far-Leap approached the flowers. Leaning over them, his tail twitching in distress, he studied the leaves without touching them. Then his eyes shot up, meeting Meadow's. "I've never known you to be serious."

"I've never had anything to be serious about." He nodded to the flowers. "Well?"

"I see what you mean."

"So you'll give them to the elders?"

With comical discomfort, the acolyte reached for the blackened plants, his hand pausing above them. Scuffling around to a different angle, he reached again, face screwing up in what might have been pain. "How do you...?"

"Oh, touching them'll make you want to pull your skeleton out through your ears," Meadow said, as cheerful as the metaphor itself. "But they won't hurt you."

As far as he could tell.

"Right. Fine. Maybe you should gather them and..."

"Nah," Meadow interrupted, to which Far-Leap scowled. "The steps are as far as I go. I'll wait in the courtyard for ol' Stonebuck."

"Yes, back to normal, I see. All right." Plucking a handkerchief from his sleeve, Far-Leap meticulously assembled the now-scattered bouquet, gathering as many leaves as he could. With some satisfaction, Meadow noted the acolyte's disquieted shiver.

Without a goodbye or even a thank you, Meadow backtracked down the weathered stone steps.

It wasn't that he hated the gods. Gods did what anyone would expect from a disconnected, self-serving deity. It was the elders and their pompous servants he despised. Anyone who could write off a child that had the "audacity" to commit a horrible accident should be written off themselves.

So Meadow did. He wrote them all off. Every one of them who chastised him for having a *child's logic* at the sophisticated age of *five aurs*.

He reached up, scratching at the base of the broken horn. It didn't pain him anymore, but the memory of it did.

As he silently fumed at the elders, he barely noticed the shadowy gnolls at the base of the temple's grand stair, and might have missed them entirely if not for their giggling laughter.

One of them whispered, "*It begins! It begins!*" In broken Faunii.

Another snarled and bit the ear of the speaker.

He'd never seen the magic-fearing gnolls at the temple before. In fact, he'd never seen gnolls at all, except in books. They looked quite dapper in their suits and leather trappings, with button-down spats wrapped around their ankles.

With his usual curiosity, Meadow sauntered over to say hello.

An absolutely massive gnoll grabbed the strap of his bandolier, and with a deft spin, the giant creature squished Meadow into an alcove, strategically out of view of the nearest patrons.

She smelled of leather and steel. On her breath wafted a combination of mint and mustard. Not unpleasant, but also unexpected, since Meadow always thought gnolls would stink of rotting meat and gore. But this wasn't a savage creature; her clothes were tailored and fine, her grey-brown pelt well-groomed and shiny. Calculating intelligence shined in her green eyes.

The other gnolls hooted and whooped as Meadow struggled to free himself.

"She is warning you so she does not have to eat you," the massive gnoll said.

"You? You're warning me?"

The gnoll bared her teeth. "No! She! *She!*"

"Oh, that's very sporting—" Meadow started. But the gnoll shook him.

"*Shh!*" she snapped. "You will stop. Stop the non-sensing."

Meadow blinked.

Irritated by the language barrier, the gnoll gave Meadow another shake. "Do-not-pursuit. That is the message. *Do-not-pursuit* or she will eat you."

Then she snapped her teeth a centikip from Meadow's nose, adding a snarl for effect. On later reflection, Meadow would wonder why she felt the need to snarl in addition to such an already crystal-clear threat—one which Meadow intended to ignore anyway if he could figure out what the warning even meant—but he'd be the first to admit he didn't understand gnolls at all. Perhaps it was their way of being polite.

The gnoll turned, and with a great push, shoved him back onto the path. Meadow stumbled on the uneven brick, nearly colliding with a group of temple patrons who graciously steadied him, so he didn't fall. One of the burlier satyrs put himself between Meadow and the gnolls, snorting a warning.

"Are you okay?" a young faun asked.

"Yeah, yeah, I'm fine," Meadow said. "We were just talking."

"Gnolls don't talk," the satyr said. "They make trouble."

When Meadow looked up, the gnoll laid back her ears, snarled again, then stalked off with her minions at her heels.

Watch Out for Unicorns

A SONG WRITTEN BY MEADOW HALFHORN

How'd you think it happened
This rainy day accord
When unicorns decided
They'd no longer be ignored

T'was a day like any other
The griffons all recall
And the manticores remember
There was naught amiss at all

Then the centaurs told the harpies

And the harpies told the elves:
Look out! The unicorns are rampant!
Run! And save yourselves!

The lesson we can take from this—
The beauty of our time
Is sometimes only skin-deep
(And often speaks in rhyme)
And when you see a pretty horse
With a horn of gold
And fur the color o' ivy
And a rage that's uncontrolled
Remember this old adage
Which I'll impart to you—
Watch out for unicorns
(And mind the dragons, too)

They rampaged through the forest
They trampled 'cross the plains
Through the nests of Roc and Tengu
Through the Pegasus' domain

Then through the swamps of sorrow
Their fur was colored green
Their envy and their hate displayed
For all the world to see

And in their wake they left a chaos
Worthy of the name:

"The Terror of the Unicorns"
Became their claim to fame

The lesson we can take from this—
The beauty of our time
Is sometimes only skin-deep
(And often speaks in rhyme)
And when you see a pretty horse
With a horn of gold
And fur the color o' ivy
And a rage that's uncontrolled
Remember this old adage
Which I'll impart to you—
Watch out for unicorns
(And mind the dragons, too)

When you hear the fauns a-whisper:
Take lessons from the past
When you hear the sphinx's warning:
This peace will never last
Take heed of this old adage
For what I say is true
Watch out for unicorns
(And mind the dragons, too)

Watch out for unicorns
(And mind the dragons, too)

CHAPTER TEN

Venom and Spite

As Benji slept, Luka fiddled with the logic board from inside her amp. With its parts splayed out on the floor around her, everything she needed lay within reach. To the casual observer, however, it would look like a disorganized mess.

She touched her welding pen to one of the circuits tethering a tiny magic capacitor to the board, severing the connection. With tweezers, she removed the capacitor and set it aside, then searched her array of components for a larger model. With a little extra power, she could create a slight buzz at lower volumes. Not enough to clip the music, but enough to give her guitar a unique sound.

It might also cause the amp to smoke or catch fire. Upgrading her equipment always came with risks, but she'd test it before going live. She didn't need an uncontrolled light show on stage.

As she found what she was looking for, Ptery peeked around the door frame, their claws gripping the wood as if it served as a shield between them and the sleeping manticore.

Benji snored and flicked an ear.

"Have you seen Meadow?" Ptery asked.

"I thought it was too quiet in here," Luka answered, perching the goggles on her head. "No, I haven't. Not for a few hours."

"Oh. A pity. I needed to talk to him about something. Something important."

As Ptery turned to leave, Luka flicked the switch on the welding pen, severing the electrical magic feed. Almost as a challenge, she said, "You could talk to me."

Ptery tutted, looking over their shoulder. "You. You and me, having a conversation that isn't small talk. Excuse the cliche, but *perish* the thought."

At least they were direct with each other, even if they didn't particularly enjoy each other's company. Still, she could never say what about Ptery set her on edge, although Benji once told her it was a simple personality mismatch and she shouldn't worry about it. Some people just didn't get along.

Shortly thereafter, Meadow told her *anyone* could be friends if they really tried and that she was a—quote—"doodoo-head" if she didn't make nice with Ptery.

Luka valued her privacy so much that she seldom sought out friendships, but she'd come to enjoy Meadow's and Benji's company. If they wanted to be in a band with Ptery, she had to find common ground. "You know," she said. "I don't think we like each other very much."

Ptery looked over their shoulder. "How astute."

"You ever wonder why?"

Ptery cast a suspicious glance at the sleeping manticore, but they backtracked, leaning on the door frame. "Perhaps it's because you're insufferable most of the time."

Luka scowled. "It's not like you've ever given me a reason to like *you*. You didn't even give me a chance. The first time we met--"

"You stunk of engine oil and sweat. I can't be held responsible for bringing it up. I swear I thought it was a compliment to you."

"In *what world* would that be a compliment?"

Ptery's tail flared, the underside of the feathers flashing a brilliant bronze. "Look!" They stomped a foot as loudly as they dared. "You were new and untested! Me and Meadow and Benji knew each other for ages until *you* showed up one day!"

Luka laughed, rubbing her forehead. "I shouldn't have brought it up. Forget it."

Ptery crossed their arms. "I already have."

"Fine."

"Great."

But they didn't leave. As Luka lowered the goggles over her eyes and resumed work on the logic board, Ptery sat, scooting closer so they could see her progress. Although it would serve them right if they blinded themself staring at the business end of a welding pen, she dug into her bag and found another pair of goggles.

"Thanks," Ptery mumbled as she handed them over.

For a while, they sat in a half-awkward silence, the only sound between them being the soft static of the welder.

"You're good at this," Ptery said.

"You've seen my A.I.nimals."

"Well, of course I have. I own one of the CA/Ts. A right little beastling it is, though. But I've never actually seen you *work*. All without magic."

She smiled. "The welder has a magic circuit in it."

Ptery opened their mouth to speak, then sighed instead. "Oh, shut up and take the compliment, would you? It's a real one this time, unless that offends you, too."

Luka arched her eyebrows. Ptery fidgeted.

For a time, the silence that followed became almost companionable. As Luka worked, she even told Ptery what she was doing. *This is my replacement capacitor. This is the circuit that connects the capacitor to the magic gate. Here's where the board plugs into the amp.*

Ptery nodded along, politely interested but clearly not invested.

As the welder buzzed and sparked, a deep, soft rumble reverberated around them, building steadily to the pitch of a violent snarl. Benji's lips curled back, revealing pearly, dagger-white teeth, although his eyes remained closed.

"He's dreaming," Ptery said, although they scrambled to get their feet beneath them. "It's only a dream."

With little warning, Benji sprang to his feet, bellowing a roar so loud that Luka instinctively threw both hands over her ears.

The crystal window cracked with a musical *snk*, tiny bits of glassy glitter flaking to the floor. Things rattled and tumbled off shelves in the adjacent rooms. Somewhere outside, a dog barked in terror.

Ptery squealed and fled the room.

Benji's bulk filled almost every kip of space, his hair standing on end, wings stretched out as far as they would go. His eyes glowed with fury as he regained his footing while the scorpion tail thunked against the walls. Though the entire room rattled, the tree valiantly withstood the onslaught, although cracks appeared from floor to ceiling.

Quills lanced through the air, their sharp ends embedding into every surface.

A sharp pain surged through Luka's arm and up her spine, carrying an almost electric charge with it that ignited every nerve in her body. Her muscles contracted, and she fell to her knees, staring at the half-kip-long quill stuck in the bend of her elbow.

Panting, Benji relaxed, his wings draping back to the floor. He rubbed at his temple, claws snagging in his mane. "I thought—I thought she was here. I saw her. I thought..."

Ptery peered around the door frame. "I told you, Luka! I told you he'd snap!"

"I didn't. I'm not—" Benji started. "I saw the sphinx! She was here!"

Blood streaked with iridescent black ran from Luka's wound. Her whole arm throbbed in time with her quickening heart. With each beat, a dark blue sludge dribbled from the hollow end of the quill sticking up in the air.

She reached for the part of herself that could deal with crises. Her cool head. Her logic under pressure. But she found it dissolving like cotton candy in a pond.

Ptery swore. "Look what you did, you *oaf!*"

"I didn't mean to!" Benji replied. "I just—they just...!"

"Ptery, shut up and help me," Luka choked. She tried to stand, but her knees wouldn't cooperate. "We gotta get the quill out. We gotta get it out, or..."

Ptery's claws scraped against the hardwood as they fled, and it was Luka's turn to swear, which she did loudly and copiously.

"I'm sorry," Benji said. "I didn't—gods. What happened? How did I...?"

The veins radiating out from the quill were turning black.

Something touched her mind. It was a distant whisper, an insistent imperative. It reached into the core of her being, seizing everything she was, and squeezed. Cracks began to appear in her resolve.

Calm, she told herself. *Like you've practiced. Freak out later. Calm now.*

"Benji," she said. "It's not your fault. I need you to focus."

If he wanted to have a meltdown later, she'd throw him a fucking meltdown party. But she could only deal with one dilemma at a time, and hers was deadlier.

The dark venom now encompassed most of her arm, turning the skin purple as it spread. Thin black tendrils wiggled toward her neck.

"Ben," she tried again. "Please."

"Yeah. All right. Okay." Benji nodded, eyebrows lowering. "I'm... I'm here. I'm here."

"Good. We need to get the quill out."

"How?" Benji whined, his golden eyes hopeless as he held up his hands. The stubby fingers would never be able to pluck the quill out on their own.

Damn it.

Luka eyed the backward-facing barbs along the quill's surface. If she grabbed it and yanked it out in one motion, maybe the adrenaline flooding her system would block the worst of the resulting pain.

She closed her eyes, turning away from the wound so she didn't have to see it. As the tip of one finger touched the quill, a gentle touch guided her hand away.

Ptery knelt next to her with a pair of pliers, gripping the quill as close to the skin as they could. The hollow shaft cracked under the pressure as it collapsed. "This is going to hurt, love," they said.

Luka nodded. "Do it."

Ptery twisted the quill without so much as a warning, then yanked it out.

She refused to cry out, despite the dizzying bite of the quill's barbs ripping through muscle. Her ears rang and her vision swam, the edges darkening and closing in, but she couldn't afford to pass out. Someone had to tell Ptery and Benji what to do.

Black blood splattered on the floor. She braced herself on her hands and knees. "Call—call a healer. You have to call a—"

"That's okay, nestling," Ptery said, taking no offense. "I can handle it from here."

"You're not trained—" Luka began.

The shimmer of a ruby-bladed dagger caught her eye, and she was possessed by such an intense fear of it that before she could wrap her head around what she was doing, she grabbed it by the handle and hurled it out of the room.

"What in the Darkrealm did you do that for?" Ptery demanded.

"I don't..." Sitting back on her knees, Luka pressed her hand to the wound. Blood welled up through her fingers. "I don't—"

She didn't want to be healed. She *couldn't allow* herself to be healed.

"Her tears are grey," Benji said, his voice distant. "That's bad, Ptery."

A terrifying wraith took hold of her thoughts and whispered sinister instructions, breaking through her pain and haze. At first, she resisted, dismissing the voice as a figment born of her fear.

Then the wraith showed her the end of the world.

Every continent across the black planet turned to ash, dust rising up into the sky and blotting out the sun. The oceans lay empty and barren, the skulls of deep-sea creatures still adorned with rotting flesh, as the scavengers had also perished in the great cataclysm.

And you are the only witness, the wraith promised. *You are alone. Is this not what you wanted?*

As Benji and Ptery argued—their conversation banal and irrelevant—Luka reached for a quill stuck into the floor. She barely registered the pain of the barbs as they dug into her palm, and she pulled the quill from the wood with a splintering *ktch.*

Yes, the wraith said. *Yes, this is good.*

She raised the quill to her throat. It would sting, but not as much as the loneliness. And the pain would only last a moment.

Benji's powerful paw closed around her wrist and slammed her arm to the floor. Her fingers opened by reflex; despite the barbs skewering her skin, the force jarred the quill free, and it rolled away. As she crawled after it, Benji awkwardly pinned her against the floor.

Flailing and kicking, she tried to shove the grey-furred monstrosity off of her, but he refused to budge.

"Ptery, what's—" Benji grunted as Luka butted her forehead into his chin. "What's she doing!?"

"Did she just try to... Open her own throat?" Ptery returned. "Is she trying to kill herself?"

They had to let her! Her life meant nothing in the wasteland Erit had become. Hope was gone. Her friends were gone.

Her friends... were here?

The wraith guided her thoughts away from the contradiction. No, those weren't her friends. They were daemons. Shades of reality. Her own subconscious fighting the truth.

Sounded reasonable.

Buried under a landslide of despair, she bit the webbing between Benji's toes. He roared in surprise and pain, releasing her to roll out of his reach.

As she reached another quill, Ptery crashed into her, knocking her over again. Her head collided against the floor, and she saw stars.

Dazed, Luka barely noticed she was teetering on the edge of consciousness. As the wraith pulled her back toward wakefulness, one of the stars coalesced into something greater. Something brighter, filled with a sense of peace and hope.

No, she said. *I can't. There's no hope. I'm the only one.*

You are not alone, the star said.

You are alone! The wraith countered.

Although she kicked and screamed and bit and thrashed, Ptery wouldn't let her go. When they began to falter, Benji took their place, lying atop her and holding her hands far out of reach of her teeth. He refused to be moved.

"Luka *stop!*" he begged.

The star agreed. She had to stop.

How could she survive? How could she go on in this wasteland? How...?

She knew how to end her life, and neither Ptery nor Benji would be able to do anything about it. The answer came to her with clarity so crystalline, she found herself suddenly cognizant.

But before she could act, the star burned the wraith away, using the last of its strength to stop her. *No,* it said. *You must hear me. This is temporary. It will pass. Think! Use my gift of clarity and* think, *damn you!*

"Ivriarck?" Luka whispered.

"Eh?" Ptery asked.

The star's form flickered, and for a wonderful moment, Luka saw the goddess—her family's namesake— silhouetted against an orb of lightning. *You must survive,* Ivriarck said. *You must attend. Your work will be critical in the coming storm.*

"She's not kicking anymore," Benji said. "I think she's... I think she tired herself out."

A memory forced its way through the dark hopelessness. Venom. Deadly. Laced with ancient magic no mortal species could replicate. So potent that even a god would falter under the weight of its despair.

Do you see? Ivriarck asked, her voice now distant.

"Don't leave me," Luka said.

"We're here," Benji replied at the same time Ptery said, "We won't."

Ivriarck did not respond. A distant phantom enveloped the star's brightness, extinguishing all but the faintest glimmer. Luka held onto that spark as the ringing in her ears tapered off into a dull whine.

Logic returned in bits and pieces.

"Her eyes are clearing," Ptery said.

Luka wondered, "Wha?"

"They were all black," Benji replied. "It was scary."

He and Ptery sat mere centikips from each other, their full attention on her rather than on each other. How? *How?* She tried to ask, because she needed to know, but couldn't form the words.

Instead, an old faetale fluttered through her racing thoughts: *The manticore waits in the woods for disobedient children. He catches them and stings them and boils them up in a soup...*

"Is it ready?" Benji asked.

Ptery held up a small vial. The liquid inside glittered red. "Yes, if we can get her to take it."

Benji raised Luka into a sitting position. At this point, she was too drained to argue. Ptery held the vial to her lips.

Clarity, she remembered, and drank it.

Benji's earlier assessment of the potion held true, as it did taste remarkably like old socks. Still, in her state, she could do nothing other than trust her healer, even if that healer was Ptery.

"I'll have to make a poultice for the gouge in her elbow," Ptery muttered. "I'm not ready to try a Cantyr yet. It might scar..."

"S'fine," Luka managed. The holes in her palm tingled as they healed. Compared to the wound where the quill went in, the tiny lacerations across her hand reacted much more quickly to the potion.

She rubbed her fingers together, the remaining blood wet and cold against her skin.

Benji eyed the red-bladed dagger, a spark of curiosity in his eyes. It still lay on the floor nearby, with a mortar sitting beside it. He seemed to wrestle with his need for knowledge, then shook his head, attention returning to Luka. "You okay? You were, uh. Scaring us for a minute there."

"No," she said.

"Of course she isn't," Ptery said, scooting away from Benji with embarrassingly candid drama. "After all that *trust* she shouldered for you! How *could* you? You monster. You... *Villain*."

The words carried less vitriol than before, almost as if Ptery spoke from habit rather than malice. Benji still frowned, looking at the floor.

"At least we know what that dreadful tail of yours does now," Ptery went on. "It would be better if the venom killed outright rather than putting us through all these theatrics. Oh, the horror!"

Luka chuckled, then coughed as a dryness caught in her throat. "Theatrics. You're the expert on that, I guess."

"I'm serious!"

"I'm not an idiot, and you're not, either." Luka leaned into Benji's warm fur, his presence alleviating the heavy weight on her chest. "I know it was an accident, and you do, too."

"Accident or not, it doesn't matter when the end result would have been the same. If we were both attacked? What then, Luka? Could Benji mix a healing potion? Hm?"

Luka wanted to tell them it wasn't the potion that saved her. It was Ivriarck, and she was worried about the dark shade that dragged the goddess away. But the combination of the venom and the potion made her tired, and she couldn't move her mouth to speak the words.

"But we did it. Together," Benji said.

"A momentary truce, nothing more," Ptery replied, stuffing their healing implements back into their bag. "Now, if you'll both excuse me, I'll be awaiting Meadow's return in a *safer* part of the house!"

CHAPTER ELEVEN

Plague

Meadow waited for the better part of three hours in the courtyard before boredom consumed him. And while he had every intention of being respectful on this visit to the temple, the sheer *ennui* drove him to action.

He reached into one of his many pouches, withdrawing a couple trumpet pods. They were seeds of his own creation. Once mature, the obnoxious orange flowers would bloom every few days and emit ear-splitting honks and squeals throughout the temple. Last time he grew them, it took the acolytes *months* to eradicate them all.

He smiled at the seeds, then crouched down and buried them beside the path. It would take a couple spans for them to bloom, and by then, they would have sent out runners all over the temple. Maybe he'd return to watch the chaos. Maybe he'd bring a camera.

Not content with such paltry mischief, he palmed the *colurus* pods he carried in another pocket. No one said he couldn't also turn the water in the temple a sacrilegious hue as he waited for Stonebuck.

Well, the *elders* said he couldn't, but they didn't count.

For maximum effect, he'd have to get into the temple, but not through the front door. The acolytes remained on high alert for *him* in particular, and if they saw him, they'd stop him.

So he'd have to find another way.

Ascending the grand stair about halfway, Meadow bypassed the priests in their gauzy green forest regalia by hoisting himself up onto the ledge of a stone planter. After sliding along the wall, he wriggled up a shallow buttress to a convenient line of open skylights. From there, it was an easy leap down into a heavily planted fountain.

As he dropped, the slick algae coating the fountain's smooth stone bed caused him to slip. The water broke his fall, splashing everywhere.

An overworked acolyte seethed as she stared at the puddles that now adorned the floor.

"Oh, good." Meadow held out a hand, which had become tangled in vines. "If you could just—"

"Stonebuck, your *headache* is here!" the acolyte shouted, stomping away. Her hooves clattered against the flagstone.

Meadow sighed. Using the sharp edge of his fingernails, he sliced through the delicate vines while "accidentally" squeezing the contents of the *colurus* pods into the fountain. As the water turned an unsightly piss-yellow, he climbed over the fountain's embankment and onto the stone walkway.

At least the tiny, raised chapel into which he'd fallen was mostly empty of patrons. He rung out his clothes, shook the water from his legs and tail, then leaned on a banister overlooking the temple's main vestibule.

Each surface, whether horizontal or vertical, hosted a flamboyant, prismatic array of mosses and lichens. Ferns and shrubbery lined the paths, which were denoted by either close-cropped sweetgrass or colorful stone. Reeds and cattails surrounded the many shallow ponds and streams which wove in and out of the temple's many small chapels.

From this height, Meadow saw the true splendor of the temple's architecture—wherever the sun streamed down through a skylight, a priest stood atop a vine-covered dais, attending to the congregation. On the busiest days, one would only have to look to the brilliant light to find help.

He backed away from the banister and slid down the mossy incline of the archway to the floor, which grew with thick yellow cowslip. Pulling up a fistful of the delicate flowers, he absently ate them as he wished he was anywhere else.

Meadow hated being in any proximity to the temple, let alone sitting *inside* it. Closing his eyes, he experienced a brief flashback of himself at the age of five aurs, ditching his guide—because his guide was one of the stiffest, most formal priests ever to dedicate himself to the goddess—and finding his way to Petalvine's stone all on his own.

Except he hadn't found Petalvine's stone. He'd found Wheriae's.

He didn't care about the temple's protocols and rules. He didn't understand that rituals must not, in any circumstance, be broken. How could he at that age? As far as Meadow was concerned, he found a stone, and because he was drawn to Petalvine, he prayed to Petalvine.

Wheriae heard. And Wheriae wanted him.

He couldn't remember much of their fight. Dreams. Flashes of visions. Angry voices screaming in his head—one who cared for him, the other only wanted to win. He had a fever. The tug-of-war lasted for days. His creche-parents thought he'd die.

"Is this why you cause so much trouble here?"

Meadow looked up. Stonebuck stood above him, smiling gently. With some difficulty, the elder sat in the grass, his antler-like horns clacking against the arch behind them. "Do you dye the fountains because if you're not causing mischief, you are thinking about *them?*"

"I don't always dye the fountains," Meadow said. "Sometimes I bathe in 'em. Sometimes I just let a bunch of sparks loose in here."

"Mm-hm. Well. You'll be pleased to know that the fountain you contaminated drained to most other fountains in this sector, and it will take days to un-spell the water. You've made several acolytes quite frustrated today, and they've had words with me."

"*Colurus* pods," Meadow said. "Home-grown for this exact reason."

"I see," Stonebuck said. He reached up to scratch at the base of one of his ancient, pronged horns. "Well, knowing the cause is half the solution."

"You think," Meadow said.

Stonebuck chuckled, stroking his beard. "Ah, but back to the matter at hand, I think. The gods closed a loophole because of you," he said. "You are the only faun ever to be claimed by two gods."

"Oh, c'mon. Others must have tried—"

"Yes, indeed. They did. But each time, they came away from their shrine with a single eye color. Purple, or red, or orange. You alone have two. You're the only one who is the conduit of two gods."

Meadow tilted his head, trying to hide a smile. "So you're saying I'm *special.*"

"Mm. Perhaps not in the way you suppose. But yes."

Meadow sat in silence for a while, staring across the chapel to a waterfall which now ran yellow. "You know, the elders didn't make it easy for me. They argued." Sometimes they argued literally *over* him as he pressed his head against the cold temple floor to stave off the pain.

But he also remembered Stonebuck leaning over him, a warm, comforting hand on his shoulder as he cried.

"It wasn't supposed to be possible, Meadow. And we still don't know why Wheriae desired you. Perhaps he sensed the power within you that we did not. Perhaps he grew impatient of so many fauns choosing Petalvine over him."

"I didn't want him. He *hurt.*" Meadow's voice broke like a kid's.

"Mm. Yes, for a god of water, he has a fiery soul," Stonebuck agreed. "It wasn't until you rejected him—when he broke your horn in retaliation—that we saw the power within you."

"You *always* did, Stonebuck."

Stonebuck chuckled again. "You made me proud, Meadow, learning so much magic on your own. I hoped you would return to the temple and dedicate yourself to Petalvine, but I fear your view of the gods is skewed because of what happened to you."

That was an understatement.

Conduits acted as magical pathways into the world, their existence serving as the way arcane forces flowed from the gods and into mortals. Meadow couldn't remember the specifics, but each conduit allowed their god a *little* more influence. A powerful conduit gave a god even greater power.

In return, the gods gave their conduits gifts. Long life. Natural magic affinity.

But when Wheriae fought for him and Petalvine struck back... *it hurt*. Of course Petalvine only wanted the best for him, but in that moment, she only wanted to *win*. It was a pain only a faun could know, as only fauns could be conduits. Meadow shivered at the memory.

But Petalvine apologized. Gave him time and distance. Wheriae...

Wheriae was relentless. Abusive.

"Do you know how you stick it to a god?" Meadow asked.

Stonebuck arched his eyebrows.

"You wash your bum in their sacred pools."

Stonebuck laughed, hearty and long, his old voice cracking as if he hadn't had a reason to laugh in a long time. "Oh, Meadow. But alas, here you are, coming through for Petalvine in her hour of darkest need. Even though you detest the gods, you understand the importance of their aspects."

"So the plants..."

"Yes. A crisis," Stonebuck said in such a way that he might have been reciting a lullaby. Calm. Ever patient. Ever optimistic. He smiled and stood, motioning for Meadow to follow. "*Your* crisis. Come with me. I'll show you."

The lush vegetation growing throughout the temple—from the hanging vines to the vast gardens, all the way to the grass-covered walls—dampened the tapping of their hooves against the stone floor. Petalvine reigned here and ensured her faithful understood her magic and purpose. Even though the temple was made of stone, it lived.

Light poured in from above; parrots and squirrels and small monkeys squabbled in the treetops. The trickle of water fountains echoed from every sub-temple and antechamber.

Clouds gathered beneath the ceiling. Soon, it would rain.

The elder led Meadow through every abbey, all the way to the temple's center. The vast pulpit, situated on a raised platform, was rumored to contain a small chip of Petalvine's horn.

Hastily constructed within the pulpit was a stone dais over which another elder stood, her face contorted in pained concentration. She bent over a bouquet of familiar black flowers, which were surrounded by a faint, sickly yellow glow. Even the leaves which had fallen from the bundle shimmered as if surrendering their spirit. Meadow couldn't take his eyes off the spectacle.

"You've prevented a disaster," Stonebuck said, "rather than creating one, as is your wont."

"What's she doing?" Meadow asked. The elder on the dais muttered as if speaking to the flowers. She trembled; a trio of acolytes approached and bid her to depart, but she refused.

"She is halting the loss of the forest," Stonebuck said. "You did well."

Another elder made his way up the stairs. Finally, the exhausted doe slumped and allowed someone else to carry her away. The glow around the flowers diminished for only a second before the newcomer began speaking to them.

"I just brought in some flowers," Meadow said.

"How many people saw this disease and shrugged their shoulders?"

"They were in my garden, though. No one else—"

"After you brought these to us, we found patches of these blackened plants throughout Faun-ir. Through divining. Through witnesses. I ask again, how many people must have seen these and passed them by? How many conduits of Petalvine thought them to be someone else's problem?"

Meadow stared at the exhausted elders who had, in such a short time, thrown together a crude, although effective, defense. A priest, standing at attention within view of the dark bouquet, caught his eye and offered a respectful nod.

Meadow turned away. He neither needed nor wanted their respect. Not after all these aurs. "The sparks were really insistent."

"Then the water god is involved. This is quite dire."

"How dire?"

"The plague seems to grow exponentially," Stonebuck explained, his voice as soft as rain. "The infected plants, in turn, affect those connected to their roots, and so on. You acted early, Meadow. But by the time we mobilized, we were forced to kill six percent of the forest to stop the spread."

Six percent! Meadow shivered. What if he'd waited 'til tomorrow?

"With any lapse in chanting, the infection attempts to remanifest. We will have someone on watch, day and night, to ensure it can't take root again." Stonebuck stepped in front of him, taking his shoulders. "Though you rejected him, the water god sees fit to call you to his service. He sent his heralds to you, and I urge you to see what he wants. Immediately."

Meadow narrowed his eyes, curling his lip. "He sends his heralds to everyone. They're pests."

Stonebuck smiled, although this smile reflected a patience bordering on frustration. "Do you trust me, Meadow?"

Meadow narrowed his eyes. He supposed he trusted Stonebuck more than others in the temple's realm. To that end, he gave a curt nod.

"You, among all fauns, are unique. And perhaps this was an accident brought about by the ancient rivalry between two angry deities. But accidents are not always bad, and you may be in the perfect position to save Faun-ir. Maybe even the world. Wheriae, after all, is Petalvine's strength..."

"And she his weakness," Meadow finished, quoting the temple texts.

The elder nodded his approval, then chuckled. The laughter carried the slightest hint of incredulity. "It's never the ones you expect," Stonebuck said. "Laurel was the last in Faun-ir to be called. Just as irreverent as you, and so *angry*. But the gods choose who they choose, even if this fell into your lap without warning. Do you remember Laurel?"

What a silly question. How could he ever forget *Laurel?* How could *anyone?* "Did you ever hear from her again?"

"No."

Then she was lost. Caught up in the affairs of the gods. Dead, probably.

Damn.

"All right," Meadow said with a sigh he hoped was sufficiently long-suffering. "Fine. I'll go see what Ol' Wet Britches wants. Gods know I can find his stone better than anyone here."

Unseen by all except the unfortunate few, a giant pale gnoll watched from the shadows of the trees as Meadow skipped down the temple's steps.

She could sense the taint of the *Interlopers* on him. He carried the stench of the New Gods. The aura of Ziro's god-touched gift wafted from him like a poison.

The gnoll thought she'd been quite convincing with her warning and knew the members of her pack had seen it delivered with faithful fervor. Why, then, did this faun pursue his folly? *Stupidity,* probably. Fauns had no sense of self-preservation and would follow their curiosity until their own demise.

It wasn't that she wanted to eat him. It was that she had to.

For the Old Gods.

Not here, though. The denizens of the forest barely tolerated her presence as it was. If she killed one of their own, they would kill in turn—as would be their right. But moreover, they might attack Ghaspir in their thirst for vengeance, and that she could not allow.

She bristled as Wheriae's chosen lackey turned down the path to the water shrine. Not even the promise of eternal servitude under the feet of *Kt'arr'ghar* would convince her to follow Meadow there. The raw abrasiveness of the water god's presence would drive her mad. Perhaps she'd even turn on her own and destroy them.

She'd heard tales of such things happening.

No. She'd have to think. Formulate a plan. And strike at the proper time.

CHAPTER TWELVE

Hammer to Fall

The sparks were back, their frog-like bodies swinging almost gracefully through the trees. They croaked now and again—not to each other, but to Meadow—as they encouraged him onward.

Here and there, a grey shock of crumbling flagstone stood out within the vibrant greenery, which was the only indication he was on the right path. Of course, Meadow would never forget the exact location of Wheriae's shrine stone, even without the suggestion of the dilapidated road. How could he? His life had changed from the moment he found it, so its presence was forever seared into his memory.

The sparks' chirps increased in intensity the farther he got from civilization.

Then, as if carved out by the razor edge of a machete, the forest abruptly stopped, and there it was. Far off the paths and surrounded by a resplendent glade, Wheriae's stone inhabited the very center of a shallow pond of crystal water. Koi swam under and around flotillas of lily pads, hinting at the connection between water and life.

At the farthest arc of the shrine, a fox started in alarm as Meadow approached, then darted into the dark forest beyond.

Wheriae's heralds thrived here. Their round bodies bobbed below the surface of the water as globular chromatic eyes watched Meadow through the ripples. They surrounded the shore, too, their little colonies constructed out of wood, stone, and furs. Little corrals built next to tiny docks harbored schools of baby koi, while rows of underwater farmland grew rich with colorful varieties of kelp.

The sparks made way for Meadow as he stepped into the pond.

The water was cool, rising just above Meadow's hocks. Some of the smaller heralds approached to investigate his hooves. The bravest of them pulled loose fur from around his ankles, then meandered off with it to do whatever sparks did with faun hair. Despite their seclusion, they showed no fear.

By now, the sun had set, though its last pink light still brightened the open sky above. Perhaps it would have been a better idea to return in the morning when the beasts of the forest weren't out in their hunting prime. Then again, Wheriae wasn't known for his patience and might take the delay as a terrible slight.

Maybe the sparks would keep the bears away.

"Hullo? I'm here," Meadow said, taking a few steps closer to the stone. He barely lifted his feet, afraid that even the tiniest splash might disturb the heralds' colony, but they didn't seem to mind. They even encouraged him onward, chirping and croaking with every centikip he advanced.

The wind stopped. The leaves ceased their rustling. The air grew heavy with purpose.

Then the sparks retreated, lining up on the shore and facing the stone. Their eyes glowed a terrible, otherworldly cerulean as shadows stretched across the pond.

Fear almost overtook him, but he'd already come so far. Nothing Wheriae did to Meadow would ever compare with the pain from his youth. He unconsciously rubbed the base of his broken horn, remembering, as he splashed onward through the deepening water.

Then he was there, staring down at the block-shaped slab of granite, which displayed Wheriae's name on it in weathered elvish runes. Moss grew in the crevasses and cracks and clung to its base, the stringy tendrils bobbing in the water. Part of a candle remained on top, though it had long since gone out. Its white wax dripped partway down the surface and puddled inside one of the runes.

"Are you gonna talk to me?" Meadow asked, in probably the wrong way. But how did one address a god? He'd never been summoned by one before. Maybe if he'd gone to God Class back at the temple, he'd have some idea.

"Hello?"

Two spouts of water leapt from the pond's calm surface, forging themselves into translucent chains in less time than it took him to blink. Staggering backward, Meadow tripped on his own tail and fell, his arms spinning through the water for purchase on the gravelly bed.

One water-chain snaked forward, twisting around his ankle and wrenching him closer to the stone. The other struck at his wrist, clasping around it like a shackle. Even though Meadow thrashed at it, the water refused to release him.

The pond bubbled as if it were boiling, but Meadow felt no heat. The sky above him turned to black; the trees faded from the edge of his vision, plunging him into a dark, bleak landscape. The chains gave another tug and pulled him under.

Down and down. Further and further, through the pond's stone bed and into an impossible depth. Deeper and deeper he went until all light vanished and the koi and lily pads were nothing but an opulent memory.

He held his breath as long as he was able as he struggled to free himself, but his chest burned with exertion. As he started blacking out, Meadow involuntarily sucked in a lungful of water, his mind spiking to the edge of panic before—

He took another breath, and another, the bubbles rising around him as he breathed the water of the curiously deep pond.

Finally, his hooves touched the bottom.

Sapphire and turquoise tiles surrounded him, inlaid with pale blue topaz stones. Blue candles floated through the depths, burning a liquid azure, defying any semblance of physical logic.

And then there was the shadow.

It rose above him, arcing back and forth, its glowing white eyes shimmering within the watery sanctum.

Wheriae. He exhaled, and the flames of the candles flickered out.

The chains vanished, allowing Meadow to move freely. Despite being underwater, he seemed bound to the floor beneath him, as if this realm was nothing more than a manifestation of Meadow's subconscious. Or the god's.

The shadow rumbled. "She stole you from me," he said, voice as deep and dark as an ancient cave. "And I always wondered... Ah, but here you are. Our *shining beacon of hope*."

He sounded sarcastic. Meadow hadn't been aware that a god could be sarcastic.

Wheriae's eyes glimmered in the darkness, sparkling off the beautifully laid tile floor.

And yet, even with his brilliance, Wheriae himself remained a mere shadow. His form changed every time he shifted, then became more streamlined as he shoved off the floor to swim. Sometimes, as the god stared at him from every possible angle, Meadow would see the hint of a leg, or a fin, or a tail, but these appendages always vanished back into the shadow's body as if they'd never existed at all.

And no matter where Meadow turned, those eyes were always on him.

The shadow settled a decikip in front of him. "I don't have much time," Wheriae said.

Meadow thought that if the god didn't have much time, he probably should spend less of it on sarcasm.

Wheriae's eyes narrowed as if he heard the thought. "You should have been mine. I claimed you." One tendril of shadow reached out, its wispy chill curling around Meadow's broken horn. "But had you not rejected me, we would all be lost."

"You're welcome?" Meadow volunteered.

Wheriae seemed to sigh, his gelatinous form deflating into a puddle of shadowstuff that crept into the cracks between the tile. Meadow could feel the god's irritation and melancholy pressing on his mind and longed to escape it, but he was trapped.

If he could swim... If he could go *up*, maybe he could escape...

"I am curled around your soul, entwined with her spirit. It is the right I claimed, the deal I struck." Wheriae shifted again, his eyes floating closer, the shimmering orbs each as big as Meadow was tall. "Thank the old ones that I did not relent."

"You hate her. Why did you stay?"

More than anything, Meadow felt the god's vicious hate warring with respect and admiration.

"It's true that I reviled her," Wheriae said. "She stole from me. She took everything. Water is life, she would say, then she'd coerce me into giving my life to her children. Because *the planet must live*. She kept me true to my task, and for that, I revered her. I loved her. She was the only one who could calm my rage! And after all that... Who praised me for holding back my temper? Who worshiped me for my magnanimity?"

One wisp of shadow curled into a fist. "No one!" he thundered, his white eyes narrowing. "I could have used the ocean to level cities. It was my right! It was my power! They would have cried out my name in terror and supplication, and I would have ignored them."

The eyes of the god bored into him again, intense and uncomfortable. Wheriae considered, then said, "I thought when she was gone, I could unleash my anger, but even her memory prevents it."

Gone?

She was gone?

"I was her strength, as she was my weakness," Wheriae continued. Bubbles in the darkness formed into a simple silhouette of a plant, while others coalesced into a droplet of water. Pieces of them cycled between each other in a constant system of give and take. "We could not have foreseen a situation in which our timeless grudge would prove to be the answer we needed. Petalvine's gift will wane within her faithful. Their magic will fail as if it never existed at all."

Finding his voice, Meadow asked, "Petalvine is dead?"

"She was taken from us by a great Shade. Darker than even the fathomless depths. More unrelenting than the fiercest tidal wave. Ah, but her suffering was short, while ours endures. Still, we fight this Shade with our very vitality!"

"Then... you'll kill it. You'll win. Right?"

An impossible sadness pressed down upon Meadow's shoulders. The mighty god looked up into the vast expanse of nothing above.

Then he said, "We are losing."

Meadow's knees gave out, and he collapsed. The cursed plants, the apprehension of the elders at the temple, the priests rushing about like ants without a queen... It all made sense now. Maybe they didn't know the reason for their unease, but this explained everything.

Wheriae closed his eyes, though the light didn't entirely vanish. Rather, it came from within the shadow, dancing around a minuscule form buried deep within—a smaller creature shrouded by its own hubris and unable to face the truth of its own existence. Was this the real god?

The surrounding ocean darkened as the light faded. Reaching forward, Meadow shook the shadow, finding its surface surprisingly solid. The light returned.

"It is chipping away at me as it did to Petalvine," Wheriae said. "But I hold the last piece of her spirit. The last hope. If I die, then Petalvine is lost, and the balance, too, is lost. You..." His eyes bore the exhaustion of his plight as they studied Meadow. "I can keep her alive within you. Nourish that tiny part of her remaining spirit until I can fight no longer. Oh, fate! My own greed and the ineptitude of a single faun have become our only hope!"

Meadow ignored the part about his ineptitude. "Aren't you *gods?*" he asked. "Don't you create fate?"

Wheriae laughed, though the sound carried more malice than humor. "Do you think you understand the gods? You barely understand yourself. Call it chance, then. Luck. Serendipity, if you must. Had we not fought over you, the world would already be under the control of this darkness, and there would be no escape."

He felt like the fulcrum of a scale. Meadow usually wasn't one for terribly fancy metaphors, but with him on one side and the end of the world on the other, it seemed a pretty apt comparison.

"Are you brave, little speck?" Wheriae asked.

"There's nothing you can do?"

"No."

Damn.

Meadow sighed, and the bubbles spiraled above him and out of the reach of the light. "Then I guess I have to be."

He sensed respect from the god for the first time, and it lifted his spirits, even if he couldn't understand why the gods couldn't save themselves. "Why?" he asked. "Why is this happening *now?*"

"I have few answers," Wheriae said. "The true nature of this Shade is unknown to us by its own design. I only know what I could glean from it before our imprisonment. Before... Before *she* died."

"And this thing has the power of a god."

"Two, currently. The rest of us are doing what we can to hold on."

"*Two?* Another god is dead?"

Wheriae growled, the sound deep and foreboding. "No, speck. How could you hope to understand? Do not ask such foolish things!"

"Okay. Fine. Right. What do I have to do?"

Wheriae's eyes closed again, for just a moment this time. His body shook as if the very act of revealing such a secret pained him. In the end, he failed. "I cannot—the knowledge is... You must figure it out yourself!"

"You have to tell me *something!*" Meadow snapped, stomping a hoof on the tile. Tiny bubbles fluttered upward, then disappeared into the darkness. "It's your lives! It's—It's *Erit's existence!* Give me something to go on!"

Wheriae roared, his voice deep and terrible, splitting through Meadow's very being. One claw darted out from the shadow, ripping open the pouch at Meadow's hip that held Benji's pendant. The moon-shaped crest floated freely, glowing with the intensity of a star as a cord of water wound through the silver bail. It coalesced into a shimmering chain. *"THE ELF KNOWS! THE ELF HAS THE KNOWLEDGE. FIND THE GODPLAIN. THE ELF WILL KNOW WHERE THE GODS REST!"*

The crest fell. Meadow caught it before it hit the floor. "Why would Benji know?"

Wheriae roared again, this time in pain. "The Shade... has gone to great lengths... to ensure we cannot reach our conduits. But some of us have tricks. Failsafes. This one—this one it has discovered. You must... Before it's too late!"

Without regard for proper reverent protocol, Meadow grabbed hold of the ever-shifting shadow. "You have to tell me more!"

"It is listening," Wheriae said, his eyes widening to an impossible size. The sanctum brightened as if the sun had fallen through the depths. "I haven't said... I haven't... I've attracted its attention. You have to go!"

Water filled Meadow's lungs and choked him as the form of Wheriae writhed. And then there was another shadow—this one far more sinister, its eyes as dark as its very being. It surrounded the god. Meadow expected him to cry out, but Wheriae's eyes glowed even brighter in defiance.

Please, Meadow begged. He floated upward as his consciousness waned. *Tell me where to start.*

Wheriae spoke no final words of guidance. Meadow experienced his agony. His exhaustion.

His silence.

The Shade stared at him, and in that gaze, Meadow felt the stirrings of familiarity.

His vision blackened, his consciousness swimming before...

He awoke.

Confused, wet, and sore, he couldn't get his bearings. He fell, splashing into the shallow pond, where he flailed against the darkness that now surrounded him. His face went under, the water stinging in his nostrils.

He tried to find some remnant of calm, but with the god's words still fresh in his memory, he could only panic for a good few seconds before rational thought took over. The Shade wasn't *here*. The blackness around him was simply the darkness of night.

And the water was cold. Coughing, Meadow climbed up onto the stone, catching his breath as best he could. He had no idea what in the Darkrealm he had to do, only that he had to do *something*.

When he closed his eyes, he could see the eyes of the Shade staring at him as if it knew who he was and what he intended to do.

Lying on his back, Meadow stared up at the two visible moons. "If you know what I intend to do," he said, as if the Shade was listening, "then please, by all means, gimme a hint. Just an inkling. Something. Because I have no idea."

He closed his eyes.

He could go home tomorrow.

CHAPTER THIRTEEN

I Don't Know What We're Talking About (And I Haven't for a While)

Ptery pulled the curtain back, checking outside for at least the tenth time since nightfall. Although wyldlights and aura possums flitted about the forest, bringing a soft glow to the otherwise dark undercanopy, Meadow remained missing.

Where was he? Faoliia's feathers, he was never gone this long!

One possum, seeing someone in the window, whirled closer and shifted from gold to green, which was the color of Ptery's aura. What beautiful little beasties they were. And so distracting! Ptery could watch their aerial antics for hours.

But *that* would be a waste of time. No, they should check on their charge again, perhaps even whip up another potion if necessary.

Luka lay across the couch from them, still wearing her blood-besmirched clothing. Ptery would have liked to remove her overalls for sanitary purposes, except the petulant patient fought against it even in her sleep. Outrageous!

Sliding off the sofa, Ptery pattered to Luka's side, liberating her arm from the blanket. Though faint against her pale skin, the quill's scar still stood out as a jagged-edged circle. A better healer could have obliterated the evidence of the injury entirely.

A better healer.

She'd be fine! Who cared if a scar remained, really? In a few aurs, the mark would fade to a pale pink, then perhaps vanish entirely.

Besides, there were two much older scars on Luka's forearm that piqued Ptery's interest. They seemed shallow enough that even a novice healer could have removed them, yet they stood out even sharper than the new injury.

Angry slashes across pale skin. Odd. Ptery ran a gentle talon over them.

Luka audibly winced under their touch, nose curling. "No. That tickles."

"Ah, are we finally waking up?" Ptery asked. "It's been a tick or two."

"Shut," Luka managed, truncating the rest of the phrase.

"Is she okay?" Benji wondered from his respectfully distanced respite across the room. "Luka, are you all right? Does it still hurt?"

She grunted.

Ptery rolled their eyes. Looking past Benji, they arched their eyebrows at the quills strewn about the empty room like terrible, tacky garland. "She's *fine*, no thanks to you."

Benji scowled, his dispirited and dejected amber eyes betraying a wounded heart that almost made Ptery reconsider their ruminations on the nature of the monster. Surely manticores couldn't fake such sincerity! Oh, but they were so crafty. So conniving. So—

"It was an accident," Benji mumbled.

"You *say* that, but I'm sure you're *thinking* about spitted banshee wings, aren't you, you toothy thing? Well, you'd only get the one, and it's scrawny, so get it out of your head."

For a moment, the beast looked shocked, then he smiled—*smiled! The nerve!*—and said, "Actually, I wouldn't mind a salad."

Something unwieldy and uncoordinated bopped Ptery upside the head. They turned their attention back to Luka to find her staring daggers at them. Incredulous, Ptery asked, "Did you just try to hit me?"

She swore under her breath, then said, " raincheck for something more violent later."

Benji laughed.

Ptery tsked. "After all I did for you."

"Not much, apparently," Luka said. "I still feel like ass."

The hollows around her eyes maintained a ghastly grey pallor, and the cloudy cast to her skin made it look as if she'd wandered just a couple steps from her own grave. Ptery couldn't help that, though. Not unless they delved more deeply into advanced spells, which could very well backfire. "Of all the ungrateful—"

"I saw it!" Benji exclaimed in a most interrupting manner.

Ptery glared. "Saw *what?*"

"The... I know what it is. I know—I've read about it before. It's the real thing. You have the ruby dagger."

Ptery glanced back at Luka—whose eyes were narrowed in confusion—then back at Benji. "What? Why bring that up *now?*"

"I just... I didn't want you to fight," he said. "I didn't know what else to say."

Luka struggled to sit up, gritting her teeth as she rested against the arm of the couch. "Yeah, I saw it, too. Fancy-ass knife."

"It's not just a knife, it..." Ptery struggled, choking back tears even though they only knew Efrit for a very brief window.

How could they explain? They possessed the words to do it, but not with the reverence the tale deserved. Efrit deserved remembrance. Honor. But all Ptery had were anger and sarcasm. That, and a real fear the gods *wanted* them for something beyond comprehension. "Efrit gave it to me. Then she died in my arms."

Damn it. They could have done better than *that*.

"Died?" Luka asked, brows lowering in suspicion. "But she was fine when she was here."

Ptery didn't know how to defend themself because they didn't understand what happened, either. Even if they'd coveted the ruby dagger since chickhood, they never wanted someone to die for it. "Look, I didn't—"

Benji held up a paw. "Luka, Efrit was *famous* in Faun-ir for living longer than any faun on the planet," he said. "By a hundred aurs! She's written about in *textbooks*. Oh, and she was in this aur's puzzle match, second round. 'Cuz Faoliia wouldn't let her die until she completed her calling."

All for this moment. All for you.

Ptery trembled.

"I don't know what it was. The calling, I mean," Benji went on, "but maybe..."

"She said Faoliia kept her alive, just to..." Ptery trailed off. Efrit's kind face and steely resolve would forever be carved into their memory. The old faun knew the will of the goddess and accepted her own fate. How? How could someone so easily accept death? "...Just to give me the ruby dagger."

"To give *you* a *knife?*" Luka asked, although her incredulity waned.

"Not a knife," Ptery repeated.

They slumped to the floor, leaning on the front of the couch. The gravity of the gift was only now starting to sink in. Some old faun they barely knew waited her whole life to give Ptery one of the most wonderful healing implements on the *planet*? It made no sense.

Because as much as Ptery loved themself, they still lacked the necessary skill for such a tool to be in their possession. So many other masterful mages deserved to own it. So many other healers could wield it in a way Ptery couldn't.

Ptery didn't deserve it.

"Are you okay?"

Benji waved a paw in front of Ptery's face, offering an encouraging smile. It took all their concentration to muster up the anger to bite back, "Of course I am!"

The gods-damned beast was too *sweet. Too kind!* Why? Why did it care?

Benji frowned, concerned. "It's just that you saw someone—"

"Oh, stop being so nice to me!" Ptery snapped, leaping to their feet. "I know what you're trying to do. The moment I let my guard down, you'll pounce."

"Ptery!" Luka exclaimed, her fingers curled into a fist. She wouldn't actually punch them. Probably.

Even so, a sick-addled rage burned in her eyes that Ptery never saw before. Obviously feeling better, Luka rose to her feet, wobbling a bit before settling on her heels.

Ptery also leapt up, standing on the tips of their talons so they could meet Luka's eyes. "I'm only telling *facts*," they said. "You can't trust a manticore. He tried to murder you!"

"I didn't try to murder *anyone*." Benji pushed his immense bulk upward until he, too, stood. The living room was getting awfully crowded, and Ptery took an involuntary step backward, certain their end had come in the form of a whole array of serrated, painful teeth.

But Benji seemed almost embarrassed, even a little confused. "It's... I was sleeping, and I was startled, and I thought—I thought the sphinx was here..."

Trailing off, he glanced at Luka for help. "You don't have to explain yourself to *them,*" she spat.

"But I want to." Benji nodded as if affirming his own decision. "What I *think* happened is... If I'm startled, maybe these quills—Maybe they—Well, you know. Like, uh. Jellyfish! Right? You know!"

Ptery didn't know, but they got the gist. "It's not comforting to know you can launch venomous quills because someone says 'boo' at you."

Disgruntled, Benji dragged the curved side of his terrifying, sharp, deadly claws across the floor. His lower lip stuck out between his two throat-crushing tusks. "I don't know what you're so scared of, Ter. I'm still... You know. Nothing has changed."

He wasn't serious. He couldn't have been serious.

It would have been wise to drop the subject and bring it up later when tempers weren't quite so high. But Ptery had their reasons, and the others knew enough to defer to their expertise, which made their arguments even more maddening. If they treated Benji with kindness, he would eventually take advantage of it. The only logical solution was to *treat the threat as a Darkrealm-damned threat!*

As for the beast, he must have known what a peril he posed. Perhaps his fright clouded his intelligence, though. After all, becoming a monster of nightmares would be enough to muddy anyone's thoughts to the point where even a liori might believe they belonged in respectable society. But the darkness would eventually devour him with all the luxury afforded by time until he forwent rational thought entirely.

That sad sack of pale fur would have to come to terms with that. Why not now? Why wait until he killed someone?

Ptery had to push, for everyone's benefit. "You're not *still you*, if that's what you're trying to say. Maybe you don't know it yet, but your..." They trailed off, waving at the remaining quills stuck in the walls. "That was an uncontrolled burst of aggression. You intended to kill—"

They spun across the floor, colliding with a wall and collapsing to the floor before they realized what had happened.

As the stars cleared from their vision, Luka stood over them, hand still curled into a fist, her entire body shaking with the effort of remaining on her feet.

Incredulous, Ptery pressed a hand to their cheek.

Luka rubbed her fist, then the anger cleared from her eyes, and she sunk to the floor next to Ptery.

Benji took a step forward.

Ptery's mind blanked. They couldn't think. Couldn't even form the words to beg for their life. As Benji's giant paw reached out, Ptery knew he was about to bring those claws down, rending their body into strips of flesh and splinters of bone. No one would even be able to identify the pieces once the manticore was through.

But the paw pressed with gentle care against Luka's chest, then drew her backward, away from Ptery. Benji's yellow eyes met Ptery's and scowled with disappointment.

"I know you're afraid. But you should... uh. I think you should go upstairs now. I think... I think Luka needs rest, and you're not—I mean, you helped before, but now..."

Luka leaned against Benji's leg, one arm pressed into his fur, her eyes closed.

Ptery backed against the wall, knees tucked to their chest. They grappled for the thin chain around their neck, one talon drawing up the tiny bauble hidden beneath their shirt. Grasping the garnet in a tight fist, they let the warmth comfort them while they wondered if they might have been wrong all along.

CHAPTER FOURTEEN

Keep Yourself Alive

The sparks! The gods-damned sparks! Couldn't they shut up for *five ticks?*

Meadow threw his hands over his ears to shut out their incessant chirping, forgetting that he'd perched himself atop Wheriae's stone the night before. Overbalancing, he fell backward into the water, where the sparks scattered in all directions as he sunk to the bottom.

His fists clenched in irritation, his fingers squeezing against cold metal.

Confused, Meadow righted himself, struggling on his elbows to the circle of wet shore around the stone so he could examine the metal intrusion in his hand. It was Benji's crest, now re-strung with what seemed to be liquid platinum. He ran his fingers along the chain, feeling an inexplicable lack of friction. Then he remembered.

That actually happened?

It couldn't have. Visions were *visions*.

And yet...

Grimacing, Meadow flipped over, running his fingers over the slash in his clothes where one of Wheriae's errant claws struck him. Under the ripped fabric was a hair-thin cut from the bottom of his rib cage to his hip. The pouch where he'd stored the crest was shredded completely.

He flopped back to the ground, allowing the mud to ooze around his extremities. Exhausted and sore, he couldn't muster the energy to move any more than he already had except to tuck the crest back into an un-shredded pocket.

The last stars of night shimmered far above in the greying sky. The faintest blue cast played at the very edges of the canopy, signaling the start of a new day. Somehow, Meadow had to get home. Or at least he had to get somewhere that wasn't on top of a god's shrine rock, in the cold, in the middle of a forest.

Around him, the sparks ribbitted their encouragement.

After rolling over onto his stomach, he leveraged his arms under his chest, pushing up with his elbows.

"Noooo," he complained, but wiggled his knees under himself anyway. If he could just *stand*, he could—

His hooves slipped on the pond's rough bed, dropping him back to his stomach, where he became intimately familiar with the taste of mud.

Face down in the silt, he once again whined, "Nooooo."

It took a long time for him to gather the strength to try again. This time, he staggered to his feet, then immediately doubled over and braced his hands on his knees for support. A weariness deep inside ate away at him as if the remnants of Wheriae's vision fought to pull him back under.

"I'm awake now," he said to no one in particular, and perhaps to convince himself.

With his hands still on his knees, he forced himself to take one step forward. His legs shook, but he remained standing.

Though Meadow never was the praying sort, in that moment, he considered asking Wheriae for strength.

"You've got your hands full, though, don't you, buddy?" Meadow grunted through clenched teeth, shuffling forward. "Or your claws. Flippers. Hooves. Whatever it is you gods have."

The sparks followed each minuscule step, gently nipping at his fetlocks. Maybe he could eat one of them for strength. Or maybe he could catch one of the koi!

He chuckled, forcing himself fully upright again. Although he wobbled, he found his balance. "It'd be... like that time..." He took another step. "Just like that time..." Another step. "Ptery dared me to eat a ham."

Such torment! Such misery! And that was just the first few hours! No, meat did not agree with faun physiology. He'd end up worse off.

Another step. Maybe he could eat some of the frogbite moss floating on the water. If he could catch it.

Another step.

He was out of energy. With nothing left to give, he collapsed on the outer shore of the pond.

Hunger gnawed at him, drawing an involuntary sob. Digging his fingers into the sand, he tried to enchant something edible from it to provide something to keep him going. But magic took energy he didn't have; consequently, nothing sprouted beneath his hand.

The grass. He could eat the tufts of grass speckling the shore.

Meadow curled his lip at the thought of it. He was a discerning faun, after all. And yet, he'd die out here in the middle of nowhere, with no one knowing what happened to him, if he didn't lower himself to the habits of a common goat.

"If any of you..." He ripped up a chunk of sod, curling his nose at it. "If any of you... *frogs...*" He spat the word like it was poison in his mouth, "...tell Ptery about this, I'll—"

He kicked one hoof at the water. The resulting splash scattered the sparks for a moment, but they soon returned to the bank, watching him with their beady little eyes.

Meadow tore off a mouthful of grass and chewed.

And chewed.

And forced himself not to spit it out.

It had a sweetness, like honey warmed over a pile of dung, with just a hint of span-old warm milk. And yet, his stomachs demanded it, so before he knew it, he was shoveling whole handfuls into his mouth.

"I hope you're happy," he said to the gathering of sparks, who noisily encouraged his feast. They were like the parents who told him to eat his boiled asparagus when all he really wanted was to bury his face in a bowl of sweet clover.

Or an apple. What he wouldn't give for an apple.

He hadn't even begun to think about the vision yet—of the Shade with the familiar eyes that looked at him through the visage of a god-killer. Petalvine was dead, and it was all that *thing's* fault. Was it even a god itself? Something from beyond Erit? An alien?

He shoveled more grass into his face. Could an alien kill a god?

Science fiction programs on the VS told him that aliens could kill *anything*. But the Shade didn't feel alien.

He dug his fingers into the ground again, willing the magic to flow through him. Wheriae said he'd keep it alive, didn't he? Of everything he learned from the god, that seemed like the most important, especially *right now*.

The magic responded slowly, searching through the memories of the soil beneath his hands. History existed in more than just textbooks. It lived on in every creature that ever walked the planet, in every bird that had ever flown overhead, and in every root that ever burst forth from a seed. Even in the eyes of the judgmental heralds.

Meadow was really sick of judgmental heralds.

"Please," he begged whatever remnant of Petalvine still existed within him. "Don't make me eat more grass."

It wouldn't have been the worst thing in the world.

The sparks were venturing onto the shore now, chirping joyously, their slimy hands on his, as if they understood what he was trying to do.

Then he felt it—a sprout under his palm. Nurturing it, calling it forth, he encouraged it to grow. In a moment, he could feel what it was, too. Radishes weren't his favorite, but it would do. It would have sustenance in it, at the very least.

He was so hungry.

How much power had it taken for the god to reach him through the veil of the darkness? His failsafe, Wheriae called the hidden sanctum. A secret not even the Shade could infiltrate. Although maybe that pathway was closed to them now.

There were tears spilling down Meadow's cheeks, though he couldn't tell if they came from exhaustion or fear. Probably both since he had no idea what to do next. He was one person, in a forest full of fauns, in a world of creatures much more powerful than he could ever be. There was no way he could save the gods.

He could get home, though.

It took way too much strength to pull the radish from the muddy earth.

He ate the leaves first. They were easiest to chew, after all. Meadow always had a taste for them, though most of his kind weren't fans of their bite. Leaf after leaf. Stem after stem. He was so hungry that he swallowed them whole. Even the root was gone before he even realized he'd eaten it.

With the small meal churning away in his belly, he willed his strength to return. "Get up," he told himself. If he could get through the forest to the temple plaza, someone should be able to get him the rest of the way home.

He lay in the grass for another minute or two, maybe five, as the sparks shimmied around his hooves and climbed across his back.

"Get *up,*" he said again, wrangling his hands beneath him.

He'd been through too much too quickly.

His hooves slipped in the mud.

The sparks chirped their encouragement.

Somehow, he was back on his feet, wavering as he tried to figure out how he'd gotten there. "Good. Okay. This is good," he said. Emboldened by his small victory, he staggered into the forest, heading toward home.

CHAPTER FIFTEEN

A Handful of Quills

Long after midnight, Luka woke with a rather brilliant plan.

Although still exhausted from her ordeal, she checked her terminal to make sure the idea was even viable. Finding she could not only do it but that it was also *recommended* for any manticore who lived in public, she rolled out of bed. Then, with some difficulty, she circled down the ramp to the main floor, only stopping now and then to stave off irritating spells of vertigo.

Upon reaching the last bend, she found Ptery still awake, staring out the front window.

Luka leaned on the railing to gather her bearings. "Meadow's not back yet?"

"Are you going to punch me again?"

"I don't see how that's relevant to—"

"Are." Ptery punctuated the word, "You going to *punch* me again?"

Luka rolled her eyes. "Only if you do something *stupid* again."

Ptery muttered something about their thankless job. "No, Meadow isn't back yet. I don't want to *cast a spell before swine*, but if he's not back by morning, I think I'll notify the authorities."

"Isn't he..." Luka waved her hand in a noncommittal gesture. "You know. Flighty?"

Ptery grunted. "*I* know him better than *you* ever will."

Fine. Ptery could pout as much as they wanted, but they still deserved to have some sense knocked into them. Luka wasn't about to apologize for decking them, no matter how much they whined.

If that's what Ptery wanted, they'd be hoping for it right into their casket.

She did notice, as she wandered into the kitchen for a glass bowl, that Ptery's face looked suspiciously un-punched. That meant they healed themself, which made sense. Luka couldn't honestly expect them to wear a badge of their own shame around for the week or more. Glancing at her knuckles, she grimaced. They hurt, but she'd make sure Ptery saw the bruise as often as possible.

Just a little reminder.

With the bowl in hand, she backtracked up the ramp until she reached Benji's empty room. He lay on the floor, blanket half-draped across one wing, with his bass laid out in front of him. With one paw, he tried to press the strings against the frets while another claw strummed at the three remaining strings. A coil of wire lay a half-kip away, both ends frayed.

His ears flicked upward as Luka entered. "I've been trying for a couple hours. There's no way. You're going to have to find someone else."

The conviction and heaviness of his voice, as well as the lack of any hesitation, suggested he'd been working on exactly what to say for the entire time he'd been attempting to play.

It would be a disservice to try soothing him with encouragement or platitudes since the problem stared them both right in the face. He could barely even hold the guitar, let alone fit his paws onto the neck of it to play the right chords. As they met each other's eyes, Benji nodded, but Luka refused. Truth or not, it seemed ridiculously unkind to rip a hole through Benji's chest and jam a handful of salt in there. He was already hurting enough.

Later. They'd have to discuss it, but *later*.

"Look," she said, picking up the bass and leaning it against the wall. The neck slid down to rest against one of the quills still stuck in the wood. It had long since stopped oozing venom, although a dried, black residue now adorned the floor. "I have an idea. About your quills."

Despite his disappointment about the music situation, Benji perked up, eyes lighting with interest. But as she explained her idea, his ears drooped lower and lower until he wore an expression of disbelief. "It *can't* be that easy."

"I think it is." She pulled her terminal and a pair of pliers out of her back pocket, then set the glass bowl on the floor next to Benji's tail. "I see manticore quills for sale all the time, right? For spells and such. Hair decoration. They must get 'em from somewhere."

Benji grunted a noncommittal agreement as she sat down next to him.

He kept his tail curled tightly into a spiral, the somewhat rubbery chitin creasing at the corners with the pressure. Luka patted the cool, tough surface. "You're gonna have to unclench, buddy."

Though he smiled and rolled his eyes, he still shook his head. "Look, someone else should do this. I don't want to hurt you again."

"It was an accident."

"But Ptery was right. What if I'd... I mean, if you and they had both..."

"Ptery's an idiot."

"But they... I... That's just it. They weren't... I'm... I'm sorry. I'm so sorry."

"Trust me." Luka met his eyes long enough to recognize his fear and concern. "Okay? That's all you have to do. Trust me. I trust *you*."

Benji scowled, one tusk pushing at his upper lip, which briefly exposed the sharp teeth beneath. Then he nodded and unfurled his tail, the remaining quills rattling like bone-carved wind chimes. "Be careful," he said.

"I will. Keep your tail still." Luka retrieved the NETsite on her terminal and gave it another quick study before closing the business end of the pliers around one of the longer quills. When she squeezed it, it cracked and buckled, a few of the smaller barbs along its surface flaking to the floor. Benji gave no indication of pain, which meant she'd found a mature, hollow quill without nerve endings or a blood supply.

She hoped.

Steeling herself, Luka twisted the quill as directed, then gave a sharp tug. It popped free of the tail's carapace, leaving a clean little divot behind.

The end of the quill leaked blue-black venom. Luka dropped it into a bowl, base-first.

"Wow, I didn't even feel anything," Benji said, incredulous. He glanced between the quill in the bowl and his tail, then grinned, relieved. "That's it?"

"The venom should become inert in a couple hours now that it's detached. We just have to keep these away from people." As a precaution, she pushed the bowl across the floor, far out of the range where she could accidentally drop her arm into it. "Unfortunately, I can only pull these long ones."

"You can't get 'em all?" Benji asked, turning his tail to look. While more than half of the mature quills were already gone and sticking out of the walls, there were dozens of smaller ones remaining.

"No, they're kinda like feathers," Luka said, poking the pliers at the smaller spines. "They have a blood supply 'til they're mature. It'd hurt. A lot. This site says manticores have cried if the wrong quills were yanked out."

Benji sighed. "Might be worth it."

Luka elbowed him. "We'll wrap the other ones. Don't worry so much, okay? The little ones don't have any venom."

They could still pack a punch if they ended up in someone's skin, she supposed. Maybe they could end up in *Ptery's* skin. By accident. She certainly wasn't imagining stuffing their nightclothes full of tiny manticore barbs.

"Why are you smiling?" Benji asked.

Luka shrugged.

Her greatest challenge became discerning the venom-laden quills from those that weren't quite mature. As she poked at each with the pliers, she had one slight mishap where she ripped out a quill just on the verge of maturity. Judging by the immediate yelp of pain, it smarted as much as the NET promised it would. The resulting wound oozed bright red blood as Benji hissed and curled his claws into the wood of the poor, abused oak.

He even swore a bit, emitting words Luka didn't even think he knew.

"Whoops," Luka said.

"You're right. You're right. The little ones can stay right where they are. Gods, there must be a way to tell the difference."

It took a bit of trial and error—and a bit of gentle testing—to determine the rather simple answer. The dark bands wrapping each quill's venom reservoir were a bit blacker on immature quills and turned a charcoal grey on those ready to be plucked. Once they figured that out, Luka quickly filled the bowl, which left Benji with a smattering of uneven, venomless quills.

Though his shoulders relaxed and his tail remained uncurled, he continued to scowl, pinching one of the still-immature quills between two claws and giving it a halfhearted tug. He winced.

"We'll probably have to do that almost every day," Luka said, studying the smaller quills, which had been even smaller when she started. The things grew fast. "But that's all right, now that we know which ones are the right ones."

"I wish I could do it myself," Benji muttered. He reached for the pliers, holding them with awkward determination in a hand unfit for the task. He could get them to close but couldn't exert any pressure.

"Why don't you?" Ptery asked.

They leaned casually on the door frame, face passive, holding a scarlet envelope aloft. Once they had Luka's and Benji's attention, they ran a claw under the flap and sliced it open.

Luka grunted, pushing herself to her feet specifically so she could appear more threatening.

Ptery ignored her and removed a single piece of newly pressed parchment from the envelope. "You don't want to be a pest about all this, of course. You ought to be able to do it yourself if you want to, right? Thankfully, I remembered *this*."

They shook out the parchment, which unfolded with a flourish. Though slightly warped from the creases in the paper, a map stood out against the light tan swirls on the surface. Meticulously penned directions adorned the corners and edges.

Efrit's letter for Benji. How could Luka have forgotten it? Dammit! She made a grab for it, but Ptery whisked it out of her reach.

"Ah-ah-ah, don't be grabby. Have patience. After you attacked me, you at least owe me *that*." They smoothed the wrinkles out as they arched their eyebrows. "I'll let you have it in a tick."

"How magnanimous," Luka drawled.

"Er, Lu. Can we just—" Benji started.

"It's not *magnanimous*; it's courtesy," Ptery replied. "I'll have you know, it took a great deal of consideration before I chose to bring this to your attention, because giving it to you undoubtedly means a manticore will remain in our band. But it's not my decision to make. Besides, maybe if he can do *the thing*, he'll take his pursuits elsewhere."

"I'm right here," Benji mumbled.

Luka grabbed for the parchment again, but this time, Ptery let her have it. She crouched next to Benji, flipping the sheet over so they could look at the map, which showed both Faun-ir and Faun-anin with the Betweenroads in the middle. There, Efrit had drawn a tiny house in green, circling it several times. "What *thing?*" Luka demanded.

"Why..." Ptery wiggled their fingers. "That thing where they can move things with their minds!"

Although Luka side-eyed Ptery with the most skeptical scowl she could muster, Benji gasped. "I didn't really think... I mean, I didn't consider..."

"Wait, they're telling the truth?" Luka asked.

"Er. Yeah." Benji flipped over his hands, studying the pink pads. "I don't remember what it's called, but it's a thing liori can do. It's, uh. You know how some species have natural magic?

Sphinxes have a lot, but manticores have something like telekinesis. I didn't think I'd be able to, uh. Do it."

Luka arched her eyebrows. "Why?"

"Because he doesn't think he's a manticore," Ptery said in a sing-song voice. "But you *are*. And the sooner you get past *that* hurdle, the sooner you can stop whining about not being able to do things with your stubby little fingers. You're welcome."

They spun on their toes and sashayed from the room.

"How'd they know that?" Luka wondered once she was sure Ptery was out of earshot. "That manticores are telewhatever."

"It doesn't matter. Well, I mean. I guess it does," Benji said. "They probably... You know when you really don't like something, so you study it as much as you can so you know everything about it?"

"No," Luka said. Most sane people would avoid studying the things they didn't like.

"Oh. Well. I know *a lot* about peas." Benji shrugged his wings, then took the parchment from Luka, holding it carefully between his thumb and forefinger. "They're right, though. If... If I can do that thing, I could stay in the band. I could still play bass. I didn't even think about it, 'cuz..."

"Well, Efrit seemed to know," Luka said. "She left this for you before she... Well. Before she died, I guess."

They both contemplated the map in respectful silence until they were interrupted by a crash from the living room and Ptery's surprised—albeit restrained—squeal of surprise.

CHAPTER SIXTEEN

(I'm Not Your) Stepping Stones

Breathe, Meadow. Just breathe.

Breathe.

His hooves dragged at the edge of an area rug, flipping half of it over. He came to rest on the rubber anti-slip surface, which tore at his fur.

When he weighed the pain against his exhaustion, the exhaustion won. He collapsed.

"Meadow!" the acolyte said. "M—Master Meadow!"

The young doe radiated confusion as she stumbled over the title, although Meadow more than earned the honorific by suffering Wheriae's foul mood. Even so, the title of Master should have been reserved for those who reveled in the presence of their god, not for screw-ups who stumbled ass-first into greatness.

In short, he understood her reluctance.

No one could deny his encounter with the god, though, even if he hadn't already spilled his experience to the elders at the temple. Aura possums, drawn by the ethereal shadow of Wheriae's touch, whirled into his living room and shifted into a dazzling rainbow of hues. They sniffed at him. Poked their ghostly noses into his ears. Then turned a blinding white as they zipped back into the forest.

He propped himself on one elbow and gasped, "You can go. Thank you."

The acolyte hesitated, but then Ptery was there, their soft, warm hands resting on Meadow's shoulder. "It's all right. I'll take care of him."

The door closed with a soft k'tp.

"We've got to get you to bed," Ptery murmured, already working Meadow's arm around their shoulders. "What on Erit—"

"No!" Meadow fought for his feet, but the room spun, introducing him to dizzying glimpses of Luka and Benji across the living room. Ptery caught him before his nose collided with the floor. "No, I can't. I can't!"

One stray aura possum tried to bury itself in his shirt. Luka grabbed it, her hands visible through its translucent body. Tame and unafraid, it nestled into her arms and shifted from white to red. "What do you mean no? You look like you've been run over!"

His thoughts raced, unable to settle on an answer. Never in his life had he been so afraid nor felt so alone. He wanted to tell them he was fine, even though he wasn't. He wanted to laugh at them for being so worried or tell them he'd been through worse.

But he hadn't.

No one had. Ever, in the history of the whole planet.

Okay, perhaps that was a stretch, but all things told, Meadow would rather have been run over.

"Benji!" he said. Possessed by a sudden burst of energy, he found balance on his hooves and nudged Ptery away. Excited, he dug into the pouch containing Benji's crest, which he immediately fumbled and dropped.

The liquid cord gleamed, winding like a river across the floor.

"You had it re-strung!" Benji pinched two claws around the cord and lifted it to eye level, staring at it in awe. "It's so beautiful. How did you afford—"

"Is that what you've been doing?" Ptery demanded. "Some of us have been worried sick about you, and you've been off playing with jewelry?"

"Clearly not," Luka said. Holding the aura possum at arm's length, she squished its backside against Meadow. It chittered and turned from red to rainbow to white. Then it sparked, teleported a centikip away, and vanished through the closed door.

"Whoa, uh, this isn't elf-made." Benji struggled with the cord, trying to find a clasp. There wasn't one. "It's not metal, either. Er..."

"Wheriae," Meadow said. "I saw Wheriae."

In the brief span of time between leaving the shrine stone and returning home, Meadow played out how the conversation would go in his head. His friends would be shocked! They'd ask what the water god wanted with him. He'd reveal his all-important mission with much pomp and importance.

They just stared.

Then Ptery asked, "You took this to Wheriae to get it fixed? Meadow. Surely there were better options!"

His manic energy spent, Meadow flopped into the nearest chair.

It took him a long time to explain everything, from the sick flowers to the ritual at the temple to Wheriae's summons. He described the Shade at length and the chill left over from his brief encounter with it. He skipped over Petalvine's death, though, only because he couldn't bear to cry again after dehydrating himself several times over at the temple.

"And," Meadow said, "The last thing Wheriae told me was that Benji'd know where to find the gods. Something about a Godplain."

"Me?" Benji blinked, his fingers wrapping around the silver moon. "I don't... The gods? Does anyone know where to find the gods? Are you sure he said me?"

"Yeah, you," Meadow affirmed, gesturing at the crest. "Well, he said the elf would know where to find the gods. Then he gave me that. You're the elf."

Though Benji was about to answer, Ptery held out a hand and interrupted. "Yes, why do you have the royal crest of the Els'ri family, Benjamin? I know you're somewhat of an archaeologist, but that crest is pristine. You didn't dig it up. Tell me you didn't steal it from someone. Perish the thought!"

Meadow took a moment to stare at Ptery in abject disbelief. In fact, everyone stared at Ptery, expressions ranging from Benji's confusion to Luka's irritated askant eyeroll.

"I'm not somewhat of an archaeologist. It's my job," Benji started. "And I have it because... You really don't know? I'm sure I've told you before. I... well. It's not a secret."

It was Ptery's turn to scowl in confusion. "You talk about everything, all the time," they stammered, uncomfortable. "Maybe you said something, but if I was busy, well. Perhaps I had to, er, tune you out. Nothing personal."

Benji pressed his lips together, then nodded. "Okay, I'll be as brief as I can. Of course you know about the Xanathic period, during which the elvish ruling family killed the Old Gods—"

"Oh, this again!" Ptery massaged their temple.

"You asked!" Luka exclaimed. "Now shut up and listen!"

Ptery grunted.

Benji mumbled a quiet thank you. "I really promise it'll be brief, but I just... There's a little..." He scratched at his mane, taking a breath as if to reset himself, then nodded. "It was the ruling elves that led the march to kill the gods. And they were called the Brilliant Elves because they were golden instead of grey. Interesting sidenote: that's why some elves are green; it carries over from a time when—"

"Benji, please," Ptery begged.

"Sorry. Right. The point is... all the Brilliant Elves were punished by the New Gods for the actions of the royal family. Really, by that time, all the Brilliant Elves were royal, whether through blood or just because, uh, well—the real point is that they all vanished except for a child named Els'ri, said to be pure of heart and without transgression, but that was probably because she was really young at the time. Of course there were regents and servants elevated in status to ensure..."

"And there were rules," Luka prompted gently.

"Right! The rules. The rules. When Els'ri came of age, she made decrees that have been followed by the Els'ri family for thousands of aurs. They're to ensure no elf ever again... Well, you see, what the royal family did, it unbalanced the planet. It nearly destroyed Erit."

"Oh, I remember that part," Ptery acknowledged, almost interested. "The Undoing."

"The Undoing. Yes. So, each child of the empire is assigned a role. Next in line. Family guardian. Keeper of secrets. You know." Benji waved a paw as if to truncate himself before continuing. "But every tenth child is... Sacrificed. Not killed. No, the empire would never... Er. Rather, they're adopted out into the world to live a common life. It's to maintain their connection to the people. And... That's me. I'm the tenth child of the emperor and empress. One of the direct descendants of Els'ri. My title is First Sacrifant Son, so I have this."

He held up the crest again, struggling to keep hold of it.

Ptery's jaw hung slack. "You're actual royalty?"

Meadow said, "How could you not know?"

"Well, that's... That's not accurate?" Benji said. "Because I'm... I have no claim to the throne. That's the point. My birth parents were really careful when they selected my dads to adopt me, though. They wanted to make sure I was cared for by someone who wanted more than the status of having a royal child. And I report back to the emperor regularly because it's my place. But I'm also welcome there, which is nice. Well, it was nice, but now, I don't... I don't know."

"But you are..." Ptery pointed at Benji with both hands, "the son of the emperor and empress."

Benji nodded.

Ptery made quite the show of fanning themself and leaning against the arm of Meadow's chair.

Apparently embarrassed by the attention, Benji averted his eyes and studied the crest as the colors of the magic-touched gem shifted from violet to blue, then back again. "I'm sorry, Meadow. I don't know how to find the gods."

Meadow leaned back in his chair, defeated. "Are you sure?"

"Why's it so important?" Ptery asked, recovering from their overexaggerated swoon. "Let the gods sort out their own problems. They're gods. Besides, Wheriae's been nothing but a gallud in your soup for your entire life. You don't owe him any favors."

Meadow clenched his jaw as an uncomfortable tightness caused his throat to spasm. Choking back a sob, he forced a smile. "I left something out," he said. Scooting to the edge of the chair, he leaned forward so he could press the backs of his hands into his eyes. This didn't stay the tears, though, and they spilled wet and warm around his knuckles. "Petalvine... The Shade killed Petalvine. She's gone. And the other gods—Wheriae says they're losing the fight."

Silence.

Disbelief.

The elders had reacted the same way.

"You must have misunderstood," Ptery began, then said, "No. Wheriae's played a cruel joke on you, is all. It's another trick to get you to use his magic. A bluff, although a rather morbid one."

Meadow shook his head. "Can't you see? The forest is dying. Plants around the whole continent are withering, and I bet it'll spread across Erit soon. Whatever this Shade did, it... I don't know. It took Petalvine's power and corrupted it. I can feel it, Ter. I didn't want to admit it before, but something changed. Maybe it was a few spans ago when I started getting these weird jolts of... I don't know what they were. Like dark, sparky, empty..." He trailed off, curling his fingers inward. "Twinges."

"I saw the corrupted plants in the forest before Efrit gave me the dagger," Ptery said.

"Could Wheriae be telling the truth?" Luka asked.

"He's not known for his truthfulness. In fact..." Benji flipped the crest over, his claw rubbing against the back. "As far as the gods go, he's easily the most deceptive. But he'd never lie about something like this. It's too serious. It's... too... Wait, what's this?" Narrowing his eyes, Benji studied the silvery pendant with renewed interest. "There's writing here. Meadow, did you...?"

"No, I didn't."

"This is an old elvish script! It hasn't been used in aurs, except academically. Of course I can read it, but it's so tiny..." Benji raised the crest closer to one eye and strained to read it.

"These are geolocal pairs. Coordinates. I wonder... Luka, can you get out your terminal?"

As Benji translated the coordinates, Luka entered them into the map module on her terminal. There were dozens of them, and once plotted out, they created a rather large circle in the Fade Desert, just outside of a city called Border.

"The elf knows," Meadow muttered. Wheriae found a way to tell him where he needed to go.

"Good, now draw lines between the coordinating pairs," Benji said. "There was a puzzle like this in a contest I was in a few aurs back. It made the location of a hidden treasure really specific. I didn't get there first, but I wasn't too far behind."

"Done," Luka said, then scrunched up her nose. "But this doesn't actually lead anywhere. There's nothing here. Just desert."

"But maybe that's where the gods are," Meadow said. He struggled to his feet, holding out a hand for Luka's terminal. She gave it to him. "Wheriae said Benji would know. I bet he couldn't say outright, so he made a puzzle he knew Benji could solve. And look! This has to be it. This has to be where I gotta go!"

"Then I'm coming with you," Luka said. "I gotta find out what that vision I had meant."

Meadow wanted to ask her what vision she was talking about, but then Benji said, "Me, too. Maybe if I talk to the gods, they can heal what Aeora did to me. I bet they can."

"No," Meadow started. "It's my Calling. It's dangerous—"

Then Ptery sighed, loudly and Interruptiously. "Well, I suppose I'll go along, too. Manticore or not, I'd best find out why Efrit gave me the ruby dagger. I'm sure it must have something to do with all this."

"Guys," Meadow said. "You don't understand. This is my Calling. It's only for conduits of the gods! I mean..." He handed Luka's terminal back to her and rubbed the back of his head. His energy once again spent, he flopped down into the chair. "I'd love to have you guys go, but I don't think..."

"You can't stop us from following you, nestling," Ptery said, their nose in the air.

Three pairs of eyes stared at him with stubborn resolve.

And Meadow couldn't argue, not because they'd won him over with their convincing arguments, but because he'd seen those eye colors before.

Well, sure, he told himself. You see your friends often. Almost daily!

But that wasn't it. Something odd and pressing tickled his grey matter, reminding him of a certain prize he'd dug out of his garden on the very day everything started going crazy. Patting his pouches, he searched for the tell-tale lump of the copper bag before finding it under his ribcage.

As he held it up, the room filled with the alluring scent of earth after rain.

"I know what that is," Ptery said, clutching at a tiny trinket on a chain around their neck. "It's one of Ziro's talismans. She uses them to carry leystones. Can I see?"

Meadow slid onto the floor, untying the bag and spilling the stones onto the rough wood. One emerald. One garnet. One onyx.

Ptery crouched, one talon passing over each in turn. They eventually released the trinket around their neck and shook their head with disappointment. "These haven't been converted into anything. They're uncut and powerless. I know healers sometimes use these as memory stones, or charge stones. But these..."

"If I'm right," Meadow said, "And I bet I am..." He leveraged himself against the chair and pressed his hoof down upon the black stone. With just a bit of weight and pressure, the whole thing split in half along a hidden axial fault, revealing itself to be a beautiful, tiny geode. Minuscule topaz gems sparkled within, surrounded by the dark shell of onyx.

Just like Benji's eyes.

In fact, each stone exactly matched the color of one of his friends' eyes.

Reaching his index and middle fingers into the bag, Meadow retrieved the hand-written note, which read Meadow, take these with you. Noticing a bit of scrawling on one folded corner, he flipped the slip over only to find more writing on the back:

Be sure not to neglect the others you might find along the way.

With hope,

Ziro

"They're Guidestones." Meadow laughed with relief. "It's you, not the stones. I'm not supposed to go alone!"

"So?" Benji tilted his head. "Does that mean..."

Near tears, Meadow nodded, a great weight lifted off his chest. "Yes. The gods seem to want all of you to come with me."

A Lost Love

A SONG WRITTEN BY PTERYLAE

In our hearts, the love we held
a sacred covenant expelled
We lost a love unparalleled...

Stolen by the fae—

A trickster queen unseelie
With her stormy gaze all steely
Wrenched our hearts right from our chests

Held them in her court aglow
A hovel in the undertow
The ocean current shadows rest
Our hearts upon her thorny breast

We lost the love—all love for e'er
sequestered in her fallen lair
Now we're husks of what we were

But at least we're lost together

At least we're lost together

Together...

Phantoms mire the night

"Escape!" I cried as eagles soar'd
"Escape!" You cried as lions roar'd
Together we could make it if we tried.

Her claws pierced arteries and veins
Our blood, our love, became a stain
It fell, a harsh and chilling rain
Upon her regal floors.

Her jealous soul held our husks to wreck
Her dark'ning chains around our necks
So into you my love I poured.

And as the light revealed your way
I knew that I would have to stay
A pris'ner of the trickster queen forever more.

And now I'm lost alone.

At least I'm lost alone.

A phantom stalks the night.

CHAPTER SEVENTEEN

The Lowly and the Lofty

They departed for the Betweenroads ten days later, on the tenth day of the span, at the tenth hour.

If Ptery had their way, they would have waited for S'rantoth, the tenth month, since ten was the luckiest number by far. But *everyone was in such a Darkrealm-damned hurry,* so they had to settle with scrounging up a bit of luck wherever they could. Never mind that Luka usurped itinerary rights from them when they planned to leave Benji behind and just rent a car.

Benji, it turned out, was too bulky to fit inside any standard vehicle. And manticores, it *also* turned out, were not allowed on public transportation.

This necessitated traveling on foot with a cow-sized mechanical pig.

Remarkably lifelike, the A.I.nimal's barrel-like torso sat atop four relatively tiny trotters, each fully jointed but nearly silent in operation. Each had a round hinge at the knee, partially hidden by a moon-shaped silver plate that caught and reflected the light of many blinking baubles along its lateral line.

Its head and face were exquisite, crafted of dozens of interlocking panels that curved in and around wires in such an intuitive way that it could barely be called a machine. Articulated triangular ears, each embedded with a sophisticated sensory array, turned this way and that to pick up signals from its surroundings.

"Why is it a *pig*, again?" Ptery asked.

Luka patted its side under enamel-stenciled letters that read *PG-SEL*. "Because this is the only thing I had available that could carry all our shit."

The pig turned, its glittering white eyes acknowledging Luka as it snuffled with its intricately crafted nose.

Ptery owned one of Luka's mechanical monsters—a small CA/T model they'd named Ny'zzri, which meant "Pretty One" in the harpy language. The first time they'd met the thing, Luka told them it would develop and grow with age; Ptery had contested that it couldn't because it was a machine, and machines only did what they were told. Just to prove her wrong, Ptery volunteered to house the CA/T for just a single month to document its progress.

It immediately turned into a pampered princess and took over their home.

After a month, Ptery had so fallen in love with its quirky personality that they'd refused to give it back.

"Does this pig work like Ny'zzri does?" they asked.

"She has an older chipset, so she's a little more influenced by user input," Luka said. "But I've had her switched on for aurs around the farm, and she definitely has her own preferences."

Meadow, seated atop it, poked his fingers between two of the panels and tugged with a rather loud effort. He'd pried an access door open a fraction of a millikip when the PG-SEL shook itself, dropping Meadow to the ground.

Benji laughed and helped him up.

"It's not a birthday present, Meadow," Luka said. "Stop trying to open it."

"Why's it got do-hickies then?" Meadow brushed himself off, stamping his hooves to get the dust out of his shorts. "If it's got hidden compartments, I should be able to see what's inside!"

Luka raised an articulated cover on the pig's side, revealing a pristine screen. The shimmering crystal surface and high-tech operating system drew a sharp contrast to the verdigrised steel and copper panels surrounding it.

When Luka pressed one of the many virtual buttons on the display, Meadow's panel popped open to reveal a steaming cylinder within. "Her coolant system," she explained. "If you'd gotten it open and touched it, you would have frozen your hand off. But be my guest."

Meadow rubbed his hand and muttered a quiet "No, thank you," after which Luka closed the panel. But not before flashing one of her *I Told You So* smiles.

Remembering their original question, Ptery asked, "*Why* is it a *pig?*"

Luka sighed.

"I mean," Ptery interrupted before she could go on a lengthy lecture about how she'd *just explained exactly that,* "why is it a pig and not a cow? Or a bear? Or, say, a small car that I could ride in while you peasants walked beside me?"

Benji rolled his eyes and Meadow nudged them with a shoulder, but Ptery was *serious*.

"Hold up, girl," Luka said, tapping the pig's side. Even without a command issued per the terminal, the pig halted, looked back, and tilted its head. For a machine, the PG-SEL moved in a spectacular, lifelike manner, devoting a moment of attention to each of the others before turning its ponderous bulk around and pressing its face against Luka's chest. She gave it another pat. "She was designed to be a truffle-hunting unit with enough space to store what it found. But the buyer wanted a dog, not a pig. Even though pigs are *much better* at finding truffles than dogs."

"So they didn't buy?" Benji asked.

"I was stupid enough to build a dog from scratch for 'em. I wouldn't do that now. I wasn't paid enough."

"Wise," Ptery agreed, scratching their chin as an idea formed. "I've just realized, you sell quite a few of these, don't you?"

Luka brushed off the question with a dismissive flick of one hand. "It all worked out, though. My girl here gave me a sort of canvas to try things out on. First, I converted her to a storage unit. That's what PG-SEL means, actually." Luka tapped the screen again, and the cargo hold on the pig's side split open and rose upward, a pneumatic brake hissing as the door reached its peak. Within, neatly situated, was all their luggage and gear. "Porcine Gatherer-Storage Edition Lugger. Figured she'd be perfect for the beginning of our trip, at least until we get reliable transportation. Plus, before we left, I installed some mage shielding that routes to all her plating, so she's essentially a magic-null zone. That'll come in handy, right?"

"Would have been better if she held my whole kit," Meadow complained. "I had to leave half of it behind!"

Luka tapped another button, and the cargo hold closed again. "Half is more than most drummers ever own," she said.

"But I'm supposed to be the drummer with a *legendarily huge* kit!" Meadow whined with all the disappointment of someone who had precisely zero transportation plans of his own. "How can I live up to that with only half?"

"You made some tough choices," Luka said with the detachment of someone who didn't exactly care.

"We would have had to leave Luka's guitars behind," Benji said. "Or my bass. Or—"

"It's not like you can *play* it," Ptery interrupted.

"Yet." Benji straightened, frowning. "The Old Manticore will show me how. I—I know it."

"You know, I'm still unclear as to why we're bringing our instruments at all," Ptery mused, leaning on Luka. "Because every time I'm at your house, there's a different set of metal creatures in your garage."

She nudged them away.

"Traveling is expensive," Benji said, missing Ptery's *very* obvious hint. "I mean, saving the world or not, we're going to have to pay for lodging and essentials. Toiletries. Books."

"Books?" Ptery asked.

"And *other* things." Benji laid his ears back until they nearly disappeared into his mane. "A quest to save the world is... Well, it's no excuse to leave your education behind. We'll be crossing into areas I barely know anything about!"

"Gods save us if you couldn't read about them," Ptery said under their breath. Benji's ears flicked.

"Playing a little show wherever we stop is the best way we can make money," Meadow said, paused, then added, "We'd make even more if I had my whole kit."

Everyone ignored him.

Ptery leaned on Luka again. This time, she grabbed their shoulder with both hands and shoved. "You would have known why we were bringing them if you hadn't slept through all the planning," she grumbled through gritted teeth.

"You haven't told them, I'm guessing?" Ptery's feathers puffed up with the pleasure of possessing knowledge that the others lacked.

She scowled. "I'm not sure what you're implying."

"You know *exactly* what I'm implying. Come on. It's better to tell them *now* before they find out for themselves. You're loaded."

Her cheeks turned red. The others stopped. The pig snuffled around on the ground as if searching for food it couldn't possibly consume.

"How...?"

"Did I know?" Ptery flexed their fingers, studying immaculate talons. "I've just put a couple things together, is all. You must sell quite a few creations like the PG-SEL here, which means you must have quite a bit of minir. It can't have just vanished. Is this why the gods want you along? I'm only doing you a favor by getting this all out in the open, so you can't be angry."

Her eyebrows overshadowed her eyes. "Oh, I can be angry."

"It's..." Benji started, then bit his lip. "Er, it's not really a secret. It's not like... I mean, we saw the same thing... What I mean to say is..."

"What he means to say is, what you do with your minir is your business," Meadow finished. "We were never gonna ask you to fund this trip. I mean, me an' Benji figured you'd be leaving it for your parents, what with the whole suicide-status of our little expedition. Besides, we always wanted to be a band, right? Well, it's literally now or never."

The redness on Luka's face faded and she leaned on the pig, which continued rooting through the underbrush as if it didn't even register her weight. As she exhaled, the little wisps of hair around her face danced in the breeze. "You didn't have to spill it all out into the open, but you're right. It's not like I have magic or claws, or some other crazy talent like you guys have. Seemed pretty weird that the gods would want a human along for no reason."

"Ah." Ptery held up one finger. "Yet you weren't going to tell us."

Luka scowled and pressed the heels of her hands into her eyes. "You idiot. It was going to be a surprise. But you ruined it."

"I? ruined?" Ptery sputtered, offended and confused, but also madly curious. They *loved* surprises.

"It didn't occur to any of you that we can't walk across the entire continent?" Luka pulled a folded blueprint from the front pocket of her overalls and waved it around. "Especially when we get to the Fade Desert?"

"It's not like we have any other options," Meadow said. "We tried to find something."

"No." Luka shook her head, unfolded the paper, and handed it to Meadow. "I mean, that's what I *thought*. Then I had an idea. I couldn't build this myself, but I have friends in Faun-anin with a huge warehouse who could."

Ptery peered over Meadow's shoulder at the skillfully rendered schematics, with hundreds of notes written in the margins. It appeared to be some sort of enormous vehicle with separate drawings for the interior and exterior, complete with paint and upholstery samples attached to the bottom.

"I call it a Kirin-Class Road Castle," Luka said. "Big enough for all of us, even Benji. I spent... Pretty much everything I had on it."

Ptery felt bad, then Meadow elbowed them, and they felt worse.

"I thought if I told you before we left, you might leave me behind."

"Never!" Benji said, butting his head against Luka's chest. It was so catlike, it made Ptery shiver. "Even if you'd told us. I mean, if we're gonna make money on the road now, we still need our guitarist. Right? If you... if you spent *everything*. That was really... It was really nice. You didn't have to."

Luka was so pleased with Benji's approval, she seemed to forget to be mad at Ptery, who started off down the road again. The mechanical pig followed, and the others soon joined.

But Luka gave Ptery a *Look* that strongly suggested her irritation.

"Well, I guess half a drum kit is better than none," Meadow said, effectively ending the conversation. He patted the pig's cheeks, and she leaned into him as if begging for more. "I'm gonna call her Pixel."

Luka blinked. "I'm not sure naming her was a problem that needed solving."

"Well, it's important," Meadow said. "I don't call you 'human,' and I don't call Ptery 'banshee.' You can't just call a thing by what it is. It's rude."

"Fine. Whatever. You can call her Pixel as long as we get where we're going before dark."

"Speaking of calling things by certain names," Ptery said, desperate to change the subject before Luka recalled their blunder, "if we're going to be playing on the road, I think we should talk about re-naming the band."

"Re-naming it?" Meadow asked. "What's wrong with *Dial It Back?*"

"*Everything*. It's not punchy enough. It's not modern enough. Look, I have some ideas, and we can take a vote."

"Pssh. Yeah, something stupid like 'Harpy Eggs' or 'Tail Feathers,'" Meadow chuckled. "It's Dial It Back. I'm sure."

Ptery puffed up, crossing their arms. "It wouldn't have been *Harpy Eggs*."

Meadow spread his hands wide as if gesturing to a marquee. "Dial! It! Back!"

"It's horrible," Luka agreed, dryly detached as if she already knew there was no arguing. Still, she added, "Who names their band a synonym for *turning down the volume?*"

"Exactly!" Meadow insisted. "It's perfect. It's ironic. People will love it."

"It's probably true to someone," Luka admitted.

"But—" Ptery said, shoulders slumping. They had to admit, Dial It Back wasn't as bad as some of Meadow's other ideas. Once, *Pancake Batter* topped the list, as well as *I'm Not So Sure We Even Need a Xylophone*. For a while, the band actually carried the name *Snorp* because Meadow liked the sound of it.

"I like it," Benji said.

"You would," Ptery countered. Overruled, they hopped up onto the hog to pout, their legs dangling over the side.

Ptery hated traveling. They especially hated all the boredom inherent to it, because one could do nothing else while traveling other than *travel*. And talk. Meadow did everyone's share of the talking, asking at regular intervals whether or not they were *there yet,* even though he knew very well how far away *there* sat on a map.

Endless trees surrounded the road, growing so thick a half kilokip outward that it became impossible to discern one trunk from another. Sure, the trees weren't as huge as they were in Faun-ir, but they also weren't as cultured. No mage of Petalvine told them where to grow, or how, or even where it might be acceptable to drop their branches. Mosses drooped from above, creating living, green stalactites above the road, while lichens decorated the shaggy bark of old weshwood horntrees. Sunlight barely reached them, though where it did, it cultivated beautiful, glowing patterns in the underbrush.

A couple hours into their journey, a rumble thundered from the surrounding forest, resolving itself into the bass growl of a mighty beast. Meadow hopped up onto the pig next to Ptery as Benji turned back and forth, his eyes scanning the trees.

But the sound didn't come from the ground. It came from the sky.

A golden glimmer sparked from overhead, the blinding shine reaching through the canopy. Just before Ptery threw a hand over their face, they caught the gaze of an eye the size of one of the planet's moons.

"Dragon," Luka whispered, reverent.

The creature passed, its tail waving like a banner and reflecting the afternoon sun into a thousand million rainbows.

"It's good luck to see a dragon," Meadow said, sliding down from Pixel's back. "Or bad. The books aren't ever clear *which.* I guess dragons mean your luck's either gonna be good or bad, which covers all your bases. There was that one time a dragon landed in the Shopping Plaza for a whole span and ate everyone's horseshoes. I suppose that was bad luck."

"What about everything in between?" Benji asked. "Not the good or the bad. Just... Normal luck?"

"Nah, not with dragons. They're weird, you know?" Meadow's fingers pried at a panel again. "I think that means it's gonna go one way or the other with us. I hope it goes the good way."

Benji bit his lip, a worried look crossing his face. "But..."

"Have you guys ever seen one before?" Meadow asked.

Luka gently smacked his hand away from Pixel's panels. "No. If it was any closer, I might have pissed myself."

"From a distance," Ptery said. "A few times. There's a red one that hangs around my home aerie, but it's never come close. Last time it passed, we had rain for a whole week. The homes at the base level flooded."

"See? Bad luck!" Proud of his observation, Meadow gestured to the sky. "But a gold dragon... I'm sure it's good luck. Gold dragons are always good luck."

"How do you know?" Benji blurted. "I've run the calculations, and the chances of us succeeding cross-referenced with all the great quests in Erit's past... Well, the number is so infinitesimally small, I had to come up with a new word to describe it!"

Everyone stared at him, even the Darkrealm-damned pig.

"Well, Mister Pessimist," Meadow said. "I guess you wanna tell us the word?"

"Oh. Well, it's a combination of Old Elvish and the gnoll simple language. Translated, it means *non-zero but near impossible*." Despite his dour warning, Benji looked quite proud of himself. "The word is *Oinguialetriq*."

"Well, *that's* another word for me to immediately forget," Meadow said, as cheerful as ever. "And it's a good thing it was a *gold* dragon we saw and not a grey one. The grey ones *really* mean bad luck. So do the red ones."

"Oh, you're just saying that because the one I saw was red." Ptery scoffed, waving one hand in a dismissive gesture. "If I'd said the one at Ge'elo was green, you'd have said *green* dragons were bad luck. I'm fairly certain they mean nothing at all."

Meadow should have argued.

He liked to argue. In all the time Ptery'd known him, he'd never backed down from an argument so easily. Usually, such conversations ended with him trying to prove his side, which occasionally risked life and limb—his own or others.

But now he stepped quietly, hooves scuffing against the shielded path and sending up sparks. "There was another faun," he said. "A little older than me. Her name was Laurel, and she was pushy. And I don't just mean a *little*. She'd make me do things over and over 'til I got them right. That was the price for being allowed to hang 'round her. She did the same thing to a lot of other fauns, too, but I was the best. She liked me the most. And I thought I loved her."

"Meadow," Benji said. "That's not—"

Meadow continued as if he hadn't heard Benji at all. "She loved being doted on, and she loved that all these people would hang onto her every word. When Petalvine summoned her, she... She threw fits. Loud ones. She yelled at her family, and she yelled at her friends. She begged the elders to find a way to let her stay, but they couldn't. The pull of the god just took over her. She stopped yelling. She stopped begging. One day, she was gone. And I never saw her again."

The others gave Meadow the respect of a few moments of silence, then Ptery said, "I didn't think fauns were... like that."

"What, you mean *selfish?*" Luka asked. "You think banshees have that market covered?"

Before Luka and Ptery could start fighting again, Meadow continued, his voice soft. "I don't know why, but it was in her nature. Maybe that's why Petalvine wanted her. Because when Laurel set her mind to something, she'd get it done for sure. But this... This she failed. She never came home. No one ever found her. The elders don't even talk about her anymore."

"I'm really sorry," Benji said.

"I think this quest is the same as Laurel's. It must be, right? It's been a long time, but if Laurel failed, maybe the gods... *fixed* things, so we'd succeed. We can't fail the same quest twice. Right? I have to believe that dragon is good luck. I *have to*."

They continued on in silence.

CHAPTER EIGHTEEN

Let's Get This Terrible Party Started

A dead ley-line cut through the forest, leaving a lush, flat, grassy plain between Faun-ir and Faun-anin. Locals called this lightning-shaped expanse the Betweenroads.

Dead ley-lines generally did not cause problems, except for a few of the more rowdy ones. If Benji recalled correctly—and he usually did—the Betweenroads ley-line rested several kilokips below the crust, placidly absorbing trace amounts of magic until it sparked.

That in itself wasn't strange because every dead ley-line sparked. Each one caused a different environmental effect in its range, though, and this one didn't seem to like trees... Or, indeed, anything more than a couple kips tall. The last human who tried to build in the Betweenroads came to the construction site one day to find the upper half of the structure missing, with no indication of where it might have gotten off to.

An orc in Balharzivit found it a month later, sitting upside-down in a latrine pit twenty thousand kilokips away from its origin.

A few people still lived in the Betweenroads, however, their squat houses scooped out of the rich earth. Grass and fancy foliage arced over the underground homes, creating rows of bumpy hills lining the paved roads.

None of these homes had addresses.

"Well, what in the Darkrealm are we supposed to do then?" Ptery asked from their perch atop Pixel.

Meadow stood next to them, hooves occasionally slipping on the steel plates as he searched across the plain. "Well, I'm not saying Efrit lied, but maybe she was, uh, misinformed? I don't see anything. All the doors I see from the road are people-sized."

"Manticores are people," Luka argued. Benji shook his head; the point wasn't worth arguing.

"I mean *small* people," Meadow amended. "Human people. Faun people. There's nothing a manticore would fit into. Say, Princey, how about if you use that sniffer of yours?"

"I'm not a prince," Benji muttered. Even so, he raised his chin, inhaling the clean air.

Elves can't find things by scent, a tiny voice in his head reminded him. *You look ridiculous. Stop. Stop it. Tell them you can't do it.*

But Benji could almost picture his broad olfactory array leeching the tiniest particles out of the air, processing them, then sending them to his brain for analysis. He detected hydrangeas in bloom at the far side of a home scoop. A pool of stagnant water rife with razebit larvae. The perfume on a woman talking to her neighbor ten kips away.

And...

And...

"Ohhhh..." Benji grimaced at the information graciously bestowed upon him by his nose. There, at the forefront of his mind, taking up all the space he possessed for thought, was the clearest image of a decaying deer carcass he'd ever conjured in his life. Not that he conjured *many* images of carcasses, but the occasional puzzle required... certain knowledge.

It smelled delicious. He very much wished it didn't.

"I knew it'd work!" Meadow said.

"Er, you *smell* him?" Ptery asked. "Revolting. It's rude to smell people, you know. You're *being rude*."

"Not... exactly." Benji ignored the admonishment, stepping off the road and into the short-cropped clover that grew wild around the homes. He followed the scent while the others, puzzled, followed after him.

As the stench grew more pungent, Luka coughed, waving her hand in front of her nose. "*Yeuch*, it *reeks*."

"It's not *that* bad, is it?" Benji turned around. He honestly couldn't tell, given his potentially... *altered proclivities*.

Luka pressed her lips together, narrowing her eyes. Dryly, she said, "Like a freshly baked ham, straight out of the oven. Delicious."

"Oh, you're *weak*," Ptery said. "It's a shame more species aren't fond of weathered meats. You *know*, my family is from desert stock. In older times, we were very good at cleaning up the desert."

"'Weathered' isn't the word I'd use." Meadow stopped, doubling over, his hands on his knees. He gagged, reeling backward a couple steps, then waved his hand for the others to go on. "This is as far as I go, guys. I can barely stand the smell of *fresh* meat. This..."

Luka shook her head, turning away.

Ptery rubbed her back, faking sympathy while rolling their eyes. "Come on now, nestling. Lean on Pixel. There you go. There, it's okay. It'll be all right."

Luka shouldered them away but still took their advice and leaned on the pig, resting her head against the cool metal plates.

Benji didn't want to go alone. Although the situation with Aeora had made him manticore-shaped, he still felt like an elf, and old biases caused a rise of fear that roiled and tightened in his chest. What else could he do, though? If he ran like a scared gallud, he might never be able to accomplish the telekinesis he could allegedly learn how to do. That meant he'd never be able to play bass again or do anything requiring even a smidgen of dexterity. Treading down the unshielded, rough road for the last few hours had made his paws so sore, he wouldn't even be able to hold his terminal without pain. He wouldn't be able to complete the written portions of the puzzles in his competitions.

He needed help.

Efrit wouldn't have recommended the Old Manticore if she didn't trust him. Right?

Sure. That made sense.

Probably.

"Okay," Benji said under his breath. The others could stay here at the farthest boundaries of the rot-stench while he ventured on, brave in spirit but *definitely* not in body. Hopefully he could hide his shaking knees from the Old Manticore.

He was just thinking about how brains were so *weird* and how you couldn't simply convince them to stop being frightened whenever you wanted to when one ear automatically flicked backward, picking up angry footfalls in the grass. When he looked over his shoulder, he spied Ptery, who stopped once spotted.

"Well, *someone* has to go with you," they said. "Someone has to protect you."

"But I've got... You know." Benji glanced at his tail, still wrapped in leather and made relatively harmless. "Uh. And the teeth and such."

"Don't be ridiculous," Ptery said. "You couldn't defend yourself against a banshee scream, and neither can this old *creature* you're about to meet. You need me. And that's final."

In addition to the rotting deer, Benji could smell a hint of Ptery's terror and appreciated them all the more for it. "Oh, okay. Okay, but if you need to, you can leave."

Ptery nodded. "Of course I can."

Unlike the other homes, the Old Manticore's was flush with the ground, with no rise above it to indicate it existed. The entrance faced away from the road, making it impossible to see for anyone who didn't already know it was there. A flat, dirt-covered circle of land dipped down toward a half-moon-shaped wall made of old planks and dirt, with a weathered door set into dried mud.

"I'm *sure* it's *perfectly safe,"* Ptery said. "If we're speaking in opposites."

The rotting deer lay a few kips away from the door, attracting flies. However, the carcass wasn't the only indication someone lived in this hole; a few odds and ends lay strewn about, like a rusted-but-functional patio set and a couple disintegrating statues of unicorns and gargoyles. A thick book, its cover scratched and fading, sat on the table.

Benji tried to ignore the bloating, furless carcass, although his mouth watered at the rancid stench. As he formed the delectable picture of his teeth closing around an extremely ripe femur, he wondered if instinct created such images in his mind or if his imagination had callously betrayed him.

Disturbing either way.

He passed a dilapidated mailbox, his stinging paws leading him toward the deer. His stomach growled as he stood over it.

"Well?" Ptery asked.

"It's—well, it's not mine. It'd be rude."

"It's a dead deer! It doesn't *belong* to anyone!"

"It didn't just end up here on its own!"

The door on the side of the scoop creaked as it opened. An orange eye stared out from the sliver of darkness. "Are you two quite finished discussing my dinner?"

Ptery backed out of the dirt circle and onto the grass, losing much of their nerve. "Dinner? You still mean to eat this? You're storing it outside. There's bugs!"

The door opened the rest of the way.

The "Old Manticore" didn't seem particularly old, though liori were effectively immortal. He looked worse for wear and quite unkempt, though, with his black mane hanging in cords all the way to the ground. His long, pointed ears suggested he'd been an elf once, though his skin was a deep, burnished bronze rather than grey. His fur, matted and ruffled as it was, appeared to be pale tan.

He smelled clean, though, which contrasted with the vile roadkill.

"Yes, dinner. I prefer it well-seasoned." Ignoring Ptery's disapproval, he added, "If I hadn't heard this young liori mention that it's rude to steal from people, I might have added you to the menu."

Ptery paled and took another step back.

The Old Manticore laughed, a hearty sound that carried the undertone of a cheerful purr. "Oh, don't be so ridiculous. The tales you've heard about me are exaggerated, I'm sure. I don't eat banshees. Your feathers get stuck in my teeth."

"But you've tried," Ptery said.

"Have I?" The Old Manticore smiled.

"Er..." Benji interrupted before Ptery could run away. "Sir, we're here because a faun named Efrit..."

"Oh, Efrit! Did you know she named herself after one of the Defeated Gods? Hah! The gall. But she earned the name, I'm sure, the tough old goat. She hasn't visited me in some time. How is she?"

Neither Benji nor Ptery answered.

"Ah..." The Old Manticore said. "It's a shame. The dying races spend too short a time on this planet. I knew the goddess blessed her with a longer life than most, but I'm still saddened to hear. She sent you to me? ...*Before* she died, I assume."

"Yes, she... said you could help me." Benji took a step forward, glancing back at Ptery, who waited outside the circle.

"If I'm doing any helping, it'll be inside." The Old Manticore looked to the sky, one paw shielding his eyes. "I *hate* this sun!"

He turned, revealing his missing tail, which appeared to have been chopped clean off. The stump that remained was less than half a kip long.

How much would that hurt?

Shaking his head, Benji followed him inside.

Despite the Old Manticore's appearance and the rotting carrion outside, his den smelled faintly of apples and roses. Although roomy, it had a cozy, enclosed feel to it and lacked windows, which made it seem smaller than it was. It consisted of only one room, built into the ground itself by means of bowed wood and plaster, which gave it a sort of upside-down bowl shape.

Furniture was sparse, save for a raised bed and a couple smaller chairs. A pile of cushions sat haphazardly arranged along one arc.

Far from being riddled with the bones of his last meals, the home contained everything one would expect from a civilized person—a small visionscreen and a shelf full of books, for example, as well as a fixed terminal on what looked to be a handmade desk to accommodate his size. Near the back was a tiny kitchenette.

Benji stared at the quaint wonder, reassured in a way he couldn't explain. This felt like *home*. A proper home, rather than the hole in the ground he was expecting when the Old Manticore first opened the door. And it meant something—about liori, about Benji himself, about the world he'd have to navigate from now on.

The Old Manticore flopped down on a plush cushion, evicting a cloud of dust that sparkled in the light streaming in from the open door. He crossed his paws in front of him and arched an eyebrow.

Emboldened by the relaxed atmosphere, Benji felt comfortable enough to ask, "Sir, what happened to your tail?"

"Occasionally, I travel to Tyl or Reinoaken for supplies," he answered. "Of course, they were outposts back when I first settled here. The truth is, they prefer a visiting manticore to be less dangerous than the average liori, so I cut off my tail once an aur."

For a moment, Benji saw all the advantages—he wouldn't have to deal with the venom or the unwieldiness of the thing. It would hurt for a while, sure, but—wait. "Once an aur?"

"Yes, it *grows back*." The Old Manticore wore an unsettlingly devious grin. "There are songs written about the horrible screams emanating from the plains when it comes time to sever it again. I'm sure you'll learn all about it from your patron. By the way..." he nodded to the door, where Ptery still stood silhouetted in the frame. "Is your friend coming in?"

"Uh. Oh. Hang on. They don't—Well, they've had a bad experience—Hang on." Benji returned to the door.

"I'm staying here," Ptery said.

"But I don't think he's dangerous," Benji returned. "I mean, he's—he's joking—"

"You naive *fool*," Ptery admonished. "He's already threatened to eat us once."

"I can hear you, you know," the Old Manticore drawled, holding a paw to his ear. "Very good hearing. And, point of fact, had I wanted to dispatch you, it would have been outside. I try not to get blood on my floors."

"Oh, *that's* fucking reassuring," Ptery grumbled.

Sitting, Benji bit his lip, looking between the Old Manticore and his friend. "I know it's scary. And I know you're afraid. But I really want you here. Okay? I don't want to do this alone. And you did—you did follow after me. I—I told you..."

"Yes, *yes*, I know!" Ptery took a deep breath, then slid one talon past the threshold. "Putting myself in an enclosed space with *two* of you beasties? You're lucky I came along to protect you, or I might just lose my nerve!"

Benji smiled. "Yes, I'm very lucky. Will you come in?"

Although they nodded, Benji scented a spike in their fear. Far from the tantalizing scent he read about in old faetales, it reminded him of bitterness and darkness. "Can we..." He turned back to their host. "Can we keep the door open? Just a bit?"

"If you must." The Old Manticore stretched, yawning and emitting a tired bellow of a roar. "You'll be chasing the flies out, though."

Satisfied, Ptery finally entered, but stayed near the far wall.

With one problem solved, Benji faced his next: what manners should one observe in the house of a liori? Should he await instructions? Help himself to a spot on the bare floor? Baffled by the disconnection between his expectations and reality, he froze for several ticks while his brain rebooted, then came to a reasonable conclusion.

Copy the Old Manticore.

Right.

He glanced at his host, who stared back with a combination of confusion, amusement, and impatience. Feeling quite on-the-spot now, Benji wrangled one of the floor cushions a quarter of a kip closer before it slipped from his fingers.

The Old Manticore sighed. The cushion lifted into the air, suspended by wisps of pale silvery white, which circled the cushion like tiny comets. It took Benji a moment to realize these wisps weren't some random phenomenon but were connected to the will of the Old Manticore.

"That's it!" Ptery exclaimed. "*That's the thing!*"

The Old Manticore dropped the cushion a couple kips in front of him. "Now," he said. "Why don't you sit down and tell me why a newly turned manticore has come to see *me* instead of studying with his patron like he should be."

CHAPTER NINETEEN

Achisthus and Telis

Benji didn't know what a "patron" was, but he could extrapolate. A newly turned liori would need someone to show them how to *be* a liori. That should have been Aeora's role, had Benji been turned by his own free will.

But he hadn't been.

"Er... She couldn't help," Benji said, lying on the cushion.

The Old Manticore stared at him, eyes hard and unrelenting, for several ticks. "Why don't we start with names, then? I'm Q'ler. If we're being formal, my name is Q'ler, Of My Own Damned Den In The Betweenroads."

"I didn't—I didn't *introduce myself?*" Benji said with a minor pang of social horror. "I'm sorry."

"*Sorry* is an odd name for a manticore."

"I mean... My name is Benji. Wild. Benjamin Wild. Of, uh. Faun-ir."

"I'm Ptery!" Ptery called from across the den. "Please leave me alone and pretend I'm not here!"

Q'ler chuckled, amused. "Right. Well. Benji is still an odd name for a manticore. Newly turned liori often choose a name which suits them better than the one they had in their old life. And you were an elf? Odd name for an elf, too. Now I'm curious."

"Oh, I was the tenth child of the imperial family." Benji dug into his mane for the royal crest. "I was adopted by humans."

"Ah." Q'ler nodded. "Yes, I am somewhat familiar with modern elvish politics. They gave you away."

The observation wasn't malicious, yet Benji couldn't help defending himself. "I love my dads. They were *very carefully* hand-picked. And... And I still see my birth parents. We're all very close. There's a reason—"

Q'ler raised his chin in a nod. "You're not here to tell me about that, are you? You'll have to forgive my curiosity. It's been many aurs since I've been home, of course."

Of course.

"How long?" Benji asked.

Q'ler smiled, patient. "Long enough to offend you with my questions, it seems." He raised a paw and rested his chin on it. Each digit revealed the yellowed, cracked tips of broken claws. "You want to know how old I am. To sate your own curiosity."

Benji looked at the floor, though he couldn't help a smile as he peered upward.

"Well, not even I can say that anymore. I stopped counting birthdays long ago."

"And why are you *here?*" Ptery blurted. "I mean, here, and not—"

"In a den? With other liori?" Q'ler paused, his expression bordering on melancholy. Still, he smiled. "Their ilk has become a culture. A forced madness. Some belie civility to the outside world while the darkness festers within. Some believe they must become vicious to survive, but it is not our nature. It's not *my* nature."

Ptery made a sound Benji couldn't identify.

"In the end, I'm not suited for den life," Q'ler concluded. "And now it's my turn, I think. Why are you here, Benji?"

"He needs someone to show him how to do that *thing* manticores do." Ptery took a step closer, but only a step. "You know, when you move things with your mind like you did with the cushion."

"Can I learn it?" Benji tried and failed to keep the hopeful rise out of his voice.

"Yes. Your patron should have taught you how to access your power," Q'ler said. "In fact, they should still be with you, keeping you close, if you are so new to this life."

There was that reference to a *patron* again. How could Benji delicately tell the Old Manticore that he couldn't consult Aeora on *any* of this? That if anyone could teach him how to be a liori, it would never be her?

"He doesn't have one," Ptery said. "Well, I suppose he *does,* but she turned him because she was pissed, then fucked off into the trees like her tail was on fire. Faoliia's tits, don't you *watch* that thing?" They gestured to the visionscreen. "Or is it just decoration? It's been all over the news!"

"I was, ah, not really *planning* on being a liori," Benji clarified.

"Turned against your will?" Q'ler asked, his voice barely above a whisper. "You weren't schooled in any way? Ah, what do they call it? There was no training? No... *Achisthus?*"

Strange that the liori would use elvish to define their turning. It meant so many things, too—all wrapped up into a single ugly word. Training. Schooling. Brainwashing.

Indoctrination.

Benji found he couldn't speak. Luckily, Ptery had plenty to say. "He won a puzzle contest against some sphinx. I suppose this is how liori get revenge—"

"No!" Q'ler roared, jumping to his paws. One claw ripped through the cushion, spilling white feathers across the floor.

Ptery shied back, thumping against the far wall.

"I'm sorry," Q'ler said. White wisps appeared around the spilled feathers, stuffing them back into the hole in the cushion as the Old Manticore paced across the short width of his den. "The liori have few laws, but this is one of them—you must never turn anyone without permission. Without *absolute consent.* Break this law, and the punishment is death."

As Benji lay stunned, Ptery recovered, braving *two* steps closer this time. Despite their fear—the bitter scent melting from them like rain—they spoke for Benji. "It must happen all the time. You can't seriously think this is a rare case? She lost. She was mad. This is what you were talking about, isn't it? That 'festering darkness'?"

"No," Q'ler said. "You can't possibly understand. There are rules. Lines that must not be crossed, or else..." His words reverted to an old elvish dialect, abandoning the common Faunii. While Benji couldn't understand most of it due to its severely archaic nature, he could pick out a few phrases, such as "*of the gods*."

When Q'ler next looked at Benji, it was with compassion rather than detached amusement. "I was also turned against my will, but it was many, *many* aurs ago. There was nothing I could have done to prevent it. Nothing *anyone* could have done. Let me be your patron since yours fled as a coward. Please."

Had Efrit picked Q'ler because of their similar situation? Benji immediately felt closer to him, even though they'd known each other for less than an hour.

"You're not lying, are you?" Ptery asked, drawing even closer. "No, you can't be. I see it now. Gods, he's right, Benji. If this happened all the time, there'd be more news vids than we could keep up with. People fleeing in terror. People other than *me*, I mean. But there aren't any liori just skulking around, crying about how unfair their lives are, are there? Other than *you*."

"I don't skulk around and cry," Benji growled.

"People rightfully have a strong tie to their identity. Their very being," Q'ler said. "Yes, this law was the promise—the one promise we made—to escape a fear-fueled genocide."

"...Seems a little... Excessive," Benji muttered.

They tried for over an hour.

Q'ler gave him a handful of calming mantras in *Gellifreyy*, an extremely old elvish dialect that hadn't been spoken for centuries. It had ties to modern elvish and even Faunii, so Benji picked it up relatively quickly, but therein lay the problem. He couldn't help analyzing the words, which drew him right out of what he was supposed to be doing.

"I can't get it," Benji said. "It's... Maybe because—because I didn't want this."

"Mm. No." Q'ler straightened the pile of books he'd been trying to get Benji to lift, then arched an eyebrow at him. "One is missing."

"He didn't telepathy it," Ptery said, waving a book in the air. They sat by the door, allowing the light to illuminate the pages of the old tome. "I got bored."

"It's not telepathy or telekinesis," Q'ler corrected. "As I told you before, the manticore's power is called *telis*, and I believe you're fully capable of achieving it."

He demonstrated again, gesturing gently with one paw. A book rose into the air, white wisps—each visible for only a fraction of a second—spun around it and held it aloft. The color of the wisps matched the stripes and spots on Q'ler's wings, as well as the markings on what was left of his tail. "We call it *telis* because it is natural magic, related only to—"

"Liori, I know," Benji muttered, hanging his head. He reached toward the book with his mind; when Q'ler released it, though, it fell to the floor. "I'm tired."

"You've been concentrating too hard. We'll take a break."

Frustrated with his inability to solve this dilemma, Benji slouched over his plate of rot-meat jerky, spearing one pungent strip with a claw. Although he still resented the notion that he found putrid meat delicious, eating it in this preserved form was much more palatable than digging his face into the viscera of a sunbaked carcass.

Q'ler returned from his kitchenette with a plate of fresh strawberries suspended by *telis*.

Much to his relief, the scent of the strawberries made Benji's mouth water as much as the rotten meat, but Ptery needed to eat something, too. "Ptery, here's some fruit. Uh... Mister Q'ler, could you...?"

"No," Q'ler said. "You're going to get it to them yourself."

"Oh, I guess I'll starve then," Ptery said, flippant, as they leafed through the yellow pages of the book.

"I..." Benji muttered. "I can't—"

"You *can,*" Q'ler insisted. "It's entirely possible that you don't *want* to."

"Of course I want to!" Benji exclaimed. He extended his mind to the plate but felt nothing click that would allow him to take it. His wings flared in irritation, knocking over the single wooden chair in the den. "Do you think I *want* to go the rest of my life unable to use my hands? I *have to learn!"*

"That might be the most I've ever heard you say without stuttering," Ptery said in a way that made it sound like a compliment and not an insult.

"I know a few things about *vadthi.*" Q'ler used the *Gellifreyy* word for a liori turned against their will. "First, they think this can somehow be *cured*. And because they think they can be cured, they're afraid learning *telis* will make them less of who they used to be. If you don't accept what you are, you'll never do it."

Benji stared. "But I..."

"You've been purposely distracting yourself. Thinking about other things. You're afraid."

Benji lay on the floor, flipping his paws over to glare at the scuffed pads that were only now starting to scab. It would take aurs for them to callus enough to the point where he could walk comfortably.

Yet he could barely fathom being a manticore *aurs from now*. Surely he could petition the gods to help him. To change him back to what he was before. He had to maintain hope, or...

He felt tears stinging in his eyes, but anxiety prevented them from falling.

"No liori has ever become what they were before," Q'ler said, more gently this time. "I understand this has hurt you in a way no one deserves to experience. But I would not mislead you on this. The trade from elf to liori is absolute. In fact, part of the process renders the victim *dead* for a fraction of a second. I imagine it's symbolic of a life irrevocably changed."

Benji could barely hear the Old Manticore anymore for how deeply his ears lay buried in his mane. "...Maybe I can come back another time."

"No, you'll get it today. For all your fear, you're clever enough." Despite his earlier statement, Q'ler *telised* the plate of strawberries over to Ptery, who pulled them from the air with such greed that a couple slices flopped to the floor.

"How many *vadthi* have you known?" Benji asked.

"In all my time, I've met less than half a dozen, including you."

"And you've taught them to—"

"A couple, yes."

"And none of them have ever been... healed? Uh. Cured?"

"No. None."

Never.

Benji realized that he hadn't come to the Old Manticore to learn *telis*. He came with the lofty hope that this ancient beast could somehow guide him to a counterspell. If anyone knew how to reverse what happened to him, it would be a liori who was so old, he couldn't even come up with a number to describe his age.

But he could never go back.

I am a liori. I can see in the dark. I can find things by scent. I can learn telis.

How many times would he have to repeat that until he believed it?

"Tell me while we're resting," Q'ler said. "Do you know the name of the sphinx who turned you?"

Benji didn't want to tattle, and yet... He could feel the great scope of the crime. He'd never be the same. He'd never fit into his own house, nor would he feel the strings of his bass beneath his fingers. His closest friends feared him. Strangers would shun him. For that, the sphinx deserved to be named. "Aeora," he said. "Of the Meerit Den."

Q'ler gave no reply. His head tilted a little, eyes never leaving Benji as if he was trying to discern if he'd heard correctly. He radiated a near-undefinable misery that filled the room, his eyes glittering in the light filtering in from the open door. "I am sorry. She's taken something from you that you can never get back."

Unable to come up with anything profound as a reply, Benji could only say, "Thanks."

"We've rested long enough. Now, you'll learn." Q'ler reached out with his *telis*, righting the chair Benji knocked over. Then he retraced his steps to the kitchen. "If I may? I believe you're concentrating too hard, as if you're learning a skill and not utilizing an extension of yourself. Imagine your arm resting on a table. Find the muscles to move it."

"But there's nothing *there!*" Benji complained. "It's not like a tail or a wing!"

Granted, it took him the better part of a couple spans to control those, and sometimes he still lost track of them.

"Hm, I see," Q'ler said. With a nod, he casually raised a handful of knick-knacks into the air, spinning them with casual disengagement. "You don't believe that this intangible part of yourself exists."

"Exactly!" Benji agreed.

Behind Q'ler, a serrated carving knife rose out of the sink, entwined in the thin white tendrils of his *telis*. "An infant only begins to walk when they believe they can let go," he said.

The knife cleaved through the air faster than Benji could blink.

Its aim would have been true. The blade would have stabbed through Ptery's eye with such force that it might have gone clean through and embedded into the wall behind them.

Instead, it remained suspended in the air, less than a centikip from disaster.

Angry, frantic cerulean wisps surrounded the blade, holding it aloft. Benji felt every bit of it, from the damp wooden handle to the deadly edge, as if he held it in his own two hands.

But he wasn't holding it. Not physically, anyway. It was as if his mind split wide open, pouring out this new knowledge as if he should have known it all along.

Ptery, breath catching in their throat, dropped the book and slid out of the way of the sharp point.

"I can feel it," Benji muttered in awe as Ptery swore excessively and profusely. The handle was still wet, the blade cold and unyielding. When he ran the pale blue wisps along the edge, he detected its sharpness, though he could feel no pain.

Realizing what he was doing, Benji dropped the knife, thankfully clear of Ptery's leg.

"You see now," Q'ler said.

"You could have *killed* me," Ptery choked, hand over their chest. They struggled to their feet, heaving deep breaths as they rested one hand against the wall.

"I would have stopped it," Q'ler said.

"They didn't know that," Benji argued. Again, he could smell Ptery's fear and their spent adrenaline. "You should have thrown it at me."

"And therein lies a problem," Q'ler explained. "Another lesson, I think. One phenomenon universal among *vadthi* is a potent venom reflecting the victim's state of mind at the point of his turning—"

"I know what it does," Benji muttered. "It—it was an accident."

"Even so," Q'ler said. "In that moment, they are distressed. They are alone. As they're at their most vulnerable, the venom takes shape."

The venom *took shape?* Benji narrowed his eyes. "It's not all the same?"

Q'ler continued. "Some manticores are elated at the point of their turning and so have venom that makes their victims unspeakably happy. Some see glorious violence in their future and possess a universally fatal toxin. But you wanted to die, didn't you, Benji? And if I threw the knife at you, might you have hesitated just long enough to make that happen?"

He couldn't answer.

CHAPTER TWENTY

As We Go Along

Meadow wiggled under Pixel, who snorted and moved away. He repeated this process several times before Pixel folded her legs into herself and lay with her belly on the ground.

Damn!

"She's programmed to make sure no one's under her," Luka said. "She's only doing what she's supposed to. You'd be pretty mad if that much steel came crashing down on top of you."

"I need an awning!" Meadow whined. "It's too early in the morning for this much sun."

"It's *way* after noon."

"Like I said. Too. Early." Meadow rose to his hooves, cracking his back and lashing his tail before stretching way more loudly than necessary. How did anyone expect him to save the world with *sunburn?*

"Everyone told you to pack sunblock." Luka fiddled with the controls on Pixel's side panel until a hatch opened and a sail-like silver cloth extended above the grass. "Benji reminded you two or three times. I remember, because you asked him why he was so hung up on sunblock, on account of him having fur and not needing it."

"Oh yeah..." Meadow chuckled to himself before ducking under the shade. Much better. "I figure I'll just use yours."

Luka arched an eyebrow before sitting next to Meadow under the awning. "It's packed. But when we get to Faun-anin, I'll get it out for you."

Meadow leaned on her, though she wiggled her shoulder enough to hint to him that the contact was uncomfortable. He didn't know why, as he could barely stand being away from warmth and closeness for more than a few minutes. She had her hangups, though, and he wasn't about to test her boundaries. Drawing his knees up to his chest, he moved a few centikips away and gazed toward the Old Manticore's den. "You think they're almost done in there?"

Luka shrugged. "I dunno. How long's it take to teach a manticore how to be a manticore?"

"I was hoping, like, ten minutes?"

Luka snorted, unlocked the screen on her terminal, and started scrolling some NETsite about new horizons in multi-magic photon focus systems.

Meadow lost interest in less time than it would take a unicorn to shit.

Bored, he turned his attention to the vegetation between his feet. His godmark already grew at the very edges of his hooves, spreading outward with its tiny tendrils, blooming in an array of minuscule yellow and pink flowers.

Without his magical guidance, however, the thin vines began to cluster together, twisting into a single, pale white rhizome. This new tendril snaked through the clover as if embarking on some sort of important, top-secret plant mission.

"That's weird," Luka said. "That's weird, right? It's never done that before."

"Yeah, it's weird." Meadow pushed forward, crawling on his hands and knees after the runaway rhizome. Although the Betweenroads lacked trees, it did have several taller plants, like shrubs and native wildflowers, so following the thin tendril took all his concentration.

When he caught up with the tapered end, he found it curled around the base of a plainslily, its leaves an inky, forbidding black. The plants around the lily were already dead, leaving a circle of bare earth around it.

"It's out here already? I thought... The elders..." Meadow sat back on his heels, plucking a handful of the transformed leaves. Although used to their wrongness, he couldn't help shivering the moment they touched his skin. As he crunched them between his fingers, they bled a deep, shadowy sludge, which crystallized and fell into the dirt.

Gross.

The opposite of iridescent, the particles gobbled up light like a void, stealing it away. Had Meadow not known the tiny shards came from the plant, he might have mistaken them for holes in reality.

"That's not good," Luka said.

"It's not," he said, plucking another leaf. Although prepared for the wrongness that leeched into him, he couldn't help a shiver. "I didn't think we'd see these here. I thought this *dying* would have to follow the ley-paths. You know what the ley-system is?"

"You know, I tried to get into magic a couple times. Never worked for me." She crouched down, running her fingers along the blackened leaves. "Is this following *you* then?"

"Ghiscaer's udders, I hope not," Meadow replied. He didn't want anyone to associate him with such a... Well. A *dastardly, evil-crusted, evil-filled creeping evil.* His godmark seemed keen on pointing these mutated plants out to him, though, so who knew? Wheriae, maybe. But Meadow would rather lick the weird not-plants than talk to the water god again.

"Then how's this out here?" Luka asked. "Something about the ley-paths?"

Meadow reached into a pouch for his terminal, but instead of his terminal, his fingers closed on a mostly-melted candy bar. That would do. Removing it, he peeled back the paper and used the end to draw a chocolate circle in the dirt. "This is Erit. Aaaand..." He drew a handful of landmasses, none of which resembled any of Erit's continents, before pointing to one in particular. "This is Kyrnis."

Luka tilted her head. "That's a gopher."

"Kyrnis. Gopher. Same thing. Here's Faun-ir." Using his finger, he drew what may have been trees in the southern portion of the continent, then circled them. "Faun-ir's a ley-field. If the planet's a big animal, the ley-fields are its guts. Heart, liver..." He circled another continent, close to Kyrnis. "Lungs." He pointed to another. "But Erit's so huge, it's got, like, ten hearts and ten livers. Ley-nodes are smaller organs, like, I dunno. Second stomachs and appendixes or whatever. Cities tend to be built on 'em." He drew lines between the circles, then branching lines to dots in between. "Ley-paths are like veins or nerves. Signals travel from the fields to the nodes, then all the way down the ley-paths. Dead ley-lines happen when there's too much magic in a certain area. They serve a purpose, like a medication. They prevent ley-fields and ley-nodes from overloading."

Even though his art left much to be desired, Meadow couldn't help feeling for the actual planet it represented. Erit was a living creature—made of rock and magma, sure—but so very much alive. Everything that happened to one part of it branched out and affected every other place, even if the repercussions weren't immediately apparent.

"I'm surprised you remember all that," Luka said, teasing.

"I know *some* things," Meadow returned. "But this was kinda my area of expertise. Like you with your machines. Back when I was just startin' out, when Wheriae and Petalvine were having a tug-of-war with my soul—"

"That's a bit dramatic."

"*I'm* a bit dramatic."

"Right, continue."

"A dead ley-line shouldn't be able to carry whatever magic is affecting the plants." Meadow scribbled a rift within his terrible drawing of the forest. "The only... *being*... that could even hope to use a dead ley-line to channel magic is a god."

"Or that Shade you were talking about."

He didn't know if there was a difference.

Pushing his fingers into the dirt, he searched for the telltale signs of surface magic. "When I was a kid, I found these *bumps* where ley-paths grew closer to the surface. They were new paths. New arteries. Faun-ir was overflowing with them." He could almost picture himself kneeling on a patch of rough dirt, nearly naked, prostrated over one of the magical bumps as he pleaded with Petalvine to give him a chance. The elders said he'd never cast anything worth casting, but the goddess had other ideas.

The ley-line sparked, but not in a way a dead ley-line *should* spark. Meadow narrowed his eyes.

"What?" Luka asked.

"It's active again. It's drawing magic from above and feeding it down into the rift." Meadow pushed his own magic downward, sensing a terrible shadow curled around the dead ley-line. Much like he experienced with the eyes of the Shade, he felt a strange familiarity. "It can't take hold in Faun-ir, so it's trying to find a new path."

Luka didn't react with cold terror, but Meadow didn't really expect her to. She couldn't feel what he felt. Couldn't sense the creeping shroud oozing through the world's magic, destroying the very blood that kept it alive. The revelation that the

Shade could reactivate and use dead pathways would keep him up at night.

For at least an extra hour. Probably less.

Meadow was a very good sleeper. The best sleeper.

"Are you okay?" Luka asked.

"Right now, yeah. I guess I'm okay." Remembering what Stonebuck said at the temple, Meadow pushed his magic into the plant, robbing it of its twisted, malformed life force. He had never used his magic in such a way before because Petalvine's magic was supposed to *create* life, not destroy it. But to stop the spread of the plague, he had to use his magic in a more novel, disturbing capacity.

The lily withered, its black leaves turning brown and dry. The stem curled in on itself as it crumbled to dust.

Meadow said, "The poor thing."

"You talk about plants like they can feel," Luka said. "They don't know what's happening any more than Ptery ever has a clue what's going on."

Meadow barked a laugh. "Well, they can feel, in a way. Different than you and me. But every plant has a personality, and none of them deserve to die to this whatever-it-is that's goin' around."

"Makes me regret those potatoes I ate last night."

"Nah, don't worry about it. You're still thinkin' of 'em like people or animals or somethin'. It's just that they're..." He struggled to find an appropriate way to say it. "They're purpose-oriented. You eat a potato and, ah, that's just part of life. That's its purpose. It's fulfilled. You know?"

Luka shrugged.

"Well, this lily's purpose was changed. It wasn't used for anything. It wasn't picked to have a place on your table to smell nice. It didn't give enough of its pollen to bees. It was ended for no reason. And I guess... I guess it was hurting."

It was hurting so badly.

"What're we gonna do about it?" Luka asked.

It was Meadow's turn to shrug. "I don't know. Kinda... Hoping that comes to me as we go along."

"And if you don't figure it out?"

Meadow shook his head and pushed himself to his feet. In the distance, he could see Ptery and Benji approaching, walking an absurd distance apart from each other. "If I don't figure it out," he said, "I think this disease'll eventually be fatal. I think it'll kill Erit."

CHAPTER TWENTY-ONE

A Song of Clay and Blood (But No Dragons)

Ptery and Benji finished with the Old Manticore so late in the day that they wouldn't have been able to make it to Faun-anin by nightfall, so they made camp. It was the perfect place, too, with a spot of bare land on which they could build a fire and a small creek where they could wash up and catch fish.

"That's weird." Ptery nodded toward a pack of gnolls on the horizon. One stopped to stare at them, eyes gleaming in the setting sun, before following after its fellows. Strange beasts, gnolls. Although Ptery hadn't ever *personally* met one, they were pretty hostile in general, so encountering one sat pretty low on the old to-do list. "You see that? What are they doing all the way out here?"

Luka opened the tent flap, stepped out, and followed Ptery's gaze. "Eh. Gnoll things. They won't come around with a manticore right here, though."

"First time I've ever been thankful for a manticore," Ptery muttered. After what the Old Manticore tried to pull, their vitriol was all the more vindicated.

Except...

They turned their attention toward Benji, who lay by himself near a creek that coursed next to the camp. He'd been there for a couple hours, staring toward the darkening sky in the east. Every once in a while, one of his little wisps would appear, splash through the water, then vanish. Sometimes he'd *telis* a rock from the creekbed, then awkwardly toss it toward the opposite shore.

Ptery shuffled toward the creek, trying their best to appear as if they didn't *mean* to meander toward Benji. That they were perhaps just preoccupied with their thoughts and happened to head in that direction without any notable intention in mind.

"So," they said, standing a reasonable distance from the dangerous creature. "So, you saved my life. I guess I should thank you."

"Oh. Well." Benji turned his head a bit, though his fluffy mane obscured his face. "I just... I like you, Ptery. I wouldn't want to see you hurt. Or... Or... Uh."

"Dead."

"Yeah, that."

Ptery sat, draping their claws down into the current. "Even after as... *Unaccommodating* as I've been toward you?"

Benji didn't answer.

Strange that he'd never shown any disposition toward anger or violence. Surely he would have expressed some inclination by this point since no beast could hide their true nature forever. Even so, since his turning, Benji hadn't spoken an unkind word to anyone. Sure, he'd vented his frustrations, and there were growls and grunts on occasion, but he never lashed out or hurt anyone on purpose. Any harm he'd caused was by unlucky accident, after which he apologized profusely.

To an almost annoying degree.

It would be impossible to fake that sincerity for so long.

Plus, he looked so forlorn now, staring at his distorted reflection in the water. His paws rested in the stream, despite the slight chill in the air.

"I suppose I'm trying to apologize," Ptery said.

Benji sniffled.

Ptery leaned forward, nearly unbalancing themself into the creek, so they could see around Benji's mane. He was *crying*.

Momentarily shocked, as Ptery didn't think liori *could* cry, they only found their voice after a significant struggle. "What's all this, then? You've finally learned how to do the thing! You should be elated!"

Benji sobbed.

Ptery felt as if someone had taken a sharp dagger to their heartstrings and cut them into a thousand million pieces. "Was it something I did? Or said? *Recently,* I mean? Do you... Wish you *hadn't* saved my life? Because I'm quite glad you did."

"It's what Q'ler said." Benji pulled a paw out of the water to wipe his face but only succeeded in making it wetter. "About... how I felt. And he was right. I... wanted to—I thought about—What I mean is..."

Benji looked up for only a second, meeting Ptery's eyes. Despite the animalistic amber of those irises, Ptery saw themself within them many aurs ago. Within those vague memories, they cried desperate tears and prayed to all the gods for a resolution they'd never receive. *Please, Faoliia. Please help me. Grant me healing. Please. Grant me peace...*

Grant him peace.

But how? How could they do anything?

Benji clenched his jaw, gritting his teeth and fighting back another sob. "Why are you here, Ptery?"

"What?"

"I know you're afraid. I can smell it. And it bothers me. I won't hurt you—I'd never hurt you. But you're here, and you're afraid, and I don't—I don't want to be... *this*. I wish I wasn't. You have to believe me."

"I..." Ptery sputtered. "I believe you."

They'd spent so much time goading him. Testing him. Trying to make Benji angry enough to show his true colors so that he'd *snap*. Then the others would see what a manticore could do when it was well and truly riled.

But he'd passed the test over and over. More times than Ptery could remember.

Benji sighed, his eyes closing. "Just let me sleep."

He pulled his paws out of the stream and flopped over onto his side. Ptery almost fainted when they saw the tender pink paw pads, as raw and bloody as ground hamburger. Instinctively reaching for Benji, they pulled back just before their fingers touched fur.

"Why didn't you tell me?" they asked. "Your feet!"

Benji didn't answer.

"How long have they been like this? Benji!"

"It got worse when we got to the pavement."

"You should have told me! I could have done something!"

"I didn't think you'd care."

The simple dismissal cut through the last of Ptery's defenses so thoroughly that tears stung their eyes. How could they have failed their goddess so terribly? Faoliia entrusted them with the most sacred of her implements—a ruby dagger—and Ptery had made such a mockery of their vocation that even someone in pain felt he couldn't seek help from the very person who should have gladly given it.

Worst of all, Benji hit Ptery directly where it hurt because they should have cared more than they did. They were friends. At least, they had been before all this *lio ri* business!

They had to get over it.

As they hurried away, Benji sobbed again.

But Ptery wasn't abandoning him to go enjoy the warmth of the fire. Ignoring Luka's quizzical glance, they ducked into the tent to retrieve a wrapped bundle and a wooden bowl before returning to the stream.

They cleared their throat.

Surprised, Benji sat up, paws splashing into the creek again. His eyes reflected so much hope that it shattered whatever remained of Ptery's heart.

"Did I ever tell you how I lost my wing?" Ptery asked.

"Uh. Which—which version? There was the one where you rescued the cub from the river, and—and the one where you fought off an army of liori, and the one where—"

"I tell those stories because I don't remember how," Ptery said. They crouched down near Benji, freeing the ruby dagger from its wrappings and taking a moment to admire its exquisite beauty. Nothing else they possessed—nothing anyone in the world could *ever* possess—compared.

It meant so much. If Ptery failed now, owning it would mean nothing at all.

Benji's ears perked up, betraying his curiosity.

Ptery shrugged. "Well, that's not *entirely* true. I remember some things. I was a child, around twenty aurs. Mature for a human, but young for a banshee." They set the dagger aside, next to a roll of bandages and the wooden bowl. Kneeling next to the creek, they dug into the silt beside the water until they found a vein of soft, wet clay. After scooping a generous lump into their palm, they deposited it into the bowl and wiped their hands on the grass. "The healers told my father that my mind wouldn't recover if they didn't separate me from the memory. So they took it and put it into this."

With one claw, they freed the garnet pendant from beneath the collar of their shirt.

"They took your memory?" Benji asked.

"It's here. And I can have it back if I break the stone." They ran a claw along the break-axis in the garnet's surface. "There's other *requirements*, but breaking the stone carries the most importance. It breaks the spell."

"Magic is so..."

"Convoluted?" Ptery supplied. They raked their fingers through the grass, searching for the right *feeling*. Weeds grew in abundance by the creek, so it would be easy to pick one and be done with it. But a carefully crafted spell manifested much more desirable outcomes.

"I was going to say 'fascinating,' but convoluted, too. Don't you ever wonder?" Benji crawled a fraction of a centikip closer, invested. "You're older now. Wiser? Maybe you could sort through the memory."

"Of course I wonder. But what I *do* remember is... Well, it's not good." Their clawtips passed over a dandelion blossom. *Perfect*. Faoliia would surely see the humor in using such a flower to heal a leonine creature and offer her blessing to the salve. Picking the fullest flowers, Ptery crushed the yellow petals between their fingers and dropped them into the bowl. "I remember that there were manticores involved. No healer could remove that fear completely since it had already been *committed*, they say. Sharp teeth and heat, the sinking sand beneath my feet. A feeling of separation. Gigantic wings like boat sails, and the blood."

Benji looked at his paws, scowling. "Why are you, uh... I appreciate that you're commiserating, but it seems like an odd time..."

"Because I wonder if those feelings are wrong." Dipping the wooden bowl into the river, they let enough water in to saturate the clay and the petals. "Benji, you saved my life for no benefit to yourself. In fact, it would have made your life easier if you'd just..." Ptery paused, rubbing their eye. They could still see the eviscerating point of the knife in front of them. "Something inside you wanted to save me, and whatever it was enabled you to do something you'd never done before."

Flustered, Benji fidgeted. "It was the right thing to do."

"Exactly."

When they flipped the ruby dagger over to use its pommel as a pestle, they found their hand was shaking.

"What are you making?" Benji asked, cutting through their fear.

Ptery stared down into the wooden bowl. "It's a salve. A special one for feet—or hands, in your case, I suppose. It will heal your wounds and expedite the formation of calluses, so you'll be able to walk without pain."

"Oh... That's very smart. And very specific."

Ptery couldn't help a laugh. "Yes, well. Faoliia's been around a long time." Ptery glanced at the red flower from the goddess' stone, still as crimson as it was the day they received it, as it nestled within the dagger's protective wrappings. "Like all gods, sometimes she grants her blessing to write a spell. As you may imagine, over the millennia, the well of creativity has dried up a bit."

To the point where Ptery had no idea what they'd do with their flower.

They crushed the clay-water-dandelion mixture into a paste. While it didn't much matter what made up the base of the salve since it was just a vector for the magic, the ritual that followed either made or broke a spell.

Wiping the pommel on the grass, Ptery flipped the dagger around, opened their hand to the blade, and ran the sharp edge across their palm.

It always made a sound. A terrible *shrrrt!* sound. Ptery ignored the shiver that ran up their spine.

Benji winced, looking away. "Healing's always been confusing to me. Why hurt yourself to...?"

Ptery held their hand above the ground as the red rivulets seeped through their fingers, down their wrist, and onto the muddy shore below. "*Yyinawg'waat,*" they spoke at the moment of contact. The paste turned a bright, unnatural blood red as the magic shimmered through it. "It's our godmark," they explained. "We're made to understand the pain of our charges to appreciate why we heal. So... Our energy goes into the earth, and the goddess's energy infuses the spell. Eventually, I'll scar. Hopefully not for many aurs, but it's what every healer bears."

Silently thanking the goddess for her blessing, Ptery turned to the river to wash their hand. With the magic extracted, the wound closed without a trace. They held it up to show Benji their unmarred palm.

"Just like that?" he asked.

"Yes. Just a moment of pain."

"Well... Thank you."

"I'm surprised you don't already know every godmark there is," Ptery said. They sat cross-legged in the grass, working up the nerve to approach the huge, deadly animal in front of them. Despite realizing the fragments of their memory might be misleading, they couldn't banish the fear.

But making the salve was only part of their responsibility. They had to apply it as well, then bandage the wounds in such a way that Faoliia would continue to show her favor. Each spell carried an extremely specific set of duties, and if Ptery failed even one of them, they would scar that much faster.

"I don't know *everything,*" Benji said. "I can't remember having to ever learn about healing for one of my competitions. That's... kinda strange, now that I think about it."

Stalling, Ptery swirled their fingers through the salve. "There's a lot more to it. Poultices, potions, and salves are much less demanding than arcane Cantyrs. Salves are more about adherence to process. And Cantyrs, of course, are more about faith."

"Faith? To the god? But everyone knows—"

"No. To my own ability."

Benji tilted his head, puzzled, ears swiveling forward in the way they did when he was trying to figure something out. "Maybe I'll get a book about healing in Faun-anin."

"Yes, well. It's quite the subject. Let me see your paws."

Benji pushed his front paws through the grass, turning them upward in a way no animal should have been able to do. It made him seem more sapient in an abstract way, and Ptery tried to see the pawpads as nothing more than a young elf's foot. After they reached into the bowl and drew out a handful of paste, though, they hesitated.

Benji offered a quiet "Oh," then, "Maybe I can do it. Or we could get Luka."

"No, I have to do it, or the magic won't hold." Taking a steadying breath, they held Benji's paw in their hand. His fur was soft as a rabbit's, even damp, and just as thick. It was far from the rough, unyielding, wiry hair they expected, and Ptery wondered if they could even lose themself within that warm pelt.

They nearly dropped the paw when they noticed the black, thorn-like claws.

Ptery met Benji's eyes again, looking for the tell-tale feral spark that might suggest a devious motive. Perhaps he'd injured his paws to draw Ptery close enough to pounce!

But his eyes held no evil. They were gentle, worried, and scared but not vicious. They were brilliant and beautiful but hid a dullness deep inside that spoke of a wound that had no spell to heal it.

Benji tried a half-smile. "You've... Uh, you've really done well, Ter! Maybe in the morning, we can—"

"I remember something else," Ptery interrupted. They lowered their hand onto Benji's palm, causing blood to ooze from the abraded skin. "As I lay healing, no idea where my wing had gone, my father told me that it was my fault for wandering off and that the liori who attacked me were having a wonderful snack about then. Then he said banshees don't need their wings for flying, so he wasn't going to pay a healer to grow mine back."

"I've heard healing a limb is expensive."

"Yes, but he could have afforded it." After coating the salve over one paw, Ptery reached for the other. "He could have done it ten times over."

"I'm not sure I like your father very much," Benji said.

"Hm," Ptery acknowledged, offering neither agreement nor disagreement. "His words motivated me to study healing. Not for myself, unfortunately. After a time, a wing or an arm or a leg... They *forget* what they're supposed to be. The lack of a limb becomes more a part of you than the limb ever was. But I lost something because of it—I struggle with balance. Banshee language involves movement of the wings, so I have difficulty speaking it."

"Then why?"

"Because I can help others." Ptery finished applying the salve to the other paw. "I can help others without charging them for it. Now hold still so I can bandage this."

"It stings a little," Benji said, worry creeping into his tone.

"It will, just for a little while. Then it'll feel cold, and you'll know it's working."

After Ptery bandaged the first paw and started on the second, Benji began to purr. It was the first time they'd really listened to the sound, which put them quite a bit more at ease. And while Benji apologized between breaths, Ptery really didn't mind it so much.

As they finished bandaging, Benji said, "I had dreams, Ptery. I... I hoped to discover something amazing, something no one'd ever seen, and write about it so I could share it with the world. Maybe I'd give talks at schools and universities. But I can't now, can I? Can I even go to digs anymore? Am I even technically an archaeologist now?"

Ptery didn't know what to say except that he was right. So few people would want a manticore at a work site. "It's all right. Dial It Back—ridiculous name as it is—will take off. You'll have that."

"I wanted to mean something."

"You will. Can you stand?"

With careful precision, always checking to make sure Ptery was okay, Benji got to his feet and put pressure on the bandages. The salve remained inside, which meant Ptery had done it right. In the morning, they'd be good as new. "Good," they said. "How are the back ones?"

"Oh, fine," Benji said. "I used to walk barefoot a lot. Uh. Before." He smiled, though the expression didn't reach his eyes. "Your feathers are puffed up."

Alas! Their wing was a snitch, betraying their nerves. Getting to their feet, Ptery pursed their lips, trying to force the feathers to lay flat again. "Right, it's a little chilly, I suppose. Now, let's get you over by the fire. It'll help the magic set. I'm not about to do this all over again in the morning. Go on, then."

The magic didn't need heat to set, but Ptery couldn't figure out a better way to get Benji to stop moping by the cold creek all alone.

As they reached the firelight, they found Meadow standing outside the tent in a sleepy daze. "Have either of you seen Luka?" he asked.

Neither of them had, of course.

"Well, that's a mystery," Meadow said, personifying the urgent concern of a very dead cow faced with the task of completing a whole stack of quarterly tax forms.

CHAPTER TWENTY-TWO

Never Write a Chapter About Travel

As it turned out, Luka's whereabouts weren't a mystery at all, and she made sure the others knew it. When the others woke, they found her safe in her bedroll, quite comfortable and warm, and not at all interested in awakening so early. Meadow asked where she'd gone.

She responded that she'd wandered off to get some air, after which Meadow pointed out that there was plenty of air at the camp. That, in fact, they were *surrounded by air*. Nothing *but* air. *Infinite air as far as the eye could see*.

Luka said she needed *regular* air, not the hot air exuded by Meadow.

Meadow gave up, and they packed for the relatively short journey to Faun-anin.

According to Pixel's map module, the complaining started precisely eighteen minutes into the walk. An hour later, Ptery groused about how much their feet hurt and hopped up on Pixel, using her as a steed. Ten minutes after that, Meadow joined them. Two whole ticks later, Ptery and Meadow fought a heated argument about who got to keep the most space atop the pig. Ptery won and made Meadow walk as punishment.

Luka couldn't wait to take ownership of their transport, although she mourned that she'd forgotten to request a soundproof room. Not for herself. One that she could stuff Ptery and Meadow into so the grown-ups could have a few minutes of blissful silence. Maybe it wasn't too late.

"Ugh, this is just *awful,*" Meadow said sometime later. "I can't feel my feet anymore. How long have we been on the road? Three days? Four at least."

Benji glanced at Pixel's side panel and said, "Two hours and six minutes. We're making good time."

"And you can't feel your feet because you've got hooves," Luka added.

"And how are *your* feet, nestling?" Ptery asked, peering over Pixel's side and batting at the tip of Benji's ear. "Bandages still holding? No pain?"

Luka narrowed her eyes at them, searching for a strange angle or a trick or even a quasi-malicious expression. Although Ptery and Benji had a lengthy conversation the night before, their reconciliation seemed too sudden. Too good to be true.

Although nothing felt *off,* she had a hard time trusting that Ptery could bury their disdain so rapidly.

Because Luka *knew people.* And she knew they would almost always disappoint, given the option.

Benji gave no indication of distress, though, instead stopping long enough to lift each of his front paws and inspect them. The undersides of the bandages were a little frayed and dirty from the long walk but otherwise showed little wear. "I feel okay," he said, continuing on.

"Be careful," Luka whispered into his ear as he passed. He gave her a quizzical headtilt.

"We'll take the bandages off later tonight after you rest a bit from the road," Ptery went on, oblivious. "That should be plenty of time for the magic to set. Oh, I can't wait to see. I'm sure they'll look wonderful."

They seemed so genuine.

But as the saying went, a satyr couldn't change its horns.

Cars passed at regular intervals, their number increasing closer to the city. As they passed the reach of the dead ley-line, houses sprung up around them, lining the curbs with adorable little gardens and handmade decor. A few shops dotted the landscape wherever there was room.

The plains gave way to forest, although the trees here were a different variety than those in Faun-ir. Thin birch and tall, red-needled riverland pines grew together in a blended canopy that created an almost confusing explosion of color all around them. Halcyon oaks appeared here and there, although most homes and shops were built *around* the trees rather than *with* them. It gave the outskirts of the city a busier, more frantic feel than the more laid-back Faun-ir.

The paved road turned to shielded dirt as they approached the city limits. A sign welcomed them to Faun-anin; under the city's name, it said, "The Ancillary to Faun-ir."

"What's that even mean?" Ptery asked.

"Ah, glad you asked," Meadow said. "I actually know this one. You know the stones where little fauns go to first connect with their god? Where they become conduits? There's only one here, and it's the one that's missing in Faun-ir. Xax's. It sort of completes the Pantheon, so it's pretty important."

Ptery shivered. "Why is there even disease magic? Or pain magic?"

"The magic exists, so it has to be channeled." Meadow nodded toward a faun passing them in the other direction. "Hey, brother! Look over here for a tick so my friends can see your weird eyeballs!"

The stranger complied and looked up, displaying his otherworldly black-red irises and glowing green pupils. He stared a little too long, though, the dark circles under his eyes starkly pronounced against his pale skin. In contrast to his pallid appearance, he offered a cheerful wave before moving on.

So unsettling.

"Some fauns are just drawn to that god," Meadow said. "And they make a choice. You can either decide to *not* be a conduit, or you accept the call and get a longer life. It's a pretty fair exchange. You don't have to use Xax's magic if you don't want to, either. Their godmark is pretty, well... You know. Bad."

In addition to the in-your-own-grave appearance, mages of pain or disease became sicker and sicker with each spell they cast until consumed by their own magic. Xax's was the most brutal of all the godmarks, although it prevented most from overusing their magic.

Most.

"I've read that the existence of therics is mostly Xax's fault," Benji said. "Humans wanted longer lives, and Xax tricked them. It was a lesson in checking your hubris and arrogance. And after all that, therics have some of the shortest lives of all the species!"

"Faetales," Ptery said. "Anyway, therics are just humans who can become beasts. They don't have shorter lives."

"They do," Benji insisted. "It's true."

"What do *you* know?"

"Almost everything!"

Ptery squealed, offended. "Not about healing!"

"Is the friendship over, then?" Luka interrupted. "For the record, Benji's right. Most therics only live to about fifty or sixty aurs. Kinda sucks."

Ptery scoffed, changing the subject with a wave of their hand. "Meadow, aren't you a dual conduit? The *only* dual conduit? I've seen Petalvine's mark. Where's Wheriae's?"

"Gills?" Meadow laughed. "I'd look terrible with gills. Nah, I've never used water magic. If you don't use his magic, you don't bear his Godmark."

"Convenient," Ptery said.

Although more chaotic than Faun-ir, everything in Faun-anin fit together in playful harmony, from the familiar plazas fauns loved so much to the walls of trees dividing everything into neat little sectors. Through the ghostly birches, slivers of sun-brightened land hinted at the open plains beyond the trees.

Farther into the city, the trees along the road grew in clusters. Suspended among them were naturally grown homes, woven together with magic and set into place one atop another, all the way to the treetops. Whitewood bridges connected each apartment, while ramps led from the ground in a spiral upward around each.

Homey but *too crowded*. It forced the residents of the forest into close proximity with each other, and all Luka could think about was getting to a hotel and getting away from all the staring eyes.

Not that they were staring at *her*. Their attention was on Benji.

His ears were pressed so deep into his mane that they were near-invisible. His head sunk lower and lower as if he intended to bury it in the ground to escape the scrutiny.

Luka offered a rude gesture in the direction of a cluster of teenagers. They giggled and disbursed.

"Now, now," Ptery said. "Don't anger the locals, or they might kick us out."

"They're being—" Luka began.

"Children. Most people never see a manticore at a distance, let alone up close. Besides, some of them are more interested in your A.I.nimal than Benji. Look."

A few people they passed almost entirely ignored Benji, although some gave him a worried glance. They seemed to spare more attention for the shining steel pig making its way down their street, though. Nothing else like it existed in Faun-anin. One kid fed her an apple, which she ate.

"Remind me to clean that out of her hold later, or it'll rot," Luka said to whoever cared to listen. "I hope there's not apple goo all over my stuff, or I'll be stealing someone else's."

"Ah, let's get you to a hotel before you kill someone." Ptery slid off Pixel's back and led a turn down a wide street that cut through the center of the city. "Besides, I can't preen without a proper hot shower. Let's see if we can't find an establishment with silk pillowcases, hm? Benji, take a look down this stretch. Tell me if you see anywhere we can stay."

Benji stepped into the intersection, gazing down the street as Ptery shuffled a kip or two away from him. "Oh, yeah, the signs are really clear. It's... It's pretty cool, actually. I can even read the farthest... Er. Okay. I see a couple restaurants. There's one that's definitely a bar..." He turned, searching down the other way. "Oh! There! The Faun-anin Roost Inn."

Meadow cheered. "Bless your eyes, Prince Fluffy. C'mon, guys, that's where we're goin'!" He skipped down the road, whistling one of his own songs.

Ptery hurried to keep up. "Make sure they have silk pillowcases!"

CHAPTER TWENTY-THREE

Doing Alright

"What do you mean, 'he can't stay'?" The very concept reeked of impossibility to Meadow, who believed all decent people should be welcome wherever they liked. Sure, he should have seen this coming since, *in theory,* liori weren't particularly welcome anywhere, decent or not. But as he'd never seen such anti-liori sentiment in practice, it simply didn't exist.

Until it did.

The satyr billie behind the counter arched a hairy eyebrow. "I mean, *he cannot stay.*"

"But he's harmless," Meadow said. "And you're making him feel bad."

Benji didn't look up as Meadow pointed at him. In fact, his head was so low, his nose almost touched the ground.

"Good, great, keep doing that," Meadow encouraged. "Maybe it'll cause, uh..." He looked back up at the satyr. "What's your name?"

"Galvit."

"Right. Maybe it'll cause Galvit to *find his missing heart.*"

"Look," the satyr said, a thin and greying beard flopping against his neck as he crossed his arms. "No liori is harmless. That is just how it is. He'll have to leave."

"'*That's just how it is*'?" Luka slammed both her hands down on the counter. "You're a satyr. Satyrs get plenty of grief, too. How do you like it?"

Satyrs were considered one of the *beast* races of Erit—because of their animal-like features, some people considered them *lesser*. Unlike fauns, who had more human or elf-like faces, satyrs very closely resembled goats. Although a worse grievance for some was that many satyrs wore minimal clothing on account of being covered in fur and having nothing in particular that needed covering.

How dare they.

But like liori, satyrs showed no natural inclination toward violence or trouble. They were also universally welcomed in faun cities, as satyrs and fauns shared a common ancestor, which predated even the elves.

In fact, if anyone should be exiled from public spaces, it would be Meadow himself. Meadow had caused so many instances of wanton chaos in his life, it would be impossible to come up with an accurate total. Yet here he stood in the lobby of a rather fancy hotel, perfectly welcome.

He considered peeing in one of the many potted plants just to show how much worse he could be than Benji but decided against it. Even though it'd be fun, it wouldn't help anyone. Except Meadow, who really had to pee.

Unintimidated by Luka's posturing, Galvit said, "Satyrs don't eat people."

True. Probably.

Luka turned away from the satyr, leaning back on the counter and threading her fingers through her hair. Meanwhile, Ptery furiously scrolled through their terminal, paying no attention to the altercation at all.

"We could try elsewhere," Meadow said.

"No, it's the principle," Luka replied. "Either we stay here, or we'll camp again. I'm not going to go searching for someone with a fucking soul."

Ptery grunted in consternation but didn't look up from their terminal.

"People are leaving." Galvit indicated the completely empty lobby, which had been empty ever since Meadow first entered. "This is bad for business. You have to go."

"Let's just—" Benji started.

Ptery interrupted by hopping up onto the counter, their talons digging into the polished wood while their wing flapped furiously to keep them upright. Red-tan covert feathers came loose and fluttered to the floor. "Ah! See, I've *found it,* you scoundrel. You can't possibly think I spent my whole life hating liori without picking up a thing or two!"

Luka stumbled backward, caught by Benji's *telis*.

"Er..." Galvit responded with the intelligence of a scholar.

Ptery held out their terminal. "Go on. Read it. I'll wait."

Suspicious, the billie took the terminal, his face growing angrier and angrier the farther he scrolled. "Fine," he growled. "But you're paying extra."

"No," Ptery said. Before the satyr could throw their terminal, crush it, or even pocket it in retaliation, they deftly plucked it from his fingers.

Galvit wrinkled his nose and bared his teeth. He snorted, lowering his curved horns. Then he bellowed, causing the insides of Meadow's ears to shiver in a way that made him want to vomit and sing at the same time.

It sounded like a goose and a llama conspired to create the most annoying honk in history.

Ptery didn't back down. "Well?"

Galvit grunted a word in Rigskit and threw a pair of keycards down onto the counter. "You're staying as far from the other guests as I can put you."

"Fine." Luka reached around Ptery to grab the cards, then gave the satyr a mocking salute. Ptery hopped off the counter.

As everyone re-shouldered their bags and headed down the long, curving hallway, Meadow asked, "What'd you show 'im?"

"Well, much to my *past* dismay—not anymore, I assure you—much of Kyrnis has rules about discriminating against the beast races." Ptery plopped one of their bags down onto Benji's back. "Centaurs, satyrs, even *sphinxes* in some cases. Areas under faun control are pretty explicit."

Despite his previous dour mood, Benji chuckled. "Remember what I said about researching things you don't like, Luka?"

Luka shrugged.

"Of course, that may not apply to manticores, but our friendly satyr doesn't need to know that. I'm not about to *camp* again where there's a perfectly serviceable hotel *right here*." Ptery indicated the walls around them. "Even if there's no silk pillowcases, I desperately need a hot bath—*with* bubbles. And there's nothing any of you can do to stop me."

They plucked one of the keycards out of Luka's hand and marched onward, talons slapping against the garish decorative tile.

"Thanks, Ter," Benji said.

Ptery waved him off, cheeks darkening. "Ah, Meadow. What did that satyr say to me, by the way? He was speaking—"

"Rigskit," Meadow said. "I think the best translation would be 'nanny who sleeps with dogs.'"

Ptery blushed harder while Benji laughed.

As Galvit warned, their room really was as far away from other people as it could possibly get. The hotel was built into one of the few Halcyon oaks in the city, which meant its halls and stairways followed the layout of the tree. One of those halls extended downward into a spiral that never seemed to end. After a strange, unnatural bend in the structure's base—at which point the tile and paneled walls ended—they dipped down into a niche where there was exactly one room, with Zero-Zero-Zero tacked onto the door.

"Does it say something about us that this is room *zero?*" Ptery asked. "It doesn't even follow the numbering scheme of the other rooms!"

"It's probably cleaner since it's so out of the way." Luka pressed her keycard onto the reader. It clicked, and the door slid into the wall to admit them. "So stop complaining."

Though more oddly shaped than usual for a Halcyon oak, the room was comfortable and clean and also quite large. Six beds of varying sizes nestled into any alcove where they would fit, while a few drawers ran up the extruded walls of the tree's interior. Although furnished with a vanity and a desk, neither showed any signs of neglect, lacking the dusty coating one might expect for a room so far out of the way.

Benji grabbed a couple pillows off the bed, arranged them on the floor, and flopped down onto them with a contented growl.

"I think we lucked out," Meadow said. "This is nice."

Meadow looked to Luka for agreement, but she was *extremely* busy trying to engage Ptery in some sort of weird narrow-eyed staring contest. Ptery, however, wasn't paying attention because they were looking at themself in the generous full-length floor mirror. So Meadow agreed with himself because someone had to. "Yeah," he said. "This is nice."

"Well, I call the shower," Ptery said. "Everyone else can stink for a while."

They made for the washroom, but Luka seemed just about to turn that attempted staring contest into a *shouting* contest, and Meadow's ears couldn't take that.

So as Ptery passed, Meadow grabbed their flight feathers. Their arms pinwheeled to keep them upright, which had the bonus side-effect of wrenching their wing out of Meadow's grasp. It buffeted against the wall with a painful-sounding *whump.*

"What was that for!?" they demanded.

"Didn't want you to relax yet," Meadow said, as sweet and innocently as possible. "Hey, Lu, can I borrow your guitar?"

"If you're going to hit Ptery with it, I have dibs," she replied.

"*...Hey now,*" Ptery said. "I just got us a room. What's all this nonsense!"

Luka scowled.

"No. No hitting." Meadow smacked Ptery on the shoulder, immediately breaking his promise. "You and I are going to go to the hotel bar to play some music. We'll try to earn enough minir to pay for the room."

Ptery whined. "I'm *tired,* Meadow! We've been walking all day!"

"You'll be fine, you baby. We brought our instruments for a reason, didn't we?"

Ptery sighed. "Fine. Whatever. No more than a couple hours, though."

Benji said, "We should come with you if we're playing."

"Definitely not." Ptery held up a hand and shook their head. "You have to stay here and rest, so I can check your paws later. They should be healed, but you've also been walking *all day*. Like me, Meadow. *I've been walking all day!*"

They didn't notice the grimace Luka initially leveled at them, nor did they notice the quizzical look on her face when they finished speaking.

But Meadow did.

Interesting.

"Your guitar?" he asked again.

After an eternity, Luka sighed and retrieved the case from its resting place against the wall. Setting it on the nearest bed—and giving Meadow a pointed glare for good measure—she opened it, revealing an absolutely stunning guitar. Though lovingly scratched from aurs of use, its elegance lay in the simplicity of the face, which was made out of a gorgeous purple wood.

"That's not the one you practice with," Ptery said.

"No, it's not," Luka replied. "This is Heliotrope. And if you break her, I will kill you."

Ptery tried: "Killing is such an imbalanced reaction to—"

"I'll kill you," Luka interrupted. "And no one will find the body." Reverently, she removed Heliotrope from its cushioned case. With no doubt in his mind that she really would kill him if he so much as broke a string, Meadow carefully looped the strap over his horns and around his shoulders. For good measure, he said a quick prayer to the gods that no random riots would break out in the hotel bar while he was playing it.

Unzipping a duffel bag, Luka pulled out a small box amp. Not enough for a real show, but for a small gathering, it would do. Compared to the guitar, though, the amp looked like *used trash* that had also perhaps been set on fire at some point.

"This's got some magic left in it. Enough to project. I was gonna fix it on the road, but it'll work for a night or two."

"Thanks. We'll be careful," Meadow said as Luka stared through his Darkrealm-damned soul and *into his very fears*.

They left as she was settling down on the floor next to Benji.

"You really didn't notice Luka givin' you the dog-eye, did you?" Meadow asked as they headed back up the long hallway.

Ptery arched their eyebrows.

"I got you out of there because she was really about to murder you, you know."

This seemed to come as news to Ptery, who covered their chest with both hands. "Whatever for?"

Meadow shrugged. "Not sure. But I'm hoping Benji talks to her about it while we're gone. I guess we'll know he got through to her if you're alive tomorrow morning."

Ptery bit their lip, worried, as they continued on toward the bar.

CHAPTER TWENTY-FOUR

Confluence

His parents named him *Walks Through Mud and Sheds Scales* shortly before his first hatchday. Had they waited a few spans, they may have named him something more related to his eternal search for a musical connection.

Like all trolls, Mud had his preferences. The green and purple colors of his pelt indicated his affinity to rock music, with a genuine lean toward ballads and just a *hint* of the harder stuff all the humans called *metal.* But nothing ever truly *reached* him, and that left a festering hole deep through his heart that should have been filled with song.

He spent most of his life searching for his music. Thus far, that usually led him to quaint bars in tiny towns on the outskirts of civilization. In these places, he'd meet the most interesting people.

"You want another?" today's companion queried. She was a djiratog faun and very tall, with warm, brown skin that reminded Mud of late fall leaves. Unlike the caprivid fauns of Kyrnis, her legs and tail were golden yellow and spotty, like those of a giraffe.

Mud grinned, looking up at her, and nodded.

The Roost Inn's bar was little more than a literal hole in the wall. It had decent lighting and a friendly atmosphere, but its rather arbitrary arrangement of tables shoved into every available space made it rather uncomfortable. It wasn't as if they needed all the tables either, given the sparse patronage of about a dozen. At least the bar provided ample space for swapping stories.

Mud still hadn't worked up the courage—nor chanced upon the proper organic opportunity—to ask his companion for her name. It'd be rude to ask now since they'd been talking for hours, but it didn't matter much at this point. They'd soon travel very different paths and leave each other's company forever. Such was the way of things.

"Well, Mud?" she asked. "What're you havin'?"

"Cantur Mystic and Fizz."

She gave him a look that suggested she had no idea what that was, then held up two fingers to the bartender, who nodded.

Two strangers, two drinks, two fingers. Two was coming up a lot today, and Mud set his mind to figuring out what else there were two of. Two barstools. Two bowls of mixed nuts and candies on the bar. Two smoothed-over divots in the wood where someone had, long ago, plunged the tip of a knife.

The bartender set down their drinks. Split in the middle by a razor-thin slice of wild beetroot, the top half of the glass was red, and the bottom a fizzy, airy blue.

The djiratog narrowed her eyes in confusion, so Mud demonstrated by taking the point of the umbrella garnish and pressing it against one edge of his beet. The blue part coalesced into the red, oozing upward and causing the entire glass to shimmer. Soon, the drink was purple.

His companion copied him.

Two colors becoming one. It seemed prophetic, although *he'd* asked for the drink, so it probably wasn't.

Out of the corner of his eye, he noticed two people meandering toward a raised platform that doubled as a stage. As they chatted with each other, they sat down under a pair of dilapidated visionscreens.

"What do you do with the beet?" the djiratog asked.

"Leave it. Toss it. Give it to me?" Mud asked hopefully.

His companion chuckled, using her umbrella to transfer the slice from her glass to his. Two beets, he noted. It was more than a passing sign at this point. The gods were playing abacus, only they seemed to be stuck at an abysmally insignificant numeral.

None of that mattered when he had a pair of beet slices to mash between his teeth, which he did with all the dignity one might expect. Which was to say *none at all* because dignity was a silly thing to expect from a perfect stranger. Besides, nothing could top the satisfying slosh one achieved when forcefully compressing cooked and softened root vegetables through one's molars. Beet juice dribbled down his chin, but the djiratog ignored it.

"And now?" she asked.

He checked to make sure she wasn't making fun of him, but her expression seemed innocent enough. He said, "You drink it."

After a cursory once-over of the fizzing concoction, she tossed it back in one gulp.

Mud was impressed. After all, it wasn't everyone who—

"Oh! Oh gods, it's burning!" the djiratog said through a self-abasing chuckle. "Oh no! Oh no!"

As she coughed, Mud asked the bartender, who'd wandered over to gawk at the hullabaloo, if maybe he could get a glass of milk for his friend.

He patted her back as she waved her hand desperately in front of her chest as if that would stop the burning. Tears streamed down her cheeks while droplets pooled on the bar under her chin.

That's when Mud noticed her eyes—and was taken by them—as they shimmered with welling tears, glowing in the dim bar light. They were a unique, deep violet. Something within them cried out from a world far beyond Mud's comprehension, and he felt compelled to comment: "Your eyes are so beautiful."

His companion coughed again, snatching the glass offered by the bartender. Milk sloshed everywhere as she desperately raised it to her lips. "Is that a pickup line?" she managed between gulps.

She looked as confused as Mud felt. "Did... you want it to be?" he asked.

Catching her breath, she replied, "Maybe when I'm not dying. *Wow*, that has a kick."

"It's the blue part." Mud rested his chin on his arm, peering into the shimmering glass. "Magic infused. Lightning magic. Strong stuff. You're supposed to sip it."

With her cheeks still dark from exertion, she held up a finger to the bartender and wheezed, "I'll stick with good ol' Faunspirit and orange juice."

Mud shrugged. It was her loss.

At the apex of his shrug, just as his shoulders were touching his ears, a strange perception overcame him. The fur of his mane stood on end with an exciting, electrical intensity, and a chill shivered through his veins. His sinewy tail contracted around the legs of his barstool, the old wood creaking under the strain.

"Are you okay?" his companion asked.

He nodded because he'd never felt more okay in his whole life. Rotating toward the stage platform, he stared at the performers—a faun with a missing horn and a one-winged banshee.

Two old injuries.

"My name's—" the banshee started, wincing at the feedback from the mic. "Gods. Well, it seems the sound equipment doesn't care what our names are, does it?"

A smattering of laughter drifted from the tiny audience. A few people nearest the bar approached the makeshift stage.

The faun rolled his eyes, his fingers meandering along the frets of his glowing purple guitar. He plucked a string. Once. Twice. The banshee adjusted their microphone, but the feedback continued.

"Something is about to happen," Mud said.

"Oh," the djiratog said. "Yes. That's why I'm here."

He side-eyed her.

She smiled. "It's all coming together. Nebula's been leading me—"

"You're a conduit of Nebula."

She nodded. "I don't know why she sent me here, but you were in one of my dreams. It's how I knew I was in the right place."

"Me?" Mud's ears swiveled toward her, but he didn't take his eyes off the stage. "I was?"

"I think so." She patted his shoulder as the microphone continued its loud whine. "Stay here. I'll be back."

She wandered toward the stage. As much as Mud desired to follow, his feet refused to cooperate, so he sat, transfixed, as the djiratog hopped onto the stage, chatted with the faun, then moved their tiny amp to the floor. The feedback stopped.

The faun played a single chord. Mud's heart leapt into his throat as the banshee nodded.

What an odd place to have a life-changing experience, Mud thought as his companion returned, hopping up onto the stool next to him. The bartender handed her a glass, which she held up to him in a half-toast before she leaned back and rested one elbow on the counter behind her.

"Well, that's better," the banshee said, offering a lopsided grin to the audience. "As I'd been saying. My name's Ptery. This is Meadow. We're going to play a couple songs for you. If you like what you hear, maybe consider a donation."

Ptery nodded to the open guitar case on the floor in front of the stage.

Then Meadow tapped out the time with a hoof. On the ninth beat, they began in unison.

They only played with two instruments—a decently-although-not-perfectly-tuned guitar and the angelic voice of a banshee—but Mud still underwent an awakening. At first, it was as if a terrible, writhing eel had gotten into his stomach, which threatened to burst out of him. Then he realized his inexplicable resistance and allowed the tune to break forth from him, although he'd never heard the song and didn't know the words.

The music became his lifeblood, each lyric etching itself on his heart and soul. He couldn't imagine being deprived of it. Couldn't even remember his life before it, as if it had always been part of him, hiding within some undiscovered corner of his being.

A dim part of his consciousness recalled his peers assuring him this would happen. One day he'd find his muse and follow it to the ends of Erit. But with nineteen whole summer cycles behind him, he despaired of ever experiencing his moment. Younger trolls than him found their song at ten aurs. Maybe twelve if they were very unlucky. His best mate even found his at the age of six! Although Mud was never the jealous sort, he sometimes resented them all in the darkest moments of his life. How could he go on being the only troll without a song?

Although the words didn't matter, Mud heard them anyway. They told the story of some poor fool being mesmerized by the eyes of a gorgon, and he recalled his own fascination with the djiratog's deep, violet eyes.

Was this all fated? Was it kismet? Destiny? Was some god pulling at Mud's strings?

Did he care?

Before he knew it, Mud was sliding off his barstool and approaching the stage. With the scant audience, he barely had to shoulder past anyone to reach it. The banshee met his eyes and winked.

They soon moved on to another song, and although Mud's fur still stood on end, he shook himself free of his trance. Dizzy, he turned back toward the bar, only to find his djiratog companion waiting right behind him.

"They're the ones," she said.

"What?"

"You felt it, too, right?" She nodded, although he hadn't answered. "There's something about them. They're the reason I'm here. The reason *you're* here."

"Their song."

"No—"

"Yes," Mud argued, then he scrunched up his face and realized his new friend had a point. "Hm."

"See?" she said. "It's weird, I know. But I've always trusted Nebula, and I'm pretty sure she's led me to the right place. With the right people."

As with most trolls, Mud did not commune with the gods. He still felt a peaceful euphoria envelop him, though, as if Nebula was speaking to him through the djiratog.

He imagined himself standing at a crossroads. One fork led home. He had his song, and it would remain with him forever.

The other fork led down a confusing path, abounding with twists and turns and the unknown. He asked himself, *did I really leave home only to find a song?* Would he truly be content if he returned now, or was an adventure more his calling?

"C'mon," the djiratog said, and Mud grew tired of thinking of her as *the djiratog*. "I'll buy us another drink. We have some planning to do."

As he followed her, he swallowed the tiny amount of pride he had and finally muttered, "I'm sorry. I forgot your name."

"That's because I never gave it to you," she said. He met her eyes, and she smiled. "It's Coriander."

In Her Eyes

A SONG WRITTEN BY PTERYLAE

There's something in her eyes that kills me
Might be that she's a gorgon
Every time I get close, it feels like my veins are on fire

Gonna turn to stone if she doesn't go
But I want her to stay, even if I'll expire
What in the world did I do to earn her ire?

It hurts so bad, but it feels so good
Want to hold her close, but I don't know if I should
Gotta let her go before I sink into the mire

In her eyes, in her eyes
Bright as a sunrise
I can't help but idolize her!
In her eyes, in her eyes
I'm completely mesmerized
Something in her eyes, in her eyes

She's so warm in my arms with her claws in my back
She'll kill me now if I don't back off
But she wants me, she says, she needs me to stay here with her

Her eyes are aflame with mistakes of the past
Know she'll seal my doom if I don't defer
Don't know if I care 'bout the wrath I'm about to incur

So here I stand in spite of it all
With the girl of my dreams who doesn't care if I fall
And in my ear, all I hear is her soft silken purr

In her eyes, in her eyes
Bright as a sunrise
I can't help but idealize her!
In her eyes, in her eyes
I'm completely mesmerized

Something in her eyes, in her eyes

In her eyes, in her eyes
I know it's unwise
Why can't she just apologize
In her eyes, in her eyes
It's forever agonizing
In her eyes, in her eyes, in her eyes

I've died
But I'm happy
In her eyes

CHAPTER TWENTY-FIVE

Halfway Between the Black and Grey

As Ptery and Meadow tried to earn their night's keep, Benji played with his *telis*. Tiny cerulean wisps danced around his claws like fairies, sparking in and out of existence. With one, he picked up his terminal but almost immediately dropped it. Luka caught it before it hit the floor.

"Good try," she said. "You're holding onto things better."

He took it from her hand. This time, he kept hold of it and even manifested a smaller wisp to tap at the screen.

Even though Ptery told him to rest, he couldn't help playing with this new skill. Talent. Power. Whatever it was. It was almost like trying to write with his non-dominant hand, except he could *see* his non-dominant hand. *Telis* flexed a new set of nerves no elf could ever fathom. It tugged at his brain like a complaining, sore muscle.

"You gonna try your bass?" Luka asked.

It lay on the floor in front of him. Unlike Luka's stunning guitar, his bass was practical and plain, although he did have the face re-done with an appealing grey-blue wood when he bought it. With his enhanced vision, he could see each scratch, each nick, each tiny imperfection. It turned the ordinary instrument into a thing of unique beauty, something no one could replicate.

But could he still play it?

He almost feared trying.

"I won't lie to you. But I *am* delaying," he said. "If I try and I can't—Well, if I can't do it, then..."

"Ptery can fuck off," Luka replied. "You're staying in the band."

"Who said anything about Ptery?" Benji *telised* the strap of his bass over his shoulders, and although a bit wobbly, he managed to rest it against his neck exactly where he wanted it. "I don't want to stay in the band if I can't play. Well, I mean, I *want*—No. What I *really* mean is that it won't matter what I want. Bands make music. And if I can't make music... It's really got nothing to do with Ptery."

"They're up to something," Luka said.

Benji tilted his head, narrowing his eyes. He lifted his front paws to show the neat, expert bandage work. If Ptery was up to anything, it was improving their attitude, which Benji appreciated so much, his heart skipped a little whenever he thought of it.

"Healing, yeah, but something else." Luka leaned against the side of the bed, crossing her arms. "No one *does that.*"

"Does?"

"You know!" Luka gestured wildly, annoyed. "A couple days ago, they would have killed you."

They wouldn't have, though. Benji knew patience would be key, and it paid off. Even though it hurt, and even though he wanted to cry more times than he could count, he realized Ptery's hate didn't stem from ignorance. It came from pain. Of course that didn't excuse everything, but it provided an explanation. Somewhat. "When we first met, you didn't trust me, either," Benji said.

Luka grumbled something, then said, "I don't like..."

Benji flicked his ears forward.

"How can you just *forgive them?*"

Ah.

"I haven't yet," Benji said. "But I think I want to."

"Just like that?"

Benji shrugged, his wings scraping gently against the wall. "Something happened last night, Luka. I got through to them. That's what we wanted, isn't it? That's what *I* wanted."

She crossed her arms, but the scowl left her face. Dark shadows became more pronounced under her eyes as her features relaxed. Benji waited for her to say something, but she didn't.

Maybe forgiving Ptery made him a doormat, but that was his choice to make. And even though the saying went "a satyr can't change its horns," it seemed like such a narrow view to take. The universe was *huge*, so maybe on some planet out in the great cosmos, there lived a satyr who *could* change its horns.

"You trust me now?" Benji asked.

Luka said, "Of course."

"Then trust me *now*."

"I'll... I'll try."

"Good. Okay."

Calling forth his *telis* again, Benji closed his eyes. He could feel the long stretch of the bass guitar's neck, and each individual fret laid into it. Four separate wisps wrapped around each of the strings, sensing their tightly-wound, cold steel surface. *Steady,* he told himself, resting one wisp on a single string.

He hesitated, then plucked it.

A crystal clear, if slightly out-of-tune, note filled the room.

Overcome with relief, he relaxed the tension in his shoulders. Even if it was only one note, it meant everything because after so much loss, he now had this beautiful, glowing blue glimmer of hope. It wasn't what he wanted, of course. But as Q'ler told him, there would be no going back; he could only find a way to forge forward.

"Can you do more?" Luka asked. "You didn't run out of the wiggly things, did you? The—"

"*Telis,*" Benji said, tears stinging at the corners of his eyes. "No. No, I just didn't think I'd be able to play."

Even in such a short span of time, his *telis* seemed more and more an extension of himself rather than the strange, foreign perception he experienced before. Perhaps putting the bass around his shoulders unscrambled the last of his hesitance, pushing him that much closer to acceptance.

What if...

What if this was okay?

He played a slow, random progression of notes, moving one wisp along the frets while using another to pluck the strings. The notes soon resolved into something more familiar.

"You're playing the song I wrote," Luka said. "'Unbroken.'"

"Well, I'm trying."

"A little out of tune, but..."

Benji laughed, employing another wisp to turn the pegs even as he continued playing. The bass slipped more into tune.

Telis, once he really figured it out, would open up so many doors for him. He'd be able to touch fire, or electricity, or maybe even reach across a room without even standing. A whole slew of scientific questions begged to be answered, and Benji would accept the call.

This is okay, he told himself, even though part of him feared those thoughts. If he accepted his fate, did that mean he condoned what happened to him? Did he see it as *fair?*

He couldn't answer that question yet.

CHAPTER TWENTY-SIX

The Mighty Road Castle

Ptery did their level best to sleep somewhere *near* Benji—as a show of solidarity, mind—but they couldn't manage it. They started with what would turn out to be a seriously strenuous slumber on a bed a couple kips away, then moved under Meadow's blankets halfway through the night. After waking from a terrifying nightmare a couple hours later, they crawled into the bed farthest away from the sleeping manticore.

Without any clue as to the time, Ptery cuddled into their comforter and tried to sleep again. Their mind danced with the twilight dreams of a rather successful, albeit small, concert the night before.

Maybe, they thought as they drifted further into the dream, they could actually make it as a—

"HEY!"

Stomp stomp stomp!

Meadow, hands on his hips, burst into the room and declared, "The door slides into the wall, so I couldn't slam it open. I figured yelling would work just as well."

"And clattering your hooves?" Ptery, heart racing, found they'd somehow jumped out of their warm blankets and now stood on the cold floor in full fight-or-flight readiness.

"Of course," Meadow said. "How else would I wake you up?"

"Quietly," Benji grunted. "It's a good thing, er, well, my tail was wrapped. There's no quills anywhere, are there?"

"Faoliia's tits, you *idiot.*" Ptery leaned against the wall, trying to overcome their sudden dizziness. "What time is it?"

"Ugh, *way* too early. Did you know the sky turns a really cool *green* color before the sunrise? Yeah. Never seen that before. Anyway, I got Benji a present!" Meadow held up a paper bag. "Handmade at this cool little tailor's hut down the street!"

"You were supposed to use that money to pay for the room," Benji noted, although his ears flicked forward in curiosity. As he stood, he curled his tail to his side and pressed his wings so hard into his ribs that it looked painful.

"One. Two." Meadow made a show of counting each of them. "Where's Luka?"

Ptery glanced at her bed, finding it empty. Odd. The last time they woke, she'd been sound asleep. Now her scattered sheets lay half-draped on the floor.

Benji stretched, newly healed and unwrapped front paws clawing forward on the floor. Jet black talons extended before him as he growled a hearty yawn, which sent a shiver of fear up Ptery's spine. They couldn't help it, no matter how hard they wished it away. Perhaps that fear would pursue them for the rest of their days.

Or...

Once again, they fiddled with the garnet around their neck.

"She probably went to see about that road castle she was talking about," Benji said, oblivious to Ptery's momentary terror.

Meadow's shoulders relaxed. "Well, she'll miss my cool gift, then! This is the best idea I've ever had, I promise." Reaching into the bag, he pulled out a strip of thick, khaki-colored fabric and said, "Lemme see your arm."

With wise hesitance, Benji held it out.

Meadow looped the strip above his elbow, opening and closing a FastTek fastener with the occasional *skrrrrritch* as he fussed with its positioning. Once it rested comfortably, he stepped back and gestured with the pride usually reserved for showing off a newborn infant. "Ta-da!"

It was a pocket. A *giant* one.

It took Benji a moment to process what he was looking at, then he broke into a grin. "Oh! This is perfect!" he said. One *telis* wisp appeared, which wiggled up and down, opening and closing the flap. This was also sealed with a FastTek hook-and-loop, rather than with ties or buttons, and *skrrrrrched* repeatedly as he played with it. "I can carry my terminal in here! And my bird guide, and—"

"That's exactly what I thought!" Meadow also beamed, pulling another pouch strip from the bag. "I got you another one for the other side."

Benji grabbed it with his *telis*, and although wobbly, he fastened it around his other arm with little difficulty.

"You're getting pretty good with that trick," Ptery observed. "I suppose you'll be able to play soon?"

Only half paying attention, Benji busied himself with shoving pocket pamphlets and other small sundries into the pouches. "Oh, yes, I practiced a little last night. Maybe by the time we get to Reinoaken."

Ptery didn't know how they felt about that. Up on stage, with lights in their eyes, unable to see what the manticore was doing because of the glare...

At the same time, they all played so *perfectly* together. It'd been spans since they practiced with Benji, and Ptery longed for his expert bass experience. He added such a beautiful basement to their music.

So yes. Maybe Reinoaken.

Ptery stared up at the shiny green monstrosity in front of them. "How in the names of the unnamed gods of chaos and order do you intend to drive this thing?"

"I drove it over here, didn't I?" Luka replied.

"And that was, what, two blocks?"

Luka scoffed.

The Kirin-Class Road Castle was a beautiful recreational vehicle—larger than a bus and brand new, with shimmering, forest green sparkle-infused paint. Metallic silver stripes decorated each side, culminating in a unicorn-shaped flourish on the back. Triple Ghiscaer drives elevated it a little over half a kip from the ground, and the newest magitechnology kept it running almost silent.

It accentuated a person's wealth and well-being, oozing class and charisma. Ptery knew this to be fact, as they knew *everything* about *every* status symbol one could possibly acquire. If you wanted to go any distance in style, this truck stood out as a glowing pinnacle of prosperity among all other contenders.

But it would be ridden in by a mopey manticore, a ditzy faun, and a temperamental human.

...And an extremely stylish and worthy banshee.

Well. One out of four wasn't terrible.

"I can't believe they got it done so fast," Luka said. "I mean, they were excited to try. None of them ever designed anything for a liori to fit into before."

"Oh, I... I think I'll..." Benji grinned, rearing up on his back legs to look in through the windows. His wings extended out to each side to balance him. "It's—they did a good job."

As his front paws dangled in the air, Ptery took a quick peek at the pads to make sure the healing held. Faoliia had no reason *not* to heal a manticore, but Ptery worried about their *own* fear. Would the goddess have sensed it? Would she withdraw her blessing for that?

But each looked as it should: rougher for wear due to the expected callusing, with none of the raw tenderness from before.

Ptery offered another prayer of thanks to Faoliia, just in case.

Meadow stared up at the road castle in awe. "It's bigger than a skybus," he said, unable to hold his tail still for all his excitement. "Petalvine would *definitely* thank you for your contribution to our awesome quest. You know, if she wasn't dead."

"Shh!" Luka shot a glance to each side, making sure no one heard. "That's a little insensitive, don't you think?"

"Ah, Petalvine doesn't care. She's dead!"

Ptery almost took the opportunity to bounce back into Luka's good graces by agreeing with her, then noticed the tears glossing Meadow's eyes.

As Meadow sniffled, everyone looked away.

"Uh." Luka cleared her throat, uncomfortable. "Okay. Okay, look, check this out. This is cool."

She pressed a button on the control in her hand, and a double door at the back split open and folded inward, revealing the interior.

Meadow, his moment of grief banished with the promise of discovery, hopped onto the ramp, which extended from the bumper to the ground. "Petals, this is *gorgeous!*"

Furnished in blues and greens, it was completely carpeted and curtained, with more bits and bobs than Ptery could hope to count or even name. Although most of the space was empty since Benji would be riding there, a couple plush chairs sat about halfway between the rear doors and the cab.

"What's this?" Meadow asked, leaning on the bumper. He ran his hand over a rough, rectangular area of metal floor right inside the doors.

"Dock for Pixel," Luka said. "She'll sit here while we ride and hold onto our stuff. Plus, she's got that mage shielding on her plating, so the closer she is to bare metal, the better."

"I think I want to travel in the back," Ptery muttered.

"Don't worry. The front's pretty loaded, too," Luka said, almost puffing up with pride. "Trust me. You'll love it. I even got custom seats where your wing'll fit so you won't smush it."

Wiggling with glee, Meadow threw open the passenger door and hopped in. He closed it as Luka yelled at him not to touch anything, then cupped a hand around his ear as if he couldn't hear her.

How unsurprising.

Ptery paced around the truck, taking mental stock of all the wonderful details. They didn't remember what every little thing was called, but they knew it must have cost a fortune. The road castle was the type of thing a *successful* band would ride around in.

"I notice," Benji said, "that you didn't have *Dial it Back* painted on it."

Luka rolled her eyes. Benji chuckled.

"I'll work on getting him to change it yet," Ptery said, crouching down to examine a pair of lenses that might have been cameras. With one talon, they peeled a thin plastic film off each of them, savoring the quiet ss*stkk* as they came off.

CHAPTER TWENTY-SEVEN

It's Late, But Not Too Late

Troll fur meant something, Coriander remembered. She learned about it back in her troll studies course some six-odd aurs ago. Maybe seven. Ten? Honestly, she only needed the course for points, and she slept through most of it.

But now here she was, with a troll roommate, who was as moss-colored as... Well. Moss, with a few purple stripes here and there for effect. And she couldn't remember a thing about troll fur.

"So. You're a troll," she said.

His fur still damp from his morning shower, Mud wrestled a t-shirt over his head, chuckling as he did so. "Very smart."

It should have been a hint for him to expand on her observation, but although she waited, he said nothing else. Perhaps she'd have to be more direct. Was it rude to ask him why he was green?

Before she could suss out a polite way to frame her question, he asked, "What is a djiratog doing so far north?"

He rifled through a bag—the only one he had—and pulled out a paddle brush. Surely it would have been easier to brush himself before getting dressed since his fur was rather long and plush, but what did she know? After all, she wasn't a troll and thus not privy to every trollish habit.

"Why's anyone leave home?" she asked in return. "Why did you?"

"I didn't," he replied. "I live in Faun-anin."

Cori tilted her head at the bag. "You're packed to travel."

"So are you."

She couldn't argue with that, she thought, as she glanced at her luggage resting against the wall. But that wasn't the point. The point was... It was... "But you were *packed,*" she repeated. "And you live here! And you're *in a hotel!*"

Coriander was sure that deserved an explanation.

Instead, he shrugged and answered, "Been waiting for the right music."

All she wanted was some sort of clear answer, even though it hardly mattered. The frustration drove her, though, and she prompted, "Quite a metaphor."

He rolled his eyes, smiling at some private joke to which she wasn't privy. As he smoothed the brush over his hair, taming the strands into something less wild, he said, "That's literal. Trolls"—he paused, indicating himself—"follow music."

The ghost of her professor echoed something similar in the darkest recesses of her memory. *Right.* Trolls had a thing for music.

They also weren't quite as big as she was expecting. Sure, Mud was bulky, especially when he hunched forward and balanced on his hands. But he was certainly shorter than her and probably not much taller than most other species. He also had a gentleness about him. Grace. Precision and acrobatic skill. While he hadn't exactly danced around to show it off, the way he moved spoke of patience and care.

"Coriander hasn't seen many trolls," he said.

"No, I haven't," she admitted.

He passed the brush into the coils of his snake-like tail as his fingers worked more fur out from under his collar. The effect made him look like he had a mane. "Lots don't understand trolls."

"No, it's not that I—" she started. "Well, it's more like... Ah, okay. No. Not really. It's just... You're kind of—Okay, I've seen trolls in town and stuff, but never really talked to..."

She trailed off because all she was doing was digging herself into a deeper hole. Sitting down on her bed, she sighed. "Sorry."

He nodded as if completely satisfied with that answer. She felt a brief surge of annoyance, both at herself and at this strange creature with which she shared a room. Sometimes he seemed barely sentient. Surely if Nebula was sending her dreams about a troll, it wouldn't be one who could barely articulate!

"I think I made a mistake," she said. "But this was fun."

Mud's blue eyes met hers, a look of shock on his face. The light flickered off the purple scale-freckles speckling his cheeks as he tilted his head. "A mistake?"

"Ah, yeah," she said, rubbing the back of her neck, embarrassed. "I think... Maybe you weren't the troll in my dream."

As he set the brush down, his expression said everything. He didn't need words to express his disappointment... Not that he seemed particularly inclined to talk much anyway. In that moment, Coriander felt she made the right call. It couldn't have been him. "I'm wondering," she went on, "If the troll in my dream was a symbol. Like... A guidepost. Telling me I'm going in the right direction."

"Ah," he said. "I'm a post."

He nodded and went back to brushing as if this explanation pleased him.

Right.

She folded the rest of her clothes, placing them carefully in her pack. Giving a cursory glance to the suitcase next to the bed, she made sure the lock was still secure. That was her most important cargo. That gave her an in. Probably.

Gods dammit. Why was Mud so quiet?

"I'm gonna go check out," she said. "I'll take your key?"

He nodded.

Gathering her things, Cori slung her pack over her shoulder and rolled the suitcase into the hall. Calling behind her, she said, "It was really nice meeting you," and then muttered some sort of thank you for the drinks. He replied in kind, and she let the door close behind her.

She hated the feeling of lonely separation that descended on her a moment later.

Really, Mud wasn't so bad, but Coriander found herself disappointed that she'd come so far only to run into... Well. That. She could tell he was smart, but he barely spoke. Surely Nebula would have meant for her to find...

What?

Who?

And what had drawn Coriander to him in the first place? Everything fit and made perfect sense, as far as she could interpret from her dream. But meeting Mud left her feeling disappointed, and she kind of resented herself for that.

At the same time, the way he'd lit up last night gave her hope. The music all but stole him from the world, lifting him into another plane; his fur stood on end as his scales produced their own glow. He seemed so alive. So electric. Just like the troll in her dream. *Of course* he was a sign that she was traveling the right path, but that was all. A sign. And she couldn't remain too angry at herself for leaving him behind.

She ignored the nagging wrongness of her assessment.

Leaning on the front desk, she waited for the clerk to finish tapping away on his terminal. As soon as he looked up, she said, "I'm checking out."

He checked his watch. "Early," he noted, but her mind was on other things, and she didn't respond. He took her keys.

Removing a loaded chip from her pocket so she could pay, she looked around the lobby. As usual, it was empty. "Do you mind if I wait here for a couple hours? I'm waiting for someone."

"Mm-hm."

Unclear as to whether that constituted a yes or a no, she said, "So I'll just sit over there, then."

"Who're you looking for?" The satyr ran her chip, then gave it back.

"There was a faun and a banshee. They played in the bar last night. Meadow and Ptery."

"Oh, they left earlier than you did. I was glad, to be honest. They had a manticore with them."

Coriander's heart sank. The whole reason she dragged herself out of bed and checked out at such a stupidly early hour *was so she could intercept Meadow before he left!*

She should have approached him the night before, but he was surrounded by fans, and she didn't want to seem like... Well. A *fan*. She needed him to take her seriously. Why couldn't she have just told him she'd been sent by a god?

How many other people would use that same excuse, though?

Cori scratched the base of one of her horns. "Ah, do you know where they went?"

He arched his eyebrows at her. "I don't tell people where the guests go. It'd be immoral. Besides, they left hours ago."

Her heart sank further, into her hooves. No! They couldn't have! "But it's only..." She checked the nano-terminal around her wrist. "It's not even nine o'clock yet!"

He shrugged.

Knowing it would come to this at some point, she pulled another chip out of her pocket, checked to make sure it was the right one, and put it on the counter. "Fifty Minir," she said. Or, she hoped it was fifty. She split up her bribe chips months ago, back in the planning stages of this little excursion, so she was a bit fuzzy on the amounts they held. "...Maybe forty."

The satyr's lips pulled into an annoyed grimace; for a moment, Cori thought she'd have to fish around in her pocket for another chip, but the clerk reached out a gnarled hand and took it. Finally. "They went north."

North. Okay. She could work with that. There were two roads leading north, so there was at least a fifty percent chance she'd get it right. "North? Definitely north. Not northeast or—"

"North," he said. "That's all I'm willing to risk. I like my job."

"Fine. Fine! Thanks!"

She reached for her bags, intent on getting out of Faunanin as soon as possible, but froze instead. With one hand poised over the handle of her suitcase, she felt Nebula's imperative as clear as a mountain stream.

She couldn't leave. Not without Mud.

Darkrealm damn it.

Coriander sighed and asked the satyr, "Can you watch my stuff for a minute?"

As he nodded, she turned back down the hall to fetch her troll.

CHAPTER TWENTY-EIGHT

The Road to Gnollwhere

Meadow disliked travel even more than Ptery.

But he liked it slightly more when someone else was driving, and he could sleep the hours away or watch silly videos on WorldVS. The awesome bus-truck-house-on-wheels Luka had purchased for them made it even more tolerable.

"You know," Meadow said, pulling up another video clip on his terminal, "you'd like Deni and Dylin, Benji. They have this show called D&D where they solve puzzles, except they do it *really badly*."

Poor Benji. He still wouldn't play when they'd arrived in Reinoaken, citing a few "no liori allowed" signs on establishment walls. He reasoned that if he couldn't stay in a hotel, he certainly wouldn't be welcome to *play* in one. So he holed up in the road castle as Meadow and Ptery booked and played another short show in a bar. Luka wandered off to do her own thing. Again.

Where was she going every night?

Didn't matter.

Well, it *did* matter. Meadow had tried to follow her out into the rainy pre-dusk afternoon, but by the time he rounded the back of their giant bus, she'd vanished. Pixel stared at him with bright, glowing eyes as he slunk back into the road castle, mystery un-solved.

A few hours later, they took to the road again with a bit more minir in their pockets.

"If they're bad at it," Benji said, his attention focused out the window, "Wouldn't it make me angry?"

"But they're really funny." Meadow stood up as the bus hit a lump of turbulence and nearly stumbled right into Benji's tail. Bracing his hand on one chitinous segment, he tried to shove his terminal in front of Benji's face. "Look, they're playing a video game here. Well, Dylin is. Deni usually watches."

Benji ignored the game, tapping a claw on the windowpane. "I've never been to the Grai Power Relay Plain before. Have you seen this? It's so... uh..."

Huffing, Meadow turned the video off and looked outside.

Creepy, skeletal towers pierced the sky at near-perfect intervals, each topped by a shimmering, rune-like amalgamation of metal and wire. Sometimes a burst of magic would zip from one tower to the next, amplify itself in an explosion of electrical magenta energy, then burst onward to the next tower. Excess energies were vented into the sky, where they roiled and thundered in a never-ending swirl of black storm clouds.

"This is where all the ley-lines meet, so the magical well is tapped by the towers," Benji said. "It's where Kyrnis gets all its power. Oh! Cool fact. It never rains here, but the clouds never dissipate. So there's no plants. See? There's nothing else like it in the world. Amazing."

The rocky, magic-altered ground, barren of any foliage at all, stretched grey and lifeless toward the horizon. Meadow shivered.

"We're about to pass the husk," Luka said, briefly glancing back through the open window between the cab and the living space. "Keep looking to the left."

Spires of magic-veined rock shot out of the ground near every tower, pulsing with pale, blue energy. Arteries of magic shifted across the dirt between one tower and the next, encircling the spires on their meandering paths.

"What's *'the husk'*?" Ptery asked, muffled through the glass.

"Huge monsters that patrol the lands!" Meadow exclaimed, holding his arms up and wiggling his fingers. He stomped bow-legged across the carpet to keep his balance and grabbed Ptery's wing through the opening. "Creatures that have been here for thousands of aurs, their bodies twisted by magic, their minds long gone! They burst out of the ground when you least expect them!"

"That's it." Ptery reached for the steering wheel. "We're going back."

"No, no, *no*," Luka said, batting Ptery's hand away. She pointed into the distance. "Look, you can see it over there."

At first, Meadow noticed nothing different, then he focused on a black patch of ground around one of the towers.

Or, rather, an *ex*-tower. The whole thing was charred and burnt-out, melted and bent at weird angles so that the tip ultimately pointed toward the ground. The wires of its runic symbol dangled downward, swaying ominously in the wind.

"That one exploded," Luka said as if ending a really twisted bedtime story.

Meadow expected her to follow up with, "and they lived deadily-ever-after."

"Tell me we're safe," Meadow demanded.

"Well, yeah, right now we are." Luka shrugged. "They just go sometimes, but there's fair warning first. You can only move so much magic through steel before it ruptures, right? I've heard the shockwave can destroy a house."

...which adequately explained the lack of civilization literally anywhere.

"It'll be rebuilt in an aur or two once the magic dissipates," Benji said. "I'd love to see one explode. From, uh. From a distance."

"Forget about the dead tower for a minute. Do you see that?" Ptery pointed out the front window toward the field. A herd of six-legged cows was making a panicked beeline toward the road.

Bathed in the magic of the Relay Plain for generations, these creatures looked nothing like normal cows. Apart from having too many legs, their horns were twisted and gnarled, their faces long and unnaturally gaunt. Sharp fangs stuck out of their upper lips while their tails dragged on the ground. A silvery electric current sparked between them with each step they took.

The herd stretched a couple kilokips to the north, lowing and undulating as they stampeded.

Luka braked as they crossed. "Well, we can't go around them."

Meadow leaned through the window into the cab, holding his terminal so Luka and Ptery could also see it. "No better time to watch a bit of Deni and Dylin! Look, they just posted a new episode."

Luka planted her hand between Meadow's horns and shoved him back into the living space.

And they waited.

Two idiots giggled from the tinny speakers on Meadow's terminal.

More waiting.

"Do you," Ptery began after a dozen or so agonizing minutes, "know how banshees were created?"

Luka looked at them as if their wing had grown back, with maybe a couple extra spares. "What made you think of *that?*"

"It's all the magic, nestling. Plus, we've been sitting here for the better part of forever, and I'm *bored*. Hearing my story is far better than listening to a couple laughing maniacs on the DragNET."

Meadow paused the video and stuck out his lower lip with much drama and put-outedness. How dare *anyone* mock his favorite NET duo, which he'd either discovered ten aurs ago or ten minutes ago? He honestly couldn't recall which, as, like Ptery said, they *had* been sitting and waiting forever.

When no one said anything, Ptery cleared their throat and sat up a little straighter. "A very long time ago, before written history, an evil human wizard decided to take up the mantle of a god. His name is lost to time—"

"Shia," Benji interrupted.

"Damn it, Benji! I'm telling it!"

Benji grinned, showing his impressive conflagration of teeth.

"Hecklers," Ptery grunted. "Yes, *Shia* gathered the brightest harpies he could find and the strongest humans from all over the planet. He bribed them with power and riches beyond their imaginations and convinced them to couple. Normally the resulting eggs would never hatch! But Shia possessed great power—more than any human ever amassed. He took his power from nearly every existing aspect and molded it into a spell. After destroying those who volunteered their... *services,* Shia hatched hundreds of hybrid eggs."

Meadow leaned through the separator window again, crossing his arms. Even Benji's ears perked up.

Ptery continued. "Some of the eggs produced monstrosities beyond the pale. Creatures so hideously deformed that not even the Darkrealm would take them. But a good number hatched perfect combinations of human and harpy, which lived and thrived in Shia's dark lair. What did he intend to do with them, with their deadly scream and razor-sharp talons? That information, sadly, is lost to time."

"Conquest," Benji said.

Ptery swore. Benji chuckled.

"I'm telling it, all right?" Ptery said. "You *need* a little mystery! Yes, they would have been used for nefarious purposes, and they would have been unstoppable. But Shia didn't take the free will of his creation, which was his greatest blunder. Once his flock was old enough, they used their weapon against him—their scream—all at the same time. We call it the Great Cry, and it broke through his shields, even his immortality. They killed him. From that day forward, they called themselves *banshees*."

"Shouldn't they have called themselves *banshias?*" Meadow asked.

Ptery slowly leaned forward and smacked their head against the dashboard.

"Someone remind me later to check how much of that's true," Luka said.

"It's true. More or less." Benji shrugged. "It's... embellished."

"It's *all* true!" Ptery insisted. "The Darkrealm take you. All of you! So what if it's a bit embellished? It's *supposed* to be a lesson. From that day forward, the gods limited the magics any one person could achieve because no single being should possess that much power!"

The cows' lowing crescendoed as more magic sparkled between them.

Benji narrowed his eyes. "Luka, can you open your window for a tick?"

She did. Benji nudged Meadow aside, sticking his ponderous head into the cab. Curling his nose and dropping his jaw, he inhaled. "Gnolls," he said.

Meadow replied, "Stop insulting Ptery."

Ptery fake-gasped.

"Do you hear that?" Benji went on, ignoring them. "There's something... A low hum. No, it's a whine. Maybe both."

Curious, Luka shut off the engine, plunging the road castle into silence.

The distant whine lowered in pitch, undercut by a rumble almost too quiet to detect. Ptery gestured toward the road, where the rocks bounced up and down as if caught in the throes of an earthquake.

"Move!" Luka ordered, pushing Benji out of the cab with both hands. He slid backward as Luka jumped through the window yelling, "Help me!" back through to Ptery. As she pushed at the window and Ptery pushed at her boots, she made it through, rolling as she hit the floor.

Stumbling to her feet, she covered the entire living area in a handful of leaps, then threw open the shutter covering Pixel's side terminal. She slammed her hand against it, and Pixel's eyes flared to life.

A nearby tower sparked with cerulean and fuchsia energy. Stripes of lightning quivered up the frame to the rune apparatus at the top, and then...

The bass thunder of an explosion, which sucked all the sound out of the air. Even the quietest whisper disappeared into the void as absolute silence descended on the plain. For several tense seconds, Meadow could hear nothing at all as the tower sparkled, then burned white-hot.

The ground rumbled, throwing spires out through its surface, evicting clouds of dirt and dust into the air.

Pixel squealed as Luka threw a shoulder against her, forcing her to remain on the metal pad near the back door.

The mage shielding! Pixel had to be touching the pad for it to work! Meadow struggled to his feet and threw himself against Pixel's side, adding his weight to Luka's.

Within ticks, the tower imploded, and its blue lightning turned into a raging fire that consumed the steel frame in an instant. A painfully bright shockwave emanated from the rune, spreading outward in a sizzling circle that threw blasts of electricity into the roiling clouds above. Lightning zig-zagged to and from every corner of the sky, producing a deafening, singular crack of thunder.

As the shockwave reached the other towers, they threw what could only be described as *oceans* of overflow magic into the clouds. As the clouds continued to build and spark, they folded in on each other as if they were in pain. Great outbursts of lightning passed between the cows, sending them into an even greater panic as they scattered in all directions.

Meadow braced himself as the shockwave passed over the road castle.

Nothing happened.

Letting out his breath, Meadow patted Pixel's flank. "Good girl."

"Are we still alive?" Ptery asked.

"Eeeiiooo! Weeiioop! Hyooowup!" went the gnolls. "Ooo-weeyoop! Wiiiuup!"

"They're close," Benji said.

Then, it started to rain.

It might have been the first storm on the Grai Plain in history, so the dead dirt had no idea what to make of the phenomenon. It was so dry and packed that the rain couldn't seep into it; instead, the water oozed around on the surface like a displaced eel with nowhere to go.

Highlighted in the glow from the flashing lightning, a pack of gnolls approached the road castle, surrounding it on all sides and steadily closing in. Their thick goggles and fang-filled grins gleamed in the darkness.

Dressed head to toe in black, well-cut rubber suits—one of the monsters even wore a *top hat*—they looked for all intents and purposes to be on their way to the theater or some other needlessly fancy function.

The leader, a huge white gnoll with glaring red eyes, hung back toward the center of the pack. She was fat and healthy, her natural teeth replaced with chunks of gleaming silver, and each of her claws tipped with glittering gold. Her underlings whooped and hollered as she shuffled forward until she was mere kips away from the open window.

"Uuwee! Uuuwee!" she said, ears swiveling back and forth.

Benji stuck his head out the window and replied, "I'm sorry, I don't understand..."

"Get down, Benji!" Meadow hissed.

But the gnoll leader, in an unplaceable accent, smiled. "Aah! Y-oou szz-peak the ol-d faun lan-gu-age!"

"Were you hunting the cows?" Benji asked. "You can have them. I think a couple of 'em... Well, you know. Uh. Died. We're just passing through."

"I-yah am Ji'irifarana'ali," the gnoll leader said. "And yy-ouu shhhhould be dead. Noww-ah I will-hh k-kill you with one fin-gerrr."

She held up the smallest finger on one hand to demonstrate. The gold point gleamed.

Benji looked impressed for all of a moment, then he ducked back into the living space and whispered, "She wants to kill us!"

"I heard that!" Ptery replied. "I vote no!"

"Me, too," Meadow agreed. "Let me see if I can close the window—"

As he reached into the cab, the gnoll leader leapt upward and clung to the door, snapping her silver-coated teeth shut a centikip from Meadow's fingers. He pulled his hand back, shaking it as if burned. Her hot breath still stung across his knuckles.

The pack whooped and laughed.

Something heavy thumped against the rear door, bending it off its hinges. Both Luka and Pixel scrambled away from it.

A round, serrated blade wedged through the crack and twisted, popping the door open like the top of a squeezed can. Several gnolls waited outside, silhouetted by the lightning, their eyes glowing through the darkness. The pale leader appeared at the now-open portal and began to climb in.

Ptery said, "Get behind me. Cover your ears."

It was all the warning everyone had. Luka and Meadow only *just* made it.

The leader, who spoke enough faunii to understand, covered her ears without a tick to spare.

And Ptery screamed.

Even with his ears covered and "safely" behind Ptery, Meadow still curled into a ball as claws of sound tore into his eardrums. Gritting his teeth, he squeezed his eyes shut, willing the piercing shriek to end.

When the scream ceased, and its dying echoes rolled across the plain, every gnoll in front of Ptery had fallen, unconscious and bleeding.

Except the leader, who slumped to her knees, a red trickle oozing from her pink nose. She stared into the road castle with a rage so intense that it made Meadow sort of prefer Ptery's scream.

Ptery, doubled over and gasping, threatened, "I'll do it again."

That's when the metaphorical burnt-out lightsphere flickered above Meadow's head. "Guys. Guys! We can *fight!*"

"Oh. Oh yeah," Benji replied.

He tensed his muscles, mane puffing up to twice its size, and charged forward. The gnolls who'd approached to pull their fallen packmates out of danger turned tail and fled, yipping what could only be gnollish curses behind them.

The leader barely rolled out of the way in time before Benji launched himself into the rain.

Meadow followed after, sloshing through the water to the right side of the bus. Several gnolls still loitered there, rattled and tense but clearly still ready to fight. One even pulled a crossbow.

Rather than rush at them, though, Meadow dropped to the ground. Digging his fingers into the dirt, he searched for the memory of the flora which used to grow in abundance there. Though the echoes of lush foliage were buried deep, they still existed and burst forth from the rock with fervor.

Huge vines entangled the surprised gnolls, suspending them a hundred kips straight up in the air. As thorny tendrils curled around their throats, they lost consciousness, their limbs dangling toward the earth.

Meadow could have killed them.

They attacked first. It would be self-defense.

What would it feel like to *kill?*

His vision wobbled and darkened. Hundreds of kilokips of water hung above him, pressing down, down, down on his chest, robbing him of breath. Crushing his bones. His spirit.

He was Wheriae, bound with immaterial chains. His mind reeled with confusion and futile anger. Deep resentment coursed through him, and also a painful sadness he couldn't shed, no matter how much he told himself it didn't matter.

How *she* didn't matter.

He struggled in a fury. With each tensing of his muscles, though, with each lash of his powerful tail, the bindings tightened.

A tendril, a shroud, circled around his neck...

"No!" Meadow shouted, returning to himself. The vines were gone, the gnolls lying still on the ground.

Breathing. Alive.

The pack fled in all directions, carrying the incapacitated with them. Soon, the leader stood alone, grimacing and barking in the gnoll language, her outrage almost palpable. But there was nothing else she could do.

She turned and ran, alabaster tail flagging her retreat.

CHAPTER TWENTY-NINE

Off Course

Coriander's car had a high roof to accommodate her tallness. Even so, the tips of her stumpy horns occasionally brushed the felt ceiling, especially if the car rocked or hit turbulence. Mud could see the divots where they'd struck over and over, leaving two little dimples against the otherwise pristine interior.

...An interior that was very interesting. The steering wheel was on the wrong side of the car! Mud worried about the legality of driving such a vehicle, but Coriander said it was hers and roadworthy, and she had a license, and it was just the way cars were where she came from. At least she was patient about it.

And also quite sullen. Not pouting, Mud noted, but quiet. Perturbed. Annoyed. The further along the road she went, the more annoyed she became until she pulled onto the shoulder and put her head in her hands.

He wanted to ask—as he'd wanted to ask for more than a day as they drove—why she returned to their hotel room in Faun-anin and asked him to come along. Unable to form the proper words, he distracted himself by counting the spots on her legs. Against her golden fur, the spots were the color of fresh-turned forest clay. A warm brown, just a shade lighter than her skin.

She reminded him of the gem called tiger's eye.

Mud reached thirty spots before she opened her door and stepped out into the warm night.

He followed, contemplating an apology. Although unsure about his specific infraction, he learned long ago that it didn't matter whether he'd committed some odd blunder or not. Fauns and humans just liked to be apologized to. Some banshees, too, and the occasional elf, but he still didn't know about liori or gnolls or other things with sharp teeth. Some of them wanted to chew on his bones no matter what he said, so he stayed out of their way. He liked remaining undigested.

Taking the time to contemplate the perfect apology, he finally settled on, "I'm sorry."

"Mm?" Coriander asked, leaning on the guard rail that ran next to the highway. "Sorry? For what?"

"You're upset about something," he said.

"Ah. Yeah. You wouldn't understand," she replied.

Mud felt very much like he'd understand if she'd give him a chance, but most people didn't give him a chance.

His apology had the desired effect, though. The tension around her eyes eased, and she slumped, forehead lowering until it rested on the metal rail. "What's with trolls and music?" she asked.

It would be insane for a troll to ask another troll that question. However, Coriander was not a troll, nor were most people outside of troll villages. It took Mud half his life to figure out why someone would ask such a silly thing, but when it clicked, it made perfect sense.

Because his friends of other species didn't feel music.

"Troll fur is the color of the music in our hearts," he said. "It is self-magic. Lost Old God magic."

"You know about the Zi'nto Ama Aragat? The Defeated?"

"Some. They gave us the gifts of self-magic, but we can't cast it. We can't pull magic from the ley-lines and weave it into spells."

She nodded, considering. "And you liked the music those guys were playing at the Roost Inn?"

"I do. Very much."

"Then... *I'm* sorry."

Mud tilted his head, ears lying back in his mane. Climbing up onto the rail, his feet hanging onto the posts, he said, "You brought me with you. Are you sorry you asked me to come?"

"No. I went the wrong way. They're not in Tyl. Or Prairieville. I went the wrong way."

Mud's stomach flip-flopped as Coriander tangled her fingers into her bristle-like hair. He asked, "How do you know?"

At first, she hesitated to explain the intricacies of Nebula's magic to him, but her frustration encouraged her voice. She revealed her knowledge bit by bit as they sat on the side of the road, watching the shiny cars speed by.

She explained that Nebula was not only the god of dreams but the god of *space*. If Coriander wanted to find something—or someone—usually all it took was thinking about them. Recently, Nebula herself commandeered this ability and pushed Cori toward Dial It Back.

And toward Mud.

But ever since arriving in Faun-anin, the strange attraction often failed or only provided a weak, insignificant pull. Nebula seemed distracted or disinterested. Cori couldn't tell which.

"The last time I really felt it was when I tried to leave you," Coriander said, crossing her arms. She turned and leaned against the guard rail, staring into the distant lights of Prairieville. "It was stronger than ever then. I knew Nebula wanted you with me."

"Maybe..." Mud tapped his fingers together. "Maybe if Nebula is distracted, the pull cannot happen, and you're actually on the right track?"

Cori shook her head. "No. I still feel them, but very far away."

"Which way?"

"I don't know."

Mud couldn't help a whine. He apologized again as Coriander glanced at him with a half-smile.

"It's not *your* fault," she said.

"Well, it is... *our* fault. Trolls dance on the strings of fate. When you tried to leave Mud, you treated Mud poorly. And the universe, the... hm." He squished up his face, trying to come up with the right word. Ultimately, he settled on the troll word for it. "The *Rrorgan*. It intervened."

She laughed. "I thought all that crap about trolls being lucky was just old faetales."

"Not faetales. Treat a troll well, and they bring good luck. Treat them with contempt, and they bring bad luck. That's where the saying comes from—"

"Always pay your trolls," she finished.

Mud got the distinct impression that she still didn't believe him, but it didn't matter. It was true. He knew it was true. That was enough. "Yes," he said.

She hopped up onto the rail to sit next to him, and neither of them spoke for a long time. Then Coriander said, "I guess we could double back and follow the other road. But Reinoaken is a hub. The roads go out from there in so many different directions..."

"Why do you follow them?" Mud asked. "The band. Dial It Back."

She shrugged. "Nebula told me to find them, so I did. She has her reasons. Only reason I can figure is that she wants me to do their sound design. Maybe they're important to her somehow, and she just wants 'em to succeed. Who knows why gods do what they do?"

"Sound design?"

Cori gestured toward the car. "All my sound equipment's in there. Terminals, software, microphones, monitors. Acoustic panels in case they want to record. Extra magicapsules for linking theater equipment to theirs. It's all the sound design stuff I own."

"That's pretty incredible."

Coriander scoffed. "It's a good guess. Well, maybe not even a *good* guess. Just a regular one."

"We have to find them." Mud hopped off the rail, slamming his fist into his open hand. "We'll find them and see what Nebula wants with them. And I'll have my song. How? How, Coriander?"

"I don't know. I was kind of tipsy when I met them, so I don't even remember their faces. I can't even remember if the one guy was playing an acoustic or an electric guitar."

"Electric. That would help? If you saw their faces?"

"That's how I connect with people. It's how I can find them in their dreams."

"Can... Coriander connect if I draw their faces?"

Her expression turned patient yet disbelieving, without a single shred of hope. "The kind of drawings you could do..."

"You think Mud is a child," he said. "Can't remember things. Maybe draws stick figures."

"No! Mud, you were halfway drunk, too. No one can see someone once and then just draw them. Even if you'd been sober, you'd never get their personalities. Their mannerisms... I need *real*."

"Wait here."

Returning to the car, Mud retrieved his bag from the passenger side floor. Shuffling his clothes aside, he found his notebook nestled safely near the bottom.

In the glow from the headlights, Mud set the notebook on the ground and gestured for Cori to come closer. She did, and as he paged through it, her interest grew until she took the book into her own hands and flipped through the drawings herself.

"I recognize these places. These animals." She shook her head, incredulous. "You did all these?"

"Yes. Look at the last one."

She obliged, turning to the last page, and admired it for a long time.

"This is perfect, Mud," she said, holding up the book. It was a drawing of their hotel in Faun-anin, complete with the stray bits of litter stuck under the shrubbery and the cracked window on the third floor. He remembered every detail, translating it onto paper with ease. The fake belfry tacked onto the oak's beautiful natural growth. The missing shingles on the gable over the unused side door. The pattern on the brick parapet above the tavern.

"I know things," he said. "Don't know why. I see things, and I do..." He pointed to the notebook. "That. If I don't, they fight to get out."

It was the only way he could describe the feeling. The urge advanced like a river, getting more turbulent over the course of days unless he sat down and rendered the thing that interested him. In this case, it was their hotel. Perhaps drawing it solved some unknown question he didn't even know how to ask.

"You can remember those guys that were playing?" Cori asked.

"The faun was Meadow. The banshee, Ptery." After a moment, he added, "I can picture them as if they're right in front of me."

Softly, Coriander hmm'd to herself, paging backward through the book. "It still won't help. Even drawings this good... There's still something missing. I don't know." Closing the notebook, she rested her hand atop it for a moment, her face blank with thought. Slowly, a smile touched her lips, then spread into a grin. "I do have an idea, though. I think we can make this work."

CHAPTER THIRTY

Wet Manticore Fur

The storm surged for less than a quarter hour, after which the magic in the sky sucked up every last drop of water remaining on the dusty earth. The black clouds once again churned overhead, flashing fuchsia lightning and hoarding their rain with greedy zeal.

Ptery found Luka inside the road castle, unconscious, guarded by a rather irate and protective Pixel. She refused to let anyone close until Meadow whispered soft assurances that they were there to help. Only then did the mechanical pig grudgingly step aside so they could move her out of the bus.

But she kept a watchful eye on everyone as Ptery tended to her and prepared a healing tonic.

"The Ghiscaer drive..." Luka muttered as she came to some time later.

"Don't try to sit up yet," Ptery said, measuring the tonic into a vial.

"Where...?"

"You're outside." Ptery huffed, glancing at the others. Unfortunately, the giant magic clouds left Benji's fur sopping wet, even after they'd evaporated the rest of the water on the Relay Plain. "I would have liked to administer care *inside,* but Benji wouldn't leave you alone, and he stinks like wet dog. No one wants *that* smell in the carpets. No offense, Benji."

Benji opened his mouth to speak, but Meadow, who sat several paces away from him, jumped in first. "None taken. I promise."

"I'm so *heavy,"* Benji whined. "You know, I bet I wouldn't be able to swim. I'd be dragged right to the bottom!"

"That's *definitely* not the matter at hand." Ptery held the vial under Luka's nose. Her eyes shot open, and she shivered at the pungent aroma. "The problem is, *you smell like wet dog."*

Benji grunted, halfway between offended and amused. "It's because of natural oils in fur—"

"Wet dog," Meadow agreed. "Sorry, buddy."

Benji said, "I'll go shake off again."

He harrumphed away from the road castle.

Sitting up, Luka took the vial and curled her nose. "The gnolls took out the Ghiscaer drive when they..." She glanced back at the rear doors of their damaged bus and groaned. "When you guys used the back bumper as a diving board, the rear drive couldn't take it. It was already too unstable. I think I went flying."

An ugly gash ran from above her eyebrow to her hairline. Ptery would have to take care of that, too, but the external injury was less dire than a possible concussion. "Drink that," they said. "All of it."

Luka glared at Ptery, then held her nose and tossed back the contents of the vial. She puffed her cheeks and wretched but didn't spit it out. Good. Making more tonic would be a pain, especially considering how tired Ptery was after adrenaline and exertion took their toll.

"I knew all along that those gnolls were up to something," Meadow said. "I told you I saw them at the temple. They told me to stop what I was doing."

"Well, if you were growing trumpet flowers again, of *course* they did," Ptery replied with half a smile. "No one wants those about."

"No, I mean, they knew..." Meadow shook his head. "*Something*. I think they knew more than I did at the time. It was weird. And I think the little grey one Benji knocked unconscious wanted to bite me."

"They *all* wanted to bite *everyone*." Benji returned, his fur fluffed out after his shake. He sat a respectable distance away and added, "Meadow, do you have any of those fire marbles? Maybe some heat'll help... Well, I wouldn't get too close, but..."

"Oh! Yeah."

As Meadow pored over the contents of his pockets, Ptery sat down next to Luka.

She glared at them, obviously still holding the tonic in her puffed cheeks. Ptery almost laughed; after all, no one wanted to keep that vile concoction on their tongue for very long. "You may be setting a record."

Her irises flashed an angry green as lightning arced overhead, but she complied. Finally.

Meadow said, "Sorry, that's just a regular marble."

"What is it you're so angry about?" Ptery wondered aloud. "I'm sure I haven't kicked your kitten or dug up your prized begonias. Do you even *grow* begonias? You don't strike me as the type to have a green thumb."

Luka gagged again, tears springing to her eyes. "It'd take too long to explain."

"This all started when I had that nice chat with Benji. Are you jealous? Don't worry. I'm not about to commandeer your soulmate. I'm not sure..." Ptery tilted their head, watching Benji as he *telised* several more plain marbles out of Meadow's pouches. "I'm honestly not sure he'd *fit...*"

Luka spit. Thankfully, she'd already swallowed the tonic.

"Ah, well." Ptery chuckled, satisfied with themself. "I see I can still shock you speechless. Now, tell me."

She glared at them again, then her shoulders slumped. "I don't know. I thought about it, but anything I think of is stupid."

"Try."

She wrinkled her nose, clearly unaccustomed to spilling her feelings. "I had a reason to be pissed at you when you were being a jerk to Benji."

"And now?"

She held up the vial. The carved crystal facets gleamed as she turned it, studying the one drop of tonic rolling around at the bottom. "How are you so *fucking annoying?"*

"You don't trust me," Ptery pressed. "And as far as I can tell, trust is vital on this little escapade. Now, we're not going to patch up all our differences overnight, but if we don't start to play nice, Meadow thinks some Shade is going to have its way with us, and I *don't* mean in the fun way. You have to talk to me, love. Or I'm not going to leave you alone."

"No, this *is* the right one," Meadow said. "Look, it's not my fault if I store my fire marbles with my stink bombs. This pouch is convenient—"

Benji uttered a rare curse.

"I don't trust you because..." Luka watched Meadow set the marble on the ground, which then burst into a comfortable, orange fire.

"Wonderful things, fire marbles," Ptery said. "A little magic, stored in a little glass ball that anyone can use. Thank the gods."

"That's it. That's the reason."

"Fire marbles?"

"No. It's how much you love the gods. Meadow, he *hates* them. But you..." Luka's fist curled around the vial with so much force that Ptery feared she might break it. Then, she let it drop into the grey dust. "How can I trust *you* when you put so much trust in *them?"*

That... was not the answer Ptery expected. "What—"

"I can't... Not right now," Luka went on. "I promise. I'll try to be nicer, but I can't tell you. There's too much..."

Ptery didn't want to argue. They desperately wanted to know why Luka would join them on this vast escapade at all if she hated the gods so much, but... She had a concussion, and maybe none of this would matter in a few hours. They'd chalk her irritation and confusion up to her injury and perhaps bring it up later if curiosity struck. "It's all right. Right now, the important thing is that you rest. And here." They held out a tiny jar filled with a scarlet balm. "Rub this on your forehead before you sleep tonight. It'll heal the cut."

She took the jar and pocketed it. Ptery hoped she used it.

All she said was, "Tomorrow morning, I'll call for someone to repair the bus." Then she stood, wobbled a bit, and wandered closer to the fire. With nothing else to do, Ptery followed.

Meadow'd already settled in, way too close to the flames, with a blanket wrapped around his shoulders. At first, it looked like he had a teddy bear in his hands, but then Ptery realized it was an entire loaf of bread.

Meadow stared straight into their eyes and took a giant bite of it.

"That was supposed to be for *everyone*," Luka scolded. She made a grab for it, but Meadow snuggled it under his blanket, out of her reach.

"*You* didn't just use all your magic," he replied. "Don't worry! I'll buy more. Bread. Not magic. I stole the bread so I could replenish my what's-it."

"Itheri," Benji supplied.

"Yeah, that's it."

Luka wrinkled her nose at him and sat near the fire. "You could grow *anything you wanted*. I learned enough to know that flora magic isn't a one-to-one ratio."

"Not now!" Meadow said. "It'd be rotten. Or purple! Would you eat orange-spotted purple lettuce, Luka?"

She grimaced.

All magic worked in different ways, and each aspect had its limits. For Ptery, it was their blood. For Meadow, it was a pool of arcane energies called Itheri. Once the pool started to run dry, it had to be replenished, or magic could get... *weird*.

Ptery had never seen Meadow run out of Itheri.

Benji must have been thinking the same thing. "I once saw you grow an entire Halcyon oak, then invent a tomato with legs that would throw *itself* at your elders."

Meadow laughed. "Aw, good memories." He horfed down another chunk of bread. "Growing a giant tree in a forest that wants to make trees is *easy*. Suspending a bunch of gnolls by their necks with vines that grew from dead earth isn't. Speaking of gnolls, did you *see* that one? The white one. She was *huge*."

"Female gnolls are always bigger than males, but she was... exceptional." Benji ran his claws through his mane, using *telis* to squeeze out more water. "She must have been very old or very—"

"Freakish," Ptery supplied.

"Important." Benji narrowed his eyes. "Well-fed. Respected. Have you ever known me to say 'freakish'?"

"It's a good time to start."

"It wasn't her size that worried me, though," Benji went on. "It was her name. Ji'irifarana'ali."

"I'm surprised you remember it," Luka said.

Benji lay down, his wings shivering in a sort of nervous tick. "The gnoll language..." He paused, tapping his chin. "The gnoll language is fairly interesting if you take the time to study it. Not only does it use audible sounds—growls, squeals, guttural enunciations—but they actually—their ears and tails are part of how they communicate. Even hand gestures. They might have... Well, *petals*. Billions of permutations of words, each attached to a feeling. And their names are often beautiful and meaningful. This one's was terrifying."

"Yeah, it was," Meadow agreed. "*Way* too many syllables. Can you imagine being a kid and having to learn—"

"No," Benji said as if Meadow was an exceptionally difficult toddler. "I was *just* talking about the important nuance behind gnoll names—"

"Look." Meadow tore a chunk of bread from the loaf and pointed it at Benji. "There was nothing nuanced about that thing tryin' to snap me in half with its teeth."

"Right, but..."

"I didn't see her at the temple, either." Meadow scratched behind his ear with the bread, then ate it, which made Ptery shiver. "Just her little minions. You know, I bet she's important or something, like a... puppet master, pulling all the strings."

Benji sighed. "Yes. It's the 'J' sound in her name. It's really rare in their language. Kinda... Reserved for things of importance or sacred concepts. All their oracles have names that start with J, so she might have once been an oracle in training.

Uh. The point is, she was given that name when she earned it. It's a reference to being god-ordained or god-touched. Her name literally means, 'A Promise to the Old Gods to Destroy.' It might be her entire purpose in life."

"Of all things, why do you speak *gnoll?*" Ptery asked.

Benji shrugged. "Puzzle contests, mostly. And my day job. You learn all sorts of things when you dig stuff up, right? But also it's a fascinating language. Oh! I bet I can speak it better now with a tail!"

"Right. Well." Ptery rolled their eyes. "The important thing is that old Boss Gnoll wasn't some run-of-the-river bully. Do you think she'll be back?"

"Wait, wait," Meadow said. "That's not important. She's got *too many syllables* in her name. I'm gonna call her J. Think she'll like it?"

Benji said, "No."

"J it is, then." Meadow stuffed the rest of the loaf into his face, then tried to speak around it. Crumbs sprayed everywhere.

Luka repeated Ptery's question. "Do you think she'll be back? With her pack?"

"I don't know." Benji looked at the ground, claws nervously playing in the dirt. "I, uh. I do know that her pack might see this failing as a reason to abandon her. But *she* seemed pretty... *determined*."

"Well, the sooner we leave, the better, then," Luka said. "I'll see what repairs I can make tomorrow, but I'll need to call for some help. We might be here for a couple days."

CHAPTER THIRTY-ONE

Our Wildest Dreams

If anything, Cori had more reason to be nervous than Mud, yet she still found herself saying, "Don't be nervous" to him. Though considered an expert on dream magic in her native Rhogot, she acknowledged that syncing someone to her dream came with a few unavoidable risks, though problems were rare. As long as Nebula went with her, Coriander and Mud would both be safe.

If only Nebula didn't feel so...

Absent.

Mud lay next to her on their modest hotel bed. Opening his eyes, he said, "I'm not nervous."

"At all?"

He flicked one ear in what seemed to be a negative response. "Should Mud be nervous?"

So much trust! Either that, or he was putting on a brave front. Cori wondered if he was capable of that, though, since he tended to be more literal and not so prone to lying. His trust comforted her and boosted her confidence. Every time she dreamsynced before, her partners found themselves unable to sleep for the longest time due to excitement or anxiety or both. Complex magic warranted a bit of concern at times.

By necessity, both of them had been awake for almost a full day at this point, so it was entirely possible that Mud *couldn't* care due to exhaustion. The best connection came to exhausted people, perhaps because they lacked the capacity to puzzle out the ramifications of dream magic as they teetered on the edge of consciousness.

Usually, she allotted a couple hours for someone to calm down enough to sleep, but at this rate, Mud would be out in an hour. Maybe even less! That'd give them the benefit of having more time in the dream. "No, you shouldn't be nervous," she answered, reaching over to the nightstand to turn off the light. Opening the reader module on her terminal, she was about to settle down with a good book when Mud snored.

"You've got to be kidding," she mumbled.

After waving a hand in front of his face and poking him several times, Cori came to the conclusion that the troll was, indeed, quite asleep. Defying all logic, his eyes were even moving beneath their lids in the early stages of dreaming.

Were all trolls like this? "Okay, that's just not..." she grumbled to herself, looking up trolls on her terminal. "Sleep habits. Sleep... Dreaming..."

Flicking through several articles, she found that each one unanimously conceded that trolls could sleep on command. They'd be perfect disciples of Nebula if they could use magic. It took Cori aurs to learn how to meditate herself into unconsciousness.

"I wonder..." she said. It felt like an invasion of privacy to study the species while Mud slept next to her, but she'd already gone down the deepcrawler hole. She might as well investigate further.

Apparently, trolls possessed a genetic memory. Or rather, certain aspects of their life's experiences were passed down from parent to child. Troll infants could speak after only a couple hours in the world. They had an innate sense of music and patterning. Short-term memories weren't inherited, but know-how was. While trolls from the same families were individuals, they often shared similar personalities for generations.

Also, their tusks indicated their sex, pointing down for males and up for females. Mud's pointed down.

"Huh," she said.

She also confirmed that most were, indeed, very literal, albeit with extremely complicated, winding thought patterns that made some believe they lacked intelligence. One article even questioned if they could be considered truly sapient.

Feeling guilty, Cori set her terminal on the nightstand and lay down.

Thankfully, she didn't need Mud in his darkest sleep to be able to guide him into lucidity. She could take the most basic flashes of images and pull his subconscious deeper, closer to what she needed him to experience.

Reaching out to Nebula, Coriander guided her mind to blankness, allowing the god to separate her from reality. It was easier now, after so long. She could almost shoulder the nervousness aside now, compartmentalizing it to deal with later. Still, the transition from consciousness into a state just beyond death always made her fur stand on end.

She'd get cold.

Pulling the blanket closer around her, she nestled next to Mud for warmth before surrendering her spirit to the ether.

She expected Mud's path to be simple—blues and shimmering silvers, perhaps, as one would expect to find in the most predictable of creatures. Unprepared, she realized her error too late as a spectrum of colors—some of which were invisible outside the dreamrealm—assaulted her senses and threatened to oust her from her meditation.

How could he possibly have such a rich subconscious? It spoke of an active mind. A quick mind comprised of layers of both creativity and intellect. Perhaps she'd found the wrong path.

She knew she hadn't.

Managing to hold onto the path despite its attempts to throw her from the dream, she pulled herself along, searching for the end of it, where she'd find Mud's aura. Its many strings wrapped around her hands, learning her, welcoming her, investigating her in return. How was she to know that she should have prepared for the complexity of this mind? How could she have anticipated?

Nebula help her.

Even faced with this truth, she pressed on, despite the complications that could arise from this indeterminate dreamwalking. She recalled her failsafe, mentally reciting her wake-up protocol in case things went sideways. Strictly speaking, this magic wasn't necessarily dangerous, but when something went wrong, it went wrong in the most catastrophic of ways.

Losing their quarry was out of the question, though. Nebula wanted Cori to find them. She *had to* find them.

The thread of Mud's path twisted and spiraled in the most unstraightforward of ways. Coriander couldn't recall whether unstraightforward was a word, but it seemed like the only logical way to describe Mud's meandering subconscious. Finally, though, she found his aura, a bright viridian spirit interwoven with millions and millions of other threads. Of course those connections were dull; after all, he wasn't connected to anyone. In all likelihood, he never had been, although, with a path as bright as his, Coriander could only assume.

Preparing herself, she stepped into his dream.

He perched high in a tree made of an amalgamation of welded sprockets. They weren't moving—not normally the case for a dream about something meant to move. This alone banished her preconceived bias of Mud's intellect. It was unlike anything she'd ever seen.

And while Coriander wasn't an expert on dream symbolism, the shimmering gears meant something. Their construction into a complex shape with a million colors she couldn't name only furthered this dilemma. She was going to have to accept the obvious: trolls were complicated.

The tiny sprockets at the ends of the branches gave way to tiny gold foil leaves. And it was on these most delicate of twigs that Mud stood, looking out into the forest far below him. It would have taken him an hour to fall to the canopy were he to lose his balance, but he appeared perfectly content in his precarious position.

"Oh, hello," he said.

Just as she questioned anyone in her dreamwalks, Cori asked, "Do you know why I'm here?"

"Mm-hm," Mud replied. "You said before we went to sleep."

Was he... *aware?* Most sync partners ignored her in favor of the fantasy playing out around them, but Mud seemed focused and ready. "Are you lucid?" she asked.

"Yeah." He poked a sprig of leaves with his toe. The gold shattered into millions of butterflies. "Sleeping is boring. Did you know you're purple?"

Cori looked down at herself, though well aware of her current appearance. She looked like *space,* or more specifically, the representation of Nebula's wings. Translucent and infinite and beautiful, filled with stars, nebulae, and galaxies. "It's my god-mark," she explained. "Everyone who uses magic has one."

"Oh!" Mud exclaimed, excited. "Yes, I've read about them. This one is very pretty."

"And I'll probably appear more in your dreams since I'm syncing with you." She scratched the back of her head. "It's just... one of those things."

"We'll go on adventures," Mud said. "Like this one."

Despite herself, Coriander smiled as the troll nimbly stepped from one branch to another. If she was putting things together properly, Mud's boredom allowed him to develop a direct awareness of his subconscious, plus the ability to manipulate it. He could affect his very dreams, something so few people could do. Amazing, really. "So why are you so high up in your tree?" she asked since they had a bit of time to kill.

"So I could see the forest!" He grinned, pointing downward where huge silver birds exploded from the treetops like whales breaching on the ocean. "I couldn't see everything when I was on the ground, so I grew this tree." As his tail curled around a branch, he looked up and pondered, "Maybe I'm too high now. I'll hit the ceiling."

Cori looked up too, surprised to find an elaborate plaster-carved ceiling close enough to touch. It stretched for kilokips in every direction.

Had it been there before?

And the designs carved into it... How were they so *detailed?* So stable?

It didn't matter. The only thing Cori really cared about was that with someone already so lucid, this dreamwalk would be more of a cakewalk. "Well, I hate to ruin your dream with work," she said. "But can you picture the banshee? Or the faun? You just have to dream them into your dream."

"And you can follow my threads," Mud said, echoing Cori's explanation from earlier. He spun around on the branch, which sagged dangerously but resisted breaking. "My paths to them."

"Yes."

Mud's thick brows lowered over his eyes as he squeezed them shut. After a moment, he blinked, rolled his eyes skyward, and the one-winged banshee slowly drifted through the ceiling and lighted upon a narrow branch.

What a wonderfully imagined construct! With any other partner, the features *might* be decent enough for Coriander to fixate on a thread, but Mud's creation was near-perfect. It was as if Ptery were here in front of them, with every freckle and feather rendered in exquisite detail.

Against her better judgment, Cori reached out to touch the construct. She'd never met a dreamer who could create something she could touch, but there was always a first time.

The edge of the banshee's wing wavered like a bad signal on a visionscreen. Her hand passed through it.

In that moment, Coriander saw her own memory of the banshee underlaid beneath Mud's. In comparison, hers was a smudged wreck of a person, its features almost impressionist in their execution. Black hair. A streak of blue where the wing was. Purple-green splotches where the feet should be.

Ah, there was the *thread*.

It was dim, a scarlet corridor of sorts, which would have led to Ptery's path had they been asleep. But the thread tapered off into a grey tangle, unfollowable. She was about to explain this to Mud when he said, "They're not asleep."

"You can see the thread?" Cori asked.

Mud nodded.

Interesting.

"Let me show you Meadow," he said.

Like Ptery, the faun drifted through the ceiling, landing gracefully on a single leaf. Meadow's bright green thread fastened itself between Mud and the construct. A luminescent corridor flared into being, surging off in the same direction as Ptery's and beyond the grey dead end. This one would lead to a path.

"He's asleep?" Mud asked.

"Yes. Take my hand."

Mud's huge hand closed over hers. After taking another moment to admire the beautiful renderings, Cori took hold of the green thread, and they were whisked away through the multiple universes that made up the dreamrealm.

In an instant, they were elsewhere, in the middle of an endless field.

Mud staggered on his feet, disoriented. Traveling the corridors wasn't for the weak or faint-hearted, but he impressed her once again. He steadied himself against her shoulder, gave a tremble of discomfort, then stood on his own without falling.

"Dizzy," he said.

"You did pretty good," she replied, ruffling the mane of fur sticking up from his head. "Watch out."

The grassy plain shifted like creeping magma into the sterile interior of an office building. The faun dashed past them, throwing file folders around like confetti. A waterfall of papers rained down around them.

Mud reached out a hand as if to call to him, but Cori took his arm and guided it back down to his side. "Not yet."

The scene changed again; they were in a school.

And again. They were in a boat in the middle of a lake.

Cori glanced down at the thread in her hand. Using one finger, she pulled a span downward, creating a loop that she held safely between a thumb and forefinger. Gently, so as not to break the connection, she let the loop slither downward, through the bottom of the boat, through the water, down into the eternity of layered universes.

Meadow's sleep deepened. His dreams lengthened. Now she could break into his subconscious.

She could barely feel Nebula, but her exhaustion wasn't insurmountable. Forcing a shift this time, she pulled the loop of Meadow's thread through her fingers. The lake transformed into the inside of a human house.

She wavered.

Why did this tax her so?

"Are you okay?" Mud asked.

"For now," she answered.

Meadow thundered down a flight of stairs, followed by a large liori manticore. It didn't seem to be chasing him, nor was Meadow overly concerned with his presence.

"Video games?" Meadow asked. The manticore nodded. The television in the living room became a go-kart with a hot dog stand attached to the back.

"Well, that's odd," Mud said.

Coriander shrugged. Dreams often made little sense the closer a dreamer got to the deepest sleep. She'd stopped questioning it long ago. Honestly, a car appearing in someone's living room was tame compared to what came out of the imaginations of some.

Before Meadow could get into the go-kart and speed off, thus prompting a chase she didn't want to deal with, Coriander took him by the shoulder.

"This one's mine," Meadow said, pointing to the couch, which now inexplicably had wheels. "You can drive that one."

He pointed to a winged vase as the manticore squished himself into the coffee table.

"Actually, I just have a question. Do you know who I am?" Coriander watched his face go from mildly annoyed to mildly confused.

Eventually, he said, "You look familiar..."

Though about to explain, Mud interrupted her by asking, "What's that?"

He pointed to the darkest corner of the room, where a shadowy octopus lurked atop a pile of rotting bones. The creature narrowed its eyes, raising its tentacles as if to attack. The fact that it had *a thread* suggested it was really here and not a dream construct.

"Oh, that's just Wheriae," Meadow sighed, describing the watery projection of the god as if it were a mere annoyance and not one of the most powerful beings in the universe. "He's grumpy because I'm not doing what he wants. Ignore him. Say..." He scratched his chin, mismatched eyes narrowing at Mud. "I remember *you*. You were watchin' our little concert that one night."

"Good job, Mud," Coriander said. The front of the house opened like a garage, and the manticore sped off in his table-car. "Meadow, is it?"

Meadow nodded, giving Cori a once-over, searching her from head to toe. His eyes widened as he transitioned to lucidity. "You're a Dreamer," he said.

The dream wavered. Those who rarely experience lucid dreams couldn't keep themselves asleep after realizing the truth. Cori grasped his thread tighter, holding his subconscious in thrall.

Confused, Meadow said, "Benji's going to win the race. He's got a head start."

Why was she so tired already? She was making mistakes.

Cori loosened her grip on the thread, and Meadow shook his head. She asked, "Where are you now?"

"Benji's house," Meadow replied.

A buzzing static embedded itself behind Coriander's eyes. Thankfully, Mud took over.

"You're dreaming right now," he said, smiling in a placid manner despite the fact that the appliances from the kitchen now had wheels and were rocketing out onto the racetrack. "Where are you when you're awake? We're trying to find you. We like your music. Can you tell us where you're going?"

Meadow pulled a map out of his back pocket. When unfolded, it covered the entire floor and became the carpet on which they were standing. "We're here." He pointed to the Grai Power Relay Plain. "Luka says we're heading here." One hoof jabbed at a city called Edge, then Meadow dragged it across the Fade Desert.

"He's very trusting," Mud asided to Cori.

She nodded. "He wants to get back to his dream. He's not entirely sure we're real."

"Can I go?" Meadow asked.

As Cori worked the thread in her hand into another loop, then tied it into a knot, she said, "Sure."

Without waiting to be told twice, Meadow jumped in his kart, speeding off to catch up to the manticore. Benji.

Strange name for a liori.

"What are you doing?" Mud asked, gesturing to the thread. She was working it into another knot. "Making sure he doesn't remember," she said. "He has to finish this dream naturally. Just..." She took a couple deep breaths as her vision started to swim. Somehow, she was running out of time. "Easier for him if he doesn't remember we were here."

"Coriander doesn't look good," Mud observed.

"Coriander doesn't feel good," she answered. Satisfied that the knot would carry Meadow the rest of the way through the dream, Cori dropped his thread. The human house faded around them, and they were left in darkness. Except for the dim purple glow emanating from the stars within her dreamform, there was no light.

She couldn't feel Nebula. Where was Nebula?

Failsafe, she thought. She had to pull them out of the dream, but she couldn't remember...

"Cori?" Mud asked. It was the last thing she heard.

All Red

THE BALLAD OF THE COLONY MISSION DISASTER

(AKA Benji's Seven Minute History Lesson)

A SONG WRITTEN BY BENJI WILD

A hundred aurs ago it's told
They left the atmosphere
For Ammit in the sky so bold
Away t'ward new frontiers

A thousand souls would travel to the stars
From their home so safe they'd venture far

The unknown loomed, but to a man they vowed
To colonize and make their planet proud.

But it was not to be, for it is said:
The first mate screamed: "Across the board, all red!"
Not a volunteer among them cried or fled.
They swore as one to save themselves instead

"All red," said Captain Yan
She calmly parsed her fear
Then raised her eyes and said to all
"We're getting out of here."

As the ship around them died, she radioed base
"All red," she said, "our ship is lost in space."
And in their darkest hour, when they'd all but lost their power
They all prepared for midnight's dark embrace.

But first a message broadcast to the crew:
"T'was an honor, all, your service here is through."
One by one, they left their precious ark
Then into darkest space, they all embarked

Free-floating as they were, they saw their ship
Across its side, an asteroid-addled rip
It listed hard t'ward starboard, then it sheared
It burned up in old Ammit's atmosphere

And rescue came too late for some
In cold and dark and dread
But had they stayed aboard their ship
All thousand would be dead.

All red, all red, their dreams would cry
For decades yet to rise
Yet in defeat, their vic'try writes:
Their marriage to the skies.

CHAPTER THIRTY-TWO

Can't Take the Sky

Benji rested outside, utilizing his keen eyesight to read a book about healing that Ptery picked up for him in Reinoaken.

The magic contained *so many facets!* There were intricate differences between potions, salves, tonics, and balms. Some were more general, others ridiculously specific. Then there were the arcane Cantyrs. Could Ptery perform them? What did they mean when they said the *power words* (as the book called them) relied on faith?

He wanted to ask all his questions in the morning, but his plans were usurped by Luka's. Before the sun rose, an enormous crane truck arrived to tow their mutilated road castle to a service center.

So Benji painstakingly *telis*-scrawled his questions in the margins of the book's pages to refer to later, then took a moment to admire his near-illegible writing. No one else would be able to interpret it, but at least *he* knew what it meant. Maybe in another few spans, his ability to control his *telis* would improve to the point where he could comfortably write research notes again!

He'd rather write with his *hands*. But lacking hands at the moment, *telis* would have to do.

As they arrived at the service center, he stuffed the book into one of his pouches. They were getting full; he wondered if perhaps he could fit another one or two pouches on his legs. Or tail.

He really should use that tail for something other than holding up decorative leather wrappings.

The service center was called GPRP-9 and existed solely for vehicles that broke down on the Relay Plain. Benji had no idea why it was called GPRP-9, as there were no other service centers in any reasonable range for it to be the ninth *of*. Considering the sturdiness of modern cars, multiple service centers would be pointless, and this one barely received business as it was.

After pondering over the question for a bit, Benji decided it wasn't necessarily a mystery that needed solving and left it at that.

It lay at the outskirts of the grey expanse, well out of reach of any exploding towers. Even so, the magic inherent to the area still affected the ground, causing huge rock formations and outcroppings to circle around the building.

But not too close. The proprietor of the establishment kept an earth mage on payroll to ensure it.

Everyone lounged in the service center in various states of sleepiness as the mechanics worked on their bus. Meadow, reclining upside-down in a severely uncomfortable chair, snored louder than a pack of coastal lions.

As Benji wondered if maybe it would be better for everyone if he nudged Meadow awake, Ptery said, "I have an idea." They climbed atop Pixel, who refused to be left outside. "Benji. This environment is the perfect place to see if those wings of yours work."

Benji froze, jaw flexing as he tried to formulate a response. He always supposed he could fly if he wanted to; it was just... he'd never considered that he might ever *want* to. His wings often remained clamped to his side where they couldn't smack into anyone or knock valuable knick-knacks off shelves. "You... You want me to... You mean... *fly?*"

"No, I mean for you to use them as giant fans to blow sailboats about in the harbor. Of *course* I meant flying!" Ptery opened their own wing, spread their arms, and added, "There's enough room in here. Open 'em up, then. Let's take a look."

"Uh..." Benji muttered, trying to find a diplomatic way to decline.

He looked at Luka for help, but she hid a half smile behind her hand and shrugged. "Look, maybe it's not a bad idea. What if saving the world requires flying?"

Ptery snapped their fingers. "An excellent point."

Meadow snored.

Dammit! Benji couldn't help a growl, though he relaxed his wings so they hung more loosely around him. "I like my feet on the ground, thanks. All four of them."

"Oh, come on," Ptery said. Though they hesitated for an obvious moment, they grabbed the edge of a wing and stretched it to its full length. "Look how well-muscled they are! I bet that's because you're pretty newly turned. But if you don't use them, you'll lose that tone faster than you can blink. And then one day, you'll want to fly, and your wings will be all withered and weak. And I shall say, 'I told you so,' and make a big deal of things. You don't want that, do you?"

"You don't want *that,*" Meadow agreed, snorted, and went back to sleep.

"I wouldn't even know where to start!" Benji contended. "It's not like there's anyone here to teach me. You can't just—You can't just take off and go! It's... It's... Ah! Like driving! Someone has to show you how it's done!"

Luka shrugged. "I pretty much learned how to drive on my own. And hey, there's no laws you have to learn when you're flying, are there? No stop signs or signals or anything."

Some instinctive corner of Benji's brain worked against him, quite eager to experience the sky. And... maybe it would be nice to soar among the clouds, to experience their temperature and moisture firsthand, and look down upon the ground without having to gaze through the window of a skycar.

Besides, if ever there were a good time to learn flight, it would be in the presence of a healer.

Benji puffed out his chest, scowled in what he hoped was determination and not terror, and said, "Okay."

"So it's settled!" Ptery clapped and hopped off Pixel's back. "Everyone outside. C'mon. Meadow? Wake up. Let's go."

They all trooped outside, Meadow lagging behind, and distanced themselves from the building and its various mechanical apparatus. A mild wind gusted from Falcon Bluff to the east, so Benji spread his wings. He tried to imagine the wind flowing over and under the shimmery-scaled membranes, achieving equilibrium and generating the lift he'd need to stay airborne.

He checked the point where his wings joined his body and how the most proximal flap extended backward, over his ribs, and ended near his hip. Although manticores weren't particularly aerodynamic, their wings were beautiful examples of natural engineering.

My *wings are beautiful examples of natural engineering,* Benji reminded himself. At times, they still seemed to belong to someone else, but they were his. He could either fold them in for the rest of his life or learn to use them.

To fly.

He shivered.

"Are you gonna vom?" Meadow asked. "'Cuz I gotta warn you, I'm not great with people horkin' chow."

"Uh, no. I'm... Well, I'm not *okay.*" Benji struggled to find the right word to describe his emotional hullabaloo but failed. "I'm not gonna throw up."

"Think they'll hold you up?" Luka asked.

He flapped them. At first, they moved in perfect sync, like they knew what Benji wanted to do. The more he thought about them, however, the less they cooperated, eventually falling out of rhythm so terribly that when one reached its apex, the other brushed against the ground.

The difference in lift versus thrust between one side and the other caused an incidental gust of wind to flip him over and send him tumbling through the grass.

"Not a great start, nestling!" Ptery called.

As Benji lay on his back, staring up at the sky, he realized that for one tick—one *glorious tick*—he'd felt all four paws leave the ground. He righted himself, spreading his wings for the second attempt.

"Wait, wait, wait!" Ptery called, dashing through the field and kicking up a whirlwind of pollen. Meadow sneezed and kept sneezing.

"Honestly, you're a flora mage," Luka said. "How are you allergic to plants?"

"Ask my parents," Meadow said.

Ptery ignored them. "This is why I said we were in the perfect place. Look around you! The rocks! They're all at perfect angles for climbing. Go on up there and get some *height*, Benji! Let that air catch under your wings so you get some free lift!"

That made sense.

It only took a few minutes to find a formation with enough of an incline that Benji could climb it. Perched atop the steep crag, he gazed down at the ground, which stretched far below. His friends, waiting a careful distance away, cheered him on, their voices lost in the wind.

He belonged here.

His heart beat faster—not out of fear, but anticipation. Here he stood, just kips from the clouds, wings extended and angled to catch the breeze as if his body knew what to do. How? How did it *know?* How did *he* know?

Did it matter?

He leapt.

The moment his feet left the rock, he remembered: *It's a long way to the ground.*

His wings did not catch the air. They didn't beat, or flap, or cooperate in any reasonable manner. They didn't carry him to the clouds.

Landing square on his chest, Benji somersaulted forward and came to a stop on his back, which knocked the wind out of him. He gasped for breath, eventually coaxing air into his burning lungs. It tasted as sweet as the most extravagant elvish pastries.

"That was good," Ptery said, standing over him. "Next time, you might consider going upward instead of down."

Benji growled. Ptery stepped back.

Luka caught up and said, "That's probably good for today—"

"No." Benji righted himself, standing on shaky legs. "I think I can do it. I *know* I can. Something feels right. One more time."

And so he found himself climbing the crag again.

Stupid. His chest hurt from where it struck the ground. He still struggled to take a deep breath. But the sky called to him, so he couldn't give up yet.

If I break something, he told himself. *A leg, maybe. If I break a leg, I'll stop.*

What an asinine ultimatum! He should stop *now* before he broke his skull!

Once again, he stood at the peak of the formation, wings extended and eyes closed so he could feel the breeze. Air circulated around him, as much a strange part of his body as his wings and tail. He owned the wind. He controlled the wind.

His front paws lifted off the rock.

Don't think about it. Open your eyes. Watch the horizon.

He let the wind take over. Let his mind drift away so his wings could think for him.

This time he didn't leap. When the wind pushed upward, Benji let go with all four feet and let his wings carry him upward. *He was doing it! He was airborne!*

Oh, gods. He was *airborne.*

He didn't belong in the sky!

His body and mind fought for control, causing him to wobble like a newborn unicorn trying to take its first steps. When his tail tried to act as a natural rudder to keep him stable, he fought it for control. When his wings adjusted for wind speed, their autonomous twitches felt alien to him, as if something else was controlling his body.

A fall from this height could kill him.

"But you're flying," he reminded himself. "You're... flying."

With instinct ensuring he didn't topple from the sky, his fear slowly turned to blind exhilaration. He flapped his wings, which carried him even higher because that was a thing he could do. He opened the great sparkling sails against the wind and stooped into a dive because he could do that, too.

His friends shouted encouragements from below, although with the wind rushing past his ears, he couldn't make out their words. Executing an unsteady turn, he tried to head back toward them but overcompensated for wind speed and looped in a full circle instead.

A muscle spasm in one wing indicated that he ought to land as soon as possible or face some pretty painful consequences. Damn! Well, it *was* only his first flight, so he'd probably have to work on his strength over time.

Right. So. How did a flying manticore land without breaking every bone in his body?

His worry and exhaustion pushed all instinctive expertise from his mind, which made Benji the sole pilot of his own body. On some level, that was a great comfort, but his knowledge of landing came from books, not experience. This high up, the mathematical physics collapsed out of his brain like a block tower kicked over by a whiny toddler.

A mess. Useless.

"Stop flapping!" he told himself. "Uh, okay. More resistance! Increase your drag, and you'll slow down."

He flared his wings again and dropped his tail. Too much drag! Somehow, this action flipped him around and upset his sense of direction, leaving him dizzy. He only regained his bearings as he rocketed right past his friends.

The lack of speed brought him closer to the ground, then gravity and his bulk did the rest. The grass rushed up to meet him as he tucked his wings in to minimize damage. Unfortunately, his remaining velocity caused him to tumble another dozen kips or so before he came to a painful stop in a patch of wild wheat.

He lay on his back, looking up at the fluffy white clouds. As much as he hurt *everywhere,* he couldn't help laughing with glee as he heard the rustle of the others running to meet him.

"Benji? Ben!"

It was Luka. Then Meadow called, "I see him! Over here!"

Oh, his wings ached. His legs felt like jelly. But he'd *flown*. Through the sky! With his own wings! None of the others would ever know the rush of it unless they chose to become liori themselves.

Being a manticore wasn't so bad. Was it?

It had its perks.

He managed to flip over as Ptery reached him, though the aches kept him on his belly. "I have to do it again," he said as he lay there. "I gotta—"

Ptery tsk'd. "Let me check you over first! Your wrist is the size of a cantaloupe. I'm sure it's sprained."

Ah, so that's what hurt. He barely felt it. "I've gotta go again!"

Meadow caught up and winced, wearing a rather telling grimace on his face. "You're not going again! Hold still for a tick and let the nice healer take care of you."

"I just need a rest," Benji said. "Just a quick—"

Ptery reached his wing and gave it a gentle tug, which sent a ripple of pain through Benji's whole body. He snarled, dropping to his elbows and knees as a tired heaviness descended on him.

Maybe he needed more than a quick rest.

"What did you do?" Luka asked.

"Found the problem," Ptery replied. "Nothing major. This joint is dislocated, and he's pretty badly bruised, but nothing is broken. Liori bones must be made of steel."

"Can you show me what an arcane Cantyr does?" Benji asked. If he couldn't fly, he could at least learn a little bit more about healing.

Ptery rolled their eyes. "We'll see. Let's get back to the service center so I can figure out what to do with you."

Ptery did, indeed, show Benji an arcane Cantyr. Rather than a poultice, they recited the words to the spell, cut open their hand, and let it bleed into the ground. Once the wound healed, they pressed their hand against the sore joints.

The damaged muscle and tendon knitted under Benji's skin. It tickled.

Ptery repeated the Cantyr several times but had to stop when they felt light-headed. "It's all I can do," they said. "But I should feel better tomorrow, and I can do a little more."

"This says there's more powerful arcane Cantyrs," Benji said, holding up his healing book.

Ptery chuckled, though not unkindly. "Ah, you're an expert now, I take it."

"Er, no. I just..."

"Healing carries a bit of a danger," Ptery explained. They looked toward the garage, where the mechanics worked on reattaching the road castle's rear doors. "If I'm not ready... Well, I could make Faoliia angry."

Benji paged through the book to the section about the limitations of the healing arts. "How do you know you're ready?"

Ptery shrugged. "I have to be able to properly assess an injury before acting. If I take too much magic, I could face consequences. I feel like it's better to... ah. Let's say *underestimate*. If I have to cast the spell again, I can."

"But..."

"Ah-ah. One day, I'll know. I'm sure."

Benji deferred, tucking the book back into one of his pouches.

CHAPTER THIRTY-THREE

Of Gods and Mice

Mud was out of his element.

He was out of a lot of things. Time, probably. Definitely his mind. And *patience*. He usually had a lot of patience! But this situation called for a bit of urgency, he supposed, so he could let his patience go. For a while.

Coriander lay draped over his shoulder, her feet dragging along the floor behind them. It was an odd floor, which Mud couldn't see or even touch because it didn't exist. Yet as he ventured onward through the inky black, his feet contacted *something* every time he took a step, and he had to give that something a *name*, or he'd go crazy, so he called it the floor.

Likewise, there were no buildings or walls or trees or other people. No cars or cities. No animals or birds or flowers.

Certainly no little metal vendor carts with shimmering imperfections dented into their mirrored surfaces. He really could have used a creme twist about now or a hot caramel-dipped pretzel. Though he couldn't feel the passage of time, his stomach certainly could, and his stomach told him he was very hungry.

Despite the stark lack of reality, Mud would occasionally notice a deep grey *static* of sorts appear in the periphery of his vision. Whenever it appeared, he'd head in the opposite direction. It made him uncomfortable.

Sometimes he'd jostle Coriander a bit to see if he could wake her up, though she never stirred. While Mud knew a lot, he couldn't figure out how anyone could sleep while sleeping, nor how to get the two of them out of this bleak place. No matter how many times he told himself to wake up and return to the real world—as he was well aware he was dreaming—he couldn't do it.

A slack, opalescent thread connected his heart and hers. Its color would shift from blue to yellow to green, then back to blue in a never-ending gradient. He couldn't touch it; every time he tried, his hand passed right through. From what little he knew about the threads, he could surmise that it had something to do with Coriander's magic and the dream.

Home. He wanted to be home.

The floor shifted in texture.

Mud didn't have great feeling in his toes since even the most refined of trolls went barefoot. Consequently, he had quite the collection of healthy calluses on his soles. But the *blankness* and intangibility of the floor developed substance and roughness that eventually turned gravel-like. Soon, it felt as though he were walking on cool, hard-packed dirt. Unable to trust his sense of touch, Mud looked down, only to find that a trail of footprints confirmed his suspicions—everywhere he touched, red soil and bracken spread out around him, transforming the dream into an overgrown path.

Gorse and thistles sprang up around his feet. Trees rocketed into the sky, their fern-like crowns turning the darkness above him into yellow atmosphere. The temperature shifted, becoming hotter. Heavier. Muggier. Feather-tufted clouds partially obscured the blazing yellow sun.

His fur withered in the humidity, becoming damp and heavy. His breathing quickened.

Then the very ground itself erupted with crags and foothills, the red stone surrounding and corralling him. Once locked into a corridor, Mud had no choice but to continue forward—the only direction he could move—as the dream constructed its mysterious reality before him.

"Coriander," he begged, his voice deadened by the thick air. He jostled her again.

She grunted and remained firmly unhelpful.

A roar, thunderous as it was shrill, ripped through the canyon and quickened Mud's feet. Though the path ahead offered nothing but a terrible, uncertain mystery, at least he wouldn't run into the teeth of an angry monster by pressing forward. He hoped.

Its percussive footsteps shifted the ground beneath him, distorting and corrupting the magic which kept the dream stable. As a troll, Mud should have been able to navigate the rough terrain with graceful expertise, but the weight of his companion over his shoulder hampered him. As obstacle after obstacle burst forth from the rock, he lost his balance and sprawled across the canyon floor, nearly dropping Coriander in the process. Rolling, he protected her from the jutting stones.

Drop her! Leave her!

The voice! Terrible, like a fiendcat's tongue over gravel, echoed within his own head. His mind swirled in pain and confusion. Though dizzy, he still managed to achieve his feet, with Coriander cradled in his arms.

You can run faster without her!

The creature roared again as if enraged at his disobedience. Though he had little energy to spare, Mud closed his eyes, trusting his other senses, and pressed onward.

No! Leave the mage behind!

The thought of leaving Coriander alone in the unhinged dream repulsed him. The idea never would have crossed his mind had the disembodied voice not suggested it, and now that the option presented itself, he could only hold her tighter. No. They would get out of this place together, or not at all.

Resting Cori over his shoulder again, he supported her with one arm and wrapped his tail around her waist to keep her secure. Splaying the fingers of his free hand across the dusty ground, he galloped on three limbs, making much better time.

The monster roared again, the rage implicit in its voice. Its footsteps also quickened, but its bulk and the damage it was doing to the dream slowed its progress so much that it couldn't catch up. Pillars of rock toppled and dashed apart every time the creature bellowed, though Mud avoided their crushing weight with deft precision.

He vaulted over a collapsing pillar and discovered the culmination of the entire dream—a single bright doorway radiating in the darkness, emanating hope and *escape*. Though far away, it seemed achievable if he threw all his energy into his awkward lope.

With every step he took, the door receded. His perception of distance meant nothing here.

Even so, threads wove in and out of the light, arriving and departing, ever infinite in their beautiful spectrum. Escape! The way out! It warmed the growing fear within him, banishing it. Gathering himself, he rushed the mysterious portal and hoped it wasn't a trap.

The ground disintegrated and fell away in front of him. He barely managed to arrest his momentum before going over and would have plummeted into the dark abyss if both his fingers and toes hadn't clamped onto the cliff's jagged edge.

Coriander wasn't so lucky, though. As Mud lost his grip on her, she flew forward and into the darkness.

As the beast roared with triumph, Mud expelled a syllable of terror and forced himself to peek over the edge. Cori dangled there, held fast by the thread that extended from Mud's heart to hers. As the ground rumbled, the thread stretched dangerously thin, threatening to snap. If it did, Coriander would vanish into the void below, lost in a darkness so deep and pure that Mud knew he'd never see her alive again.

He raked his fingers desperately across the thread between them, willing it solid. If he could hold it, he could easily pull her up, then they could figure out what to do together. They could reach the glowing door and leave this horror behind.

Every time he grabbed at it, his hand went right through it.

Time ticked away. The thread stretched thinner while the all-consuming blackness dragged Coriander down.

Mud grasped at her thread, trying to pin it between his fingers and the dream-ground to gain some purchase, but it remained intangible. He dug his nails into the dirt until he felt agonizing pain.

"Please," he begged.

Let her fall! The voice intoned. *You must trust me! You must! I am the god!*

That. That was not Nebula.

I will cut the thread for you!

The reverberating footfalls grew closer. Mud knew he had to rescue Coriander and flee before the creature reached them, or neither of them would ever awaken.

"Please!" he said again.

Trolls did not worship the gods. They were aware of them, of course, as one couldn't deny the existence of the deities any more than one could deny the existence of a particularly annoying neighbor. But no troll ever prostrated himself in servitude to the gods nor offered platitudes to appease them. They had no need to since their magic came from within—their luck, their music, the color of their fur... No god could give or take that away.

Worshiping gods was a waste of time when you wanted nothing from them.

Now though, as Mud lay on his belly, persisting in his futile endeavor to grasp the thread, he prayed for the first time in his life. "Nebula," he cried. "Please hear me. Please listen to me."

I hear you, the voice hissed in his mind. *Let her fall!*

Mud whipped his head violently to banish the demon from it. Angry, the monster roared again, nearer now. Minutes away, if that. He closed his eyes and tried again. "Nebula, you've led your servant this far! You can't let her die now!"

The thread brightened.

"Help me save her," Mud pleaded.

No sooner had the words left his mouth than his hand collided with the thread, now a physical object in space. He wrapped his fingers around it and pulled; his hand turned translucent and starry, swirling with an infinite, violet galaxy within. When he reached with his other hand, it underwent the same phenomenon.

He ignored it insofar as aesthetic interest went. It was beautiful, but he cared more about how the change enabled him to pull Coriander to safety—as carefully and slowly as he dared, so the thread wouldn't snap before he could save her. As soon as he could grab her arm, he did and hauled her the rest of the way up.

The jagged stone tore at her dreamform, spilling stars into the ether. The glowing points highlighted a path across the chasm all the way to the door.

The disembodied demon-voice screamed its frustration.

Fear gave him strength, and he lifted Cori easily into his arms. With tentative caution, he slid his foot onto the path. When it contacted the starry surface, it, too, turned purple, and

Mud understood that he had a limited capacity to interact with ineffable aspects of the dreamrealm. It was enough that he could hope to carry himself and Coriander across the chasm to freedom.

When he transferred his full weight onto the path, he found it to be perfectly solid.

The enraged roar drew ever closer.

At first, Mud made his way carefully—one small step at a time, kipping toward the glowing doorway with painful concern. He pre-planned each step, testing the durability of the path before committing himself. But then Coriander began to squirm in half-conscious panic as she muttered his name.

He looked behind him to find the monster of his nightmares. The eater of trolls. The Dym.

It was larger than he expected, towering far above the remaining columns of stone. It had no eyes nor any other logical features, only an amalgamation of clawed legs on a serpentine body. At the front, a gaping saw-toothed mouth continued to roar rage and obscenities Mud had never heard.

Millions of threads connected to it, but some of them flared with such heavenly light that he couldn't help noticing them and counting—as trolls were wont to do. It seemed important. The number felt *significant*. Dire.

Apocalyptic.

It placed half a dozen of its foul many-jointed legs onto the star-path. The path held.

Despite the star-path's meandering route to the door, Mud loped along as quickly as he could. Though he feared falling into the darkness, he feared the Dym even more. To be consumed by such a monster meant to lose your soul.

They wouldn't make it. The Dym was faster.

"Stop," Coriander said. "Put me down."

Mud hesitated, but only for a second. She possessed intrinsic knowledge of this place, more than he could ever hope to understand. He had to trust her.

Despite his terror, he set her down. While she stumbled at first, she soon gained her feet and stretched both arms toward the creature, which now towered above them like a massive, living skyscraper.

It never stopped roaring. Every time its feet crashed onto the star-path, another portion of the canyon fell away behind it until there was nothing left. Yet Coriander never flinched.

"What are you doing?" Mud demanded.

"Put your hand on my shoulder," she said, and he did as she asked. "I need to pull from you—I'm sorry. I'll explain later."

He felt a twinge in his heart and a sort of *jolting* behind his eyes. The purple on his hands crawled up toward his elbows as Coriander curled her fingers toward her palms.

A shimmering violet sphere surrounded the Dym, silencing its roar. When Cori whipped her hands apart, the bubble burst, severing the thread connecting the Dym to the dream.

Cracks appeared in its visage, spreading like spiderwebs to its massive bulk, then down its limbs. Glowing light sprang from each fissure.

How dare you defy your god? The voice screamed. *You were mine!*

It grabbed for the frayed end of its thread but vanished before it could take hold.

Breathless and wordless, Coriander sank to her knees and rested her horns against the path. Mud picked her up and carried her the rest of the way through the shimmering door.

CHAPTER THIRTY-FOUR

Spectre

With some difficulty, Ji'irifarana'ali reached up and turned her spitted beef haunch so it wouldn't burn. Rather than releasing the succulent aroma of cooked meat, though, the blaze emitted the acrid scent of oil, causing Ji'iri's nose to wrinkle. At least her fire kit represented the gnoll ways. Even alone, in the middle of nowhere, she would never use the new magics to start a fire.

Even if this one stunk of machines.

A wound of contrition ran from her elbow to her wrist, inflicted by her own pack as a symbol of her incompetence. She'd never be able to use that arm again and was effectively cast out of the Ghaspir due to the superstitions of her second in command. Perhaps she pushed them too far and too fast, but subtlety wasn't her strongest attribute.

How was she to know that the others would see the banshee's cry as a warning from the True Gods? That they'd take it as a sign to follow the Speaker's instructions to the letter?

And how could she have predicted that they would take the faun's mercy as the True Gods' own mercy? After all, the Speaker said their quarry would be *kind*. And kindness flowed from the True Gods!

Well. As far as Ji'iri was concerned, the Speaker would be the death of the Ghaspir. No hou-hou—outsider—would ever be allowed into their city. If the True Gods took interest in hou-hou, it was only because they were a danger to gnolls. And a danger to gnolls must be eliminated.

Carefully reaching into the fire, she retrieved the hottest brand she could find and pressed it against the gaping slash on her forearm, cauterizing it. Unable to help it, she cried out, her voice ringing through the plains. No one would hear her. Her pack had run home.

They should have regrouped and killed their target. Letting them live would bring ruin to their city. But her pack—like the rest of Ghaspir—trusted the oracles and the Speaker.

Damn.

She allowed herself a moment of sadness. Ostracized from her kind, she would have to find home and hearth elsewhere. Not with hou-hou. Alone.

Gnolls lived in clans. It was their way. How could she possibly endure?

The ground shook. At first, she believed it to be a simple earthquake—quite common on the Relay Plain and its surrounding fields. But the shaking increased in intensity until she rose to her feet to stabilize herself, planting both hands on the ground.

Something dark erupted from the fire, sending the wood and her dinner flying.

The tremor ceased, leaving an odd, huge, bud-like structure in the middle of the campfire stones. Unlike normal plants, this bud wasn't green or red or blue but a deep onyx so pure that it sucked light out of the air and destroyed it.

Magic emanated from it. At first, this caused her hackles to rise, and she bared her teeth. Then, she felt the touch of the True Gods.

A sign! A sign of her *faith!*

Ji'iri approached the bud, reaching out to it, basking in the sheer power it exuded. Although cautious, she placed her uninjured hand on it, shivering as a rush of peace and hope invaded all her senses.

"Please. Speak to me. I serve you."

It didn't speak, but it *communicated*. She saw perhaps a dozen shadows... No. *More!* Surrounding the blessed True Gods, holding them captive, as they had been for millennia. Their pain reached her, but also their promise and will. Never before had Ji'iri experienced such elation, but how could she have? The True Gods were supposed to be *dead*, destroyed by the elves who called themselves *liberators*. But her people knew the truth.

Ji'iri believed the old poems, even if the Ghaspir strayed from their teachings.

Their grace. Their power...

The vision waned, but she did not feel abandoned. Instead, she felt renewed. Whole.

The flower blossomed, its black petals spreading out like falling trees. They turned to ash and withered to the ground, leaving a macabre pedestal behind. Black ichor dripped from the edges, oozing to the ground where it congealed into jelly-like masses.

In the center of the pedestal lay a cube etched with the letters of a language she'd never seen. The thing hummed with the power and will of the True Gods, and sparks slithered along its sharp frame.

Ji'iri couldn't help a moment of hesitance. The True Gods were the shining beacons of her people. Golden and green, red and white. Yet she felt their eternal song coursing from this death-plant like the hymn of a zealous choir.

When her people wrote about the Gods, they did not refer to *darkness*.

"Ah! But I've passed the test," she said. "You are shrouded in darkness because you are captive. I won't doubt you again."

She did not know how the cube worked or what it could do. But she knew she must deliver it to her prey so the True Gods could work through it and possibly even work through *her*. The fur along her spine stood on end as she shivered, pleased to finally be recognized for her devotion.

With a trembling hand, Ji'iri reached for the strange device. She almost expected a revelation as to its inner workings but felt nothing except the gentle approval of the gods.

It was enough.

Cradling it in her elbow, she knelt before the pedestal, uttering the prayer of obedience. She would do as asked. She would do it with haste. She would do it without thought to her own glory.

"And I swear," she said, lip curling into a snarl, "I will not fail you."

The pedestal crumbled to ash.

CHAPTER THIRTY-FIVE

Attitude City

The clouds rolled in, and with them came a chilling cold. Luka let Meadow drive the now-repaired road castle so she could rest in back with Benji. She told everyone it was an excuse to make sure he wasn't in pain after his flight, but they all knew the truth—she just wanted to spend time with him. And also get her tired eyes off the road for a bit.

So she relaxed against Benji's side, his wing draped across her lap like a blanket. The warmth and the rhythm of the road made her sleepy; as she began to doze, she shook herself conscious, as she did not want to let Meadow drive completely unsupervised.

They'd end up in the ocean. Or the *sky*.

Notably, the Kirin-Class Road Castle had no flight capabilities, but if anyone could figure out a way to mess up that grievously, it'd be Meadow.

In order to distract herself, Luka reached for Benji's crest, flipping it over to admire the old elvish script engraved on the back. Although tiny, she could make out some of the flourishes and symbols, which shimmered and sparkled like water.

Hard to believe the beautiful, infinitesimal instructions spelled out a set of coordinates. What would they find there, in the middle of the desert?

The Godplain?

Their inevitable demise?

Nothing?

She couldn't decide which option was worst.

The window into the cab opened. Luka braced herself for the news that they'd fallen off the planet.

"Uh," Meadow said. "Hey, Ptery and I were listening to the radio, and it cut to a severe weather warning. They're saying there's gonna be a moonstorm."

Luka swore. "What kind?"

"Lightning. But we can keep going, right? Pixel—"

She swore again. "No, the charge in her mage shielding won't last through a whole moonstorm. She's got an hour at most."

Ptery peered through the window. "So what do we do?"

Damned moonstorms and their unpredictability. Unique to a very specific stretch of Kyrnis, they formed when cool, wet air from the Rona Ocean collided with the hot, magically-charged atmosphere pushing south from the Fade Desert. Storm residuals sometimes made it as far south as Faun-ir.

Although the lightning variety wasn't the *worst,* driving through one in an ungrounded vehicle could be risky. If only it were snow, then they could have glided right over it with barely a hiccup.

At least the warning explained the clouds and the cold.

"We can stay in Edge," Benji said, tapping a claw against his terminal screen. "It's close, and it's huge. And since it's right in the heart of moonstorm territory, I bet it has depots for buses and trucks and stuff."

Luka sighed. They might have made it halfway through the Fade Desert if it weren't for the storm. It was all for the best, though, since she preferred to stop in the early evening so everyone could rest and eat and so she could attend to her own needs.

"You think we could play a set?" Ptery asked.

"In a moonstorm? Everyone'll be staying home. I mean, we could try." Luka tapped her chin. Summoning people to a get-together in a moonstorm might benefit them less than taking the night off. If someone got struck by lightning...

"Let's... skip playing Edge," Benji said. "I'm not ready yet. By the time we get to Border... I promise I can do it."

"Uuugh," Meadow groaned. "That's what you said in Reinoaken. You gotta jump in with both feet! Or all four, in your case. All... seven limbs?" He turned around to look through the window, and the road castle briefly veered off course.

Ptery backhanded his shoulder.

"Let's just concentrate on safety tonight, okay?" Benji said, his voice hardly above a murmur. "We don't want anyone to get hurt."

"Fine, fine." Meadow waved a dismissive hand. "Give me directions, Princey."

The paved road became quaint cobblestone as they neared Edge, though modernization still encroached on the lazy, idyllic setting. The spaces between the paver stones were filled with custom-cut, shimmering black tiles, which, after some deliberation, Luka identified as tiny solar panels.

With some research, she discovered Edge separated itself from the power grid decaurs ago and ran entirely on the sun's energy. The solar batteries were housed in block-sheds outside the city, and power lines ran underground.

Tourism necessitated the deception. Visitors expected a laid-back town where they could relax on the edge of the desert with their families. Introducing a high-tech environment carried risks, so the powers that be chose the best of both worlds. Guests could still experience a rustic setting from hundreds of aurs ago while still having all the conveniences of home.

Within the confines of an enormous, flourishing city.

Benji shivered as they crossed into the city. Luka arched her eyebrows, but he only shrugged and said, "Just a weird feeling. I think."

"Whoa. Hey, guys, look." Meadow tapped on the windscreen. "You can see Phoenix Temple already."

It rose above the streets like immense flames, each section of the tower sparkling in a different shade of red, orange, or yellow. Although Luka didn't enjoy tourism like the others, she couldn't wait to see the crystal facets up close.

Fog already cloaked its highest spires, though, as clouds continued to encroach. Lightning flashed above, arching across Edge's many intricate lightning rods. They'd have to find a place to stay as soon as possible.

With surprising skill, Meadow maneuvered the road castle through the narrow residential streets, reducing the speed to little faster than a crawl. As rain started to splatter against the windows, the tension within the bus increased to the point where not even Ptery spoke.

When an enforcement car pulled in front of them and turned its lights on, everyone let out a synchronized groan of frustration.

The car's door opened, and a yellow blur leapt from it and into the sky, vanishing before Luka could get a decent look. Then something thumped against the roof of the bus, its feet tap-tap-tapping across the steel surface.

Ptery muttered, "Hm, interesting," opened their door, and slipped outside.

"Where'd they go?" Meadow snapped, voice rising in panic. "What's on the roof? Is it the gnolls? Are the *gnolls back?*"

"Have you ever seen a yellow gnoll?" Luka asked.

"Not *yet.*"

No sooner had Meadow punctuated his tiny sentence than a grinning, upside-down feathered face appeared in the driver's side window. Meadow squealed and nearly leapt across the center console as the sudden harpy tapped gently on the glass.

Meadow, breathing heavily, shook his head.

Rain fell in large splashes against the windscreen.

"Come on, then," the harpy said, her voice muffled through the barrier. "I'm with Edge's Enforcement department. And you're in need of a bit of chastisement. No big deal. Not even a citation. Feathers to gods."

Even reassured, Meadow still refused to get any closer to the door and maneuvered his tail into position to press the button. The window stuttered downward as the harpy rolled her glowing amber eyes.

"There we go." The officer turned her neck at an almost one-hundred-eighty-degree angle so she could look at them upright. "Our Frox Biofilter detected a liori in your bus, and by-freesin, it was right. Look! A liori, right there in your cabin. Oh, you're a lucky manticore, you are! The biofilter kills liori from the H'grit den, but you're still alive, aren't you?"

Benji blinked. "Kills? That must have been what I felt when—"

"Yes. We have an agreement. They don't come into the city to cannibalize the residents, and any residents silly enough to wander into the desert are free game. *Even so.*" She flipped around, crawling down the side of the bus until she stood on the ground. "No liori allowed. Just in case. You'll have to leave."

"But... The moonstorm," Meadow protested.

The harpy shrugged, her wings shaking off the rain. "It's quite literally not my problem."

Luka slid open the back window, intent on arguing with a bit more sense than Meadow or Benji, when Ptery wandered around from behind the bus. Luka covered her ears, expecting a scream.

But instead, Ptery spoke softly, and the harpy froze, the grin falling from her face. "What did you say?"

Luka uncovered her ears.

Ptery said, "Who are you running from?"

The black scales speckling the officer's face and arms—the godmark of the fire gods, Kaneer and Shastaa—glowed red. Minute flames danced across her talons. *"How did you know?"*

"Don't do anything stupid, nestling." Ptery indicated a handful of onlookers with a wide sweep of their hand. The cluster of humans and fauns were far enough away that they probably couldn't hear the conversation but were certainly near enough to witness an Enforcement Officer setting someone on fire. "No torching us alive. We've got witnesses. I'm not going to tell anyone, but you're going to hear us out."

"Bribery!" the officer spat.

"You're threatening to send us to our deaths. Essentially. Maybe." Ptery nodded up at the clouds. "At least listen to me. If you want to take us to jail after... Well, I guess we'll at least be out of the storm."

The harpy chittered, a deep squall building in her throat. But she said, "Fine."

"That faun"–Ptery pointed through the window—"is on a mission *straight* from Petalvine herself. His name's Meadow. You can check with the flora temple in Faun-ir if you want."

"I will! And the manticore?"

"He's along because the gods want him to be. So am I. So's the human."

The harpy twitched, grimacing. No one ever wanted to contradict the gods, but how many times must an officer hear "I'm on a mission from the gods" as an excuse? After several long ticks, she leapt back onto the road castle, wing claws gripping the door frame as she pushed her neck through the open window. Her rear talons squealed against the paint as she held on.

She gave Meadow a once-over, then tilted her head to look through the window into the back.

After mostly ignoring Luka, the harpy focused on Benji. Specifically on the crest, which still sat atop his mane. "Ah, you're the one from Faun-ir. The *vadthi*. Benji Wild."

"Yes, ma'am?" Benji squeaked.

The officer uttered a low *bah-whoop*, which suggested defeat. "I can't let you *stay,*" she said. "The people will see—"

"The battery sheds," Ptery suggested. "They're plenty big enough for our bus to fit, aren't they? And you can lock them from the outside. Just make sure to let us out in the morning, and I *promise* we'll be on our way. We don't want to be here anymore than you want us here."

The officer clicked and whistled. "Yes. Okay. And I will call Faun-ir. If they don't know who you are, I'll—"

"They *will,*" Ptery said. "Ask for, er..."

"Stonebuck," Meadow said.

The officer bobbed her head in a nod. "Fine. All right. Then follow my car, and keep the liori out of sight!"

CHAPTER THIRTY-SIX

Rain Must Fall

Each linear row of energy towers in the battery shed had huge gaps on either side, with thick, glowing gold conduits feeding from each bay into the ground. Sometimes a conduit would pulse or fade, depending on the energy needs of any particular sector. Some barely glowed at all—perhaps attached to new construction or even vacant buildings.

Fascinating. Benji wandered up and down the rows for a long time, hypothesizing how the batteries might store solar power, then how they might feed electricity in equal portions to the whole city. He could easily look the answers up on his terminal, but he found it far more entertaining to try to figure things out for himself before verifying his thoughts.

His musings about the workings of Edge also helped him *not* think about how he could have died without warning. What if the biofilter killed *all* liori, and not just those from a certain den? How did it know one liori from another?

The concept of functional immortality seemed less daunting now that he'd almost died.

"Hey, Benji!" Meadow called. "Come help us set up a tent. Luka won't let us run the heat in the bus, so I'm gonna start a fire. It's cold."

Benji set his wonderings aside. "Is that wise? Uh... In here? In the... you know. *Closed building?*"

"I got another couple fire marbles." Meadow held up the tiny spheres, which glinted in the golden light. "No smoke."

Right. No smoke, but what If something caught fire?

Benji kneaded his claws into the cement floor. So... Not a *high* chance of an out-of-control blaze. But no one fully understood the extent of Meadow's unique chaotic talents, not even Benji, who'd only been his friend since childhood.

At least Meadow had picked the most open space he could find to park the road castle and set up camp.

As Benji and Luka helped set up the tent, Ptery sat on the rear bumper of the bus, moping. They'd been quiet since the confrontation with the harpy officer but wouldn't say why. So as the tent came together enough to stand on its own, Benji wandered toward Ptery, confident that the others could finish making camp without him.

"What happened?" Benji asked. He sat, curling his tail around his feet. Since his wings still hurt from his test flight, he let them relax, billowing across the floor.

"Isn't it obvious? I got us a place to stay. Not a *good* place, mind." Ptery looked around at the stark accommodations as hail pinged against the shed's metal roof. "Loud. Cold. *None* of us will get any sleep. But it's better than being in a gliding electrocution chamber."

"You said something to that officer," Benji pressed, "that made her change her mind."

Ptery closed their eyes, chuckling without humor as they pinched the bridge of their nose. Shaking their head, they pulled one leg up, wrapping an arm around one knee. "Ah, well. I committed a terrible offense. Hm." They shrugged, tilting their head briefly in a self-executed concession. "Not *terrible*. It certainly wasn't *nice*, though."

Benji sat. "I don't mean to be, ah, rude. But..."

"I am not exactly the nicest person, am I? Perhaps I'm growing a conscience in my old age. Perhaps I care more since I realized..."

"Realized?"

"Yes!" Ptery threw up their hands. "I realized that it's possible for me to be *wrong*, love. I've never considered it before. *Clearly*, I am a pinnacle of all things good and right in the world, and nothing I've said has ever been..."

Benji rolled his eyes.

"Ah, you're not buying it."

"No."

Ptery sighed. Dramatically. More dramatically than necessary. "Well, if you must know, then I need to tell you about harpies first."

Benji waved a paw. "Ah, we... covered harpies in a competition a few aurs back. Really interesting! I don't think I'd find it very... Comfortable? It wouldn't be very comfortable to be the only male in a whole nest, though."

"Aerie," Ptery said. "You know, a lot of people think harpies can only be hens, but that's silly, isn't it? At least you understand that. Truth is, on average, only one in forty chicks that hatch are male. And in some bloodlines, it's one in a *hundred*. The hens call them princes because they're little treasures and bottle them up in *beautiful* cages where they live out their lives like pampered pets. Some of them inevitably run away to live as hens, but they're so *precious* that there's always a bounty for their return."

"Aaah, I see." Benji nodded. "And the officer was..."

"I didn't see any other option. I was afraid."

"How'd you know?"

"Well, it's the same as with banshees, I suppose. There's no outside *difference* between hens and princes. So the question is, how do they tell each other apart? You know, for when it comes time for making little ones." Ptery shrugged. "Not that it matters much in our society. I'm sure it's a remnant left over from evolution. Personally, I find it terribly strange, but since banshees come from harpy stock..."

Benji said, "You're talking about pheromones."

"Now she'll spend months looking over her shoulder, wondering if I contacted a local aerie to turn her in. But I wouldn't. Gods, I wouldn't. How could I ever send someone back to that? If she'd called my bluff, we'd all be burnt to a crisp."

"She could have done that anyway."

"I guess." Ptery, elbows now resting on both knees, ran their talons through their hair. "Thanks for, you know. Listening."

Unsure of what else he could possibly say, Benji nodded toward the fire. "I can't feel it, but... Meadow and Luka tell me it's really cold in here, so—well, you could—If you want, come over and sit by the fire? Luka has popcorn and marshmallows."

Ptery smiled. "I like you, Benji."

Confused by the non sequitur of the admission, Benji couldn't form a single word between his brain and his mouth. While trying to think of something nice to say in return, he stared at Ptery like an idiot.

Ptery waved a hand. "You go. I need to think for a while."

Benji nodded. "You know, you... might have saved our lives."

"I know. But we also might have been fine."

Leaving Ptery to their brooding, Benji ambled off toward the camp, checking once over his shoulder to see whether or not Ptery was following.

They weren't.

Wind slammed against the shed door, causing it to shudder in its track. It held, though any more gusts like that might break it wide open, despite the officer locking it. Meanwhile, the torrent of rain was so heavy it came down in a solid sheet, making the row of skylights on the corrugated roof look more like silvery waterfalls than glass.

The endless flashes of lightning created a headache-inducing strobe effect in the darkness beyond the reach of the firelight.

"This is my first moonstorm," Benji said, reclining near the fire. Luka rose to her knees, wrapped her blanket around her shoulders, and scooted over to lay against him. He wrapped his wing around her, gently purring in the warmth from the fire.

Meadow followed, huddling against his other side. Benji wrapped a wing around him, too, and slowly, Meadow's violent shivering tapered off into a contented sigh.

Benji checked the back of the bus again, but Ptery still sat there, alone.

"Maybe tomorrow we can check your tail for..." Luka yawned, voice raspy with exhaustion. "...quills we can pull out before we leave."

Distracted, Benji didn't answer.

"Don't worry about Ptery," Luka said as Meadow started to snore. "They're probably pouting 'cuz we weren't put in a five-star hotel."

"Be nice," Benji replied.

"When I'm more awake. Promise."

She lapsed into silence. Soon, her breathing turned rhythmic and slow.

And Ptery still didn't come to the fire. Their talons scraped against the metal bumper as they shivered, their foggy breath rising into the cold air.

Though grateful for Ptery's intervention, Benji tried to imagine the terror the harpy must have felt. She wouldn't have been able to go to any of her fellow officers, as revealing her secret to the wrong person may have potentially caused life-changing consequences. Did she have friends? Family? Would she be forced to leave Edge out of fear that Ptery wouldn't hold up their end of the bargain?

Should he have cared? The officer seemed almost disappointed that the biofilter didn't kill him.

His thoughts turned more surreal and detached in the earliest stages of hypnagogia. He always liked that word. It had a good feel to it. *Hypnagogia.* Early sleep hallucinations. Not dreams. Vivid, colorful, safe. Benji broke apart the syllables as little yellow harpy-shaped birds fluttered in and out of the edge of his mind's eye.

They could fly. So could he.

He could fight a gnoll.

He could move things with his mind.

Better. This was *better.*

Despite the thunder and the cracking of the hail against the shed, Benji drifted off. Almost immediately, the little yellow harpy-birds started calling his name.

"Ben?"

His ears flicked, and he ignored them.

"Benji!"

The insistent voice cut through Benji's slumber, even though the thunder couldn't. Reluctantly, he opened his eyes, raising his head from his paws.

Ptery stood a kip away and looked to be on the verge of tears, shivering even with a heavy blanket wrapped around them. They rocked back and forth, feet treading in place as if trying to get tiny snippets of relief away from the cold floor.

Another crack of thunder shook the shed.

"I want to stop being afraid," Ptery said. They knelt down in front of Benji, holding out their clasped hand. "I *need* to stop being afraid. Or I'll freeze to death."

"I won't hurt you," Benji said.

"I know. I know. But I need you to help me do something." Opening their hand, they revealed their garnet necklace.

Their memory. The one taken from them after their injury.

"I need to know what happened," Ptery went on, placing the garnet on the floor between them. "Something feels wrong, and I need to fix it. But this won't break open unless someone is there to witness the memory. I'm told it's a safeguard... In case it's more than I can handle and someone needs to return me to the healers."

Honored, though a bit unsettled by the prospect, Benji found himself saying, "Why me? Why not Meadow? I mean, of course I will, but things—well, things have been, uh. Rocky..."

"Because Meadow isn't you. It has to be you."

Benji's analytical nature demanded answers besides "*because*," but the question died before he could ask it. Some things didn't need to make sense. Some things, you *felt*. "Okay," he said. "What do I do?"

"It's not difficult. The magic binding the memory to the stone responds to will. Of course, I never thought I'd want to break it, so I'm not completely versed on the *details*..." Ptery's hand hovered a centikip from Benji's cheek. "But it requires contact."

"Okay. All right."

Ptery didn't move. Cold radiated from their hand.

"Ptery?"

"This is awfully close to where the teeth are," they said but finally rested their hand on Benji's cheek.

"Now what?"

"Look me in the eye. Yes, like that. And now, I believe we will the stone to break. Together, now..."

"Wait."

Ptery's deep scarlet eyes narrowed in confusion. "Are you backing out? Must I do this with Meadow?"

"No. What do you want me to do if you can't handle it?"

Ptery considered, then said, "I'm ready. I know I am. But if something... Goes wrong, don't take me to my father."

Not particularly reassured, Benji nevertheless pictured the garnet breaking.

And then, he was someone else.

CHAPTER THIRTY-SEVEN

Once and Never More

Ptery high-stepped through the streets with all the confidence of a fool.

If they, a child, appeared as if they *meant* to be wandering Qalisti at night, well, no one would question what they were doing. Right? And then no one would even *think* to spirit them back to their frustrated father.

They may have underestimated the indifference of strangers. However, all that mattered was that no one bothered them, and no one would dare harm the starry-eyed scion of a District Councilate.

A District Councilate whose voice echoed in Ptery's ears: *Should you find yourself lost in Qalisti, follow the lights to the market. Someone there will help you.*

Ptery wasn't lost, but they *did* need help—of a sort—and the market seemed the best place to find it.

Luminous orb-lights lined the streets, guiding the young banshee's way. Glowing faintly green under the stars, they brightened the shop stalls and art installations of the city's denizens, all of whom relied on Ptery's father, Evialor, for guidance. They loved him, and in turn, he provided liaison services between them and some of the other, more distant species of Erit.

Like the liori.

For many aurs, Ptery *begged* their father to take them to see the beasts, but Evialor insisted that liori were dangerous and were no proper guests for a *child*. Well! With no one to watch Ptery at home, they had to travel *together* to the desert, and Ptery intended to seize this opportunity with all their talons. They'd meet a liori and prove that even the beasts of the desert could be perfectly civil.

"I know I'm right," Ptery muttered, pausing at one of the booths to check out some of the handmade candy lions. A shame they hadn't thought to bring a minir chip with them. Their father would never approve of such a purchase, though, so it was all for the best.

The harpy behind the counter watched them with a shrewd eye, then shooed them onward when Ptery loitered for too long.

The narrow street soon widened, terminating in a bizarre open bazaar that shone with the light of day.

Although dust hung in the air, kicked up from the packed red-earth street, Ptery had never witnessed anything so beautiful. Enormous steel and glass buildings surrounded the market, rising so high into the sky that the tops seemed to disappear into the clouds. Ad boards and handmade decor sparkled from every available wall while magelamps floated high above, casting down heat and a golden, sunny glow.

And the *people!*

Humans and fauns. Harpies and banshees. Fae, satyrs, duarrow, and trolls. A lone orc in their heat-armor. Some species Ptery couldn't even name. They all browsed the countless stalls and stands, searching through an impossible variety of groceries and gifts. Consumables and keepsakes. Necessities and indulgences.

Forgetting for a moment the reason they came, Ptery stared in awe at the infinite wonder.

Then they saw the manticore.

He wandered the stalls like the others, deadly tail held proudly over his head as if it couldn't harm a soul. Some people gave him a wide berth, while others shuffled around him without offering a second glance.

Ptery's wings fluttered, feathers puffing like rising dough.

Dodging around the crowd, they kept the manticore in sight as much as they could until they emerged from between two stalls and stood face-to-face with the beast.

He towered over Ptery, pale green eyes staring downward as tawny, brown-speckled ears swiveled forward. "Did you need something?" he asked.

Ptery, frozen in awe and a healthy dose of fear, shook their head.

Perhaps that would have been the end of the encounter. It seemed like it should have been. After all, Ptery had no words to offer, and the manticore was clearly busy with his shopping. But the beast searched the crowd as if looking for something very specific, then looked back down at Ptery.

And waited.

It took a few ticks, but Ptery found their voice. "I wanted to meet you! Well, not *you* specifically, but I've never seen a liori before, and my father brought me here on business, so I thought..."

"Then you should come with me," the manticore said. "I'll take you to the den."

At twenty-two aurs old, Ptery was at the apex of their childhood, falling toward the wild mystery of the adult world. However, being the sheltered child of a dignitary carried its drawbacks, namely that they'd never learned not to trust strangers. Strangers, after all, loved Evialor and could never possibly do anything to harm the Councilate's family. To ensure their position, Ptery clarified, "My name is Pterylae. I'm Evialor's scion. Most people call me Ptery because it's easier to say. That's what I've been told."

"Then I'll call you Ptery," the manticore said.

How strange that he didn't offer his name.

Ptery asked, "Who are you? You should tell me your name, you know."

The manticore, already in the process of turning away, dipped one wing and looked over his shoulder. "Me? Oh, I never picked a name. I used to be Orvin. I guess I still am. Come with me. Come on, hurry up."

A tiny voice in Ptery's head spoke up, warning them of the danger. They shouldn't go. They'd already met a manticore, and that should have been enough. But the opportunity to meet more, to ask them about themselves, and to maybe even learn how they did that *thing* with those swirly lights...

They dug their talons into the packed earth. If they said no, they may never get another chance! When their father heard about this little excursion, he'd lock Ptery in their hotel room *forever.*

Well, that left only one clear option.

Orvin led them through the market and onto one of the surrounding, narrower streets. Although darker here, Ptery wasn't afraid, as no one would mess with them when in the company of such an imposing friend. "Do you come to the market often?" they asked.

Orvin nodded and increased his pace. Ptery hurried to keep up.

"What were you looking for there?" Ptery persisted. "Don't liori have what they need in their dens?"

Orvin didn't answer the question. Instead, he replied, "We need to get this over with."

The red earth gave way to the grey sands of the Pilicoarse desert, and finally, Ptery stopped, confused by the manticore's reticence. "Get *what* over with? I thought you were taking me to meet your family?"

"Of course, yes, but..." Orvin gestured with a huge paw. "But they're waiting for me, just at the edge of the city. Come with me. Hurry."

But Ptery was not stupid. Naive, perhaps, but much smarter than a newborn chick. "Actually, we're pretty far from the city now... My father will be missing me. I should—"

They found themself surrounded by a number of strange, glowing red wisps, which matched the color of Orvin's wings and tail. With some difficulty, as if he hadn't been using this power for very long, he dragged Ptery onward and into the desert. By this time, Ptery recognized the danger and screamed as loud as they could, but they were young, and they'd never seen the use in developing their deadly scream.

After all, who would harm the scion of a Councilate?

"Let me go! What are you—" Ptery struggled against the wiggling wisps, but every time they dodged around one, another appeared to take its place. "What are you *doing?* My father will—"

The wisps jerked, and Ptery fell to the ground, acquiring a bitter mouthful of sand.

"Sorry. Don't struggle. Please," Orvin said. "Please. You don't understand."

Ptery very much *didn't* understand, which was why they struggled! "If you'd let me go, I... Listen, if you go on your way and let me go home, I won't even tell my father what you did!"

Orvin raised a paw, gesturing toward himself and tugging Ptery behind a rocky formation. The city disappeared from their view. "Listen. Listen carefully. I need to take you away. Your father isn't a good person—"

Taking advantage of their closeness, Ptery flipped onto their back and clawed at Orvin's chest with the sharp talons on their feet. The wisps vanished, and while Ptery struggled to gain a foothold on the loose sand, they were still able to find purchase and flee.

Filled with the denial of youth and assured that nothing terrible could possibly happen to them, Ptery knew they were free, that they'd escaped some terrible fate that they could tell their friends about later. The city lights rose before them, growing closer and closer in their vision.

Something sword-sharp pierced their wing.

As they cried out, a great weight pushed them face-first into the sand. "I wanted to help you. I swear. Remember that. But he's *here* now. He's watching. He—" Orvin paused, then tore.

A warmth spread across Ptery's back, accompanied by the sound of bones splitting and breaking. Of muscles rending from flesh. Feathers snapping under the stress. The pain seemed distant and unreachable, though, as if this terrible nightmare plagued someone else.

Not them. Never them.

"He told me he could heal me," Orvin said, his voice tugging at the blackness at the edges of Ptery's consciousness. "I'm not supposed to be a manticore. He said if I taught you a lesson..."

"No, please. I need..."

What did they need? Their mind swam with confusion as the sand turned red around them. They tilted their chin upward because their father would be angry if they returned all bloody.

And there they saw the impassive face of Evialor, watching from between two abandoned, crumbling buildings.

Detached.

Ptery lost consciousness.

The vision ended.

Ptery woke, warm within the comforting blanket of Benji's mane. Neither of them spoke as the memory faded around them.

Ptery understood now, even though they didn't back then. Not entirely, anyway. Their father hadn't taken the memory from them to relieve trauma. He took the memory because he'd been seen.

Little bits of conversation returned to them as they sat in the dark, cold barn, the rain pattering against the metal roof far above. The healers couldn't just take the *end* of the ordeal because the curiosity would drive Ptery to break the garnet too soon. It had to be the whole thing.

"I was so angry," they said after many minutes. "I refused to see my father. But he had money and influence, and the healers did what he wanted them to do. And I guess I filled in the gaps in my memory with..."

"Fear," Benji said.

"Yes. I suppose."

Sometimes, on the darkest, most lonely nights, their wing still hurt. It hurt now. Or, rather, the memory of it caused a terrible wringing ache they couldn't banish. Their torn muscles spasmed, twitching beneath terminally ingrown feathers, which would never lay properly against their scarred skin.

"He was like me," Benji said. "Q'ler used the word *vadthi*. A liori turned against their will."

"I think so, yes."

"What he did was wrong, but..."

Ptery nodded. The face of terror, a liori face that had invaded their nightmares for half their life, turned into a scared, mewling little cub. A cub too frightened to refuse Evialor's demands and too hopeful over the promise of a cure. "I think... maybe he wanted to take me away. To help me."

Benji said nothing.

"You know, I left home at thirty-two aurs. There were times I wanted to leave earlier, but my father said... He said I couldn't make it without him. That my life was so tied to his that I'd soon return without a minir chip to my name. I believed him. He told me..."

Ptery trailed off, remembering the shouting match in the hospital as frantic nurses tried to bandage what was left of their wing. It was the moment Ptery vowed to become a healer. To help others.

"He told me healing was an unworthy profession. That I could never excel at it because, on some level, I would always recognize my *place*. My stature in the community. My own self-importance. I think he hoped his doubts would come true."

"He isn't a good person."

"Yes, I know that now," Ptery replied. "I've really known that for a long time. I wonder how my life might have been different if I let Orvin help me."

"You were a chick. You didn't know." Benji tentatively placed a paw on Ptery's shoulder.

It was warm and comforting, and they felt none of the repulsion they expected. An echo of old fear still remained, but it barely mattered anymore. "I'm sure my father had that young manticore killed."

"Could he do that?" Benji asked, incredulous. "I... I feel like... It would..."

"He could do whatever he wanted. He still does." Ptery gathered the broken shards of the garnet. Rocking their hand back and forth, they watched the light play off the rough edges and the shattered facets.

For twenty aurs, they'd been mad at the wrong *thing*. For twenty aurs, they let fear dictate their biases because what else could they possibly do? Ptery could see the claw marks on the remaining stump of their wing, but they couldn't see their father's hand behind it all.

Anyone would have believed the same.

"Thank you, Benji. For your patience. For... Being here with me tonight." Although Ptery smiled, it wouldn't be long before the tears spilled down their cheeks.

They buried their face in Benji's mane and cried until they fell asleep.

CHAPTER THIRTY-EIGHT

Sixteen Threads

After an extra day of rest, Mud drove. Strictly speaking, he detested driving, but Coriander was in no condition to do so. He also would have preferred allowing her to rest for another day or so, but in her more cogent moments, she revealed the horrible truth about *Runaway Dreams*.

Dreamwalking itself allowed the dreamers to remain tethered to their physical body, but in a Runaway Dream, the soul was completely detached, existing on its own without an anchor to the physical world. In such a situation, the dreamer lost their sense of time and place. Their subconscious became their entire reality.

Runaway Dreams generally occurred when a dream mage didn't adequately prepare for whatever dream they meant to enter. It was the most dangerous part of dreamwalking, and though it occurred so infrequently as to be non-mentionable, it almost always led to the death or disablement of those involved.

Unless you found the *way out*. Which Mud had. Somehow.

In any case, they lost time to the dream. A whole day and a night, to be exact, though it felt so much shorter. Coriander told Mud to stop trying to resolve the time difference. He'd never be able to do it, and trying to figure out how mere minutes in the dreamrealm translated to hours in the real world would eventually drive him crazy.

It seemed like sound advice, so he stopped.

But they still had to make up time, or they'd lose Meadow and his friends entirely. Cori refused to miss the band due to a dreamwalking screw-up and had been about to sit behind the wheel herself when Mud intervened.

He really, really detested driving. But he also preferred that whoever chose to drive didn't also go on to crash the car in a terrible melty fireball of death, and so here they were.

Mud held his hand up to the window, studying it. Although it had been as purple and starry as Coriander's in the dream, it lacked any sort of sparkle now. He couldn't even see the sun through it, which disappointed him to no end. Once given the rare gift of being able to see through your hand, you ought to be able to keep it.

"You'll get used to it," Coriander muttered. She lay with the passenger seat reclined, empty eyes staring at the felt ceiling. "Eventually, it'll seem normal."

"You're awake," Mud said.

"Mm-hm. I do that sometimes."

"How's Coriander feeling?"

She made a noncommittal grunt that Mud understood to mean "okay-ish."

He had so many questions but hated to interrupt her recovery with things that most people should already know. While he hadn't actually *conducted* magic, he thought he could feel it within himself now, and he didn't hate it.

He couldn't help asking, "What is magic supposed to feel like?"

"Nebula's presence is cool. Like a fall day."

He nodded. Crisp. Expansive. Comfortably suspended within space. That's what he felt.

"Mud, there's something I need to tell you."

He arched an eyebrow, daring a split-tick glance away from the road. Cori's eyes seemed clearer, her color much less ashen than before. Still, the dark circles under her eyes suggested she still suffered the effects of the botched dreamwalk. "You should sleep," Mud said.

She shook her head. "I didn't have a choice... In the dream, I saw that Nebula had... had *chosen* you. And the creature..."

"The Dym," Mud corrected.

"It could have severed us from reality. It wasn't natural. It wasn't... It wasn't supposed to be there. Did you see the threads?"

Mud clearly remembered the threads. Thousands of them—millions, maybe—all connected to its vastness. Some threads were pale, but others shone like stars. "There were very bright threads," Mud said. "And very not-bright threads. I counted the bright ones."

Coriander smiled, shifting the back of her seat into a more upright position. "Counted them."

Maybe it seemed silly now, but if the Dym really existed in the dreamrealm, and it really had people connected to it, Mud felt as if he ought to have counted whatever he could. "There were sixteen."

"Hm," Cori muttered. "I feel like I've heard that number before."

Mud shrugged. "Yes, it is reasonable to count to sixteen. There are a lot of sixteens."

"It's something else," Cori said. "You sure there were sixteen?"

"I counted them several times." He paused, tilting his head. "When Coriander banished the Dym from the dream, the threads went with it. All of them. How did you do that?"

"That's what I wanted to talk to you about." Cori bowed her head, looking at her hands.

She explained that by necessity, any one dreamwalker only possessed so much power. Although Coriander was quite strong compared to others who used the same magic, she couldn't have possibly hoped to banish something as imposing as the Dym from the dream on her own.

And all gods, she went on, championed several magics, some major and some minor. While Nebula was the deity of dreams, she also carried other aspects, such as gravity, telekinesis, and even *the void*. Because each one held so much power, any mage wishing to pursue the study of Nebula's magic could only pick one. And while some people could access magics from *several* gods—there might be a mage of fire *and* water, for example—Nebula would never allow this from one of her mages.

"I didn't have time to explain in the moment," she said. "I'm sorry."

Though Mud wasn't stupid, it took him several ticks to put all the pieces of the puzzle together. He still didn't entirely understand when he said, "You pulled from me."

"Yes. I... locked you into a path. I chose dream magic for you. I had to."

They wouldn't have made it to the door to escape from the Runaway Dream if she hadn't, though that was hardly the point. Rather, it *should* have been the point, but Mud couldn't contain his excitement over the revelation itself. "Do you mean I can do that?"

Without preamble or thought, Coriander simply said, "Yes."

"...Oh."

"I should have asked. You should have been given a choice. Most people... Well. Most people would choose telekinesis. But without committing you to dream magic, I wouldn't have been able to—"

"It's okay," Mud said. "I think Nebula might have chosen, actually. You just pushed it along."

"I wondered if I saw the mark on your hands. I thought you said trolls couldn't use magic."

"We can't."

Cori narrowed her eyes and stared at the ceiling of the car. "If you can't, then I wouldn't have been able to pull from you. How...?"

"Because I prayed to her. I begged her."

When Mud glanced at Cori, she was scowling.

The road whistled beneath them as they sped onward toward Edge. Despite the somber mood, Mud could barely contain his excitement. What if he became the first troll to have control over magic? What would the others say? Was he *special?* Was he unique? How had he managed to reach the god, despite all his magical... inertness?

What did *sixteen* mean?

Mud slowed the car as they entered Edge. It was one of the larger cities in the area, and while it held some of the largest centers of industry on Kyrnis, it also reminded him of *home.* Quaint, comfortable, slow. Its residents greeted each other in the streets before retiring back into their row houses that nearly abutted the sidewalks. Even the shops had a homey feel to them.

Clean-up crews scoured the streets for fallen branches, and a few water mages guided standing water toward drainage ditches where it could flow into the nearby river. Safety barricades placed here and there along the streets blocked off construction crews that worked diligently at fixing damaged buildings.

It looked like there had been a recent storm.

As Mud found a suitable-looking hotel—with a pool! He slowed the car and pulled into the lot. Cori protested, but Mud insisted because her skin looked grey and sad. If she was going to sleep, she should do so in a proper bed, where she could be warm and cozy.

"For a few hours," Cori grumbled. "We don't want to waste too much time."

"A few hours," Mud agreed.

As they got out of the car, Cori looked toward the horizon, where the Fade Desert stretched infinitely to the North. "Mud, the dream doesn't lie."

"Hm?" Mud asked.

"Everything we saw. The Dym, the threads. I wish I would have been awake. I feel like we experienced something important, and I slept through it. And *you*... I really saw you for the first time, Mud."

"I have been here the whole time."

She chuckled without humor. "What I mean is... I didn't understand you. I didn't really understand trolls, I guess. I thought..."

"You thought Mud was simple. Stupid."

"Not stupid. Never stupid. I promise. But I did underestimate you, and I *am* sorry for that."

This apology felt real. Mud couldn't say how he knew, only that Coriander didn't seem like the type to apologize lightly, nor did she stand to gain anything by it. Plus, despite having only neophyte connections to the magical world, he *kind of* understood what she meant when she said that she saw him for the first time. While the dreamrealm wasn't exactly a window into anyone's soul, it was more pure than anything Mud had experienced thus far. If not a window, it was at least a reflection.

"Thank you," he said.

Coriander rested her head against his shoulder, staring out into the lifeless desert. "It's hard to gain Nebula's trust," she said, changing the subject. "You can be her conduit your whole life and never tempt her magic. But you did it."

She didn't sound jealous or bitter. In fact, she sounded awed and proud. Mud twitched an ear in her direction, trying to keep his tail from curling in pleasure at the compliment. Even with his considerable effort, it still twisted around itself like a pretzel. Coriander paid no attention. Still embarrassing.

"I can teach you how to focus your magic. At first, it might seem a little wild and unpredictable, but you can train it and tame it, kinda like an animal."

"You don't owe me anything," Mud said, even though the prospect of learning magic made his heart soar.

"I do, in a way," Coriander replied. "In a lot of ways, actually. I forced magic into you, for one—"

"You needed to—"

"And I'm not gonna pass up the opportunity to train the first-ever magic-wielding troll."

Mud laughed. "An honor for you."

Even though Cori was exhausted, she also managed a chuckle, then gave Mud a gentle pat. "Of all the gods you could have prayed to..." She trailed off, muttering to herself before asking, "Wait... How many bright threads did you say were attached to the Dym?"

"Sixteen. Why?"

"Maybe it's nothing. Coincidence."

"Why, Cori?"

She shook her head, eyes narrowed as she debated with herself in quiet undertones. "It's just that there's sixteen gods."

CHAPTER THIRTY-NINE

The Fade Desert

Three-thousand four-hundred and seventy-six aurs ago—or maybe seventy-seven; Benji couldn't remember the exact month—a magical accident rendered the Fade Desert completely devoid of life and sustenance, evaporating even the underground aquifers. While time had introduced some life and water back into the region, it still remained one of the driest places on the whole planet. The devastation even extended onto multiple continents, and textbooks suggested the incident creating it might have killed millions of people.

Benji *thought* he loved the Fade Desert, but as it turned out, he just loved the *history and lore* of it. Once fully encircled by the kilokips of dead land and unnatural lack of life, he very much wished he was *out* of it.

But he was stuck there. For hours.

As the road castle glided over the broken, fragmented road, all anyone could do was talk or sleep. While Meadow drove, he managed to convince Ptery to spill what was bothering them, so Ptery told everyone what they'd discovered by breaking the memory stone the night before.

Luka threatened to murder Evialor, then she and Ptery hugged.

It was nice to see them bonding and getting along.

Eight hours in, with Ptery taking a stress-induced nap on one of the road castle's fold-out beds, Luka and Meadow switched places, and Luka drove. But even with Meadow hanging out in the living space with Benji, the emptiness around them sucked all potential for conversation or games right out of the air, and they lounged in silence for the next stretch of the drive. The only interesting thing to look at was the other cars, which also sped through the desert as fast as possible.

Once the sun set, even the scant intrigue of the endless desert disappeared.

"The EWPS says we're coming up on the coordinates," Luka said, her voice flat and tired.

"We should just call it the 'Oops.'" Meadow stood, stretching. "EWPS has too many syllables."

"It's less than 'Erit World Positioning System,'" Benji noted.

Meadow cracked his neck. "Ugh. That's true. If I had to say *that* every time, I'd forget what I was saying halfway through saying it. Yeah. I'm gonna call it 'Oops.' You'll remember what I'm talking about."

"You and *syllables*." Luka pulled off the road onto a well-kept exit. "The coordinates are near a rest area. I'll stop there."

"A rest area?" Meadow asked. "Lemme guess. It's just a patch of sand with a couple chairs half-buried in a dune."

"No, someone built an oasis," Luka replied. She tapped the screen on the dashboard. "Could be what we're looking for?"

Ptery woke, sitting up and rubbing their eyes. "I'm not sure an oasis in the middle of the Fade Desert is the same thing as the Godplain, nestling."

But what if it was? Wheriae must have known *something* when he etched those coordinates onto Benji's crest.

This couldn't possibly be a gallud's errand.

Broad-leafed palm trees sprung up around them, lining the exit and introducing some much-needed color to Benji's exhausted eyes. Beyond them, the moon reflected off a broad body of water, which must have been the central spring of the rest area.

Although he longed to leave the bus and stretch his legs, he imagined he'd have to stay inside to preserve the feelings of the non-beast species staying at the oasis. Or... at least to preserve his *own* feelings. He was too tired from the long drive to weather their misplaced discomfort.

Then he saw all the liori.

A black-furred sphinx flew by the bus before landing next to the enormous spring, lined with all kinds of people seeking respite from the desert. She leaned against another sphinx, who was engaged in deep discussion with a pair of fauns and a couple tiny fae. A manticore with its deadly tail casually curled over his back served refreshments to a flock of harpies stretched out on lawn chairs.

Trees and sculpted shrubs surrounded the water, actively tended by groundskeepers wearing bright green uniforms. A cobblestone path led away from the oasis and toward a block of open-fronted cabins. A campfire burned in the center of them, where dozens of strangers shared conversation and food.

A manticore waved at Luka, and she stopped, rolling down her window.

"Greetings," the manticore said. "I'm Reclesti. My den and I built this oasis for all to enjoy. No harmful magic, no necromancy, no fighting. Would you like a cabin?"

Luka glanced back at the others, shrugged, then said, "Sure."

Green wisps of Reclesti's *telis* appeared, jotting something down on a ticket, which he then tore off and handed to Luka. "Cabin sixteen. Right down the road and turn left. Welcome!"

Ptery leaned through the divider window and asked, "Just like that? Does it cost anything?"

"Doesn't appear to." Luka handed the ticket to them, then maneuvered the bus down the road as indicated.

Although the cabins appeared open at first, the front panels could be opaqued and solidified, which gave the occupants privacy whenever they wanted it. More than half the occupied cabins were currently open, though, as the campers mingled and exchanged stories from the road.

After unloading the bus and laying claim to a corner within cabin number sixteen, Benji wandered toward the campfire. It burned at least ten kips high—maybe more—its glow touching every cabin surrounding it and even glinting off the oasis down the road. A few people roasted kabobs in the open flames, although most sat a reasonable distance away from the heat and smoke.

Benji situated himself in an open patch of sand and hay. No one backed away from him or leveled a hostile stare in his direction, which was a welcome change from the normal.

Someone even offered him a marshmallow. When Benji held out his hand, the fearless banshee popped the fluffy little cylinder on the tip of his claw, then waltzed away to offer marshmallows to everyone else.

It didn't take long for Meadow to catch up. Sitting down, he stole the marshmallow, ripped it in half, and gave the larger half back to Benji. "There's a stage here, past the oasis," he said. "A little small, but it's a nice-looking platform. I bet we could play."

Although *here* would be the best place for Benji to reintroduce himself to playing live music, he still muttered, "I don't know..."

"Aw, c'mon." Meadow popped his half of the marshmallow into his mouth, then re-stole Benji's portion. "You gotta do it *sometime*. There's a lot of people here. We could make some minir."

"I'll think about it."

"Good enough for now."

As the fire burned, Meadow leaned against Benji, chatting with anyone who would listen. Eventually, he flagged down the marshmallow-distributing banshee and acquired another half dozen marshmallows, which he refused to share. To lay claim to them all, he stuffed every single one into his cheeks at the same time.

Benji, content to people-watch, took note of everyone coming and going from the open sandlot: A troupe of fauns with brown skin and near-black coats. More liori than he'd ever seen in one place. Bright-feathered harpies flying high above the oasis and nesting in the trees. Tiny fae having heated discussions with enormous trolls.

Within minutes, Meadow gathered a small crowd of these vacationers and challenged them all to guess just how many marshmallows he could fit into his face. So far, the highest reasonable guess was fifty.

Shaking his head and rolling his eyes, Benji wandered away from the fire. He didn't want to be around when Meadow inevitably discharged a pile of marshmallow goo from his strangely ponderous stomachs.

He didn't get too far, though, when a glint of light caught his eye, drawing his attention to a gold-rimmed telescope set up atop a shallow dune. A rainbow-feathered banshee stood next to it, adjusting the eyepiece before looking through the lens.

Stars. Benji loved the stars.

He glanced upward at the blanket of pinprick specks filling the sky from one horizon to the other, each shimmering in the thermals created by the hot desert air. There were so many stars here that he couldn't even pick out any constellations. He knew where they were, of course; he hadn't solved dozens of puzzles about the cosmos without retaining a little information. But finding individual stars among tens of thousands proved terrifyingly futile.

As Benji realized just how tiny he was in the universe, he heard the banshee exclaim, "Beautiful!" and his ears flicked toward them.

What did they see that he couldn't?

He only hesitated for a moment before stepping off the dirt path and into the loose, white sand. As he drew closer, the banshee's dark eyes met his for a moment before they went back to the telescope.

"There's so many..." Benji said. "I mean, of course there are. Without—Without all the light from the city. But, er... Is there something...?" He scanned the sky, but couldn't make out anything unique among the endless expanse of stars.

"Only the coolest thing in the universe," the banshee said. "Take a look."

They stepped aside, gesturing to the telescope. Benji shuffled closer and sat down, wrapping his tail around his feet and bowing his head so he could look through the eyepiece.

He let out an involuntary gasp after using his *telis* to adjust the lens. There it was—billions of kilokips away soared the Dragon's Tail comet, its two pink and blue tails stretching farther into space than any comet ever observed on Erit. With everything going on, Benji had forgotten all about his intent to study it.

"This is the first night it's visible with a standard telescope," the banshee said. "I just *had* to come to the oasis to observe it. I mean, I'll never get another chance, since it only orbits close enough to Erit every—"

"—seven-hundred aurs," Benji finished. With the exception of the elves and a few very long-lived animals, no one alive today would have seen it on its last pass. Not even Efrit, the oldest faun who ever lived! "I wonder if my birth parents saw it last time it was here."

He could imagine the emperor and empress standing atop a terrace, comforted by the warm glow of the Dragon's Tail comet as it reached its perigee.

"I bet. No one can miss it. That's what I've heard, anyway."

The lump at the banshee's feet, which Benji had previously taken for a pile of supplies covered in a fluffy blanket, yawned loudly and startled Benji from his wonder. Then it rolled over onto its back, flopping across his front paws.

"Er..." Benji said.

"Oh, that's just my barycapa, Steve. He won't hurt you. He just likes warm things. And I'm Alephyr."

Alephyr scooted Benji aside and went back to looking through the telescope.

"Benji," Benji said. "Thanks for letting me look. I can't believe I almost forgot about it."

"Well, it's good luck to see it, I've heard! Just like seeing a real dragon." Pausing his observations, Alephyr scribbled something into a notebook.

It seemed forever ago that Meadow and Ptery had argued about whether or not dragons were good luck. The memory made Benji smile. "Is that true? If—if you see a dragon..."

"Oh, yeah." Alephyr grinned, resting one arm across the telescope. Their wings fluffed up with the pride of dispensing knowledge, while Steve snored. "Well, every time *I* see one, something good happens, so I gotta figure they're lucky."

"Well... I suppose I could use a little luck, so I hope you're right."

"Trust me. I know comets. And this is a lucky one."

As Benji shuffled his paws out from under the barycapa, he noticed an ashen-skinned elf slide through the dune's dark shadow. Her orange eyes burned brighter than any fire in the camp.

"...Zeera?" Benji muttered. It couldn't be. What would she be doing so far from Lunarilis?

"Hm?" Alephyr asked. "Were you talking to me?"

"Ah, sorry. I have to go. Thanks again for showing me the comet."

Alephyr said, "I hope the Dragon's Tail brings you that luck you're looking for. Nice to meet you!" and went back to his studies.

Benji tailed after the elf, keeping as close as he dared. She seemed to be searching for something, allowing her gaze to rest on each person around the fire before moving on to the next. Each motion she made carried a fluid grace as if she moved faster than the average person could perceive.

No one paid her any attention. Except Benji.

He tried to sneak after her so he could verify whether she was who he thought she was before calling out her name. But a manticore could only move so quietly, and it wasn't long before her ears stood straight up and she turned, fixing Benji with a suspicious, bright-eyed glare.

"It *is* you!" he exclaimed. "Zeera, it's me. Benji!"

Her suspicious glare turned confused until she recognized him, then she didn't hesitate. Crossing the couple kips between them in less than a tick, she threw both arms around his neck. "Ben! I thought you were in Faun-ir! What are you doing in the desert?"

"We're... ah..." He wrapped her in a hug, careful not to crush her. "It's a long story. You want to come sit with us? Maybe... maybe we can catch up. It's been a long time. Things—things happened."

She stepped back, studying him. "Well, of course I knew what happened to you," she said. "Not much escapes me or the royal guard. But seeing you in person..."

"Who's the vampire?" Meadow asked, coming to stand alongside Benji. He held six partially chewed marshmallows in one hand.

"Meadow, this is Zeeraliana, ninth child of the empire," Benji said. "She's my sister."

Meadow offered her a marshmallow. She wrinkled her nose and waved him off. "Ah, it's *norsfar,*" she said. "Vampires are a bit different. Where are you staying?"

Benji led her back to their cabin, where Luka and Ptery had made a smaller, more manageable campfire. Roasting atop it in a pan were a few choice meats and veggies from Pixel's hold. Meadow reached into the ground and grew some tiny ears of corn, which he also threw into the pan to cook with everything else.

As the sun dipped farther below the horizon, the sky darkened from deep blue to black, and stars appeared in all their glorious brilliance. Without any civilization to hide them, even the tiniest stars shone as bright as faelights, completing constellations that couldn't be fully appreciated in the city.

Meadow opened a can of broth and poured it into the pan. Once it all cooked long enough, he portioned soup out to anyone who wanted some. Zeera passed, of course, joking that she hadn't eaten solid food in a decaur. It just didn't taste good anymore.

"I've never seen the sky like this," Ptery said as they ate. "I've traveled a lot. But I've never been anywhere like this."

"And there's the Isotyre arc of the Silver Cloud galaxy," Benji said, pointing out the streaks and tangles of pink and cyan that decorated the sky. "You can't see that from the city. Not even if you're on an observation deck in Faun-ir. When I was little, my dads took me to the desert so I could see a *little* of it, but we didn't go this far."

"Never realized there were so many stars," Luka said.

Sometimes a meteor streaked by overhead in sparkling, silver clarity. Even the faintest of them blazed brilliantly as they exhausted themselves and burnt out in Erit's atmosphere. After so many aurs, Benji could finally confirm that the beautiful pictures in his books weren't embellished, but neither did they do the *real* night sky any sort of fair justice.

Zeera pointed to the moon, Ammit, in its waning phase. "There's people up there, looking back at us."

"Hmph. Not with quite the same wonder, I suspect," Ptery said.

Benji laughed. "Are you actually impressed?"

Ptery leaned back against a rock, nestling their arms behind their head. "And if I am, does that cloud your impression of me?"

"Improves it, I think."

"Ah. Well. Good."

Luka set her bowl aside, folding her hands in front of her. Ever suspicious, she fixed Zeera with a polite, albeit intense stare. "Weird that you'd just run into your brother here, isn't it?" she asked. "Of all the places..."

"Yeah, kinda," Zeera agreed. "I'm here because the captain of my sect noticed a traveling artifact. An old one. The kind made by the Bright Elves before the fall of the first empire."

"And it's here? In this camp?" Ptery asked. "I wonder if that's what..."

Luka elbowed them.

"I don't think it's here *yet,*" Zeera said. She took a sip of moonshine and curled her lip, revealing two sharp fangs. "Darkrealm, *that's* got a kick. I'll need more of this before I leave."

"So why are you *here?*" Luka persisted.

"Because of how first-empire artifacts were made, they leave a path into the past *and* into the future," Zeera said. "It's just a matter of getting far enough ahead of whoever's traveling with the thing and intercepting it."

"And you can just follow the trail?" Meadow asked.

Zeera shrugged, grinning. "I mean. Yeah. I'm a norsfar."

Although similar to vampires, norsfar fed on magic, not blood, and the empire always employed a few of them to keep the emperor and empress safe. Rogue magic could spell disaster for unwary royals, which meant someone had to be on hand to detect and eliminate it.

Benji had always envied Zeera's tracking skills. At one point, he even thought maybe he'd like to become a norsfar, but the ritual made him nervous.

"Now," Zeera said, setting her moonshine aside. "What's my little brother doing in the middle of the desert with his friends?"

"Well, it's not a *vacation*, if that's what you're wondering," Ptery said. "Very important business. Strictly confidential. Need-to-know only."

"We're looking for the Godplain," Meadow said.

Luka lowered her head into her hands.

"What?" Meadow said. "If she can tell us all about the artifact-whatsit, we can tell her what we're looking for, right? Maybe *she* knows where it is."

Zeera offered a tolerant smile. "Well, the Godplain's a myth, isn't it? Why are you looking for it?"

As the fire burned lower, Benji did his best to explain their quest, with Meadow interjecting the important parts about Wheriae and his odd coordinates. He showed Zeera the royal crest, with the tiny symbols emblazoned across the back—symbols only Benji could read.

"Wheriae told me that 'the elf' would know where to find the place where the gods rest," Meadow said. "I thought it'd be Benji, but he could only read the little numbers."

"And they led us here," Benji added.

"We're going to search around once the sun comes up to see what we can find." Ptery looked around, then back to the fire. "But it doesn't feel very Godplainy, does it? One would expect there to be a bit more reverence and pomp about."

Zeera's expression turned from tolerantly humorous to concerned. "I heard the temple sent a faun on a quest to discover the reason for the dying flora. That was you? All of you?"

"Yeah! Pretty cool, huh?" Meadow asked. "Problem is, Wheriae wants me to go somewhere, but he won't tell me where that place is. You know, maybe we're also supposed to find this artifact, too. Miss Zeera, you wouldn't mind if we took a look at it before you ate it, would you?"

"You think the artifact might lead us to the Godplain?" Ptery asked.

"Wait," Zeera said, holding up a hand. She stood, her eyes burning into Benji's as she studied him as if trying to read his thoughts.

Could she do that? He shrunk back, looking at the ground, unable to maintain eye contact.

"What if..." Zeera went on. "What if Wheriae sent you here to find *me?*"

A smattering of screams came from the direction of the oasis. The panic escalated into a cacophony as people began to flee.

Then, a haunting *"Iiooowoop! Yooowoop!"* echoed from every tree and cabin wall.

CHAPTER FORTY

Gnolledge is Power

Meadow's unfortunate thought process followed a very confusing line.

First, he reasoned that if people were running *away* from The Big Scary Thing By The Water (henceforth known as The Thing for ease of summary), he ought to run away, too. He could not save the world should he be killed.

Second, he wondered if The Thing might be *part* of his involvement in saving the world. It sounded like a gnoll, and gnolls seemed to be a common theme in his life lately. Kind of like recurring colors in poems, only furrier and with more teeth.

Third, if The Thing (probably a gnoll) was the goal, he should at least consider running *toward* it. Or perhaps consider meandering carefully in its direction so as not to get eaten.

Last but most importantly, he wished he could go back in time and undo his decision to eat so many marshmallows. Saving the world would be harder with a unicorn's weight of sugar in his stomachs.

"Get *back* here!" Ptery hissed, grabbing Meadow's shoulder. They pulled him into the shadow behind the wall of their cabin, where Benji and Zeera also hid. "That giant beast of a gnoll *followed us!*"

Meadow peeked around the corner, momentarily spying the impressive white-haired gnoll. "You mean J," he said as Ptery grabbed his horn and yanked him out of sight again.

"Ji'irifarana'ali," Benji corrected. "Don't let her hear you call her J."

Another volley of screams rose from the oasis. A manticore skimmed the cabin's roof, then dropped to the ground, putting the structure between himself and the attacker. He ignored Meadow and the others and ran into the desert. Fauns and humans fled behind him, their feet sinking into the soft sand.

One of them left a trail of blood behind them.

A bright explosion of orange fire lit up the sky, followed by the gnoll's unusual laugh. *"Hyoooop! Iiiooowoop!"*

"We don't know that she followed *us* here," Meadow said. "She might have just coincidentally ended up at the same camp. You know. In the middle of the desert."

"THERE-RRR ISS A BANSHEE-YA! A LIIORI!" The gnoll screamed, so everyone could hear her. *"A FAUN-AH! AND-RR, A HUMAAHN! BRING THEMMM TO-RR ME, AND I-YA WILL SPARRRE THE RRREST!"*

Ptery and Benji both stared at Meadow, their expressions somewhere on the spectrum between terrified and I-told-you-so.

"*That's* just bad timing," Meadow said.

Zeera asked, "Why would *gnolls* be looking for you?"

A sharp scream erupted from the direction of the huge central campfire, then abruptly ceased as the person making it was silenced. A chill ran from Meadow's ears to his hooves.

He didn't know if Wheriae sent him here for this purpose or if the god had some other idea in mind. Regardless, Meadow couldn't allow innocent people to die because they got in the way of a gnoll with a weird grudge. He crouched, checking around the corner again.

J lacked her pack. She stood alone, a strange, rainbow-glowing cube in her hands.

"It's just the one," Meadow said, looking back at the others. "Where's Luka?"

"Hiding, I hope," Benji said. "She disappeared as soon as—as soon as people started—"

"Good," Meadow said. "I'm going to do the same thing I did before. The oasis should be able to grow enough vines to catch one single bad guy. Ptery, find Luka and make sure she's okay. Benji, you and your sister head for the desert with the others. Keep the cabin behind you so she doesn't see you."

"No, I'm staying," Zeera said. "That gnoll has the artifact I'm looking for. I either need to contain it or see that it's destroyed."

"That?" Ptery jerked their thumb at the cube. "That cube is the artifact? The *ancient elvish artifact?* Why in the Darkrealm does a gnoll have it?"

"I don't *know.*" Zeera shrugged one shoulder. "For all anyone can figure, it found the thing buried in ruins. They just turn up sometimes! That's definitely it, though, and I'm not leaving without it."

"Fine," Meadow conceded. "But—"

"Well, of course I have to help," Ptery interrupted. "After all, if we're taking a murder-cube away from a homicidal gnoll, my scream is the best weapon we have."

That made sense. "Okay. Benji, you find—"

"I think—" Benji started, his glowing eyes meeting everyone's in turn. "I think we're probably in this together? Uh, four against one?"

Meadow never could give orders anyone would listen to, so he shouldn't have been surprised when the others completely disregarded everything he said. Then again, he selfishly did not want to be alone when facing J and whatever weird artifact-weapon she carried. He nodded.

J's whoops drew closer.

"I have a plan," Ptery said. "We surrender. That thing won't be able to tell an elf from a human. No offense, Zeera."

Zeera shrugged.

"Then J lets us approach," Ptery continued, "and I hit her with a scream. Meadow, you tangle her up, and Zeera, you grab the artifact."

"Er..." Benji curled his tail in front of his front paws, unwrapping the bindings. "Look, I think we should be careful. If it was that easy, someone would have done something like that already, right? There were dozens of people here." After a pause, he muttered, "Darkrealm, I pulled all the quills yesterday..."

"They were all too startled," Ptery answered. "We're not. We have a plan. Okay?"

They looked at the others, who nodded.

"But fan out," Zeera said. "If we're far enough apart, well. If something goes wrong..."

She left the sentence unfinished.

Meadow took a deep breath, steeled himself, then called, "Okay! We give up! We're coming out!"

J screech-snarled in triumph as her quarry appeared from behind the cabin. Her sharp, silver teeth gleamed in the firelight. The well-tailored suit she wore now sported rips and stains; one sleeve was missing, leaving snakelike threads twisting out from the damaged shoulder pad. An elaborate necklace comprised of brass beads and steel animal skulls hung around her neck, the baubles jangling against each other like a demented, macabre wind chime.

Though stained with dust and grime, her pelt was the purest white, setting her apart from other gnolls. Her red eyes glared maliciously, smiling in the dark.

It was the strange, textured box in her well-manicured, gold-painted claws that held Meadow's attention. The runes and letters on its surface, though corroded by time, emanated a peculiar wrongness that filled his senses and made all his hair stand on end.

The leader of the oasis den, Reclesti, lay unmoving some distance away, surrounded by a pool of blood. Several others also lay scattered around the clearing—some who probably just got in the way and others who looked like they might have been trying to stop J from hurting more people. In addition to the central campfire, a few smaller fires also consumed the dry cabin wood and thorny desert trees.

J was only *one gnoll*. How could she have done this on her own?

Had the *cube* caused this?

Meadow caught Ptery's eye and shook his head. They needed to know what the artifact did before proceeding with the plan.

As everyone spread out, surrounding the gnoll in a quarter-circle, Meadow tried and failed to keep his tail from lashing against the sand. At least his knees weren't shaking enough for anyone to notice. "So," he said, holding up his hand in a half-hearted wave. "I see you got yourself a neat little toy."

"A *toy?*" J spat. "Thiss-ah iss a prresent from the *Trrue Godss.*"

"Right. Okay. Cool. That's fun. What's it do? Can I try it?"

J laughed, her *whoops* echoing from the walls of the abandoned cabins. "Therrre are no worrds-ah in yourrr rr-language-ah."

"Oh, we have a few words," Meadow said, lazily scratching an ear as if he didn't absolutely want to piss himself. "I mean, I like the word 'unnecessary.' Maybe 'overkill.' I'm very fond of 'please, stop, I think people are dead.' You know. All very good things to say."

She narrowed her eyes, tilting her head. "Youu-ah talk too fasst."

"Yeah, they've told me the same." He gestured at the others. "How about if you put that cube-thing down, then you, me, and my friends sit around the fire and have a nice chat about why you want to kill us, huh? We could make hot dogs. It'll be fun."

Meadow's godmark struggled to grow in the desert, but he could feel the little tendrils trying their damnedest to find purchase. He sank his hoof down into the sand, pushing his magic with his foot rather than his fingers. If he could control the little vines just enough to pull J off her feet before she noticed them...

She noticed them.

Meadow should have understood her feint, but even if he had, there wouldn't have been enough time to warn the others. With both hands still clasped around the glowing cube, J leapt forward, her teeth snapping shut a few centikips from his nose.

Meadow stumbled backward, unable to maintain his balance in the shifting sand. The giant gnoll loomed over him, grinning, letting gravity do the work for her as Meadow fell.

He pinwheeled his arms, feet flying up in the air as his shoulders thumped against the ground. Thankfully his head struck the soft sand, but his left forearm crunched against a rock as he flailed. It snapped at an angle that might have been interesting if it didn't hurt so darn much.

His cry of warning became a scream of agony.

Then Ptery, ever rash despite their intelligence, screamed with the full power of their debilitating voice.

Meadow dove against the ground, using the desert to cover one ear while his good arm covered the other. Even so, he should have heard *something* painful. But Ptery's scream had a hollow, vacant quality, reverberating and echoing with an otherworldly ring until it vanished entirely.

Ptery coughed, gagged, and grappled at their throat as the gnoll giggled with unrestrained glee. She flipped the box around, pointing a golden-colored face toward them. The surface of it shimmered and undulated like a swarm of angry hornets.

"Myy-ah turnhh," J said.

A sound like thunder ripped through the quiet oasis, causing ripples to distort and disrupt the sand. Cobblestones broke free and went flying while boards on the side of the cabins creaked, splintered, and cartwheeled across the sand like tumbleweeds.

Though not as precise or streamlined as a banshee's scream, the noise carried a more *physical* sort of power, one that tried to rupture from the inside out. Meadow, unfortunately, lay directly at the center of it, and the initial shockwave lifted him clear off the ground. As he tried to regain his bearings, he careened into the side of the nearest cabin and, due to the already compromised integrity of the wood, crashed right through it.

Something in his hip popped in an excruciating manner.

Ow.

But he'd had worse! Well. Maybe not as bad as a broken arm at the same time as a dislocated hip.

"Meadow!" Benji cried as the burning room spun.

Not as bad as a homicidal gnoll bent on his destruction.

J's laughing cackle drowned out Zeera's shout of challenge. A burning beam fell just a kip and a half from Meadow's leg.

Yeah, he probably hadn't had worse than being ass-up in an on-fire cabin made entirely of dry wood.

But the *emotional* pain...

No, Meadow decided. This was probably as bad as he'd ever had it.

Benji roared, the rumble carrying incredulous shock and anger.

Meadow had to get back into the fight before someone else got hurt. Breathing as if he'd just run a marathon, he reached for a cracked beam and braced it under his uninjured shoulder. He leveraged himself to his feet and dragged himself outside.

Ptery crouched by the huge fire, some of their flight feathers singed. Benji stood on the other side of the gnoll, ready to pounce. Zeera circled behind, a thin rapier clutched in one hand.

"Ouuwoop! Auuwoop! Ouuiipp!" J called. "Again-ah!"

"Don't, Ptery," Benji said, his voice drowned out by the roar of the fires. "That thing eats sound!"

Meadow dropped to the ground, fighting against the blinding pain to dig all his fingers into the sand. Just a bit below the surface, his hoof-like fingernails dug into what might have been fertile clay, and within it lay instructions for an *incredibly* limited selection of species. The deeper he went, the more he found until his magic latched onto an ancient species of grapevine.

Good enough.

He *expected* the plant to burst forth from the ground and wrap J up in its tendrils.

But the gnoll laughed. The side of her cube glowed a sickly, termite-wiggly green. She barked, and Meadow was once again hoisted off his feet, tangled in the same prickly vines he tried to call forth himself.

As J stretched her arms, the vines stretched, too. Meadow thought she might tear his hip right out of its socket.

She only stopped when Benji's *telis* appeared, trying to steal the artifact. The glowing face of the cube turned white. The wisps vanished, only to reappear again to shove Benji off his feet.

No magic, even innate magic, would work while J held the artifact. They had to get it away from her.

Meadow chewed through the vines holding his limbs. He thanked the gods for the strength of faun jaws as he dropped to the ground. His left leg, now numb from hip to hock, barely supported his weight, but at least the pain was gone. Shoving the makeshift crutch under his shoulder again, he limped toward the others.

Benji and Ptery still flanked her on two sides. As Meadow joined them, they spread out just a little further.

J did not seem fazed, but with her attention on Meadow, Zeera took the opportunity to attack. She leapt, briefly transforming into a bat, then dropped down atop the gnoll. With fluid grace, she swung her rapier, knocking the cube from J's hands.

Meadow would have been impressed with seeing his first demonstration of norsfar transformative powers had he not been dizzy with hurt.

"Now, Ben!" Zeera ordered.

Benji hesitated. Meadow couldn't blame him, the poor guy, since he'd never really been in a situation where he was supposed to *bite someone*. However, in that brief half-tick, J threw Zeera off and rolled through the sand. By the time Benji pounced, she was clear of his claws.

Zeera shifted to bat again, spun between Benji and J, then grabbed the artifact just as her wings turned back into hands. She dodged J's claws and somersaulted out of the fray, tossing the cube to Ptery.

Then she stood between J and Ptery, staring at the gnoll down the length of her blade.

Although J did not immediately attack, Meadow watched the proverbial cogs turning behind her hateful eyes as she glared at each of them in turn. He dropped his crutch again, digging his fingers into the sand. Without her cube, she wouldn't be able to counter his magic—

With a flash and a flourish, J freed the dagger from the thong around her ankle, spun around, and plunged the silver blade into Benji's neck.

Although Ptery cried out in disbelief, Benji stood his ground like a sturdy rock as J stared at him in confusion.

Oh.

Meadow laughed. The blade couldn't cut through Benji's thick mane!

Undeterred, J recovered more quickly than anyone could act. She ripped the dagger upward, drawing a roar from Benji as she tore out his hair. Grabbing onto his wing, she flipped onto his back and stabbed downward, directly into the soft muscle between Benji's shoulder blade and wing.

His front half dropped into the sand as he screamed.

J ripped the dagger upward again, launching a red spray of blood into the air. As Benji rolled, she vaulted off his back, sailing over Zeera's head.

Her target? Ptery. And the cube.

It would have been a perfect time for Ptery to scream had they not been paralyzed with fear.

J's arm twisted behind her head, fist curled tight around the pommel of the dagger. With the energy from her leap, she'd be able to split Ptery in half with the blade before anyone could rush to the rescue.

Meadow wanted to look away, but he couldn't.

In the space of a single breath, a shadow passed overhead, colliding with the J and tackling her to the ground. The... *creature*... wrapped a near-infinite number of arms and legs around the rampaging, snarling gnoll, then held on just long enough to rip long gashes through J's leather cuirass and into her chest.

Regaining her feet, J kicked at the creature, who flipped through the air like an acrobat and landed on its feet.

It was a *theric*. A giant spider theric! Its greenish carapace sparkled with iridescent beauty in the firelight.

Baring her teeth, J crouched, retrieving a second dagger from a strap around her other ankle. The gnoll growled deep in her throat as she circled the new challenger. The theric, arms wide and shoulders hunched, rotated to meet its opponent at every turn, silent and patient.

Then J bolted.

The theric straightened in surprise but gave chase a tick later. Despite the wild weaving of the gnoll, the spidery beast kept up with amazing alacrity, zig-zagging across the desert as it pursued.

J, falling to all fours, made a beeline for Ptery, who yelped, dropped the cube, and shielded their face.

Bleeding and desperate, Ji'irifarana'ali's hands closed around the artifact. She hefted it over her head in victory, a mad grin plastered on her face.

And then the cube *exploded*.

A sickly green bubble of magic surrounded the gnoll, catching the fragments of the ancient device before they could fly away. The bladed shards sunk into her flesh as she screamed in a mixture of panic and pain. As the magic closed in on her, her back arched in agony, and her legs gave out beneath her.

But she didn't die.

Vines the color of poison and death burst from her arms. Her fingers. Her chest. Her throat. They coalesced into another *being*, leaving little of the original gnoll exposed. Acting as a parasite, the plants commandeered their host's legs, pulled her to her feet, and forced a roar from her throat.

It sounded like a whole choir of the Darkrealm-damned—souls cursed to wander between one life and the next, never finding solace with their god.

Holy shit.

A twisted vine whipped out toward the theric, knocking it aside as if it was nothing more than an exceptionally leggy ragdoll. Another grabbed Zeera around the throat and threw her into the burning wreckage of one of the cabins.

Another vine snaked around Meadow's ankle, lifting him several kips into the air. He dangled upside-down, squealing as his capture bore the unforeseen consequence of popping his hip back into its socket.

He might have thrown up had the subsequent relief not calmed his stomachs.

As Meadow tried not to cry, one last vine tied itself around the end of Benji's tail, right at the joint before the venomous sting.

And it squeezed.

And *squeezed*.

Benji roared in pain as the entire telson just popped off, rolling across the ground like a ball.

J's eyes, still visible through the tangle of vines, were wide with horror. She quivered and trembled within the mass as if trying to escape. The vines curled around her jaws, manipulating them as if she was nothing more than a puppet, while her voice rasped, *"I WILL KILL YOU MYSELF!"*

In the periphery of his vision, Meadow saw two more people—a djiratog and a troll—standing just past the reach of the firelight. The doors of their car were open as if they'd been driving by and decided to spectate the fight like it was some sort of sport.

Idiots.

Run, Meadow tried to say, but a vine curled around his throat, cutting off his air. J lowered him down until they were eye-to-eye.

Her hijacked fangs glimmered orange in the firelight.

The edges of Meadow's vision closed in, his pain fading into a distant memory.

He apologized to Petalvine. To Wheriae.

Because he tried. He really, *really tried*. He *knew* nothing short of Erit was at stake, and for once, he wanted to make the gods proud. He wanted to make the elders proud.

He wanted to mean something.

"I think we are too late," Mud said, his voice trembling with regret. "The Dym is *here*."

Coriander shook her head. Although surrounded by the creeping tendrils of the shadowy monster in her dream, this creature lacked the immense size of the Dym. Plus, clumps of fur and scraps of leather poked out between the wriggling black vines. The Dym was made only of darkness.

"We must do what we can," Mud said. "For Nebula. To save their song."

The vine creature was formidable and strong, holding Meadow suspended with what seemed like little effort. All around it, people were bleeding and possibly dying. If Coriander and Mud rushed in with no weapons and no battle experience, they'd be destroyed.

But...

Together.

"Mud, I have an idea," Coriander said. "Take my hand."

He did.

Like any of the gods, Nebula frowned on the use of magic to affect free will. That meant only the masters of dream magic, who'd dedicated their lives to Nebula for decaurs, could cast sleep spells on their own.

But sometimes, she allowed for a special *trick*. A consensus among mages.

Unlike what they did in the dream, Coriander could not *pull* from Mud, but she could *pool* with him.

"This will be your first spell," she said. "Focus your thoughts, and will that thing to fall asleep."

J's eyes rolled back in her head, the mass of vines sagging like a tangle of frayed yarn. After wavering back and forth a few steps in each direction, she collapsed to her knees.

The killing stalk around Meadow's throat fell away, flopping onto the ground with a dull *pap!* Then, as he sucked in a much-needed breath, the vine around his leg also relaxed.

He had less than a tick to react. Instinct took over, and he thrust out both arms to catch himself.

Bad idea.

He collided with the ground, left arm buckling, his vision swimming white-hot as the pain radiated through every single neuron in his body. His stomachs heaved, disgorging a decent portion of his dinner.

As a final insult, the vine-creature fell on top of him.

Though J's movements remained sluggish, she seemed to be recovering. Something had to be done to stop her rampage.

He could only think of one answer.

"Ptery!" Meadow croaked, his throat struggling to form sound. "Do it!"

"I can't!" Ptery called back. "I'll hurt you!"

A vine rested across Meadow's throat again but lacked the tenacity to squeeze. J's frightened eyes stared into his, her mouth working on its own, separate from the control of the vine-creature. *"It-ah... it is not-aah... a true god! It... is... an... impostor!"*

A net of tendrils closed around J's face and sucked it back into the twisted nest of horrible darkness.

The sharp edges of thousands of thorns cut into Meadow's skin. The word *"BLEED,"* deep and ominous, emanated from somewhere deep within the tangled mass.

It was so focused on ending Meadow's life that it dropped its guard and left its back exposed. Its once vivacious vines now lay still all around it, except for those pressing into Meadow's skin.

An opening.

The theric screeched, leaping onto the creature and slashing at the vines with all four clawed hands. Black ichor, thorns, and leaves flew from the creature until the theric exposed fur.

Hissing, it plunged its decikip-long fangs directly into Ji'irifarana'ali's neck.

The vine-creature screamed in shock and rage, bucking from Meadow and whipping its vines in a frenzy. Though it struggled against the spider theric's eight limbs, it couldn't break free.

The black vines crumbled, exposing the broken gnoll beneath them.

J wavered, gagging, foaming at the mouth and bleeding from her eyes as she struggled to remain on her feet. As the venom ran its course, though, she convulsed and dropped to the sand. It was only then that the theric let go, backing away to allow the gnoll to die.

Meadow massaged his throat, sitting up with some difficulty. "Don't run," he said, reaching for the spider-creature, who was already looking for an escape. "Don't run, please. I already... I think I already knew."

It hesitated.

Delirious with pain and exhaustion, Meadow nevertheless pushed himself to his hooves so he could give chase. Though he stumbled on his first step, the theric caught him before he hit the ground.

Meadow said, "Thanks, Luka."

With a final jerk, the gnoll lay still, her lifeless eyes reflecting the stars.

CHAPTER FORTY-ONE

The Healer

No one died. Not even the den's alpha, Reclesti, nor any of the others who initially tried to stop J's attack. Ptery attributed it to the gnoll's inexperience. They *understood* magical items. You couldn't just put a powerful relic in the hands of a layperson and expect expertise. Had J trained to use the cube competently, the outcome might have been a lot worse.

Meadow called it dumb luck.

Reclesti declared the miracle a blessing from Aurapax, the god of light and the desert. As the residents of the oasis returned in ones and twos, then by the dozens, he promised a celebration to thank the golden god for his protection.

...All while the den's master healer urged him to sit down so they could repair his gaping head wound.

The den's resident liori worked to dig trapped people out of the rubble while mages of various disciplines repaired as much structural damage as possible. Any healers, even novices and apprentices, tended to cuts, broken bones, and burns. While injuries ranged from minor to grievous, everyone would survive. All things taken into account, it *was* a miracle.

Those who ultimately defeated the gnoll fared slightly worse than average, however. They all sat around a fireless faelight orb as Ptery checked their injuries, ranging from cuts and scrapes to burns and broken bones. Zeera *looked* the worst with charred skin covering nearly every centikip of her body, but she assured everyone that norsfar healed quickly on their own.

As she doused herself with a Wheriae-blessed canteen full of endless cold water.

Luka was magnificent and terrifying. Beautiful and deadly. Still in her spider form, she sat near the faelight orb with the others, the pale white light glimmering off her carapace, turning her green or purple depending on which way she moved. Like a centaur, her upper body remained *mostly* humanoid, with her abdomen resting on the ground behind her.

In her four arms, she held a redver—a type of eyeless vulture. A flock of them had descended to feed on the dead gnoll, so Luka took the opportunity to grab one of the red-feathered pests. She'd been intermittently plunging her fangs into it to feed for the past half hour.

Gross, but interesting.

She could not talk in her theric form. After a series of gestures and painstakingly-typed messages on her terminal, it turned out that she couldn't immediately shift back to human, either. Not until she finished eating to regain her energy.

"Are you hurt at all?" Ptery asked.

She fixed them with eight luminous green eyes and shook her head.

"Good. As soon as I'm done fixing everyone up, you have a story to tell. Don't think you're getting out of it."

Luka bared a mouthful of conical black teeth and looked away.

After assessing the damage, Ptery unwrapped the ruby-bladed dagger and got to work.

They knew the words to almost *every* necessary arcane Cantyr, but they feared Faoliia's rejection. What if they cast a more complicated Cantyr, and it didn't work? What if they weren't *ready?* It would suggest an inability to master more complicated Cantyrs, like ridding a body of magical poisons or cancers.

Or regrowing a limb, the ultimate healing that only the most dedicated masters could perform.

"Okay, Benji," they said. "Let me take a look at your shoulder."

Benji rolled partway onto his side, stretching his wing behind him and out of the way so Ptery could see the wound. Its clean edges still oozed, but J's knife had missed anything vital. The blade was just too short to pierce through the powerful shoulder and wing muscles.

Ptery's father once told them they were too flighty, too unmotivated, and too irreverent to ever master the more powerful Cantyrs. How could the healing goddess ever see favor in a lazy, disobedient child who could barely pay attention in school? Faoliia would laugh and watch with amusement as Ptery scarred their beautiful umber skin.

In all their years of study, Ptery only ever used one arcane Cantyr—a minor healing spell which they couldn't fail. In fact, it rarely failed for anyone. Acolytes and novices could often be heard using it to practice and also to garner favor with Faoliia. Although using it carried little risk of scarring, it also required *several applications* to repair more serious injuries, like the ones faced by Ptery's friends.

They could do it, though. Taking a deep breath, they sliced their palm and allowed a river of blood to splash into the sand. At the same time, they spoke the proper words. "*Yyika ayakmi kc Yyika ayakari.*"

Pressing their non-bleeding hand against Benji's thick fur, they waited for Faoliia's blessing. It appeared as a red glow, which briefly suffused the injury, then dissipated into hundreds of twinkling little motes of light.

They repeated the process twice.

After the third time, they felt a dizzy little high. A warning.

But Benji's wound was closed and scabbed over.

"Much better, thank you," Benji said.

"It's as good as I can do." Ptery opened their hand. The deep cuts were gone, leaving behind a smear of red. "The bleeding has stopped. The muscles are knit. It won't leave a scar. Now for your tail—"

"No, don't bother," Benji said with a sigh. He curled it around, revealing a mass of strange, blue, web-like regenerative tissue where the telson used to be. It was no longer bleeding. "This thing apparently heals on its own. Too bad for me."

Good for Ptery, though, with as much as healing took out of them. They leaned against a half-burned tree so they could rest and catch their breath.

"My turn!" Meadow said.

"In a minute," Ptery replied. Meadow pouted.

"Ptery is pale. You should eat," the troll named Mud said. He, along with his companion, Coriander, had joined them around the faelight after the battle. Neither had been explicitly invited, but no one asked them to leave, either.

"This *really* hurts, though." Meadow pointed to his arm. The compound break left a minor laceration and terrible, puffy bruising spreading across his skin. With as chipper as Meadow seemed, Ptery suspected some severe nerve damage underlying the gruesome surface, masking much of the pain.

It was probably more than Ptery had the capability to heal.

"Let me just..." They stood, waiting for a wave of vertigo to pass. "Let me check—Zeera, are you sure you're all right?"

"I know it *looks* bad, but I really will heal up on my own. I guess If you still have the energy, I wouldn't mind some help with this one." She pulled up her bloodstained pantleg, revealing an ugly slash from ankle to knee. "Sharp bit of wood got me when the gnoll threw me through the cabin. If you fix this, I can look for whatever bits are left of the artifact."

"Not many, I suspect," Ptery said. They knelt next to her, studying the cut. Thankfully, it wasn't too deep, just ragged and likely to become infected without intervention. "I think most of the pieces went into old J over there. Any idea why it exploded?"

"Artifacts from the age of the golden elves are *notoriously* difficult to destroy," she mused. "So I don't know." As she idly scratched at her chin, blackened ash fell away to reveal healed, grey skin beneath. Disgusting, but Ptery was transfixed.

"Texts hypothesize they're created by the old gods themselves," Benji added. "Made out of elements that aren't even native to Erit."

"And only specifically tailored magic or a god's curse can break them. Usually," Zeera said.

"That vine-thing that ate J wasn't a god." Meadow pointed over to where the gnoll's body lay. "She told me before she died. I think it was the last thing she said."

"Interesting," Zeera said. "If I can find a piece and bring it back to the coven, maybe we can find out what happened to it. Get some answers. If nothing else, whatever's left of it needs to be contained."

Made sense.

Steeling themself, Ptery sliced into their palm again, repeating the healing process and speaking the Cantyr. *"Yyika ayakmi kc Yyika ayakari."*

"What's it mean?" Zeera asked as Ptery pressed their hand against her leg. The red glow returned, surrounding the cut. Although it pulled the edges closed and stopped the bleeding, it didn't entirely heal it. The spell wasn't powerful enough for that.

Exhausted, Ptery sat down in the sand, reached for Zeera's canteen, and poured the cool water over their hands. "Directly translated, it means 'Life—meager (me) unto Life—meager (you).' It's some ancient harpy language, I think." They sighed, eyes half-lidded as they stared at Meadow's arm. "I don't think I can heal a break that bad. We'll have to get one of the other healers."

Meadow pouted *harder*.

"Odd way to say it," Coriander observed. "The syntax is strange."

Ptery rubbed their wet hands on their shirt, leaving behind a red smudge. Glancing at Coriander, they tried to determine her sincerity, although she seemed more curious than derogatory. "Harpies put importance on certain words. *Yyika* is 'life.' Or... One of the words for it. Mm." They flapped their hand dismissively. "They've a lot of words for 'life,' oddly. It's the most important part, so it comes first."

"I think I see your problem," Meadow said, scratching his chin. "You keep doing the one that means *small*. You just gotta say one that means 'big heal,' and you won't have to do so many."

Ptery studied the backs of their arms. Rather than the usual warm brown, their skin had paled several shades. "Healing magic doesn't work quite like that," they said, wistful. "Oh, it'd be so easy if I could just wave my hand and demand a stronger heal from Faoliia, but she has her rules."

"I read the book," Benji said. "That healing book you got me. Remember? I bet you could do a stronger heal, especially with the ruby dagger. And especially because—"

"Oh, do you know more about healing than I do now?" Ptery snapped.

"Yes, actually," Benji said with a shrug. "Logistically, at least. You've been doing this for most of your life, and you're *good* at it, Ter. Your dad was wrong, okay? You're a born healer. I could feel the power when you healed my sprain, and I felt it now."

Ptery shivered when Benji brought up Evialor. Never a *dad*. Only a father and only because he had to be.

But... Benji was probably right.

"If you're wrong, I'll scar," Ptery said.

"I'm not wrong. Look, Faoliia believed in you enough to give you that dagger, right? Have some faith in her, too. Trust me, and trust her."

Luka huffed, stood, and tossed the shell of the redver aside before wandering off toward the bus. Despite the chaos from J's attack, the road castle thankfully made it out of the fight unscathed.

"Where does Luka go?" Mud asked.

"She doesn't like the gods very much," Ptery answered, even though they still didn't know why.

Benji got up to follow her, but she squealed and pointed back to the faelight. Cowed, he laid his ears back and re-settled himself in the sand. "She'll be okay."

Ptery closed their eyes. Despite Luka's displeasure, they felt Faoliia's favor in Benji's encouragement, which was a good sign. *Plus*, they didn't even have to look up the words because they'd known them for aurs.

Still, trying a new heal, and with everyone watching...

"You can do it," Benji repeated.

A warm breeze ruffled Ptery's feathers. It was either a sign or a stray thermal from the large campfire. Ptery took it as the former and shuffled over to Meadow, who held out his arm.

Never had Faoliia rejected one of Ptery's spells, even though she often refused to favor other healers with the same level of experience. Consequently, Ptery remained completely unscarred.

But what if...

The truth settled on Ptery like a thousand tons of stone. They didn't believe in themself. Not really. They'd only ever cast spells that could not fail.

Benji believed in them. Meadow clearly did, given the hopeful glint in his eye. Coriander and Mud didn't strike Ptery as the types who reveled in the defeat of others, even though they'd all just met. Maybe they believed in Ptery, too.

"Right," Ptery said, running careful fingers along the length of Meadow's arm. Putting it off wouldn't raise their chance of success. After a deep centering breath, they sliced their palm.

Deeper. The spell required *more*.

Determined, they curled their hand into a fist, allowing the sacrifice to trickle into the earth. One drop. Two. As the second droplet made contact, they spoke the *Cantyr: "A'Aiyy'Og'Wii."*

Ptery had their doubts. So many doubts. So many stories of healers pushing too far and too fast, pursuing the more complicated heals like the bone-mending *Cantyr* they just performed. Their mind filled with the healers of legend, covered in so many scars from their failures. Yes, eventually, Faoliia would leave her *mark* on Ptery, but they feared it would come too soon. Their father told them—

Their father said a lot of things.

Please, Ptery prayed. *Let it work.*

They rested the palm of their other hand against Meadow's arm, and a veritable explosion of red light pulsed from it.

Meadow breathed a contented sigh of relief.

It worked.

"Look, I can move it right again!" Meadow bent his arm at the elbow and shoulder at the same time. "Still a little sore..."

It *worked!*

So many pathways opened before them now, all because they took a chance and listened to their friends instead of their father. They could cast a *complicated spell.* A real spell. One with an initial fail rate of half! Checking their palm, they found the wound completely healed and felt Faoliia's smug favor in their heart.

She believed in them. They could believe in themself, too.

"Uh, Ptery." Meadow waved his hand in front of their face. "It's still sore!"

"Er. It will be for a little while," Ptery cautioned, grabbing Meadow's arm and lowering it to his side. "You have to give the healing time to set. Please."

"But it's like it was never even broke!" Meadow said, holding it out to Mud.

The troll poked it. Meadow allowed it, turning this way and that so everyone could get a good look. Mud said, "I've never seen healing in action before."

"And the ruby dagger," Coriander added.

The implication of the observation was clear as she spoke the name of the instrument in reverent tones. She believed Ptery to be a skilled healer just because of the very implement they possessed.

Maybe they were. And now there were so many other spells they could try, should the need arise. As they looked around at everyone, though, they hoped the need would never present itself.

For now, they needed to rest, or they'd pass out.

Sitting cross-legged in the sand, Ptery re-wrapped the dagger in its bindings, taking special care with the red flower. The petals still shimmered as if freshly plucked from the earth, the potential magic still safely tucked within. What spell could Ptery possibly create when healing already had such a rich, thorough history?

Perhaps the gods had plans.

Fate. Bah.

With the ruby dagger stowed, they leaned against a rock that was still warm from the heat of the day. Conversation faded around them as they began to drift off, the fragrant desert air lulling them into the most relaxing slumber...

"Hey! Hey Ptery!"

Ptery scrunched up their nose and tried to ignore Meadow.

"Pteryyyyyyyyyy!"

With the legendary patience of Ghiscaer's silent priests, Ptery resisted picking up a rock and using it to break off Meadow's other horn. "Xax's venom. Yes, Meadow?"

"Oh," Mud said. "They are grumpy when you wake them up."

Meadow rolled his eyes. "They're almost always grumpy. Hey, Ptery, guess what? These two?" He pointed at Coriander and Mud. "We saw them in Faun-anin. They were at that little concert we did. You remember?"

Ptery scratched their chin. They did remember Mud's green fur and Coriander's *excessive tallness*. "Oh yes. You're following us, then? Our first fans?"

The prospect excited them enough that they momentarily forgot about being cross.

"We were guided," Coriander said. "Nebula has been pushing me to find you. It's a good thing we did, too. As soon as we drove up, we knew you needed help."

Meadow snapped his fingers. "I saw you two, then J got all wiggly and let me go."

Coriander nodded. "It's dream magic. I couldn't do it alone, but with Mud, we could cast it together. It was supposed to make that *thing* fall asleep. But it was Mud's first spell, so it went a little sideways."

"First spell?" Meadow paused. "But trolls aren't..."

Mud offered a shy grin. "Mud is a troll who can do magic. Nebula gave it to me. I don't know why."

Ptery met Meadow's eyes, then Benji's. They all seemed to share a similar concern—too many *weird things* were happening for all this to be coincidence. Too many god-related things.

Interesting, but terrifying. The word "fate" danced around in Ptery's thoughts again and they didn't like it.

"I'm sorry to have appeared the way we did," Cori said. "We planned to meet up with you sooner. But that monster you were fighting... I think it tried to trap me in a dream. It didn't want me to find you."

"The Dym," Mud said.

"We've been calling it the Shade," Meadow added.

Cori narrowed her eyes. "Do you know what threads are?"

Meadow shook his head, but Benji said, "It's how you find people in dreams. Their connections."

Coriander nodded. "The creature that invaded my dream had sixteen threads connected to it. Mud counted. Nothing should have that many threads tied to its life force."

"There's sixteen gods, not counting Chaos and Order. And no one does." Zeera frowned, then amended, "Fifteen, with Petalvine dead."

No one said anything for a tick, then Coriander asked, "Petalvine is dead?"

"It's... not exactly common knowledge, nestling," Ptery said, "But yes."

"She was killed by that Shade." Meadow bowed his head, kicking at the sand. "And I don't think killing the gnoll stopped it. It's still alive somewhere, and now we know it's aware of us."

Mud said, "But there were sixteen threads. There were sixteen, I'm sure."

Coriander ruffled the fluff on his head. "Maybe we need to find out why."

Meadow stood, limping on his sore hip. Ptery would have to fix that, too, once they rested. Not tonight, though. Tomorrow morning would be soon enough.

"That's why we're all the way out here in the desert," Meadow said. "I'm supposed to figure out why all the plants are dying and why Petalvine's gone. If I don't... Uh. I'm pretty sure Wheriae's gonna eat my face. You know, besides the whole planet dying and all. We're going to the place where the gods rest. It's called the Godplain."

"Then we're coming with you," Coriander said. Mud nodded, resolute.

"One problem," Ptery said. "We don't know where the Godplain is."

"Wheriae gave us coordinates." Benji held up his crest. "But they led us here. And the Godplain... It's not here."

"Actually..." Zeera tapped her fingers together, biting her lip. "Are you sure those coordinates are from Wheriae? He sent you here?"

Meadow nodded.

"Right. Okay," Zeera said. "I wasn't being entirely honest before. The emperor and his family are the guardians of the Godplain. It's... A very old secret. The whole reason that the gods let the empire continue to exist after the elves killed the Old Gods. I know where the Godplain is, and I'll tell you how to find it."

CHAPTER FORTY-TWO

A Kind of Magic

Having sufficiently fed on the redver enough to restore her internal magic reserve, Luka shifted back to human well out of view of the others. She found her unburnt clothes still in the pile where she left them, thankfully, and dressed before anyone could follow her.

Then, she wandered over toward the dead gnoll, ignoring the stench inherent to hours-dead corpses. Although someone had covered J with a blanket, Luka could still see the outline of a real, actual person.

A person she'd killed. She'd never killed before, save for the chickens and rabbits she had to catch so she had the energy to shift. It didn't bother her as much as it should have. Then again, perhaps the gnoll deserved to die, which lessened any feelings of remorse she might have had.

It couldn't have been reasoned with. Right?

She did the right thing.

"You could have told me."

She looked over her shoulder. Benji stood a couple kips away, eyes downcast.

"I wanted to," Luka said. "I didn't know how."

"I was there when it happened." Benji looked up at her, tilting his head. "I mean... after. In the hospital. You didn't have to tell me then. We barely—I mean, we'd just met. But maybe if you'd told me when I turned, when I was attacked—Sorry. That's selfish."

"It is. A little." Luka smiled, ruffling his mane as he sat next to her. "You're right, though. I almost told you then, but it'd been so long, I couldn't think of a way to bring it up."

"It's okay, you know." Benji leaned against her. "You can trust us. Even Ptery."

"I know."

"Good. Are you okay?"

Luka shrugged, digging her bare feet into the sand and soaking up its warmth. "Just trying to figure out what to tell everyone. Now that Ptery's fixed everyone up, they'll all want to know. Well, Meadow will, at least. I can't tell 'em nothing."

"I hate to say it, but... You're right," Benji said. "Reason I came over here is 'cuz Meadow's trying to get me to tell him things I don't know. But I'll be with you, promise."

She stood, brushing the sand off her overalls. "I love you, you know," she said.

The admission came out of nowhere, but it was the right time to say it. Even in the deep dark of the desert, surrounded by the stench of dead gnoll. After all, they'd all just had a little taste of the danger they might find on their journey, and if she didn't tell Benji she loved him now...

What if she never got another chance?

She expected him to be flustered or look away, but he beamed, butting his head against her chest and drawing her into a powerful embrace. "I love you, too," he said. "But you knew that. I knew that. And I'm always here for you, no matter what."

Luka had nothing else to say.

They returned to the faelight and sat down. Benji wrapped one wing around her, and she pulled a blanket over her legs.

"So," Luka said, and everyone turned to look at her. Although she didn't entirely trust Zeera and the newcomers, they saw her theric form too, so she needed to defend herself to them, as well. Just in case. "So. That thing I did."

"It's quite the secret," Ptery muttered. "I'm surprised you kept it for so long."

They lay wrapped in their sleeping bag, eyes half-closed and ringed with dark circles. For the first time ever, Luka felt a powerful, glowing respect for the healer; she had never realized how much of a sacrifice healing demanded. They always acted like it was easy or no big deal. Maybe even something they studied casually in their spare time out of boredom.

As much as she hated Ptery's love for the gods, she couldn't hate Ptery.

"I think Meadow was onto me," Luka said. "At least, he suspected. A couple times, it was hard to sneak away. But I try to spend an hour or two shifted every day so I never forget. Complacent therics..." She trailed off. Benji bumped her shoulder.

"Complacent therics?" Coriander prompted.

"Therics have to spend twenty-eight hours in their alter form every cycle," Benji explained. "Er... If they don't, they go feral on the night of the new moon. They lose their minds."

"I decided right from the start that I wasn't going to become like the theric who bit me," Luka said. "I wasn't going to attack someone. Not ever. So I make sure to shift every day. If I keep a schedule, it'll never happen."

"You were attacked?" Ptery whispered.

"Most therics aren't," Luka said. "Most therics ask to be changed 'cuz there's power in it, right?"

"For many species," Zeera added. "Humans become therics. Elves become norsfar. A little bit more negative for others, but still."

Luka nodded. "Now that we know the limitations and the rules, it's pretty easy to keep yourself out of trouble. But sometimes, therics still go feral, and—"

She'd never get that night out of her head.

"Do you want to tell us what happened?" Ptery asked, voice surprisingly gentle.

For so long, Luka hadn't wanted to tell anyone. It was supposed to be a secret only she, her parents, and her doctors knew. If people didn't know, they couldn't hurt her with the knowledge, and she could maintain friendships from a comfortable distance.

But now the secret demanded release. She wanted to tell them.

Maybe she wanted their pity.

"It was a few aurs back, before I met you guys," she said. "There were rumors, but I thought they were just campfire stories. You know, one kid says he sees a feral theric, then *everyone's* talking about it, and it's on the news, and there's warning signs and reward posters. 'Cuz if you go feral, you're stuck that way for a whole month."

Ptery sat up, scowling.

"I didn't believe 'em. I thought it'd be impossible for someone to go feral 'cuz we've known how to avoid it for decaurs. Like, *how stupid could you be* to forget, right?" She shrugged. "So this one night, I asked my brother—"

"You have a brother?" Meadow asked.

"Had," Luka replied.

The others said nothing, allowing a natural moment of silence—save for the crackling of the large campfire—to settle over the camp.

"His name was Claey," Luka said, smiling at the memory. "We were twins, but I was older by a couple minutes, so sometimes he felt like he had to listen to me. Or maybe he just humored me. I dunno. He wasn't ever into building stuff like I was, but he loved to read. He was so smart. I think you woulda liked him, Benji."

Benji half-smiled. Luka continued. "There'd been a storm the night before, and there's these rocks... Ah... Kinda electrically charged. Sometimes I'd tell Claey that it felt like stealing from Ivriarck 'cuz she wouldn't let me learn magic. I tried a few times... Electrical. Metal. Anything that would help me with what I did, but I could never learn. When there were storms, though, I'd go out looking for these rocks left behind when lightning strikes the ground. I could dig 'em up and power my projects with them. They hold a charge forever. I've never had one run out. Pixel runs on 'em, in fact. Claey went with me, and just as we were starting to dig, I was attacked from behind. I didn't even hear the thing coming."

"That gash on your arm..." Ptery said. "The one you never let me try to heal. I thought you were being a distrustful cow, honestly."

Luka arched her eyebrows.

"Ah, sorry," Ptery muttered. "It makes sense now. You can't heal theric-inflicted wounds."

"This isn't even the worst one," Luka said. Her back was a mess, and for a long time after the attack, she couldn't move her shoulder. But while the external signs of her injuries remained, she healed within. Mostly. "It was a bear, I think. That's what the wanted posters said, but I never got a good look at it. It pushed me down, and it was standing on me. I woulda been dead right then if Claey hadn't thrown a rock at it. One of those electric ones. It shocked the thing. Pissed it off."

"Oh no," Benji muttered.

"Yeah..." Luka replied. "It went after him. It just left me there, and I watched it just... tear into him. It dragged him off. He was calling for me, and I just..."

"Luka was hurt," Mud said. "What could you do?"

"I dunno. Somethin'. I mean, looking back, I feel like I could have..."

Benji nudged her again.

"They took me to the hospital, and I slept through the search," she went on. "They found his arm and part of a leg. They think the theric ate the rest of him. Therics are like that, you know? When they go crazy. There's no reasoning with them. No getting through to them." She couldn't help a laugh. "All this time, Ptery's been afraid of Benji n' they shoulda been afraid of me."

Ptery looked away.

"I met Benji when I was in the hospital," Luka went on. "He was cleaning the floors. He'd stop in every day to see me."

"So he knew?" Meadow asked. "You knew all this time?"

Benji shook his head. "No. She didn't say anything for *days*. Then she told me she missed her guitar. I got her parents to bring it in for her. She showed me how to play."

Luka nodded. When she'd thought she'd never be happy again, as she'd wondered how—or if—she'd be able to attend Claey's funeral... as she thought about how it'd be easier if she'd just died, music came to her mind.

If Benji hadn't come to see her every day, maybe she wouldn't have made it. They had a bond back then, maybe because he never asked questions even though he'd seen her scars. He must have suspected some sort of magical injury for her to be in the special ward, but he never intruded. And when she threw her existence into her music, he just sat and watched her play for hours.

He brought her extra ice cream from the kitchens. He made sure to throw her sheets in a heater before bringing her a new set.

Ptery said, "At least we know why you had that vision and why old Ziro wanted Meadow to bring you along."

Benji shot them a look, but Luka laughed. "Yeah. I kinda suspected. I can kick ass if I need to."

"Quite," Ptery agreed.

"I bought the Road Castle to cover it up," Luka said. "I thought maybe if I led you guys in a different direction, you wouldn't suspect anything else. But then... I didn't have much of a choice. I couldn't just..."

"It's quite an interesting form," Ptery said. "I don't think I've ever seen a spider or any insect. I've mostly seen lions and leopards and wolves and the like."

"A few birds," Meadow added.

"That's because I'm a magical dead-end. A Terminus Theric," Luka said. "I can't spread the curse 'cuz magic can't pass through me, so I've got the venom instead. It's why I couldn't learn magic no matter how much I wanted to. And if you're a Terminus, you're a bug. Or a spider. I hear there's one guy who's a starfish somewhere on Rhogot."

"The poor fellow," Ptery said. "Well, it was quite the entrance you had. What a way to tell us. Well played, love. Well played."

Luka smiled. "You're not the only one who loves drama."

Ptery tossed their hair. "I don't *love* drama, nestling. I *live* drama. There's a difference."

"And now you know why I hate the gods," she said, with a pointed look at Ptery.

They narrowed their eyes.

"I wanted to learn magic. I thought there was something wrong with me, but all this time, I just... *couldn't.* I'm magic-null, which means I can't cast it. But I can be affected by spells. So I'd pray to Ivriarck and Qit every night for their help, and this is what they gave me. A fucking curse. And you..." She gestured at Ptery, unable to keep the resentment out of her voice. "You're a miracle healer."

For once, Ptery was speechless.

"I loved them as much as you. I swear. Even had a little shrine to Ivriarck in my backyard, so I don't understand..."

Her face was wet.

Was she *crying?*

She hadn't cried about this for *aurs!*

"Uh," Benji said. "Could you all leave us alone for a few?"

"Yeah, sure," Zeera said. "We'll just be over by the road castle."

Coriander and Mud stood as well. "It's nice to meet you," Cori said.

"C'mon, you two!" Ptery called. "I'm going to show you how to push all the buttons on the dashboard! It makes Luka *so mad!*"

Luka sighed.

"Mud will prevent the banshee from pushing all the buttons," Mud said.

As they followed the others toward the bus, Luka muttered her thanks.

Once everyone was out of earshot, Benji took her hand, curling his paw around her fingers. With his *telis,* he gently caressed the back of her hand. "I think you probably saved our lives tonight."

Only because she had to. How could she just sit by and watch that gnoll kill everyone? If she had, she wouldn't have anyone to keep a secret *from*. At least now she'd be able to shift in front of the others to get her time in. Then she could read and play on her terminal instead of running off into the dark to hide, like some criminal.

Luka shrugged. "You would have figured it out."

Benji bit his lip, then said, "I do wish you would have trusted me. Before. I know why you didn't, but..."

"But I never *distrusted* you, either. Maybe I was embarrassed about it. I don't want anyone to look at me and think of me as... that thing."

"Embarrassed? But you're *magnificent!"* Benji blurted out the compliment, then his cheeks turned such a dark shade of black he looked like a charcoal brick.

"I wouldn't call that *magnificent—"*

"Don't." His *telis* brushed against her lips. "You don't see yourself as I see you. As the others see you. You're beautiful, Lu. And... and how could anyone—How could anyone not think—I mean..."

Tripped up on his words, he fell into silence.

"I didn't keep it from you to hurt you, I promise."

"I know. Like I said before..." He pressed his forehead to hers again, closing his eyes. "If anything happens to you, you don't need to go through it alone ever again. I'm here. I promise."

Tears stung her eyes as she wrapped her arms around his neck, holding him close. He rested a paw on her back, careful of his strength, before he embraced her in earnest.

Then Meadow ruined the moment by shouting, "Hey, Luka! Can you make *webs?!*"

"You can't kill him," Benji purred.

She knew. But it was fun to imagine it sometimes.

CHAPTER FORTY-THREE

Dial it Back

A couple days later, well-rested and newly healed, Meadow tested out his repaired leg by hopping from one rock formation to another. Ptery said they wouldn't fix him again if he fell, but Meadow had all the confidence in the world that they would.

Reclesti, the alpha liori of the Oasis Den, sat at the base of one of the formations just as Meadow reached the apex of a particularly daring leap. "Are you in a band?" the manticore asked. "I saw you unloading your instruments when you arrived."

Meadow skidded down the rock, executing a terrible landing. He would have fallen face-first into the sand had Reclesti not caught him with one giant paw. After recovering,

Meadow did his best to pretend he *meant* to stumble. "Yeah! And hey, great to see you up and about. I thought you were... you know. Dead?"

Reclesti laughed. "It takes more than a crazy gnoll to kill a manticore. Although I can't remember most of what happened. Thank you for saving the oasis."

"Ah." Meadow waved a hand, embarrassed. Luka did most of the work, after all. Meadow just flailed around a lot and broke both bones in his forearm. That hurt. "You mentioned our band."

"Yes. Look, some of the residents are shaken up a bit. It's no wonder. Many of them make their home here, and a couple families lost most of their possessions in the fire. I was hoping a little music might lift their spirits."

Meadow's ears perked up. "You want us to play?"

"Would you? We can pay."

Meadow would have done it for nothing, just for the experience of having a sizable audience. They might need the minir on their journey, though, so he nodded. "Yeah! We'd love to. Just tell us when and where to be."

Benji's breath came in rapid bursts as everyone waited backstage.

The hyperventilation started as soon as Meadow told everyone they had a gig and worsened as they set up for the concert. When Coriander, who turned out to be a brilliant sound technician, told them they were good to go, Benji swore quietly under a frenzied whimper.

Now, in the small pre-concert space afforded to them, Meadow could actually feel Benji trembling.

"You okay, buddy?" Meadow asked, his sequined shirt sparkling in the low light. It was clear to the others that Benji was absolutely losing his nerve. His eyes were wide and unfocused, his wings dragging along the floor wherever he went.

Benji shook his head.

"C'mon." Meadow rubbed his shoulder, smiling. "We got you all dressed in your sparkly cuffs and whatnot. Deep breaths. You can do this. We've been waiting for this for aurs, Ben! We got a gig! Our first big break!"

Everything Meadow said went into one tufted ear and right out the other.

"They'll—they'll run away," Benji said. "They'll see me, and they'll be afraid. And what if—" He turned to look back at his tail. "Oh, right. No quills. It's gone. Okay, that's okay. Good. But if they don't like liori—"

"It's a den *full of liori,*" Ptery said. "You've just got stage fright!"

This audience wouldn't be like the ones Benji was used to. Meadow recalled the decent but sparse crowd from the puzzle competition, and even those hundred or so spectators made Benji nervous. This time he'd be playing a bass, *with paws*, in front of many more people.

"But... I'm..." Benji backed up into a temporary wall, which rolled backward. "I can't do it. What if I can't play? My *telis...*"

Luka, dressed in the flashiest outfit Ptery could force her to wear, knelt in front of him. He should have towered over her, but he was so squished inward with fear that they were eye level. "Hey," she said. "You can do this. I've seen you *writing*. You can play a guitar. I know it."

"I don't know why I'm—" Benji started, but Luka hushed him.

"Sometimes trauma isn't what you want it to be," she said. "You can't decide what bothers you and what doesn't. Last time you were in front of a lot of people, you were attacked."

"But we're—and I should have—"

She shook her head. "Look at me. Something happened to you. It was just a few spans ago, right? And you're scared. I get it. Sometimes I'm still afraid of what people'll think of me. But fuck 'em. If they want to make a big deal about it, they aren't welcome here. They can leave."

"What if Ptery was right?" Benji asked, his golden eyes wide with terror. "What if I see all those people and I just—what if I snap? What if—"

"You won't," Ptery said. "If anyone should be afraid of that, it's me. Not you."

Benji, lost in his fears, didn't hear them. "There's just so many people out there. And if they run, they could—what if someone dies? What if someone's crushed, or—or what if—"

Meadow couldn't understand stage fright himself. He *loved* to be the center of attention. The more people watching him, the better. He could sympathize, though. "How do you prep for your competitions?" he asked. "There's people watching then, too."

"But I don't have to play a bass with *telis,*" Benji whined. "Oh, gods..."

He continued to oscillate between his worry that people would be afraid of a liori and his fear that he'd disappoint everyone by being unable to play.

Until Luka, her voice deadpan, said, "Well, then I guess we take that chance together."

She looked sick; a greenish glow spread across the bridge of her nose and down her cheeks, but she had their attention. "I only have two, maybe three minutes to talk at this point, depending on how long I can hold this off."

No, she wasn't sick. Her face was actually turning green. Ptery swore.

"Are you shifting?" Meadow asked. Did they all somehow trigger it with this backstage stress? He wasn't even sure that was a thing with therics. Just in case, though, he added, "If Benji promises to calm down, can you stop it?"

"I'm doing it on purpose," Luka said. Her skin took on a strange luster as her face formed an indent right down the middle. Her canine teeth were already showing past her lip and turning midnight black. "And no, I can't stop it once it starts."

"Wonderful," Ptery grumbled. "Now we'll have *two* of you out of commission."

Luka went on. "I've never played a guitar in front of a crowd while shifted, so this'll be the first time. Benji, you won't be alone."

His jaw was slack. "But—I didn't mean... You shouldn't feel like you—"

"When have I ever done anything I didn't want to do?" she asked.

He paused, pressing his lips together, dubious.

Luka winced as one of her arms increased in bulk, tearing her silken sleeve, then the seam of her shirt down one side.

"Oh," Ptery lamented. "That shirt was expensive."

"I told you I didn't want to wear it." Luka actually smiled, holding up her arm as it split in two, right down the middle, like tearing paper. Surprised, Ptery stumbled backward, their fall only broken by the fact that Benji happened to be right behind them.

"Did—did that hurt?" Benji asked.

Luka shook her head. "It used to, back when this first started happening. If you fight it, it's... unpleasant."

"You'll give me a heart attack if you keep doing that," Ptery said. "Then there'll be three of us down. Meadow'll have to be a one-man band. And we all know how that'll turn out."

"Hey, I could do it!" Meadow argued.

She ignored them both, her attention still on Benji. "People think therics are monsters, too. So if we're both monsters on stage, I thought maybe you wouldn't feel so bad. Not that I think they'll care either way."

"You're not a—" Benji started almost automatically. But it was hard to deny the sentiment as her nose pushed into her face with a sickening crunch and disappeared.

"Did *that* hurt?" Meadow asked.

She rolled her eyes just before they turned a uniform neon green.

It was fascinating to watch, if not a bit disturbing. More eyes appeared, each the same stunningly vibrant green. Her other arm split. As her chest widened, the fancy, expensive shirt tore entirely; she covered herself with her arms as if to keep her modesty, but her chest had already flattened into four hard plates.

"If I'm not a monster, then you aren't," she said, her voice weakening. "I mean, I guess we—Kh. Hh. I guesshhhkk... Sssor-ry—hh—" Her lip curled as the greenish-grey chitin worked its way down her neck. Every time she tried to speak, she had to gasp for breath, revealing the black interior of her mouth and a million cone-shaped teeth. "I won'tkh—"

Her voice tapered off into a squeal, like nails on a chalk-board.

"That's why she doesn't talk, I'd wager," Meadow said, el-bowing Ptery.

She turned away from them, coughing.

"Oh, gods," Ptery muttered under their breath. "Luka, your back."

It was crisscrossed with scars. For a moment, they were pink, but as the grey-green carapace worked its way down her back, they turned stark white, gouged into her skin, unhealed. The reason for her affliction rested over one shoulder—a series of very clear puncture wounds from the teeth of some large creature.

No one had commented on these old injuries after the at-tack. Perhaps they'd all been too worn out to even notice them.

Meadow shuffled to her side, putting a comforting hand on one shoulder, which was starting to sprout course, almost sharp spines. One of her hands, now a three-fingered talon, rested atop his.

She was shaking.

Her face no longer had any human quality to it. Except for the shape of her eyes, Meadow could barely tell it was Luka at all. Her soft red hair formed into clumps and hardened, stretching into spikes that stood on end, quietly rattling against each other like a particularly eerie wind chime.

Both of her legs also split in half, stretching and segmenting into spindly spider legs. She nearly stumbled but managed to regain her balance just as her backside ballooned into an abdomen. Caught off-guard, Meadow bumbled out of the way as Luka squealed what might have been an apology.

No one said anything. Luka didn't even move, not even to breathe. She was eerily still, although the tips of her hairs trembled just slightly with her nervousness.

"I suppose I should say something comforting, but now there's two of you who won't go on, and I'm rather livid," Ptery said, talons tapping on the floor with irritation. "And I could probably sing without bass, sure. But without guitar..."

Luka finally looked over her shoulder, then turned slowly, all eight bright eyes focused on Ptery.

Ptery shrunk back. "Big spider," they said. "Sorry."

Luka's eyes smiled in a way that suggested she was quite entertained by the reaction. She also—somehow—looked as tired as Meadow felt watching the shift happen. Reaching for her guitar, Heliotrope, she gently separated it from the stand and draped the strap over her shoulder. A moment later, the side panels lit up in their brilliant, eye-catching purple.

"You can play?" Benji asked. "Like that?"

Luka shrugged, her attention on Benji for just a few extra seconds before she pointed to his bass.

Benji shook his head. "How do we deal with it if we can't play?"

"Who cares?" Meadow said. "They're all out there for a good time, right? Even if we suck, they just want to smile. So we'll give 'em a show."

This time, Luka stepped forward, moving fluidly on four legs. She picked up the bass—plain compared to her own flashy guitar—and held it out. Benji took it in his paws, indecisiveness on his features before he slung it over his shoulder and under a wing. "Okay. Yeah," he said. "Right, let's do it."

"Finally," Ptery muttered, mopping their brow with their usual dramatic flair.

With a giant theric added to the mix, it took them a bit longer to shuffle from what served as their green room to the stage's right wing. Once they made it, though, Meadow peered around the edge of the open curtain to see just how many people they'd be playing to. Reclesti told him they'd have a decent audience.

Meadow estimated at least five hundred.

"I see Coriander and Mud," he said. "They're in the sound booth, giving me a thumbs-up. Oh, there's Zeera. She's a bat. Hanging from a tree about ten rows back."

Benji hunkered down next to Meadow, his ears pinned back. Despite his great size, he seemed so small. His claws dug nervous divots into the floor as he purred subconsciously—not from contentment, but with fear.

"It'll be okay," Meadow said, patting his shoulder.

He snapped out of whatever nightmare scenario he was imagining, his wings trembling. Taking a deep breath, he said, "I know."

Luka towered almost a foot above him now, green carapace shimmering in the overhead spotlights. Her focus was on the stage, her chin held high as she ignored Ptery's constant staring. To be fair, it was hard not to stare, considering less than an hour ago, she'd been a short, temperamental little human mechanic. Meadow rested a hand on one of her arms, giving the hard shell a pat.

"Y'all right?" Meadow whispered.

She looked down. The two eyes that were the right shape offered a smile while the other six stared, unblinking. The smallest pair was so tiny, Meadow could barely see them through the bristles over them.

Honestly, she was kind of pretty. Terrifying, but pretty.

"Right. Well, nestlings. I suppose we ought to get out there," Ptery said. They squeezed between Meadow and Luka, bravely stepping out on the stage, despite having no read of their audience.

A smattering of applause greeted them.

Luka squared her shoulders and followed.

Meadow heard the strange, collective gasp from the crowd—unified as if they'd been planning it. The gentle murmurs became high-pitched, verging on panic. To be fair, Luka's theric form was one of the most intimidating creatures Meadow had ever seen, far beyond the comparative simplicity of a liori.

How could they know she wouldn't hurt a fly?

Well, maybe a fly. She was a spider, after all. She'd probably hurt a gnoll, too, since she already had. Probably not a human or faun, though, Meadow hoped.

Struck with an idea, he followed Ptery to their mic at the front of the stage rather than ducking behind his drum kit. He hoped this would be one of his better ideas and not like the one that led to Petalvine's auxiliary temple being filled with cow-shaped flowers that bellowed obscenities all day.

Oh, he'd suffered for that one.

Ptery graciously stepped aside and handed Meadow the microphone as he reached for the stand. Even if their multi-talented singer could work the crowd into a frenzy without batting an eye, it wasn't a frenzy they needed right now. It was calm. And Meadow could dispel the crowd's rising fear.

Before he could say a word, though, Benji slid onto the stage, perching himself as near to the wing as he could. Compared to Luka's appearance, the audience seemed merely curious, as they were used to liori.

Although he relaxed, his nervous purring registered through the mic and transferred through the speakers.

Kudos to Cori's sound system, Meadow supposed.

Right. Well. It was the biggest gathering they'd ever played to, and with people already jostling nervously, they were about to lose everyone.

"Okay!" Meadow said. "Thanks for coming. We're—"

Before he could finish, Luka mis-stepped; her unwieldy abdomen unbalanced the top amp on her stack, which sent it crashing to the stage floor. The microphones squealed in protest, their feedback drowning out Benji's rumble.

Benji growled, both front paws covering his ears.

Despite her face being a hard shell, a pale white blush sprung to Luka's cheeks. She moved fluidly to pick up the amp, legs working in absolute harmony. It was amazing watching her move so easily, though it made Meadow realize that she'd been suffering alone with this curse for years—enough time to learn this beautiful grace.

Ptery's feathers were fluffed again. "It's over, dear. We should leave before—"

"No," Meadow said into the mic. "No, don't worry about Luka. She's 'armless. I mean... Harmless. She's got a few arms, doesn't she?"

The audience didn't seem to know what to make of that. A few of them chuckled.

As soon as Luka got her amp stacked, she reciprocated Meadow's joke with a rather rude gesture.

A few more people laughed.

"Yeah, see, she's all right," Meadow went on. "Usually, we save this bit for closer to the end of the show, but, ah... since we're all here, and since you all look like you've seen a monster"—someone in the audience barked out a hearty laugh—"We'll do the intros now, I guess? Ptery?"

Ptery crossed their arms, rolling dark eyes. "By all means, take over."

"Right. You've met Luka. When she's not taking care of your pest problem, she's playing guitar. Or breaking our amps. Equally entertaining."

Luka rolled her head across her shoulders, partially-lidded eyes focusing on Meadow in mock irritation as she played a quick sting on the guitar, four arms moving in tandem.

"And over here's Benji. He doesn't want to be a manticore anymore than some folks want him to be one. Trust me on that. But you rub his belly, and he's fine." Benji groaned, but the nervous purring stopped. He swung his bass around, raising one paw as his telis plucked out a quick succession of notes. For now, the audience seemed placated, if not won over.

Ptery's talons were starting to tug at the mic stand as if to pry it away from Meadow. In response, Meadow removed the microphone from the stand and absconded with it across the stage. "Our feathery frontperson and fantastic vocalist is Ptery, who's very impatient."

"I'm not," Ptery said. "You're a ham."

"See, that's actually true," Meadow replied. "I'm Meadow. Usually, I'm behind the drums. But sometimes, I want to remind the audience that I exist, so I steal Ptery's thunder. They love it. Really."

"Give. Me. That." Ptery made a grab for the mic, either brilliantly playing into Meadow's banter or becoming genuinely irritated. Sometimes it was hard to tell.

Meadow had their audience back. Their curiosity had taken over the void left by their fear, and it seemed—for now at least—they were willing to stay and hear the music.

"We'd like to play a bit for you tonight if you'll let us. I know we're no Emerson's Puzzle or King, but we're... uh."

Oh. His friends would kill him. They'd kill him, but it was brilliant! He had to run with it. The opportunity would only come once, and if he didn't chase it, he'd lose it forever.

Dial It Back just didn't work anymore. Maybe it had when they were a banshee, a faun, a human, and an elf. But with everything they'd been through so far, the old name just wouldn't roll off Meadow's tongue anymore. Even though he'd thought of it, it had to go. From this day forward, let no one utter the name ever again!

After enough of an expectant hush passed, he said, "We're The Bestiary."

Following a confused silence, they received the cheer they'd always wanted.

Unbroken

<u>A SONG WRITTEN BY LUKA IVRIAN</u>

You say you think that I'm broken
And I know that you're hopin'
That I'm really not copin'
That I'm really not broken—

If you can just...

Get in my head
Mess around in my mind
You say my secrets I'll shed
That I'll make you mine.

But I say—

I'm fine!

Don't!
Need!
Your!
Brand!
Of!

Help in my life!
I'm not some quest to be completed
Don't like the way I'm being treated

By the likes of you!

You tell your friends that I'm broken
That you tried and you tried
You wedged your way right inside
Even though I'm not open—

Then I say that I've spoken
I'm really not broken
Again and again
And your growing disdain—

Turns to lies and vitriol
All takes a toll on my soul

But you can't stop now—
If you can't have me then how
Can you just let me go?

And you try to destroy.
Release is not an option
If I'm broken then you'll shatter me
The rest of the way

I repeat—I'm not broken
It's just a myth that you're holdin'
You slam your fists on my walls
But I'm still standing tall

And I'm not broken

I'm fine

Unbroken

EPILOGUE

Another Letter to the Emperor

Dear Emperor Gwilym,

I hope this letter finds you and the empress well. May your reign be long and peaceful.

As I'm sure you well know, things are different with me now, and learning how to write again was a challenge. I sincerely hope this letter is legible, all things considered.

I've made some discoveries about myself, but also about the people closest to me. One can't exactly judge by what's on the surface alone. Although I always knew this in theory, seeing it play out in front of me has been eye-opening. As it's my duty to impart my wisdom to the empire, take heed of this lesson: every person hides demons. Not even the emperor or empress can possibly know everyone's story.

I learned that a young, brash banshee grew up without parental love. I see the sadness in their eyes sometimes, whereas before, there was only pride. But Pterylae is healing now, and moving forward as best they can. They've filled the hole in their life with the love of their friends, and they're better for it.

I learned that a woman who kept her friends at arm's length did so because she feared rejection. But when we found out what Luka was, we could only love her more for it. She's slow to trust, but she is also healing, and I will be there for her every step of the way.

And I learned that my childhood friend, Meadow, who only ever cared for himself and his circle, might be the only person who can save the world. He's taken up the mantle with surprising reverence, considering his attitude toward the gods.

Ah, the gods.

Emperor. Father. I regret to inform you that the goddess Petalvine is dead.

I know little of the cause, only that the machinations of a great Shade have rendered the pantheon helpless. Wheriae, the great god of water, reached through the void to leave instructions with a simple faun who was in the right place at the right time. We are all caught up in it—myself, Pterylae, Luka, and, of course, Meadow.

I don't know where this will lead.

We've already had our first test. I've attached a report of the defeat of Ji'irifarana'ali, a matriarch gnoll of what I assume must have been the Ghaspir. We've sent her body back to the gnoll city for last rites. We feel it was only proper.

She carried a darkness within her, though. At the last moment, she whispered the truth to Meadow: The Shade that haunts us is a false god.

Thankfully, our journey isn't all dour. Despite the pressing dilemma, our band had its first concert in an oasis in the Fade Desert. It was a success, and some of the audience even asked for autographs afterward. I think the world will need music and entertainment if we're all to face what is to come.

I hope we are able to play more. Though I admit to having a bout of stage fright, I did enjoy the experience.

My sister, Zeera, will be sending her own report, along with what is left of the artifact she was sent to find. I asked her to stay with us for a while, and she agreed. We'll be heading to the fairgrounds in Border to celebrate the Rebirth of the Phoenix festival before continuing on to Lunarilis.

I wish you had told me of the existence of the Godplain, although I do understand why you didn't. Sometimes it is difficult for me, being outside the family. I can only hope my service and knowledge have done the empire some good.

Please tell Empress Thaykha that I send my love, and I shall see you soon.

With respectful affection,
Benji Wild
First Sacrifant Son of Imperial Lunarilis

GLOSSARY of TERMS and PRONUNCIATION GUIDE

WARNING: CONTAINS SPOILERS!

IMPORTANT PLAYERS

- **Benjamin Eugene Wild, AKA Benji** :: *(BEN-jah-min YOO-Jeen WILD / BEN-jee)* (He/Him) One of the main characters; once an elf who was turned into a manticore by the sphinx, Aeora. He is gentle and intelligent, and follows Meadow on his quest not only to help, but to discover a cure for his curse.

- **Coriander Starseeker, AKA Cori** :: *(Cor-ee-AN-der STAR-see-ker / COR-ee)* (She/Her) A secondary character; a djiratog faun who is talented with sound design. Sent by the goddess Nebula to find the main characters.
- **Luka Eva Ivrian** :: *(LOO-kah EE-vah IV-ree-an)* (She/Her) One of the main characters; reserved, always low-key angry or frustrated, but very loyal. Human. Extremely talented with machines and computers. Last name "Ivrian" is derived from the goddess Ivriarck, who is the goddess of electricity.
- **Meadow Halfhorn** :: *(MEH-doe HAFF-Horn)* (He/Him) One of the main characters; a faun who is tasked with discovering why the goddess Petalvine has died. He also must discover why a mysterious being called the Shade is destroying the planet's plantlife. Meadow is missing half of his left horn.
- **Pterylae, AKA Ptery** :: *(TARE-uh-lay/TARE-ee)* (They/Them) One of the main characters; a banshee with a dark past they have forgotten. They are missing their left wing. Brash and unforgiving, they are nevertheless a talented healer who has the goddess Faoliia's favor.
- **Walks Through Mud and Sheds Scales, AKA Mud** :: (He/Him) A secondary character; a troll who is generally very trusting, but not naïve. Is searching for his song.

ANTAGONISTS

- **Aeora of the Meerit Den** :: *(Ay-OR-uh of the MEER-it Den)* (She/Her) The sphinx who turned Benji into a manticore, and then vanished.
- **Ji'irifarana'ali, AKA J** :: *(Jee-EER-ee-fah-RAH-nah-AH-lee)* (She/Her) A giant white-furred gnoll who is bent on destroying the heroes through any means.
- **Shade, the** :: *(Shayde)* An unknown creature or thing who has captured the gods.

GODS

- **Aurapax** :: *(OR-uh-pax)* (He/Him) The god of light.
- **Drowlian** :: *(DROH-lee-un)* (She/Her) The goddess of darkness.
- **Faoliia** :: *(Fay-OH-lee-uh)* (She/Her) The goddess of healing.
- **Ghiscaer** :: *(GISS-kare)* (She/Her) The goddess of air, sky, and wind.
- **Ivriarck** :: *(IV-ree-ark)* (She/Her) The goddess of lightning.
- **Nebula** :: *(NEB-yoo-lah)* (She/Her and They/Them) The goddess/deity of sleep and dreams.
- **Petalvine** :: *(PEH-tal-vine)* (She/Her) The goddess of flora.
- **Phoenixes, the** :: *(FEE-nixx-ez)* (She/Her) The phoenixes are named Kaneer (Kan-EER) and Shastaa (SHASS-taah) and are the goddesses of fire. They are married.

- **Wheriae** :: *(WHARE-ee-ay)* (He/Him) The god of water.
- **Xax** :: *(Zacks)* (They/Them) The deity of pain and disease.
- **Ziro** :: *(ZEER-oh)* (She/Her) The goddess of earth.
- **Defeated, the** :: *(Dee-FEE-ted)* The four "Old" gods who created the world. They were killed long ago by elves. Most gnolls still believe they live and call them the True Gods.

OTHER CHARACTERS

- **Alephyr** :: *(AWL-eh-fer)* (They/Them) A banshee Benji meets in the desert. He's an astronomer and his assistant is a barycapa named Steve. **Kickstarter reward Cameo!**
- **Claey** :: *(Clay)* Luka's twin brother. Deceased.
- **Efrit** :: *(EFF-ritt)* (She/Her) A faun. Extremely old, and said to be the best healer Faun-ir has ever seen. She took her name from one of the Defeated.
- **Els'ri** :: *(ELS-ree)* (She/Her) The last brilliant elf, spared by the gods for being pure of heart. Became the first elvish empress of the new age. Her blood carries down to the current ruling family. Deceased many aurs ago.
- **Emperor Gwylim Els'ri** :: *(EM-per-er GWIL-im)* (He/Him) The emperor of the elves. Benji's birth father. Surname is taken from the last brilliant elf, Els'ri.
- **Evialor** :: *(EV-ee-ah-lore)* (He/Him) Ptery's father.

- **Far-Leap** :: *(FAR-leep)* (He/Him) An acolyte of Petalvine with aspirations to become a priest. He does not like Meadow.
- **Galvit** :: *(GAL-vitt)* (He/Him) A satyr billie who runs the Faun-anin Roost Inn. Tried to refuse Benji as a guest, until it was pointed out to him that he couldn't do that.
- **Harpy Officer, Unnamed** :: *(Har-pee Off-iss-er)* (She/Her) Although not given a name, this yellow-feathered officer nearly put our heroes out in a severe storm because they had a manticore with them.
- **Laurel** :: *(LOR-uhl)* (She/Her) A conduit of Petalvine who left Faun-ir many aurs ago. Only mentioned.
- **Orvin** :: *(ORR-vinn)* (He/Him) A manticore from Qalisti.
- **Q'ler** :: *(Kler)* (He/Him) An extremely old manticore and Benji's patron. Unkempt, and lives alone instead of in a den with other liori. He cuts off his tail once per aur so he can travel to settlements without making people afraid. Sarcastic and dry.
- **Reclesti** :: *(Reh-KLESS-tee)* (He/Him) A manticore whose name means "good home" in old elvish. He runs the Syren Oasis in the Fade Desert that serves as a rest stop for weary travelers. He's well-loved and takes the "no fighting" policy in his den very seriously.
- **Stonebuck Ravenfeather** :: *(STONE-bukk RAY-ven-feh-ther)* (He/Him) An elder faun. Extremely patient and wise. He is close to the end of his lifespan.
- **Zeeraliana** :: *(ZEER-uh-lee-AHN-uh)* (She/Her) Benji's sister, also known as Zeera. She is the ninth child of the

emperor and empress and has chosen to become a norsfar to serve the empire.

LOCATIONS

- **Ammit** :: *(AH-mitt)* One of the moons of Erit. Colonized.
- **Balharzivit** :: *(Bal-HAR-zih-vitt)* An orcish town located within an active volcano. Mentioned only.
- **Betweenroads** :: *(Buh-TWEEN-rodes)* A plains town between Faun-ir and Faun-anin that lies on a dead ley-line. The ley-line teleports away anything that grows over a certain height, so there are no trees here. All the houses are scooped out of the ground.
- **Border** :: *(BOR-derr)* A large city at the edge of the north side of the Fade Desert.
- **Darkrealm** :: *(DARK-relm)* A place past death where the recently-deceased are said to wait to be collected so they can pass on to the afterlife. As the name suggests... It's very dark.
- **Edge** :: *(Edj)* A city on the southern border of the Fade Desert.
- **Erit** :: *(AIR-It)* The planet on which the story takes place. About the size of Saturn, with unstable seasons. It fills the entire habitable zone of the solar system's sun.
- **Fade Desert** :: *(FAYD DEH-zert)* The largest desert on the planet, which spans several continents. Centralized on Kyrnis. The result of magic gone wrong millenniaurs ago. There is little water to be found above or underground, but the ecosystem is slowly recovering. The

Fade Desert boasts its own unique species unlike any others on Erit.

- **Falcon Bluff** :: *(FAL-kun Bluff)* A township bordering the Grai Power Relay Plain. Mentioned only.
- **Faun-anin** :: *(Fawn-AH-nin)* A forest city neighboring Faun-ir.
- **Faun-ir** :: *(Fawn-EER)* A forest city, said to be the original birthplace of all fauns.
- **Ge'elo Cliffs** :: *(Geh-EL-oh Cliffs)* A banshee city. Ptery's home. Only mentioned.
- **Ghaspir** :: *(GASS-peer)* The only gnoll city on Kyrnis. Nearly impossible to find, though the rough location is noted on maps. Only mentioned.
- **Godplain** :: *(GOD-plane)* According to Wheriae, the place where the gods rest.
- **Herractir** :: *(Hare-AHC-teer)* A city. Only mentioned.
- **Kyrnis** :: *(KEER-niss)* The continent on which the story takes place.
- **Liori Dens** :: *(Lee-OR-ee Dens)* Cities or towns inhabited by liori. Generally low-tech.
- **Lunarilis** :: *(Loo-ner-ILL-iss)* The capitol of the elvish empire, located at the northernmost part of Kyrnis.
- **Pilicourse Desert** :: *(PILL-ih-corse DEH-zert)* An extension of the Fade Desert onto the continent of Qilinster. The capitol city of Qalisti is located within it, near the Kipanic Sea.
- **Prairieville** :: *(PRARE-ee-vill)* A village. Only mentioned.
- **Qalisti** :: *(Kall-EES-tee)* The capitol of the continent, Qilinster, which is across the Kipanic Sea from Kyrnis. It is

a desert city, which is home to many different species, including liori. Unlike most continents in this sector of the planet, Qilinster is unified under the rule of one city. It is generally peaceful and prosperous.

- **Reinoaken** :: *(Rine-OH-ken)* A city which the main characters only pass through.
- **Rhogot** :: *(ROE-gott)* The continent south of Kyrnis. Only mentioned.
- **Stone** :: *(Stone)* A place where young fauns often go to commune with their chosen god. Young fauns become conduits at stones. Most faun settlements, cities, and towns have at least one. These are usually unkempt and allowed to grow wild.
- **Syren Oasis** :: *(SI-ren Oh-AY-sis)* An oasis/rest stop in the Fade Desert run by the manticore Reclesti and his den.
- **Temple** :: *(TEM-pull)* Most faun cities contain one or more temples, where people may come to worship or attempt to communicate with the gods. These are generally very old and were built when the faun cities were established. Faun-ir has a temple to every god except Xax.
- **Tyl** :: *(Till)* A town. Mentioned only.

SPECIES

- **Aura Possum** :: *(OR-uh POSS-um)* An ethereal creature who dwells in the forest. They float/levitate, and change color when near a person to match the color of their aura.

- **Banshee** :: *(BAN-shee)* Originally created as a hybrid of harpies and humans by the wizard, Shia. Have since become their own successful species. Banshees' main weapon is their debilitating shriek, which can incapacitate or even kill.
- **Barykapa** :: *(BARE-ee-kap-uh)* A large, docile rodent with horns. Often kept as pets, although not considered domesticated.
- **Brilliant Elves** :: *(BRILL-yant Elves)* Golden-skinned elves transformed by magic. Could be born randomly to pale elves. Also known as bright elves. Extinct.
- **Colurus Pod** :: *(CULL-er-uss Pod)* Capsules containing strong, concentrated dye from the Colurus flower—another of Meadow's creations which blooms in many colors. In water, the dye reproduces on a molecular level, so it's very difficult to remove.
- **Deepcrawler** :: *(DEEP-craw-ler)* A sapient species which lives underground. Most surface-dwellers don't know much about them, except that many of them worship Xax.
- **Duarrow** :: *(Doo-AR-oh)* Short, stocky humanoids who generally live underground.
- **Dracotherex** :: *(DRAY-ko-THARE-ix)* A reptilian creature with chisel-like teeth.
- **Dragon** :: *(DRAH-gunn)* Strange, serpentine creatures that aren't purposely destructive, but can interrupt daily life depending on their whims. All attempts to com-

municate with them have failed, although they are clearly intelligent. Dragons are referred to as a force of nature, much like wind or rain. They are also responsible for the existence of the DragNET.

- **Faun, Caprivid** :: *(Fawn, CAP-rih-vid)* A half-humanoid, half animal person. Fauns choose their own names around the time they become conduits. Males are called bucks and females are called does. Top half is human-like, bottom half is goat. Long tail.
- **Faun, Djiratog** :: *(Fawn, JEER-uh-tawg)* A half-humanoid, half animal person. Fauns choose their own names around the time they become conduits. Males are called bucks and females are called does. Top half is human-like, bottom half is giraffe. Extremely tall.
- **Frogbite Moss** :: *(FRAWG-bite Mawss)* Tiny floating plants, often eaten by sparks or herbivorous frogs. Can also be eaten by sapient species. It's somewhat sweet, but not very filling.
- **Gallud** :: *(GAL-uhd)* Small creatures with a snake-like body, a bird-like head, and tiny wings. Generally considered pests. Meadow used to breed and raise different varieties.
- **Gnoll** :: *(nole)* An intelligent, secretive hyena-like species that is rarely seen in society.
- **Halcyon Oak** :: *(HAL-see-on Oke)* A tree molded by certain faun shapers into a home for fauns. They are usually large enough to house several families. They are alive and contain spirits.

- **Harpy** :: *(HAR-pee)* A sapient person with the body of a large bird of prey and the face of a human. Harpies are mostly female, although occasionally a male is born to them. Males are called princes are are generally kept sequestered away for breeding purposes. Very matriarchal.
- **Liori** :: *(Lee-ORR-ee)* Sapient lion-like creatures with extreme sexual dimorphism.
- **Liori, Manticore** :: *(Lee-ORR-ee, MAN-tih-core)* The male liori, which have manes, bat-like wings and long tails. The telson at the tip of the tail contains venom, and attached to it are quills, which also contain venom. The type of venom varies based on the manticore's mood at the time of their turning. More dominant liori have longer tusks. Can use *telis,* a telekinetic power, to move objects.
- **Liori, Sphinx** :: *(Lee-ORR-ee, Sfincks)* The female liori, which have feathered wings. Sphinx may have one or many psychic or psionic abilities, including telekinesis, mind-reading, empathy, and others. May very rarely have the ability to predict the future. Less dominant sphinx have more lion-like faces, where more dominant sphinx have human-like faces.
- **Norsfar** :: *(NORZ-farr)* An elf that is bitten by a theric becomes a norsfar instead of a theric. Norsfar are essentially vampires which feed on magic in blood. Norsfar do have a way to make more of themselves without being bitten by a theric in a highly secretive ritual. They

can become rabbits during the day, and bats at night. Benji's sister, Zeera, is a norsfar.

- **Orc** :: *(Ork)* Rarely seen on Kyrnis; large humanoids who live in very hot environments.
- **Pale Elves** :: *(Pale Elvs)* Elves with skin in various dark colors like grey, purple, or blue. The original elves. Pale elves are now just called "elves," as the brilliant elves are now extinct. Some interbreeding with brilliant elves led to green-skinned elves, though they are relatively rare.
- **Razebit Flies** :: *(RAYZ-bitt Flys)* Small insects which feed on magic within blood. Much like mosquitoes.
- **Redver** :: *(RED-verr)* An eyeless desert-dwelling vulture. Extremely acute sense of smell, but very little self-preservation instinct.
- **Satyr** :: *(SAY-terr)* Related to fauns, but with much more goat-like facial features. Still humanoid and very intelligent. Satyrs are naturally strong and while they are capable of holding less physical careers, their restlessness often leads them to athletic pursuits. Males are called billies and females are called nannies.
- **Spark** :: *(Spark)* Heralds of the god, Wheriae. Frog-like, slimy, and yellow. Most people consider them pests. They seem to be semi-intelligent and live in villages wherever Wheriae's stones are located.
- **Static Cow** :: *(STA-tik Cow)* Carnivorous cows that live on the Grai Power Relay Plain and predate other creatures in the ecosystem to feed on their magic. Docile to non-relay-plain inhabitants.

- **Theric** :: *(THARE-ik)* Were-creatures. Must spend a certain amount of time in their alter-form each moon cycle or they will be forced to transform and lose their ability to think and reason. Therics come in many forms based on the innate magic of the person. Some humans become therics on purpose. Humans bitten by therics become therics themselves.
- **Troll** :: *(Trohl)* A furry humanoid with arms that are longer than its legs. Trolls have an affinity to music and their fur color reflects the type of music they personally prefer. They have a semi-genetic memory. An innate magic can cause bad luck if you are mean to a troll, and good luck if you are nice to a troll.
- **Trumpet Pod** :: *(TRUM-pet Pod)* The seed of a flower created by Meadow. When they bloom, the orange flowers blare like trumpets until removed. They reproduce with runners, so eradicating a plague of them can take a long time.
- **Wyldlights** :: *(WILD-lites)* Small insects which glow in the dark. Sometimes used in lanterns.

TECHNOLOGY

- **A.I.nimal** :: *(A-I-Nih-mal)* Luka's creations. Crafted of metal, plastic, and magic, these creatures actually think for themselves.
- **CA/T Model** :: *(CAT Mah-dol)* A type of A.I.nimal. Cat-shaped. Meant to be a mouser, but often develops its

own personality. Ptery owns one named Ny'zzri, which means "pretty one" in the harpy language.

- **D&D** :: A channel on WorldVS where two friends named Deni and Dylin play games and solve puzzles. They're not particularly good at it. This is Meadow's favorite thing to watch.
- **DragNET** :: *(DRAG-net)* Stands for "Dragon Neural Experience Technology. It's essentially the internet, but it originates from the mind of a sleeping dragon. People can manipulate the DragNET (making NETsites and the like) and the sleeping dragon occasionally sends the only known communications between sapient species and dragons. These communications are usually "Hello," or "Can someone scratch my shoulder?"
- **Erit World Positioning System** :: *(AIR-It Werld Po-SI-shun-ing SIS-tum)* AKA the EWPS. It's GPS for the planet, and runs on DragNET technology. Meadow calls it the Oops.
- **FastTek Fasteners** :: *(FAS-Tekk FAS-en-ers)* It's Velcro with a different name.
- **Frox Biofilter** :: *(Froxx BI-oh-fil-ter)* A device that surrounds the city of Edge which warns enforcement officers of any entering liori. It is programmed to kill liori from the H'grit den.
- **Ghiscaer Drive** :: *(GISS-kare Drive)* The primary mechanism that makes cars work. Causes vehicles to hover a short distance above the ground and moves them along roads with compressed air magic.

- **Grai Power Relay Plain** :: *(Grai POW-er REE-lay Plane)* A location on Kyrnis where a series of tall metal towers transfer magical power from the ground ley-system to buildings across the whole continent. Located centrally. Most cities have a receptacle for power distributed by the relay plain.
- **Heliotrope** :: *(HEE-lee-oh-trope.)* Luka's guitar. If you break her, Luka will kill you.
- **Kirin-Class Road Castle** :: *(KEER-inn Class Rode CASS-uhl)* A large camper-like vehicle with all the comforts of home. There are other classes, but this one is the most technologically advanced, the largest, and the BEST.
- **Magitechnology** :: *(MAJ-ih-tek-NAH-lo-gee)* A combination of magic and tech. Most tech incorporates some kind of magitechnology.
- **Minir** :: *(Min-EER)* Money. Stored on data chips or cards.
- **Module** :: *(MAH-jool)* Essentially an app which runs on terminals.
- **NETsite** :: *(NET-site)* Essentially a website.
- **PG-SEL, AKA Pixel** :: *(Pee-gee-Ess-Ee-Ell/PICKS-uhl)* Stands for Porcine Gatherer-Storage Edition Lugger. A pig-shaped A.I.nimal designed by Luka. Carries everyone's luggage, and can also hunt for truffles. Named Pixel by Meadow, because she needed a name.
- **Skybus** :: *(SKY-buss)* A car that flies high in the air and utilizes magitechnology to stay aloft. Much like an airplane.

- **Terminal** :: *(TER-min-uhl)* Devices that connect to the DragNET and to each other. Each terminal is essentially part of the same system with sectors to keep everyone's individual information safe. Terminals come in may varieties, including handheld, nano, desktop, and slate, each with roughly the same capabilities.
- **Visionscreen, AKA VS** :: *(VIH-zjon-screen)* Analogous to a television, although with some holographic and three-dimensional capabilities.
- **WorldVS** :: *(WERLD-VEE-Ess)* YouTube, but for the DragNET.

MAGIC

- **Achisthus** :: *(Uh-KISS-thuss)* The process by which a liori creates another liori. Involves crushing the heart.
- **Artifact, the** *(ART-ih-fact)* A cube given the the gnoll, Ji'irifarana'ali. It seems to originate from ancient times and will take any attack used against it and turn the power on its attackers. Extremely powerful.
- **Cantyr, arcane** :: *(Can-TEER, arr-CANE)* A healing spell. Verbal. More powerful than physical potions or poultices, but much harder to master. Also called power words.
- **Conduit** :: *(CON-doo-it)* A condition of being for most fauns and some satyrs. Conduits channel magical energy into the world. The magic they channel is based on their patron god, which they choose around 5-7 aurs of age. Being a conduit grants a faun a double lifespan.

Meadow is the only faun who is a conduit for two gods—Petalvine and Wheriae.

- **Dreamrealm** :: *(DREEM-relm)* A sub-universe of subconsciousness where dreams exist. Follows absolutely no rules of physics and is extremely confusing.
- **Dreamsyncing** :: *(DREEM-sink-ing)* One of the magics granted by the goddess, Nebula. Allows a dream mage to directly connect with another person who is in close proximity to them in order to guide them through the dreamrealm.
- **Dreamwalking** :: *(DREEM-wah-king)* Dream mages within the dreamrealm are said to be "dreamwalking."
- **Fire Marbles** :: *(FIRE MAR-bals)* Sold at the checkout line at almost every store, these convenient little marbles will start a self-contained magical fire anywhere, which will burn and stay warm for several hours. Somehow the fire generally "knows" what it is and isn't supposed to burn, but recommended best practices state to still be careful.
- **Godmark** :: *(GOD-mark)* A certain attribute all users of magic bear. This differs based on the type of magic used. For example, flora mages cause small flowers to grow whenever they stand on earth. Fire mages have fire-colored scales on their arms.
- **Herald** :: *(HARE-uhld)* Direct servants of the gods. Usually a person. Sometimes a whole species.
- **Itheri** :: *(ITH-er-ee)* The pool of arcane energy inherent to flora mages. Finite, but can be replenished. More complicated spells generally use more, but more talent-

ed mages can optimize their Itheri use. Itheri can be depleted not only by magic use, but by physical exhaustion. It can be recovered by sleeping and eating.

- **Ley-field** :: *(LAY Feeld)* A large pool of magical energy. Faun cities are usually built on or near them.
- **Ley-line, Live** :: *(LAY Line, live)* A narrow channel where magic flows. Generally occur when there's too much magical energy in an area. Ley-lines alleviate strain.
- **Ley-line, Dead** :: *(LAY Line, ded)* A narrow channel where magic no longer flows, except in spurts called "sparks." Sparks can lead to strange phenomena in the area.
- **Ley-node** :: *(LAY Node)* A pocket of magical energy close to the surface. Can often be reached by digging.
- **Ley-path** :: *(LAY path)* Larger rivers of magical energy, which branch into ley-lines and connect Ley-fields.
- **Ley-system** :: *(LAY sis-tuhm)* The entire ley network.
- **Leystone** :: *(LAY-stone)* A small rock sometimes used by mages of Ziro that can hold magic or a spell.
- **Mage** :: *(Mayj)* A magic-user.
- **Moonstorm** :: *(MOON-storm)* Moonstorms occur in a very specific part of Kyrnis. They form when cool, wet air from the Rona Ocean collides with the hot, magically-charged atmosphere pushing south from the Fade Desert. This creates a magical storm that typically happens from early evening to dawn. All moonstorms cause a severe drop in temperature.
- **Moonstorm, ice** :: *(MOON-storm, Ice)* The most dangerous type of moonstorm. Rain freezes upon impact

with the ground, and large hail may fall, causing severe damage to vehicles and homes. Sometimes randomly produces coconut-sized hail. Cities which experience ice moonstorms generally have reinforced structures such as metal screens that cover windows. Shelters are also provided.

- **Moonstorm, lightning** :: *(MOON-storm, lite-ning)* This type of moonstorm causes copious sky-to-ground lightning and is considered the second most dangerous type. It is strongly recommended that no one drives through these storms and instead seeks cover before they begin. Buffeting winds cause accidents, and the lightning cannot be grounded through normal means.
- **Moonstorm, snow** :: *(MOON-storm, sno)* The least dangerous type of moonstorm. Causes a heavy snow that generally melts by morning when the temperature rises. As cars are built with Ghiscaer drives, they can easily float over any accumulated snow.
- **Telis** :: *(TELL-iss)* Manticore telekinesis. Inherent to the species, but requires learning to master. Manifests as small wisps of light which match the color of the manticore's markings.

TIME

(Presented from SMALLEST unit to LARGEST unit)

- **Tick** :: *(Tik)* Analogous to 1 second.
- **Span** :: *(Span)* A period of ten days.
- **Aur** :: *(Or)* 13 months or 418 days. Analogous to a year.

- **Decaur** :: *(DEK-or)* A period of 10 aurs.
- **Centaury** :: *(CENT-or-ee)* A period of 100 aurs.
- **Millennieaur** :: *(Mill-en-ee-or)* A period of 1000 aurs. (Plural: Millennia)

DISTANCE

(Presented from SMALLEST unit to LARGEST unit)

- **Millikip** :: *(MILL-ih-kip)* About 1 millimeter.
- **Centikip** :: *(CENT-ih-kip)* About 1 centimeter.
- **Decikip** :: *(DESS-ih-kip)* 10 Centikips.
- **Kip** :: *(Kip)* About 1 meter.
- **Kilokip** :: *(KILL-oh-kip)* About 1 kilometer.

OTHER DEFINITIONS

- **Calling** :: *(CAW-ling)* Specific to conduits. Occasionally a god will demand service in exchange for the gifts of long life and good health. A faun recruited by a god to do a special task is said to have a Calling.
- **Creche** :: *(Cresh)* A polyamorous relationship of fauns who raise children together. Not all members of the creche reproduce, but they are all seen as "parents" to the young. Some creches can reach 14 individuals or more. Very few fauns are monogamous.
- **Councilate** :: *(KOWN-cill-at)* Very much like an ambassador. Also provides liaison services between certain species and others. Seen as very wise and very important by the cities they serve.

- **Dial It Back** :: *(Dile it Back)* The name Meadow gave the band consisting of himself, Luka, Ptery, and Benji.
- **Dym** :: *(Dimm)* An ancient, monstrous enemy to trolls. Some say it was a real creature, others say it was a fae-tale. Somehow, though, this creature exists in the genetic memory of the whole species. It lived by feeding exclusively on trolls.
- **Emosis** :: *(Ee-MOE-sis)* A phase all therics go through where they are unable to control their transformations.
- **Faetale** :: *(FAY-tale)* A fairy tale/fable/story.
- **Faun: Acolyte** :: *(Fawn AK-oh-lite)* A faun who has entered the service of a god. This service usually starts when the faun is very young.
- **Faun: Elder** :: *(Fawn EL-der)* Leadership of a faun settlement, city, or town, generally agreed upon by consensus and not a vote. Not necessarily old. All elders are also priests of one god or another, but not all priests are elders.
- **Faun: Master** :: *(Fawn MASS-ter)* A faun who has been favored by a god for some reason without first passing through the ranks of acolyte or priest. Not an elder. In general, extremely talented with magic.
- **Faun: Priest** :: *(Fawn Preest)* A faun who has dedicated their life to a god and who has been hand-picked by that god. Generally very gifted with magic. Priests give religious guidance and can lead rituals. Occasionally priests are trusted with creating new magic.
- **Faunii** :: *(FAWN-ee)* The "common" language. Most people of the world speak some dialect of it.

- **Gellifreyy** :: *(GELL-ih-fray)* An old elvish dialect.
- **Geolocal Pair** :: *(Jee-oh-LOH-cuhl Pare)* Extremely specific coordinates.
- **Rigskit** :: *(RIG-skitt)* The satyr language.
- **Ruby Dagger** :: *(ROO-bee DAGG-er)* An implement created by the gods themselves to be used for healing. While mortal-made daggers work well, owning one of the few ruby daggers ever made signifies favor with the goddess, Faoliia.
- **Sacrifant Son** :: *(SAC-ri-fant Son)* The tenth child of an elvish royal family. Not kept and raised by the empire, but instead given to an adoptive family, to be raised in the world.
- **Serkitball** :: *(SER-kitt-bawl)* A sport with extremely complicated and varied rules. Most professional players don't even know them all. Sometimes played in anti-gravity.
- **S'rantoth** :: *(Ss-RAN-toth)* The tenth month.
- **Vadthi** :: *(VAD-thee)* A liori turned against their will.
- **Xanathic Period** :: *(Zan-AH-thik PEER-ee-od)* A period in the planet's past where the elvish ruling family killed the Old Gods. This is also known as the Undoing.

Finally...

- **Bestiary, the** :: *(BEST-ee-air-ee)* The new name Meadow suddenly gives their band in the last goddamn chapter of the book.

www.ingramcontent.com/pod-product-compliance
Lightning Source LLC
Chambersburg PA
CBHW020302030826
48979CB00027B/1997/J

* 9 7 9 8 9 8 9 4 2 2 6 2 3 *